PRAISE FOR DOLORES REDONDO'S PLANETA PRIZE-WINNING *ALL THIS I WILL GIVE TO YOU*

"Emotionally vivid . . . *All This I Will Give to You* has much to reveal . . . Ms. Redondo unfolds her lengthy saga at a steady pace, with an abundance of detail. The patient reader will be rewarded with revelations both dramatic and poignant."

—Tom Nolan, *Wall Street Journal*

"If you're a fan of Stephen King's character-driven writing style and his patient spinning of suspense, you'll love this novel from Dolores Redondo."

—Jalyn Powell, Sci-Fi Movie Page

"The Galician setting, its scraggly landscape persistently misted in a gentle rain, is a pleasure to spend time in."

—Daneet Steffens, Seattle Review of Books

"Yes, it is that good."

—Glen Seeber, *The Oklahoman*

"*All This I Will Give to You* is the first great thriller of fall."

—Elizabeth Entenman, HelloGiggles

"*All This I Will Give to You* is a surprising, deep, and unforgettable story."

—Jason Schott, *Brooklyn Digest*

"*All This I Will Give to You*, a Spanish bestselling sensation from Dolores Redondo, uses a taut psychological thriller as framework to get at the complexities of a nation in transition."

—CrimeReads

"The best crime novel in translation I read this year."

—Mark Sanderson, *Evening Standard*

PRAISE FOR DOLORES REDONDO'S INTERNATIONALLY BESTSELLING BAZTÁN TRILOGY

"Myth and reality blend and blur in this sophisticated and razor-sharp thriller. All of the skeletons are banging on the closet doors to be set free, and free they are in this gritty, fascinating, and compelling story. Already number one in other countries, this one will be making its way up our bestseller lists too."

—Steve Berry, *New York Times* bestselling author

"Redondo tells the ancient tales in a hypnotic voice."

—*New York Times Book Review*

"A fascinating protagonist."

—Isabel Allende

THE NORTH FACE OF THE HEART

ALSO BY DOLORES REDONDO

All This I Will Give to You

The Baztán Trilogy:

The Invisible Guardian

The Legacy of the Bones

Offering to the Storm

THE NORTH FACE OF THE HEART

DOLORES REDONDO

Translated by Michael Meigs

This is a work of fiction. Names, characters, organizations, places, events, and incidents are either products of the author's imagination or are used fictitiously. Any resemblance to actual persons, living or dead, or actual events is purely coincidental.

Previously published as *La cara norte del corazón* by Destino in Spain in 2019. Translated from Spanish by Michael Meigs. First published in English by Amazon Crossing in 2021.

Published by Amazon Crossing, Seattle

www.apub.com

ISBN-13: 9781542022323 (hardcover)
ISBN-10: 1542022320 (hardcover)
ISBN-13: 9781542022316 (paperback)
ISBN-10: 1542022312 (paperback)

Cover design by David Drummond

Printed in the United States of America

First edition

For Aitor and June, for waiting "to take a longer dip" so they could be with me. I'm honored.

For Eduardo—always—for everything.

For my agent, Anna Soler-Pont, for her contributions, her counsel, and her tireless, unending effort. Thanks for being the "bad cop" for my novels and the reliable counselor in my day-to-day. Heartfelt appreciation; "Onward!"

To Maria Cardona, for putting inspiration, determination, and joy into the task and showing me that with a smile, everything can be done "better." Thanks for making it look easy.

To Ricard Domingo. You still have the ability to see the invisible. For the many years.

To the memory of José Antonio Arrabal, who ended his life in seclusion but not in obscurity. Thank you for reading my work right up to the end.

THE NORTH FACE

This novel is part of a series inspired by the north of Spain. Some of the stories feature Amaia Salazar as the principal character; others focus on different characters and plots that intertwine to create a shared world in which the north—not always just a point on the compass—is the common thread.

Because the most desolate place on earth is the north face of the human heart.

PROLOGUE

Elizondo

Amaia Salazar was twelve years old when she went missing in the forest for sixteen hours. They found her in the early morning, eighteen miles north of the place she'd wandered off the path. She lay unconscious in the pouring rain, and her clothes were scorched and smeared with mud like those of a medieval witch pulled from a bonfire. In stark contrast, her skin shimmered white, pure and icy, as if she'd just emerged from a glacier.

Amaia always insisted that she remembered almost nothing of her ordeal. She recalled losing her way, but after that, her memory flashed the same image over and over. The effect was the exact opposite of Reynaud's nineteenth-century praxinoscope, the spinning device that displayed a sequence of still images to create the illusion of movement. Her own blurred mental pictures froze everything into a single scene. Sometimes she wondered if she had really wandered all that way through the forest or had only stood there hypnotized by the sight of a single tree, staring at it and burning its primitive maternal form into her mind forever.

She'd gone out with her dog, Ipar, on a Sunday morning like any other with a group from the Aranza hiking club she'd joined that spring. She liked the woods, but she'd signed up mostly to please her aunt Engrasi, who'd been insisting for months that she should get out more.

They both knew she couldn't just go play in the village. For a year she'd gone nowhere outside their home except back and forth to school and to church on Sundays with her aunt. The rest of the time, she stayed inside, reading by the fire, doing her homework, or helping with the cleaning and cooking. Anything to prevent being seen outside. Any pretext to avoid what she would face in the village.

She told her rescuers that all she could remember was staring at that tree. But that wasn't entirely true. The tree remained etched in her memory, but so did the storm . . . and the hut in the forest.

She awoke in the hospital to her father looming over her, his wet hair plastered to his forehead. His eyes were red and raw from weeping. When he saw her lids flutter, he leaned over, his face anguished, hoping she would recognize him. She choked on a surge of immense tenderness. She loved her father, her protector, more than ever, but before she could tell him so, his warm lips brushed her ear and he whispered, "Amaia, don't tell anybody. If you love me, do that for me. Don't tell."

All her love, everything she'd ever felt for him, squeezed her heart till it ached. But the words to express her feelings withered and became painful memories congealed around her vocal cords. At last she nodded, incapable of speech, promising silence, promising to keep the deep, dark secret that ended her love for him forever.

PART ONE

A composer is always thinking about his unfinished work.

—*Stravinsky*

The dead do the best they can.

—*Engrasi Salazar*

1

Albert and Martin

Brooksville, Oklahoma

Albert was only eleven. He wasn't a bad boy, but he disobeyed his parents the day of the murders. Not to defy them, but because he really thought nothing was going to happen, like the last time and the time before that. For hours, the forecasters had warned that an enormous storm was brewing. Warm masses of moist air were colliding with cool dry winds from the north, which could generate tornados. It was the same old hysteria they'd heard all spring. His mother kept the TV in the kitchen turned way up, even though the weatherman kept saying the same things over and over. She didn't let him lower the volume or change the channel. His parents took this stuff about tornados very seriously, and for the life of him, Albert couldn't see why. They'd never been hit by a tornado; their house had never been damaged. He told them that Tim, the younger Jones boy, wanted him to come over and play that morning, but they refused. He would have to stay inside. The Joneses' barn had been flattened by a tornado three years before, and the same thing could happen again. They all had to stay close to the storm shelter in case the alarm was given.

Albert didn't protest. After breakfast, he left his cup in the sink and slipped out the back door. He was about halfway to the Jones farm when the atmosphere changed. That morning's cloud cover broke, churned, and went crazy. The sun shone erratically through the torn and whirling clouds. Intense shafts of light cast long shadows across the ground. A deathly calm settled over the land. The birds fell silent and farm machinery sat idle and untended in the barns. Albert strained his ears but heard nothing but a dog howling far in the distance.

Or maybe it wasn't a dog?

The first violent gusts struck as he came around the bend in the road and spotted the Jones farm. He broke into a panicked run, scrambled up the front porch stairs, and grabbed the doorknob, turned, and pulled.

Locked! When no one came to answer his pounding, he raced around the house to the kitchen door that was always open—except today it was bolted. Cupping his hands around his eyes, he peered into the kitchen. Nobody there.

Then he heard it. He took two steps and poked his head around the corner of the house. A howling funnel was barreling toward him across the deserted prairie, a locus of black destruction clad in a swirling coat of cloud and dust. Awed by its swift progress, Albert stood fixed to the spot, hypnotized by its power. Flying dirt blinded him and tears of pure panic filled his eyes. He looked around desperately for some place to take shelter.

He knew the Jones family had a storm cellar, maybe behind the barn, but it was too late to go back that way. Desperate, he raced toward their sturdy chicken house, glanced back for an instant and saw the monster still advancing, and then ran as fast as he could, praying they hadn't locked the coop. He twisted the heavy latch, a crude metal plate mounted on a sturdy spike. He plunged inside and pulled the door shut behind him.

Albert found himself in near-absolute darkness, but his eyes adjusted to the dim light seeping through the cracks. He panted and wheezed, half choked by the stink of feathers and chicken shit. Fumbling through his pockets for his inhaler, he remembered leaving it on the table by the television. He fought back panic as he heard the howling beast outside change its tune. Was the horrible noise abating? Had the monster turned from its course?

Albert threw himself on the ground, heedless of the warm excrement that immediately soaked his trousers, and peered through a screened vent set low in the wooden wall. If the funnel had indeed altered direction, just for a moment, it had changed its mind again and was back on track. He saw it advancing, tearing across the prairie, a living thing compounded of everything it demolished along its path. Albert looked back into the interior and only then, as his eyes once more adjusted to the gloom, did he see the chickens. The hens were huddled all together in a silent, compact heap in the far corner of the chicken house.

They knew they were going to die, and he was seized by the same horrible dread. Shaking uncontrollably, he dragged himself to the mound of poultry. He made himself as small as he could and pushed deep into that warm living pile an instant before the tornado hit. The birds' silent acceptance of their fate exploded in cackling, thrashing screams that sounded almost human. Albert yelled with them, calling for his mama, feeling the air being sucked from his lungs. In that wild moment, he remembered the diagram the allergist had used to explain how the sacs in his lungs sometimes collapsed and denied him oxygen. He kept yelling, emptying himself completely, his voice reduced to a high, thin, useless shriek. Albert knew his end had come when the beast outside drowned out his pathetic squeak. The last thing he felt as the chicken house blew apart and showered debris everywhere was the warm, convulsive spurt of urine as he peed his pants.

The shining sun stood high in a clear blue sky. Not a single cloud marred the perfection overhead. Martin paused, feeling dampness in his carefully combed hair. He brushed his hand across the nape of his neck and was annoyed to find his shirt collar wet as well. With the tip of one polished shoe, he cleared away some splintered wood and rubble so he could put down his briefcase. He wiped his neck with a fine white handkerchief, then carefully folded it and tucked it in his back pocket before checking his appearance again. The crisply creased trousers and polished shoes were satisfactory, but the tailored dark-denim jacket had been a mistake. He knew oppressive heat typically followed tornados, so he should have chosen something lighter. Everything around him had been destroyed except for the untouched little red barn by the steps to the underground shelter where the Jones family had taken refuge.

He picked up his briefcase and headed that way. The storm shelter's heavy metal doors had been flung back. A stout chain still dangled from the interior handholds, evidence of the family's hurry to escape their dark refuge. He descended the steps and paused for a moment to take in the scent of the basement, a rich mixture of mold and decay with a faint smell of urine. His heart accelerated. The shelter was deserted. Martin ascended the steps and went toward the farmhouse. Or, rather, what was left of it.

Albert woke up slowly. Even before he opened his eyes, he knew he couldn't move. A tremendous weight lay across him. He heard faraway voices, surely the Jones family, and he tried to call out to them. The pressure on his chest was so great that after only three labored breaths, he passed out again.

He came to in a flood of dazzling light. He didn't know how long he'd been unconscious. He told himself not to panic. If he became hysterical, he'd pass out again. Trying to assess his situation, he realized he was pinned. He saw a section of the coop's roof on him, but he felt something else on top of that, something terribly heavy. The roof fragment wasn't very wide. He worked his left hand around the edge and touched something lying across it, probably one of the heavy wood uprights. He panted. His forehead burned, scraped raw by flying fragments of wood, and his nose was full of blood and snot. The upright wouldn't budge. He couldn't move his left leg. It was broken—and he just knew it was shattered.

Albert wanted to cry but knew blubbering could kill him. He focused his whole being on controlling his emotions so as to fend off an asthma attack. With great effort, he breathed as deeply and as regularly as the heavy weight permitted. He imagined his mama's voice—*Very good, Albert, you're doing very well*—and the way she patiently talked him through his attacks.

The thought of Mama made him want to cry again. His eyes brimmed with tears, and he felt like a stupid little kid. *Stop it,* he told himself, and an involuntary shudder jerked his destroyed leg. He gasped in pain and lost the little control he'd established.

After a moment, he again focused on counting his breaths, doing his best not to think of his mama. Eventually he regained a semblance of calm. He twisted his head to the right, scraping his forehead as he tried to see through a gap in the heap of smashed wall panels.

Albert was a country boy. Even though he couldn't see the sky from his position, the slant of light told him it was early afternoon. The tornado had swept away every trace of cloud.

Because Mr. Jones had cut the grass the day before, he had a clear view of the man walking across the field. It wasn't Mr. Jones; this man was carrying a briefcase, and a badge on his chest flashed in the sun. Albert gulped air and tried to shout, but produced only a hoarse wheeze. The man turned in his direction and scanned the wreckage scattered across the farmyard. Albert was sure the man was going to help him, but just then, a hen that had been lying inert to his right revived with a squawk and scrambled through the gap into the yard. The man looked away and continued toward the farmhouse. Albert broke into tears. He didn't care if he choked. He was going to die anyway.

The closer he got, the clearer their laments became, the same wails he'd heard dozens of times before. The actual words meant little. All survivors of catastrophe, every single one, sounded the same. That wet, strangled voice as if their throats had been cut, the miserable pleas when rescuers appeared. They wasted their dwindling energy rooting through the devastation for something familiar, anything at all to help assuage their survivor's guilt.

A teenage girl was picking through the debris, collecting colored scarves. She waved them overhead like a gymnast, tracing trails of dust before wrapping them around her neck. She was the first to see him. She called to the family and pointed in his direction; her long fingers were tipped with gleaming black nail polish. They gathered and gaped at him through an opening that had been a window. They watched him cross the farmyard, ankle deep in splintered wood.

Martin took great pleasure at the sight. There were two boys, one a teenager and the other probably not yet twelve. The bigger boy wore a T-shirt printed with a picture of a rock band, and the little one's hair was really too long for a male child. Farmer Jones didn't disappoint him either; he sat moaning and sniveling on the steps of what had been the front porch. Martin saw the bottle of water, the chocolate bars, and the revolver Jones had put down. The man held his head in his hands, a picture of impotence. An elderly woman seated beside him, probably his mother, consoled him and rocked him in her arms like a baby. A woman in her forties stood nearby, her bold gaze directed at Martin. Young Mrs. Jones, no doubt. Slim and pretty, with her hair dyed an unnatural scarlet. She had one of those stupid little dogs in her arms. It squirmed, yapped, and whimpered.

Martin made sure his badge was clearly displayed. Glad to see him, they all dropped what they had salvaged and instinctively gathered where the front door had been, even though the wall on that side of the house was gone. Mrs. Jones was the first to move forward. She adjusted her low-cut blouse and fluffed up her hair without letting go of the dog, then started down the steps. She favored

Martin with her best smile. He smiled back, despising her with all his soul for being the font of evil, horror, and steaming corruption that had called down the wrath of Almighty God. He offered her his hand and knew exactly what he was going to do. He usually started with the old women, but this time, he was going to kill young Mrs. Jones first.

Albert heard the shouts and the shots. His eyes widened in astonishment and he forgot his tears.

Maybe, just maybe, this really was his lucky day after all.

2

The Character of Mountain Folk

FBI Academy, Quantico, Virginia
Wednesday, August 24, 2005

Amaia Salazar shifted uncomfortably in her seat in the second row. She'd been among the first to enter the large hall for today's lecture, knowing this room might well prove to be too small because there was so much interest. This morning's presentation was different from the classes for the group of European police officers; today's event was a lecture open to all FBI agents and trainees at Quantico. She'd denied the adjacent seats to two agents in suits by projecting a profoundly unfriendly look and frozen out a couple of grinning trainees in their distinctive blue polo shirts. She didn't want company.

Special Agent Dupree's lecture was of far greater interest to her than anything else in the exchange program. The speed with which the room filled was evidence she wasn't the only one who felt that way. A middle-aged German police inspector greeted her with a smile and settled at her side. Gertha was the only other woman in the Europol delegation. Considering the chilly reception both officers had received from their male counterparts, it was hardly surprising she'd stuck close by Amaia's side. Amaia had been somewhat standoffish at first. Gertha had seemed pleasant, but she'd been entirely too chatty for Amaia's taste. Not that the German officer was one of those who bores you to death or badgers you with questions. Still, in the course of two meals and the bus trip from the airport, Gertha had related practically her whole life story.

"Mountain folk," Gertha said. "They are different."

"Excuse me?"

"I think you come from the mountains, like my husband. It's hard to get him to talk."

"Actually, I'm from a valley!"

They'd both laughed at that. In the four days since then, Gertha had gotten more than just a few words out of her. Perhaps it was due to the reassurance of opening up to someone she'd probably never see again, or because Inspector Gertha Schneider knew how to listen. Gertha had become a sympathetic ear for confidences and revelations Amaia had never shared with anyone. They'd talked until the wee hours of the night more than once. Gertha headed up a homicide investigation team of forty-five officers, thirty-eight of whom were men. She'd had her share of conflicts when she took charge, but she was singularly free of resentments.

Before Gertha said anything, a man in a suit dropped into the seat on the other side of Amaia.

"Assistant Inspector, I've been looking everywhere for you. I thought you'd be in the break room with the others." He gave her a smile to let her know his aggrieved tone was just an act. The smile lasted maybe a bit too long. Amaia deliberately looked away.

Emerson had been assigned as her point of contact, the agent responsible for orienting her, helping her get the most from the course, accompanying her, introducing her to her instructors, and using his own devices and passwords to provide access to the material she needed for the assignments. From time to time he got a bit too friendly.

"I came early to get a good seat. This is a subject that particularly interests me."

"Seems you're not the only one." Emerson looked around the room, almost full by now. "Looks like our agent Dupree has a lot of fans. Ever hear him speak before?"

"I went to a lecture he gave in Boston three years ago, when I was a graduate student. I stood in line, got his autograph and a quick handshake. The schedule says Dupree's going to conduct our seminar this afternoon. I want to be ready."

Emerson raised one eyebrow and gave her a patronizing smile.

She saw he was dying to tell her more. "You know something I don't?"

"Special Agent Dupree has his own style. His teaching methods can be unusual. He's not an instructor; he heads a strike team. He does lecture from time to time, and sometimes he drafts an article for the Bureau's intranet. It's really unusual for him to agree to help train the Europol group."

"You work for him, don't you?"

"Not exactly . . . ," Emerson was pained to admit. "Sometimes I travel with his team. I'd really like to be assigned to his unit, and maybe someday I will be. Right now I'm on the communications support team with Agent Stella Tucker, who works for Dupree. So I do work for him, but only indirectly. Profiling requires lots of different skills. They mostly use field agents on their strike teams, but quite a few support functions are based here. We back up the field agents looking for bad guys."

He said "bad guys" as if talking to a child and gave her another one of his phony smiles. He changed his tone when she didn't react. "Agents stationed here support all three strike teams. I specialize in data analysis. It doesn't sound sexy, but it's vital for their work."

The conference room light dimmed, and the buzz of conversation died away as if controlled by the same switch. A spotlight came up on a bare lectern.

Agent Dupree emerged from the right side of the stage and walked into the pool of light. Dupree was slim and elegant, his short hair carefully combed, just as she remembered. The dark circles under his eyes emphasized the pallor of his complexion; he looked like a man who never got enough sleep. He wore a perfectly tailored midnight-blue suit, a matching tie, and a white shirt. He was clean shaven.

Dupree took his place behind the lectern. He appeared to have no text or notes. Amaia wondered if he'd had a script pre-positioned on the lectern; if so, that attention to detail might be a clue to his character. She made a mental note to watch to see if he picked up any papers afterward.

The brief bio in the course program said he was forty-four years old, a native of Louisiana with degrees in law, economics, art history, psychology, and criminology. For the past year he'd headed one of the three working groups at the FBI's Behavioral Science Unit.

Dupree raised his chin, put one foot forward, and shifted his weight to the other. His hands rested easily on his hips as he looked out at the faces in the auditorium.

He reached out and tapped the microphone. A thunderous sound filled the hall. He leaned forward slightly, looked up, and spoke to someone she couldn't see at the back of the auditorium. "Could you please put some light on the audience? When I can't see them, I feel as though I'm just talking to myself." His voice was resigned. "I feel like that often enough already."

The lights brightened just enough so Dupree could make out their faces.

He surveyed the rows of seats as if looking for someone. When he got to Amaia, he kept his gaze on her for a couple of seconds, then looked down at the lectern. The eye contact had been brief. She supposed he'd been studying someone behind her, but then she realized Agent Emerson was watching her. He hadn't missed it.

Dupree looked up. "We all know the importance of establishing a victim profile, analyzing the criminal's choice of known victims. But today I'm going to discuss the importance of identifying and registering *possible* victims as a means of detecting an unrecognized serial killer. We will first consider the type of victim chosen by the killer and cases in which the existence of a murder is in fact unknown."

A shiver of excitement went through the room. Dupree looked at Amaia and directed every word to her. "One often supposes that a crime is the means by which a murderer purges his own suffering, since many killers were victims before they became executioners. Of all the possible assumptions, the most dangerous is the notion that, deep down, killers want to be caught, so their crimes are merely desperate pleas for recognition of their own suffering. This is certainly not true in the case of mental illness, but that is another question entirely."

Amaia heard Emerson mutter in astonishment. "What the hell . . . ?"

Agent Dupree paused and looked around at the rest of the audience. "This hypothesis asserts that exhibitionism and savage behavior are cries for attention. Criminals resort to the same behavior again and again in their effort to be something, to be someone, to be important; their egotism is their undoing. Because they want attention and recognition, they take risks and make mistakes that give them away.

"But watch out. Assumptions are the investigator's greatest enemy, and there's ample proof that not all serial killers are compulsive and disorganized. Some of them are conscious of their own deviant behavior. Some serial killers, knowing something about police methods, use ruses and deceptions to throw us off the scent. This type of killer stages the scene carefully. He lays red herrings; he sends us down blind alleys. He takes his time and picks his opportunities carefully. He can go on murdering for years. He covers his tracks, maybe hides the bodies of his victims; perhaps he makes his murders look like accidents, suicides, or simple disappearances. Or maybe he selects vulnerable, marginalized individuals whose disappearances won't be noticed: drug addicts, prostitutes, the homeless, illegal immigrants. Outcasts."

He addressed the left side of the hall, where Amaia and her colleagues were seated. "The vast size of the United States gives the murderer a large territory to operate in. You in the European Union have had open borders for a decade now, so you face a similar situation.

"This killer has no intention of getting caught. Notoriety doesn't interest him. He has his reputation and social status already."

Dupree paused and fixed his eyes on Amaia again. He grinned. "Like the devil himself, he gains his satisfaction and power from the fact that we don't believe he exists."

A stir went through the room.

Agent Emerson was staring at Amaia, but she kept her eyes on Dupree and pretended not to notice. Gertha was harder to ignore when she leaned over and whispered, "He is talking directly to you."

Dupree surveyed his audience. "Homicide detectives have their methodologies. They're trained to look for discrepancies that raise questions in the usual areas of inquiry: jealousy, sex, drugs, money, inheritances, who stands to benefit, the possibility of blackmail. But serial killers don't fit the usual categories; their gratification is psychological. We have to understand how the killer rewards himself, so as to determine what needs he's satisfying. This presentation and your next training exercises will focus on the identification of common elements and discrepancies related to victim types, apparent accidents, murder scenes, and missing-person cases. Above all, we consider elements that might suggest that an apparent suicide or accident is nothing of the kind. We may in fact be looking at a murder or even one in a series of murders.

"How do we study a serial killer who hides the evidence of his existence? How do we create databases with information unknown to us? How do we describe the behavior of a phantom, a hidden predator who is thrilled by the fact we don't even know he exists?" He looked around, as if expecting someone to reply.

"Victimology," Amaia breathed.

"Victimology," declared Dupree. "The science founded upon studies not only of actual victims but also of suspected victims, as well as those who disappeared into thin air. In such cases, victim profiling is necessarily an abstract science, for our investigator's intuition must tell us whether a victim does in fact exist. Analysts must keep in mind a wide range of variables, including physical characteristics, psychological factors, social position, and character traits. Clues could be suggested by character weaknesses, physical anomalies, or even unique physical features. We consider the family around him. If he has none, that's significant as well. And, of course, illnesses and pathologies, medical treatments, and any available information concerning behavior, personality, tastes, and affinities. The work is grueling, certainly, but it's necessary whenever a detective has even the slightest suspicion a victim may exist. It doesn't matter whether there's a body or not. Complicating the task even further is the fact that our memories are fallible, and we may overlook things. We must document each prospective case fully, watching for common characteristics or incongruities, clues that signal that a disappearance may in fact have been a murder."

Dupree pressed a button on the lectern. A screen behind him on the stage lit up with the image of a handsome but extremely thin young man in a suit. The black-and-white photo looked like an old newspaper clipping.

"Back in the 1980s, the English researcher Noah Scott Sherrington of Scotland Yard began putting together a database of possible victims. He collected information about women, fugitives, missing persons, and runaways. You'll get a copy of his case file after this presentation. The most striking aspect of his work was that Inspector Sherrington didn't have a shred of evidence that these women were dead. Not a single body or body part or even any indication they might have been kidnapped.

"Sherrington was looking at an economically depressed coastal region where the weather was atrocious most of the year. London was a huge draw, compared to working in a local cannery if you were lucky enough to get a job. That's why many young women left. Technicians and manual workers assigned to the area for short periods found the little ladies eager to leave for a better life in the big city.

"By setting up a database for those missing girls, Sherrington was able to draw up a map of the actions of a hypothetical predator. It took him years. He eliminated the names of women who had turned up elsewhere in the country. A clear profile of the typical victim emerged. His conclusions were specific and horrifying. Today, Inspector Sherrington is recognized the world over as a pioneer of victimology for his achievement of proving the existence of a previously unknown serial killer.

"Sherrington had so refined his work, he was virtually one hundred percent sure which women were runaways and which had been murdered. He achieved this without the support his work deserved.

"Using Sherrington's research as a foundation, the police went to work with their usual methods, locating and reinterviewing witnesses, reconstructing the women's movements, sifting through the case files and Sherrington's profiles."

Dupree paused. He gave Amaia a look so challenging that some in the hall turned to stare at her. "Following his instinct and based on his flawless investigation, Sherrington had eliminated all suspects but two. At the time he referred to this as 'a hunch.'"

"'A hunch,'" Amaia repeated under her breath. Now she understood the connection.

When the Judicial Police promoted her to assistant inspector only six months earlier, she'd inherited a cold case involving the disappearance of a young nurse trainee at a hospital who'd just started her assignment. Officers who interviewed her acquaintances there concluded her disappearance was voluntary, but the girl's mother disagreed. She raised a racket with tearful television appearances and appeals for help made through the press. It was a difficult case; no one wanted anything to do with it.

Except Amaia. She reviewed every detail of the investigation and quickly focused her attention on a staff surgeon. He hadn't even been considered as a possible suspect, though they'd interviewed him because the girl's coworkers remembered seeing her with him. The doctor was eliminated as a suspect both because there was no evidence of a relationship and because he had a sterling reputation. He was from a Pamplona family of distinguished medical practitioners.

Amaia's supervisor dismissed her suspicions out of hand. "I know the family. It's unthinkable." She didn't bring up the subject again, but she shadowed the physician for weeks in her off-duty hours. He eventually led her to a secret apartment where he was keeping the young woman as his sex slave.

She wasn't his first victim. His arrest resulted in the discovery of evidence implicating him in the disappearances of at least two others. In her case report, Amaia wasn't able to specify the factors that had roused her suspicions. She wrote that she'd "had a hunch."

Dupree surveyed the crowd. "Sherrington's hunch obsessed him. He trailed those two suspects for weeks, first one and then the other. One wild, stormy night on his way home after monitoring one suspect, he stopped at a traffic light. The other suspect happened to cross the intersection in front of him. On an impulse, Sherrington followed. It was pure chance; the inspector had no idea the murderer was on his way to dispose of a victim. Sherrington's profile lacked one vital detail: he hadn't determined how the killer got rid of his victims' bodies. A later review of the case notes revealed the brilliance of Sherrington's conclusions. Unfortunately, no one supported his work or even paid any attention to it.

"Alone late at night in a furious storm, our inspector saw the killer unloading the body of his latest victim, a young woman who exactly fit Sherrington's profile. Elated that he'd caught his murderer red handed, Sherrington tried to arrest him, but the killer was bigger and stronger than he was. They struggled and Sherrington collapsed, falling victim to a heart attack triggered by stress and an undiagnosed cardiac anomaly. Hunters chanced across Sherrington the next morning, and he was evacuated to a hospital where a risky heart operation saved his life. The killer had escaped by the time the inspector regained consciousness. Even so, Sherrington's analysis had so precisely established the murderer's methods that the police were quickly able to locate the bodies of nine other victims.

"Because of his severe heart condition, Inspector Sherrington was placed on permanent disability leave. To this day, the Sherrington database is a model of victimology. Sherrington's principles are valid whether the crime is obvious or the murderer staged the scene as an accident or a suicide."

Dupree looked around. "Agents, cadets, thank you all for your time. Colleagues from abroad, the coordinators will give you a folder with details of Inspector Sherrington's investigations. Study them. They will be the subject of your next seminar. This concludes today's lecture."

Special Agent Dupree left the stage. The audience sat in silence. The auditorium lights came up and left them blinking.

Amaia got to her feet but didn't move as she focused on the stage and the exit through which Dupree had vanished. The attention he'd focused on her had made her feel both strangely flattered and oddly threatened. She realized too late she hadn't remembered to watch whether Dupree had picked up notes on the way out.

Gertha gave her a hearty slap on the back. "Girl, that's what I call getting yourself noticed!"

Lost in thought, she heard Emerson exclaim, "How about that, Assistant Inspector! Looks like you really impressed the boss!"

He was jealous as hell.

She turned to look at Emerson as if awakening from a trance. Something in him had changed. He'd done his duty as her mentor and more, even though she'd had the impression he'd been less than pleased to be saddled with a female cop in a class that was almost exclusively male. Emerson was one of those alpha males who hates to lose. A couple of times, he'd tried gazing deep into her eyes and charming her with his brilliant smile, but now his mouth was a slash of displeasure. His chin jutted out and he was puffed up like a bantam fighting cock. Amaia put one hand on his shoulder and pushed him gently aside. She stepped past, leaving him disconcerted and offended, as if she'd poked him with a pistol instead of her index finger. She made her way around the chatting agents clustered along the rows and in the aisles. She exited the hall, on her way to the stage door.

Emerson called out behind her. "Salazar, you can't leave now! The seminar starts in fifteen minutes in room 3, all the way across campus. We have just enough time to get there!"

He caught up with her as the stage door opened. Dupree came out into the corridor with another agent at his side. Men in the hallway shook Dupree's hand and congratulated him as he made his way through the crowd.

Amaia raised a hand. "Agent Dupree!"

Dupree turned but looked straight through her. He nodded at Emerson, just behind her, and called him by name, then turned away and continued down the hall.

Amaia stood stock still and watched him go. "Arrogant son of a bitch!"

She knew Emerson had heard her. She didn't care.

3

Intentions of the Gale

Quantico, Virginia

They'd already dimmed the lights by the time she got to class. Agent Emerson stopped at the door, turned, and stalked back down the hall without a word. Inside the conference room, a storm was raging. A video on the huge screen showed rain pelting down and winds gusting, ripping off roofs and sending them flying through the air. Power lines were down, and huge waves battered the coast. Trying to avoid notice, Amaia found a place in the back. A second, similar television news video followed and then came a series of still photos of tornados, typhoons, hurricanes, and other natural disasters.

"Natural disasters!" a woman's voice rang out in the back of the room.

Amaia recognized the slightly nasal voice of Agent Stella Tucker. Though Tucker was hidden in the dark, Amaia remembered her clearly as a fifty-ish African American woman with a strikingly beautiful face. She wore her hair cut short like a marine, perhaps to contrast with the exuberantly fleshy body that made her appear shorter than she actually was. Tucker was one of Dupree's colleagues. She was his chief liaison with the media, families, and victims. Dupree was the only member on the team with more seniority than Tucker.

"Disasters leave dozens of victims, and inevitably the dead have multiple injuries. Standard operating procedure for disasters requires rescuing survivors as quickly as possible and disposing of decomposing bodies to limit the danger of disease. That's part of the reason why everyone involved in rescue work and investigation is under tremendous stress. These are scenes of pure chaos, places where rapidly developing events can easily cause an investigator to miss indications of a crime. Some bodies are crushed. Others may hang from trees, so battered that their clothes have been torn off.

"On your desks you have a folder with all the details about the next exercise. This past spring, during one of the hottest Marches on record, tornados and storms struck many parts of the country. One of those storms battered a small settlement near Killeen, Texas. Dozens of people were killed, including the Mason family: father, mother, three teenage children, and the elderly grandmother who lived with them."

The screen lit up with a picture of a typical Texan farmhouse with a smiling family posing on the front porch. The disaster photos that followed were of poor quality, presumably taken by an inexperienced amateur. The victims' injuries hadn't been photographed close up. A couple of the wide views showed the bodies lying close together, indicating they'd probably huddled there before the roof collapsed. Amaia imagined them trying to reassure one another, fighting back their fears. Debris, wood fragments, and a few bulky pieces of furniture lay across the bodies.

Tucker let them take in the images before she continued.

"There was a rush to bury the dead, common after natural disasters. At first, no one saw the deaths as suspicious. The coroner issued death certificates and didn't order autopsies.

"About a month later, freezing winds from Canada and pockets of warm air from the Gulf of Mexico collided, generating violent storms, a supercell that had the potential to produce tornados. This one exploded over Oklahoma, and a tornado took out the Jones family farm near Brooksville."

Another farmhouse appeared on the screen, this one photographed from the air. The next photo showed everything in the same scene smashed to bits.

"The Joneses were found dead inside their ranch house. The father, his elderly mother who lived with them, his wife, and their three children, all the same ages and sexes as the Mason family."

The death scenes were shown side by side on the screen. The similarities were astonishing. In both images, the bodies lay very close to one another under a scattering of dust, debris, and overturned furniture. Amaia didn't know the geographic coordinates of the two farms, but she had the impression the bodies might be oriented in the same direction. She made a mental note.

Agent Tucker paused and listened in evident satisfaction to the murmurs of the European police officers. The next set of images was of excellent quality. Even an untrained observer would be able to see these were taken by a professional.

"If the rescuers had followed the same procedures with the Jones family as were followed with the Masons," Agent Tucker continued, "these murders might easily have escaped detection. The entire family was found in what had been the living room. The bodies were in decent shape, and the trauma that had destroyed their skulls could easily have been attributed to falling rafters or beams."

The French officer next to Amaia spoke up. "These death scenes resemble each other. We see that the first one did not provoke suspicion among local and state authorities. The photographs suggest the first investigation was not the responsibility of the FBI. What was the reason to see the second case in a different manner?"

Agent Tucker let the silence settle in to make sure she had everyone's attention.

"A witness," she said in a whisper perfectly audible from her place in the back of the room.

Amaia smiled. This Agent Tucker clearly knew exactly how to capture their attention.

"A twelve-year-old boy, a friend of one of the farmer's children," the agent added in her normal voice. "Despite the weather alerts, he sneaked off to see his friend. The storm hit before he could get to a shelter, so he hid in the chicken house. The tornado that struck the farmhouse didn't touch the nearby barn, but it did blow down the coop. The boy wasn't seriously injured, but he was trapped for hours by a heavy wood panel. He was able to breathe, but he was immobilized, and the weight on his chest kept him from calling for help. He said he heard the family come out of the storm shelter by the barn after the storm had passed. He couldn't see them from where he was, but he knew their voices. Then he saw a man cross the field toward the house.

"Soon after that, he heard shots, screams, and more shots, followed by a terrible silence. Terrified, he heard someone shifting the debris, then nothing. He described the man as tall and thin, with the gait of a young man, and carrying a briefcase. He had some sort of badge. The boy said the man came out into the yard, put his little case on the ground, stood before the wreckage of the farmhouse, and raised his arms. In silence he waved his arms slowly and rhythmically as if conducting an orchestra. The witness said he looked like a composer, so that's the name the investigators have adopted."

Everyone in the room was quiet, but they tensed like bloodhounds suddenly catching a scent.

Amaia turned and looked for Agent Tucker. Her face was scarcely visible in the dark, but Amaia saw her satisfaction at their reaction.

"Contrary to what you might expect, the killer didn't remove the weapon. We found it next to the bodies. A Smith & Wesson 617, twenty-two caliber, registered to the father. The autopsy established that they'd been shot in the head and then the bodies were struck with a blunt object or objects in an attempt to make it look as if they'd been killed by falling debris. We found evidence to support the boy's version of events: the family took refuge in the storm shelter by the barn and they'd all been executed at close range. The rubble-strewn scene in the house was staged to suggest the fatal wounds occurred when the house collapsed.

"One of the Oklahoma investigators recalled a front-page newspaper photo published a month earlier of the Mason family. Remember: the Masons were buried without autopsies. The sheriff who'd handled that case said a pistol was found by the bodies, a twenty-two caliber owned by the father, but they thought it was irrelevant. We obtained an exhumation order. Postmortems confirmed that gunshot wounds, concealed by blows to the head, were the causes of death."

Autopsy close-ups showed the injuries and abrasions.

Tucker left her place in the back of the room, stepped to the door, and turned on the lights. The grisly images faded and almost disappeared. Amaia and her classmates blinked, trying to adjust to the sudden brilliance.

Tucker paused theatrically and looked around the group. Amaia sensed the agent was trying to provoke a strong reaction. "The sheer violence of gales of more than 250 miles an hour makes any flying object a potentially lethal projectile. The killer was certainly aware of this, for all the wounds were inflicted postmortem. In two victims he plugged the bullet holes with stone fragments. In others he used wood splinters."

Amaia, seated closest to the door, was near Tucker. She saw the hint of a smile on Tucker's face as class members murmured among themselves. Tucker saw Amaia looking at her and the smile vanished instantly.

Tucker pointed to the thick folder in front of Amaia. "The Oklahoma investigators suspected this was a case of kidnapping, a federal crime, because the victims had been held in their own home; that's why they called in the FBI. The documents on the desk before you contain all the details we have—information from the neighbors, the witness statement, photos of the crime scenes, short biographies of both families. To keep you from just groping around in the dark, we've given you the entire case file as it stands. It describes our efforts to establish links between the two crime scenes and the two families, which have been unsuccessful so far except for the obvious correspondences of sex, age, and family structure. This is an open case, and we are actively investigating. This file is confidential. Nothing in it has been made public. We believe the perpetrator's goal is to remain undetected. We don't think he's seeking notoriety; he is apparently satisfied that his crimes haven't been recognized.

"Our greatest advantage is that he thinks we don't know he exists."

Gertha objected. "Is it not reprehensible to wait for him to strike again and abstain from informing the press—thereby encouraging him to continue?"

"We're convinced he's not going to stop. Publicizing our investigation will only make him change his modus operandi. Given the vast area across which the killer moves, we'd never be able to catch him if he did. Our only chance is to get there ahead of him. Your mentors will assist you as needed, but they will offer no suggestions or comment on your work. They'll provide digital access to any relevant information or data in our systems. You will draw up three profiles: the first behavioral, the second geographic, and the third victimological. You will deliver your written conclusions no later than noon tomorrow."

Barbagallo, the Italian inspector from the Carabinieri, waved his folder. "Excuse, please, Agent Tucker, not to complain about your presentation, but the schedule states Agent Dupree is to present this class . . ."

Amaia smiled and silently shook her head, remembering how Dupree had deliberately ignored her in the hall.

Agent Tucker, already at the door, paused with her hand on the knob. She clearly relished the moment. "He already did. Who do you think prepared the lecture?"

4

Ward Funeral Home

Cape May, New Jersey

The cadaver was in terrible shape. Mary Ward pinched its cheek with her bare fingers. The layer of skin over the cheekbone peeled away, leaving a raw spot that looked like a patch of bad sunburn. She rolled the epidermis in her fingers. It had the gummy texture of old rubber cement. She sighed. Frozen cadavers were always bad news, and this one was no exception. She wiped the remains with a damp sponge and leaned over to check the reservoir of the dehumidifier she'd left running overnight next to the treatment table. She emptied the collected water into the sink and decided to leave the machine running, despite the noise, as she worked on poor Mrs. Miller.

She dusted the body with desiccant and turned her attention to the hair. She checked the photo they'd given her for reference and noted with real regret the deceased's abundant mane of chestnut hair. The woman in the picture was smiling at the camera and hugging one of her boys. She remembered him well; the Miller boy had died six months earlier in the big storm, along with his parents, his grandmother, and his two siblings.

Most of the family had been buried almost immediately, as was often the case after disasters. But Mrs. Miller's mother, who was in Spain, had a heart attack when they informed her of the catastrophe, and she had moved heaven and earth to make sure her daughter wouldn't be buried until she'd recovered enough to see her one last time. Now the authorities had delivered a body that had been in the deep freeze for six months, and they expected the Wards to perform a miracle.

Mary used a hair dryer to blow away the desiccant. After testing various pigments, she mixed up a sticky flesh-colored paste and applied it to Mrs. Miller's face. She smiled in satisfaction as she spread it first with a sponge and then with a fine brush.

As she daubed the mixture along the jaw line, she noticed a little lump, probably a broken or dislodged tooth, not uncommon in such deaths. She sighed and put aside the bowl and the brushes. She inspected the subject's oral cavity with a flashlight, probed with forceps, and was surprised to find everything intact. She ran her fingers along the jawline again. There was definitely something there, a loose fragment of some kind. She worked it along the lower jaw and trapped it against a rear molar. She knew she had to be careful, or the object, whatever it was, would vanish down Mrs. Miller's throat. With great care, Mary inserted tweezers and guided them along the rear teeth. She held the object in place with pressure from her fingers until she was sure she had it firmly gripped. She extracted it and held it up to the light.

It wasn't the first time Mary Ward had seen a bullet, but God knows she hadn't expected to find one in the mouth of the late Mrs. Miller.

5

Insolent

Quantico, Virginia
Thursday, August 25, 2005

Amaia followed Agent Emerson along the corridors. He hadn't explained; he'd only told her to follow him. She knew she wasn't going to get any information out of him. He'd refused to meet her eyes, and now he was walking a yard ahead of her. Their tenuous rapport had been irreparably damaged the day before, so she asked no questions and concentrated instead on memorizing the labyrinthine path she was taking. Her guide was probably trying to disorient her. She was almost certain of it by the time they reached the end of a narrow hallway and took an elevator down to the basement.

The doors opened onto a large space with cubicles, desks, and agents absorbed in their work. Emerson gestured toward a couple of straight-backed chairs by one of the offices off the central space. He rapped lightly on the door and went inside, leaving her outside alone. Several of the busy agents watched her with interest. One of them made eye contact with her, then glanced toward the ceiling. She followed his gaze and saw the blinking red light of a closed-circuit video camera. She was being watched.

On the other side of the door, Emerson greeted his colleagues but received no reply. He settled into a chair in the corner. He'd expected to see Dupree, Agent

Tucker, and Agent Johnson, but he was surprised to find two other men next to Dupree, also studying the monitor showing the woman waiting outside.

Assistant Inspector Amaia Salazar was a good-looking young woman with long blond hair that she put up in a ponytail, unobtrusive earrings, and polished shoes. She sat with her back straight and her head held high. Dupree saw her glance up at the camera. She didn't seem bothered by the knowledge that they were observing her. He read that as a sign of authentic, hard-earned self-confidence.

Agent Johnson, standing at one side of the desk, opened a folder and read aloud from it. His voice was deep and his tone was calm and knowledgeable. His bristling but neatly trimmed and prematurely white mustache and beard gave him the air of a Victorian physician. He hadn't gained an ounce of fat in the thirty years since he'd entered the FBI Academy. He might even have lost a few. He was proud that he could still wear the same suits as he had back then.

"Amaia Salazar, twenty-five years old, graduated summa cum laude from Boston College. Law, sociology, and behavioral science—specialization in criminology, with a minor in nonverbal communication. Finished her MS, returned to her country, joined the police."

One of the men next to Dupree nodded, unimpressed. Jim Wilson was the director of the Criminal Justice Information Services Division (CJIS), overseeing the National Crime Information Center (NCIC), which he had helped establish. NCIC files contained data not only on murders, rapes, and armed robberies, but also information about parole violators, gang members, terrorists, missing persons, stolen identities, and more. He'd persuaded law enforcement agencies from across the globe to contribute files to his compendium. All told, the database contained at least twelve million records.

The other man was Michael Verdon, director of the Criminal Investigative Division. Everyone knew he and Wilson were old friends. Both were close to sixty, had been in the same class at the Bureau, and wore matching comb-overs that did little to hide their increasingly shiny pates. The similarities ended there. Michael Verdon had the figure of an athlete and a deep tan like that of a marine. He could have easily still passed the physical tests required of incoming trainees. In contrast, Wilson was one of those men who looked in shape only from behind. His potbelly was as big as a six-month pregnancy. Wilson and Verdon had collaborated in the 1980s on the Descriptive Index for Latent Identification (DILI), a pioneering program that collated features of any given crime with information already in the system, flagged similarities, and linked them to possible suspects. In the beginning, the DILI had access to fingerprint data only if an individual had been in prison or was incarcerated. The DILI was prehistoric by today's standards, but it had established the parameters used subsequently for forensic databases around the world.

Michael Verdon put into words the question that was bothering all of them. "Why didn't we recruit her straight out of college? Boston's been the source of some of our best agents." Wilson nodded, studying his copy of Salazar's file.

Johnson also nodded. "The boss took a look at her." He jutted his chin toward Dupree, who was still watching the monitor. "And we tried. Everything fit—good background, adopted by an elderly American couple, educated in the US from the age of twelve at some of the best boarding schools, dual citizenship: Spain and the US. A couple of boyfriends, nothing long term. No drugs, no weapons, no scandals. The dean contacted us about her. Salazar presented a brilliant thesis on . . ." Johnson checked the file. "Here it is: 'Scientific Interpretation of Nonverbal Communication Relevant to Minor Children at Risk.' But when we approached her, she said she wanted to go back to Europe."

"To Spain," Dupree added, breaking his silence.

"To northern Spain. Pamplona. Even though the National Police or the Guardia Civil would have been glad to have her, she opted for a smaller force, Navarra's Judicial Police. Not much more than a bunch of backwoods state troopers."

"And now we've got her back," Verdon mused aloud, not speaking to anyone in particular. He left Dupree's side and took one of the chairs by the door.

"Yeah." Johnson smiled. "Actually, we never really let her out of our sight. We weren't surprised to see her hit the ground running. She's the youngest assistant inspector in the country, and she really should have been promoted again already. Her career is taking off, but—"

"But they don't know what to do with her," Agent Tucker said sharply. She tossed the file onto the desk. "No good deed goes unpunished. Especially when a woman's involved."

Johnson raised an eyebrow, but that was his only reaction. Tucker never passed up an opportunity to call out anything that smacked of sexism. Johnson assumed, as everyone did, that Tucker had received her share of insults and abuse, but he knew she was ambitious and had her sights on becoming Dupree's successor. She hadn't discriminated on her way to the top: she'd trampled on everyone, regardless of race or gender. For the last two years, she'd supervised a unit of three criminal investigators, one man and two women. She tolerated Emerson because she'd identified him as a consummate ass-kisser with a flair for recognizing talent.

Emerson shrugged. "In any case, the crime rate in that region is pathetically low; I doubt she's seen any bodies there except suicides and murdered wives. She's probably gotten rusty."

Dupree looked up as if surprised to find Emerson there. His reaction made it clear that Emerson was off track.

Tucker told him why. "You're wrong. She hunted down a predator, one of the nastiest and most elusive types of killers, all on her own. She freed his most recent victim and proved he'd kidnapped and murdered two other women before that."

Emerson's jaw tightened.

Verdon put into words the obvious question. "Why would someone with her education and training want to go back? What was she looking for in Spain?"

"She was waiting," Dupree replied.

"Waiting, but for what?"

Dupree said nothing. He smiled to himself and kept his eyes on the young woman on the monitor.

Johnson took over. "When we send out invitations to European police forces, we usually ask the top brass to nominate their candidates. But we were specific with the Spaniards: we wanted Assistant Inspector Salazar." He smiled.

"We're lucky she doesn't know it," Dupree added.

Wilson had listened without comment. He went to the door that opened directly into the adjacent office, grasped the knob, and turned to look at Dupree. "You know my opinion. She turned us down once; brilliance is no excuse for insolence." He jabbed his bloodless finger toward the desk and a document covered with colorful sticky notes. "If she can justify this—*and* you can explain to me why it's genius and not arrogance—you'll have my full support for whatever decision you make."

"Thanks, Jim," Dupree replied. "I appreciate that."

"Thank me after she explains herself. I'll monitor the interview from my office."

Dupree nodded and waited for Wilson to close the door behind him. "Johnson, bring her in."

They seated her in a chair facing Agent Dupree. In her peripheral vision, she saw Johnson and Tucker on her left and Emerson on her right. Out of her field of view, seated directly behind her at the door, was a man they hadn't introduced. Dupree didn't offer to shake hands; he didn't greet her at all. He sat leafing through the report before him. She recognized it immediately from the various colored notes she'd applied to the pages.

She flinched a bit when Dupree launched into his comments with no preliminaries. "Yesterday Agent Tucker gave you the dossier for an exercise analyzing an active case. Your job was to prepare three profiles: behavioral, geographic, and victimological." He jabbed a thumb at the clock on the wall behind him, where the hands pointed to nine forty-five. "The instructor gave you until noon today, but you turned in your work only three hours later." He raised the document to show it to her. "That would be a record, except for the fact that you gave us back the same dossier decorated with about half a dozen Post-it notes and the same number of short comments."

Amaia sought to respond. "Sir—"

Dupree held up a hand to stop her. "Your first note reads, 'Details about the third case not provided.'" He gave her an inquiring look. "Tell me, Assistant Inspector Salazar, what makes you think there's a third case?"

She swallowed hard before answering. "Sir, it was a comment made by Agent Tucker during her briefing."

Dupree lifted an eyebrow, inviting further explanation. Amaia saw Agent Tucker sit up straighter when she heard her own name mentioned.

"At one point in her briefing, Agent Tucker said, and I quote, 'Given the vast area across which the killer moves.' Sir, maybe a Greek or an Italian might think that the four-hour drive between Texas and Oklahoma is a long way, but no one in the United States would. Agent Tucker's statement led me to think there was probably another case that hadn't been described."

"Your instructor told you she'd given you all the available information," Dupree insisted.

"Would the FBI really disclose all the details of an open case simply for a student exercise?"

Agent Tucker leaned forward so Amaia could see her face clearly. "The premise is that there are no more details; those we gave you were enough to complete the exercise."

Dupree saw the momentary twitch of skepticism in Amaia's face. He prompted her. "It appears you didn't accept that premise."

"I believe that everything points to the existence of at least one additional case. That was the basis for my comment."

Dupree leaned back in his desk chair and studied Salazar for several seconds. Something had changed in the tone of his voice when he next spoke. "On March fifteenth, all members of the Mason family were found dead inside their farmhouse near Killeen, Texas, after a violent storm ravaged the area. The local police followed standard procedure after a disaster and the victims were buried within twenty-four hours. There were no autopsies.

"On April twenty-sixth, a tornado destroyed the Jones farmstead near Brooksville, Oklahoma. The bodies of Mr. Jones, his wife, their three teenage children, and Mr. Jones's mother were found in the wreckage. In this case, we had a witness, a boy trapped in a collapsed chicken house. He heard gunshots and screams and then saw a man waving his arms like someone directing an orchestra. The witness named him the Composer.

"The Oklahoma Department of Public Safety called us in, and we managed to get there before the scene had been disturbed. All the bodies were covered by debris, even though the witness claimed—and evidence later substantiated—that the family had taken refuge in the cellar when the storm hit. The witness stated he heard them come out. He knew them well, and he recognized their voices. All the bodies were supine with their heads oriented toward the north. They'd been killed by shots from a small-caliber firearm confirmed to belong to the father. Each individual had ligature marks that suggested they'd been tied hand and foot. The victims evidently weren't bound for long, and the killer removed the cords and took them with him. He sought to disguise the gunshot wounds by battering the bodies.

"We then obtained an exhumation order for the victims in Killeen. You may not be familiar with the effects of embalming. Draining blood and replacing it with embalming fluid can obscure certain marks on the skin, but a month after the deaths, the bruising was evident under ultraviolet light. All the bodies had been bound hand and foot. The police in Killeen had thought the deaths were accidental and therefore had had no reason to investigate further."

Dupree leaned forward and leafed through Amaia's submission. "In your second note," he continued, picking up the little square so that it adhered to his index finger, "You write, 'Saves them from the destruction,' 'He's their rescuer,' and 'Arrives when they need him most.'"

A sigh showed them she was nervous. Her voice emerged thin and choked, "Thanks to the witness . . ." She cleared her throat, swallowed, and started over. "Thanks to the witness, we know the killer arrived at the house immediately after the tornado. He got there ahead of the rescue teams, the police, and the firefighters. The family had survived but they'd lost everything. They were overwhelmed. The killer presents himself as someone who's come to help, someone bringing them salvation—in more than one sense of the word. That's the only explanation why a family of three adults and three teenagers would be unable to defend themselves against this man. If, as Agent Tucker told us, he arrived unarmed and then used the father's gun to kill them, he had to get close and win their confidence, so as to overcome their defenses."

Emerson interrupted her. "You're not adding anything new. If you'd bothered to study the report, you'd know we dismissed the possibility that the perpetrator was on the rescue team. According to the witness, the Composer carried a briefcase and wore a badge."

Dupree pointed to another sticky note, this one yellow. "In your third note, relating to the position of the corpses and the ligature marks, even though you weren't informed that the bodies were aligned with their heads to the north, you wrote, 'After killing them he cares for them. That's his mission. To maintain that mission, he's determined to hide his crimes and not get caught. Not just to remain undetected. He's obsessed with endowing the dead with dignity.'"

Amaia had seen Emerson shaking his head in disagreement as Dupree read out the note, but Johnson was the one who countered her argument. His voice was calm, as always, and he spoke in the manner of a learned professor seeking to dialogue with a student. "I do not agree with that point. The individual we seek is a hunter, a predator who wants to stay hidden. We don't believe that disguising his crimes has anything to do with the victims. He does it for himself, in order to remain unperceived. He succeeded in disguising the murders of the Masons, and he'd have gotten away with the Jones murders too if there hadn't been a witness."

Dupree looked up from the report. With a lift of his chin he invited Amaia to respond.

"I believe he hides his method of execution by gunshot for a different reason. I think he perceives his own method as undignified or even cowardly. In some twisted way, he's trying to reestablish order, to endow the dead with dignity; he doesn't seek to degrade or shame them. That's why he disguises the wounds. He makes their deaths look accidental, a result of divine will. Perhaps he sees himself as carrying out God's work, finishing up what God sent the storm to do. A fair number of people still believe that natural disasters are divine punishment. I believe the killer's exploitation of natural disasters to carry out his murders isn't evidence of a desire to hide his crimes. Rather, he sees himself as an instrument of God's holy wrath."

Tucker and Johnson exchanged quick glances, while Dupree remained seated behind the desk. He took a deep breath. "I'm not entirely convinced. Our approach to this case takes into account the ritual behavior typical of 'annihilators,' killers who murder entire families. But I have to say that your reasoning is as original as the way you presented your report."

Her knee started to jiggle. Amaia placed a hand on that leg as she sought to regain her calm. She had known exactly what she was doing when she presented her conclusions. She'd provoked them deliberately, and now she had to deal with the pushback.

"Here's one thing that particularly caught my attention." Dupree pointed to the yellow note posted at the bottom of the boy's witness statement. He read it aloud. "'Does the boy go to church regularly? Has he ever attended a funeral? Would he recognize church liturgy?'"

Amaia had held her breath as he read. When she inhaled again, it was with a quick snort. She blinked and was about to explain, but Dupree raised a hand to forestall her. He picked up from his desk a document printed on FBI letterhead. "Yesterday, after reading your *brief* note, Agents Johnson and Tucker flew to Oklahoma to find out. They interviewed the witness and his parents. Agents . . ." With a wave of his hand he gave them the floor.

"This family doesn't go to church," Tucker said. "The father thinks religion is absurd, and he had plenty to say on that score." She read from the document she had in hand. "'He explained that his family does not attend church. In response to our question, the boy stated he has never attended a church service or a funeral.'"

Johnson spoke up. “We showed him video of a church service. The boy recognized the gestures immediately. He told us the Composer did exactly the same thing.”

Amaia exhaled, her reaction signaling that she’d been counting on such an answer, but Dupree was the next one to speak. “The killer was not directing an orchestra or composing a symphony for the dead; he was praying for them, carrying out a farewell liturgy.”

Amaia’s voice was scarcely audible. “A Dies Irae for the repose of the dead.”

Dupree looked past Amaia and caught Verdon’s eye. Verdon nodded. The boss returned his gaze to the young woman. She was beginning to feel uncomfortable.

Amaia held his gaze as long as she could. Though aware it might be a mistake and a sign of weakness, she lowered her gaze. She looked up only when he spoke again.

“The next note says, ‘Executes them with the father’s gun. Not a coincidence. Knows the gun’s in the house.’”

Emerson swiveled on his chair. “Then how does he find it in the middle of all that confusion? Anyone could assume there’d be some kind of firearm in a farmhouse, a shotgun or maybe a hunting rifle, but in both cases it was a small-caliber weapon. Even supposing he had some way of knowing about those guns, how was he going to locate them in the wake of a tornado?”

Amaia didn’t respond to Emerson. She kept her eyes on Dupree until he signaled he expected her to reply.

“When a violent storm is threatening, families are going to take various safety measures: collecting food, flashlights, water, weapons . . . They probably had everything in a bag or suitcase they brought with them into the storm cellar. And as I mentioned before, the killer didn’t come across as dangerous or threatening. That’s the only way to explain it, unless”—she paused, fully aware she was about to clash with Tucker—“unless the killer had his own weapon, held it on them, and forced them to surrender theirs.”

One of Dupree’s eyebrows shot up. “If he’s already armed, why use the father’s gun?” He scribbled a note across the bottom margin of the page.

“That’s part of his ritual. For some reason he sees it as important.”

Emerson got to his feet, unable to contain himself. “All of which brings us back to an annihilator, an exterminator of families who has to commit his crime with the father’s gun.”

"Why punish the other members of the family?" Tucker asked.

"They probably stand for members of his own family," Emerson replied. "He punishes them in place of those who knew he was being abused and did nothing about it. He satisfies his psychological urges by taking control and disposing of them as he wishes."

Amaia considered this. "He could be an annihilator. But, as a rule, the annihilators who kill whole families as a demonstration of power and control were subject to terrible abuse as children—physical, emotional, and, in most cases, sexual. Those killers usually torture their victims to inflict upon them the same suffering they themselves were forced to endure. If he's choosing families because they remind him of his own, he has to be identifying with one of the members. In most documented cases, the killer leaves that person alive. The spared individual escapes unless he presents a threat, and the killer never tortures him. He does inflict great pain on the others, and he doesn't disguise the injuries, indignities, or humiliations. Just the opposite: he arranges the scene to highlight what he did to them. Annihilators want the world to see what they did and understand the torments they themselves went through."

Johnson agreed. "I'm intrigued by this line of reasoning. Maybe this time, we've encountered something completely different. All the family members were executed, their injuries disguised, and none of them was subjected to any visible indignity. He treated them all the same."

Amaia nodded. "The only differentiating factor is that the father owned the gun. That's all. I don't believe this case involves an annihilator, although it might look that way at first. He's an evangelical assassin. He identifies those who have sinned and redeems them with death. And now we know he prays for them afterward."

Emerson was adamant. "I don't believe that's relevant. Maybe he's repentant. But the rest of the profile points to an annihilator. We all agree on that."

Amaia saw Tucker tilt her head slightly. Emerson didn't have the support he thought.

"Cognitive bias," murmured Amaia, annoyed.

"What do you mean by that?" Emerson challenged her, offended.

Amaia took her time. She didn't expect them to make it easy, but she hadn't thought they'd want her to accept their views simply because they were FBI agents. She chose her words carefully. "I mean that when you draw up the profile of a killer, you have to be careful to avoid false-consensus bias. It's human nature to look for evidence we can interpret to confirm our beliefs; it's just as human to neglect anything that contradicts our views. It's the same with consensus. There's a tendency to assume that the theory we propound has more support than it actually does. Often we don't question our own assumptions, and that's a mistake. Sometimes lots of people have the same opinion, and they're all wrong."

Emerson stared at the floor. Johnson's sigh of disgust was loud in the silence.

Dupree frowned slightly and stared at her. It was clear this discussion wasn't to his liking.

Amaia could tell he regarded her as no more than an opinionated rookie—or less, since she wasn't an actual FBI trainee. Well, it was true she was just a small-town cop from rural Spain, but she insisted on being treated with respect and knew how to stick up for herself. She'd done what she could to complete the exercise, even though she was convinced they'd left out important information. She heard a rustle behind her and saw Dupree acknowledging a signal she couldn't see from the man seated at the door.

"Go on," Dupree ordered her.

She nodded in acknowledgment. "It's the fact that he prays for them that makes him different, and that distinction changes things. We still don't know whether the praying is significant. It could be decisive. We can't dismiss it just because it doesn't fit the standard profile of an annihilator. We need to go deeper." She spoke directly to Dupree. "And I suspect that's what you think, as well."

He raised his eyebrow again, but his skeptical look quickly turned to one of amusement. "Oh, really? What makes you say that?"

"I don't think it's a coincidence that you devoted yesterday's lecture to killers who disguise their crimes."

Dupree didn't respond. He leafed through the dossier Amaia had decorated with sticky notes. Finally, he closed it and looked at her. "There are two more notes. In the one related to the victimological profile you say, 'Same sexes, ages, relations.' Wouldn't that tend to confirm the unit's analysis? If he's a family exterminator, he'd require the same cast of characters you mention. Each family member would stand for someone he knew, for his own family, so as to give him the opportunity to exact his revenge."

Amaia shook her head in disagreement. "He's not seeking revenge; he's looking for atonement. The cast of characters doesn't matter to him, but completing the set of victims is extremely important. It's the family, the concept of family per se. He's an evangelical killer, but he doesn't kill the dog, because the animal's not part of his creation. I'm sure that he didn't touch any pets."

She noted sounds of discomfort. Sighs, shifts of position. She'd put all her chips on the table. Her bravado had captured their attention, but she was aware of the risk she had taken.

Amaia sat up straighter. This was winding down. If she didn't speak now, she'd never have another chance.

"Sir, I couldn't deliver the profiles without getting the answers to my questions. Information is missing, sir—"

Tucker cut her off. "You could have completed the exercise with the information you had."

"Knowing information had been withheld confirmed my conclusions," she replied quickly. "Completing the exercise without all the relevant information would have meant accepting a fraudulent or misleading scenario. The dossier given to us did not mention that they'd been tied up or that the boy saw the killer was wearing a badge." She regretted her words as soon as they were out of her mouth. She heard the door behind her close. The man who'd sat behind her had just left. She had a foreboding that the closing door had shut off any possibility they'd ever take her seriously.

She half closed her eyes and exhaled slowly before daring to look at Dupree again. He was holding up the last sticky note, the blue one she'd placed on the geographic profile.

He waved it at her. "'Latent variables'?"

She paused to calm herself and then explained. "Latent or hidden variables, sir. Variables not directly observed but inferred from other information present and visible in the situation. The latent variables indicate he's done this before and perfected his method. I'm certain there's at least one other case."

Emerson smiled malevolently. "Based on what evidence?"

Amaia turned toward him and even allowed herself a momentary smile before replying. "Based on a mathematical model. If you're really a data analyst, you should be familiar with the method."

"I know what they are," he muttered.

"In this case," she plunged ahead, "they are inferred from Agent Tucker's declaration that the killer moves across a vast territory." She remained in the same position and watched as signs of discomfit appeared on Emerson's face. His eyes refused to meet hers, focusing on the middle distance.

"You couldn't be more wrong—"

"Actually, she's right," Dupree interrupted. "There is another case. Last February a violent storm swept across the coast near Cape May, New Jersey. The Millers, a family with an identical age and gender composition, were found dead inside their home. As in the Mason case, they were buried without autopsies. Mrs. Miller's extended family lives outside the United States. When they heard what had happened, her mother had a heart attack. She wasn't able to travel until last week. Meanwhile, Mrs. Miller's body was kept frozen at the express request of her family. Mary Ward, the proprietor of a funeral service in Cape May, thawed the body and began to prep it for a possible viewing. While applying makeup to the face, she noted a lump along the jaw that turned out to be a twenty-two-caliber bullet. We haven't yet been able to obtain exhumation orders for the other family members because of the length of time since their deaths, the opposition of the heirs, and the intervention of an extremely conservative judge. The judge told us that photos taken of the scene should be sufficient for our investigation." Dupree opened a drawer, took out a maroon folder, and placed it on the desk in front of Amaia. Inside, a thick packet of photos showed the interior of an oceanside cottage destroyed by wind and water. The bodies of the family were grouped in the main room of the cottage. The victims' crushed skulls contrasted with their otherwise unscathed bodies.

Amaia went through the photos carefully, almost reverently, touching them as little as possible. She was brought back to the present by Agent Dupree's voice.

"Assistant Inspector Salazar, early this morning a twister devastated a wide area in Texas. The bodies of the Allen family, including a father, mother, and three teenagers, two boys and a girl, have all been found dead in the wreckage of their home. Since both the father and the mother grew up as orphans in foster homes, at first glance, this case doesn't look like it fits the killer's profile. We are headed to Texas to take a closer look at the scene and we want you to come along."

Amaia nodded obediently.

6

Itxusuria

Alvord, Texas

The grassy yard in front of the Allen house showed hardly any sign that a tornado had recently passed over it. The ground-level basement windows were intact, and so were the front porch steps. Pots filled with a profusion of tiny purple flowers flanked the front door. Only when she looked up did Amaia realize the single-story house no longer had a roof. The structure had been peeled away completely. It looked like a turtle with its shell ripped off.

The driveway was jammed with vehicles, evidence of the enormous number of police, firefighters, paramedics, and funeral home employees gathering on the premises. Amaia trailed behind the FBI unit along the narrow path the local police had cleared, but they had to stop because of the crowd. Agent Emerson, directly in front of her, looked back for an instant, then elbowed his way into the living room without waiting for her.

Amaia didn't care. She knew they couldn't do anything until the room was cleared. Nobody seemed to be paying attention to the rest of the house, so she decided to check out the other rooms first. Her jacket was too large, but at least it bore the distinctive yellow FBI initials across its back. After searching its various concealed pockets, she found a pair of latex gloves, pulled them on, and walked down the hall toward the back of the house.

The roof was gone, but the house's interior seemed almost untouched. The kitchen was a different story. Pictures hung askew, long jagged chunks of wood had been ripped from the structure, and piles of debris from the now-missing roof were coated with dirt and dust. Electrical cables, twisted and useless, dangled across the broken walls. Amaia saw that the windows had imploded and left glass scattered everywhere. An unfinished meal sat on the table. The kitchen chairs were overturned, evidence of a hasty flight just before the storm hit.

On her way across the front yard she'd scanned the exterior of the Allens' tidy farmhouse for signs of a storm cellar. Dupree had said on the flight to Texas that this family wasn't an exact match for the victimological profile of their killer, but Amaia thought the fit was too close to be mere coincidence. A husband, a wife, and three children—two boys and a girl, the same ages as the Mason and Jones children. The entire family lay dead in the main room of their home, even though the pattern of damage suggested they could have survived simply by sheltering beneath the furniture. The FBI needed to verify the orientation of the bodies and locate the father's pistol.

If the Allens were victims of the Composer, as she suspected, they'd have ridden out the tornado in a shelter. By the kitchen door, she found another, identical door that opened onto the basement stairs. She rummaged through her jacket and came up with a small flashlight. She went down without touching the railing, careful to step on the outside edges so as to avoid compromising any possible evidence. Dust swirled in the air. Very little light filtered through the basement windows. The ground-level openings, narrow slots high in the ceiling of the basement room, were almost completely obscured. At first, she thought they were caked with dust or mud, but then she saw that brown paper had been taped across them.

Her flashlight beam revealed carefully labeled plastic bins filled with flashlights, batteries, a transistor radio, jugs of water, and canned food. There was even a little camping stove with a bottle of propane. She found a bulky old sideboard against one wall. On it stood two cans of beer, two diet sodas, half a dozen other canned soft drinks, and a couple of plastic bottles of water. A small padlock hung unsecured from the sideboard's bottom cabinet. She pushed the doors open without touching the handles and immediately smelled the familiar odor of gun oil. The firearm wasn't inside, but boxes of .22-caliber slugs were stacked at the back of a shelf. She saw several sleeping bags and pillows in a heap along the wall farthest from the windows. A gold-colored toiletries bag, similar to a makeup kit, lay beside them. She squatted, peered into it, and found it full of medicine.

Amaia went back upstairs and took the hall toward the living room but was literally boxed in by two Texas state troopers. A male voice with a heavy Texan accent was insisting that everyone except the FBI and the crime scene technicians clear the premises. She flattened herself against the wall to let the state troopers pass. Each wore a broad-brimmed cowboy hat. They were so burly that their shoulders spanned almost the whole width of the hall.

She finally got a look at the living room. The mess and confusion around and over the family were greater than elsewhere in the house. Technicians in their distinctive white coveralls and masks were busy collecting photographic evidence, snapping pictures of every object as they removed it. The victims' heads were ugly, dusty gray mashes of coagulated blood. All were oriented toward the north, and in the same order as in the other cases: the wife, then the three children in chronological order of birth, and finally the husband. The FBI team waited in a silent circle as the work proceeded. A tall man with a Stetson hat, white shirt, dark tie, dark jeans, and boots stood next to Dupree.

Dupree caught sight of Amaia standing in the doorway. He swiftly crossed the room toward her, a dangerous and angry look in his eyes. He said nothing until they were face to face. He was furious. "Where the hell were you?"

She was taken aback. "I was—"

Dupree snorted like a bull, seized her by the arm, and perp walked her outside.

She tried to explain. "I couldn't get in. Agent Emerson left me behind, the hallway was blocked, and I took a moment to—"

"I am not interested in excuses," he snapped. "Emerson is an idiot. But I made a big gamble bringing you here, and I didn't do it just to show you how we work. I wanted you to keep your eyes open. Get in there and try to understand that family's terror! I want to know how the Composer thinks. Don't let them intimidate you. I've got your back."

Without waiting for a reply, he turned on his heel and went inside.

Amaia bit her lip, exhaled through her nose, and followed him in.

The techs had finished uncovering the bodies, and the FBI team was squatting to watch as they listened to the medical examiner's first impressions. Amaia walked over to stand directly behind him.

"They've been dead for less than five hours. No hematomas evident yet, but there are traces indicating they were tied up. Surprisingly little loss of blood, considering the extent of the cranial injuries."

Agent Tucker spoke. "So the head injuries were inflicted postmortem?"

"Can't be sure of that yet. We'll have to wait for the autopsies. But what I can tell you is that these are fatal injuries." With two fingers the doctor delicately pushed aside the smaller boy's hair so they could appreciate the violence of the blow that had deformed his skull.

Tucker persisted. "They were all fatally wounded the same way, their skulls crushed. Were they killed in this room?"

"Well, you saw how they had to be dug out from the debris. But the fact that they gathered here doesn't prove they weren't injured elsewhere in the house. I've seen similar situations in house fires. When panic hits, family members look for one another, it's normal. And all too often they die together as a result."

Dupree added a note. "With all heads oriented toward the north."

The medical examiner shrugged. "Okay, well . . . that's unusual, but . . ."

Amaia shook her head and joined in. "There's no blood anywhere in the rest of the house. I checked." She was speaking only to Dupree. "Not a single drop to suggest they could've been hurt elsewhere. With head injuries this serious, they'd have bled profusely; there'd be a trail of blood."

Johnson followed up. "There's nothing on the clothing. If they'd been upright when struck, staining would have been inevitable."

Amaia stepped forward and leaned over the youngest victim. She pointed to the mass of gore covering the back of the boy's head. "If you look closely, you'll see there's a bubble maybe half an inch below the point of impact."

The medical examiner pushed aside the boy's hair there. "Could be a blood clot."

"It's not," she contradicted him. "That's a gas bubble. Examine the very edge of the wound, on this side, and you'll find two little black spots. That's residue typical of the collar of abrasion formed from a gunshot at point-blank range. It's almost invisible because of the battering. But a skull is hard bone, and it prevented the gas from dissipating within the body. That's why this bubble formed."

Dupree nodded in satisfaction.

"You might be right," the medical examiner acknowledged reluctantly.

"They all died from shots to the head, shots disguised afterward by these blows," she asserted.

Johnson intervened. "While there are many similarities with the other cases we identified, we still haven't found the pistol. And there's no grandmother."

"The family took shelter in the cellar which can be accessed from the kitchen." Amaia still spoke only to Dupree. "They were prepared. They had water, food, batteries, a transistor radio, and flashlights, all sealed in plastic bins. The gun was kept down there. I couldn't locate the firearm, but I saw an oiled cloth, a cleaning brush, and several boxes of twenty-two-caliber ammunition. They spent the night down there, but I don't think they got much sleep. The bedrooms up here are a mess, but it's obvious the beds weren't slept in. There are six sleeping bags downstairs and open drinks. The beers were probably for the father, the diet drink for the mother, Coke for the kids, and water for someone else. A sixth person."

Emerson appealed to the others. "It's pretty damn reckless to assume that an extra sleeping bag and bottle of water prove the presence of a sixth person. They could've put down all the sleeping bags they had, and any of them could have been drinking water."

Dupree's look invited her to respond.

She did. "On the floor by the sleeping bags there's a little cloth case full of pills and tablets, the sort of medicine a senior citizen would take. Blood thinners, blood pressure medicine, tablets for arthritis, sleeping pills. The elderly carry their medicines with them wherever they go, and they take their pills with water. Add to that the fact the water bottle has obvious lipstick traces. Neither the mother nor the girl is wearing lipstick."

"There's a problem, though," Tucker objected as she pushed herself to her feet. "There's not a trace of this person. According to their files, neither spouse had living parents. Both were orphaned at a young age, and they were in foster care in their teens. Neither had any other family."

Amaia left the house. Winding her way through the vehicles blocking the drive, she got far enough away to get a wider view of the property. The dirt road to the Allen farmhouse connected it to a state highway about two hundred yards away. From the edge of the highway, she scanned the rolling plain.

The crop, probably soybeans, had been harvested, so the absence of machinery wasn't unusual. She remembered seeing a fridge magnet from the Alvord Farmers Co-op. The only structure in sight was the ravaged farmhouse, and they'd been told that the closest neighbors were more than two miles away. She looked up at the passing clouds and started back toward the house.

A state trooper was leaning against a patrol car. She gave Amaia a friendly look and nodded toward the farmhouse. "Unbelievable, right? Looks like a turtle with its shell ripped off."

Amaia's lips twitched in a faint, wry smile. "I thought the same thing when I saw it. Too bad there's a threat of more rain."

"Oh, don't worry about that. A company from Oklahoma will be here in an hour or two with an industrial tarp to cover it. After the examiner takes the bodies out, we'll go through the place room by room and inventory everything. It goes to a warehouse until the case is closed. After that it goes to the heirs. That is, assuming there are any."

Amaia gave her a real smile this time. "Pretty efficient!"

The friendly woman extended her hand. "Alana Harris, state trooper."

"Assistant Inspector Amaia Salazar." She touched the FBI badge pinned to the front of her baggy jacket.

The trooper grinned at her. "They didn't take too much trouble getting you the right size, did they?"

Amaia returned the grin and pointed toward what was left of the farmhouse. Dupree stood with a Texas Ranger on the front porch watching them. "Any idea where the roof wound up?"

"Sure!" was the cheerful answer. "It's a bit less than a quarter of a mile from here." Harris pointed. "You're lucky. Three years ago, a storm following Hurricane Helen tore off part of the church roof and left it on a silo two miles away."

Amaia nodded in thanks. She headed around to the back of the Allens' destroyed home. In contrast with the front yard, the field behind the house was littered with splintered wood, clothing, and smashed furniture. A six-armed standing lamp stood incongruously upright in the field, all of its bulbs intact. The roof was nowhere in sight.

"You'll have to go down yonder to see it," her new friend called after her. "It got stuck in a hollow."

Amaia turned and waved her thanks. She saw that Dupree had left the supervising ranger on the porch and was headed in her direction.

She strode forward single mindedly, aware Dupree was behind her. There was no sign of the roof, but when she turned back, Trooper Harris waved her on.

The hollow was about six feet deep and seventy-five feet wide. And lo and behold, the roof was there, almost intact, still fastened to the joists that had anchored it to the farmhouse. The grassy field had been trampled by someone; the track ahead of her was as obvious as boot prints in a snowdrift. She turned and saw a similar grassy trail in her wake.

Dupree caught up with her and stood silent at her side. Behind them, the rest of the team emerged from the house and headed in their direction.

Amaia slipped down the slope, went forward on all fours, and looked under the edge of the roof. She stood up immediately and signaled to Dupree and the others. She commented to their huddle, "Where I'm from in Spain, there's an old belief that the sacred space of a family home includes the foot or two just outside the walls. They call that outer perimeter *itxusuria*. If a family member was denied Christian burial in the village cemetery, they buried that person at home. In the shelter of the eaves."

She stood watching as they spread out, crouched, and peered under the stranded roof. Someone took out a high-tech flashlight. Its dazzling beam played across the shrouded space until it came to rest on the bloody face of an elderly woman.

"There she is," Amaia said. "The grandmother."

7

Doubt

Quantico, Virginia
Friday, August 26, 2005

Seated before a computer, Amaia again tried to keep her attention on the instructor's explanation of how to structure case summaries in order to enter them into the international victimology registry. She was tired. She'd been up almost all night drafting her report and conclusions, and despite her best efforts, she knew that most of what was being said in class was escaping her. Her thoughts kept returning to her hypotheses, most of them disputed by the agents in Dupree's unit. A good deal of her thinking was outside the box, driven by intuition.

But when all was said and done, that was what Dupree had demanded of her when they separated. He wanted three profiles on his desk by eight.

Amaia delivered them at seven. She checked her watch; it was past noon. She couldn't get her profile of the killer out of her mind: *White male, forty-five years or older. He has killed before using the same method. Organized and patient, waits for the right opportunity, unlike killers who seek victims. Caucasian who kills in his own racial group. Religious believer who may think the church is too indulgent of sin.*

The class ended. The next one was underway before she had time to catch her breath.

Amaia was deeply fatigued, but she knew that was the price for being right, the unwelcome privilege of knowing where to find the piece that completed the puzzle. Irreverence for authority, the ability to detect the undetected and arrogantly contradict received wisdom, the courage to present those insights without ceremony or restraint—none of this was easy; it exacted a price.

Her discovery of the dead woman under the roof had sparked an open confrontation with Dupree's team. The debate wasn't theoretical anymore. The instant the light struck the smashed face of the old woman in that improvised tomb, Amaia felt the pieces of the puzzle snap into place and reveal the ferocity of the predator who had composed these dark tableaux. This crime scene was virtually untouched, unlike the living room, which had been trampled by so many law enforcement agents. She let her mind drift and saw the killer's pursuit of the old woman, as well as the threats and coercion that forced her into this dark place.

He definitely wasn't an annihilator. She was absolutely sure he wasn't. His goal wasn't to destroy families but instead to assemble one perfect family, its perfection cemented in death. Her intuition and ideas sparked an explosion of the resentment the FBI team had had trouble stifling since the meeting in Dupree's office.

"They don't have grandparents!" Johnson rebuked her, face to face, visibly angry but carefully controlled. "They were orphans; the parents of both spouses died long ago. Agent Tucker told you that!"

"This is the grandmother. Check it out and you'll see," she insisted. She stalked off toward the farmhouse.

"We did check!" Tucker called out angrily, following her. "I checked personally."

"Then check again!" Amaia told her.

"Do you understand who you're talking to?" Tucker snapped. "You have no authority here."

Amaia stopped in her tracks and fixed her eyes on the ground, seeking calm. She was boiling inside. She was undecided whether to walk away across the field or just turn around, grab Tucker by the collar, and shake her until she saw the light.

She did neither. Without retreating an inch, she lowered her voice until it was almost inaudible, obliging the agents to lean in close to hear what she was saying. "Forget the official records. Ask the neighbors if that woman lived with them."

Agent Johnson almost staggered back in astonishment at that. He glanced openmouthed at Dupree, trying to gauge the boss's reaction.

Emerson, at the end of his patience, looked around. "What kind of nonsense is this?" he exclaimed, throwing his hands up.

"Check again," Dupree ordered calmly.

"But, Dupree, we already have the information!" Johnson protested.

"Verify it."

Dupree sent her away so he could speak with the others. She sat in the car, the naughty girl forbidden to play with the rest of the kids. She watched Dupree, Emerson, and Tucker, all with their backs to her; she could tell from their gestures they were arguing without raising their voices. She was certain they were talking about her.

She saw Johnson return from questioning a group of neighbors who'd congregated nearby. He said something to Dupree, and then the group turned simultaneously and looked in her direction.

Amaia got out as they approached the car. Dupree deputized Johnson with a wave of his hand.

Johnson admitted she was right. "The woman under the roof is Belinda Wright, a childhood friend of Hugh Allen's mother. She took Hugh in when he left foster care. Hugh lived with her and her husband on a little farm nearby until he married and set up here. When Belinda's husband died years later, she moved in with the family. She wasn't really his mother, but she might as well have been."

Dupree imagined the sequence of events. "Somehow the woman managed to get out of the house, or maybe she was already outside when the killer arrived. He caught up with her in the field, murdered her, and dragged her to the roof and shoved her under it." Dupree gave Amaia a look that showed he was impressed.

Tucker's tone was considerably less adversarial when she next addressed Amaia. "Now I understand what you meant with 'the cast of characters.' It's not so much that he's looking for a family that exactly matches; instead, he wants one he can use to populate his scene. But it's hard to imagine he's choosing them by figuring out where a natural disaster is likely to hit."

"That's not quite it," Amaia objected, starting to hit her stride. "It's not that simple. We have to keep in mind it's gotten easier to predict exactly where a storm or hurricane is going to hit. He knows that too. The hurricane tells him where to go. It's God speaking to him. God and the weather forecasters anyhow," she amplified with a rueful smile. "I believe that's how he beats everyone else to the scene. He's in the area before the hurricane arrives, waiting for God to give him the exact coordinates."

Emerson clicked his tongue in disgust. "Let me see if I've got this right," he said with false affability. "You're imagining the killer doesn't choose a family but instead a place—the place where a natural disaster will strike. Sure, they're no longer that hard to predict, but only up to a point. But if that's how he chooses the scene, how does our Composer find families that match his criteria once the weatherman tells him where to go? Does God tell him where disaster will strike even before the weather bureau does, so he'll have enough time to identify candidates? Or do you think it's all some sort of mystic hocus-pocus like burying bodies under the eaves of the house?"

"That's idiotic reasoning," she answered firmly. "And I'm not making assumptions, I'm building a case from the facts. It doesn't matter what I believe. The important thing is whether *he* believes it. That's the power of faith. If this killer justifies his actions as God's will, or he's at least convinced that God doesn't see him as a murderer but as a just man, he'll attribute to divine guidance events the rest of us think are insignificant. And he'll have developed his own methodology for selecting his victims."

Tucker spoke. "We're still in the early stages, and we don't yet have all the information, but evangelical killers believe they're ridding society of the worthless, the perverse, and the miserable. They usually prey on prostitutes, drug dealers and addicts, and anybody they perceive as immoral. We're just starting to look into the Allen family, but we've combed through the lives of the others, and I can tell you now they don't fit that profile. They're ordinary families with their good points and bad points, but as far as we can see, they weren't the sort an evangelical killer would condemn as immoral. Nothing suggests they were guilty of anything."

Johnson objected. "In the Wuornos case, the killer murdered prostitutes' clients, punishing the men, not the women. The sin an evangelical killer identifies might not stand out at first glance."

Tucker considered that, then turned to Amaia. "Then you're suggesting one or several family members did something, manifested some behavior, that meant they deserved to die?"

"The murderer thought they deserved to die," Amaia cautioned her. "We have to remember he doesn't see the world as the rest of us do. Anything any one of them had done—even the children—might strike him as immoral. But that can't be all of it, since he doesn't take out only the offending family member. He punishes them all. He sees them all as responsible."

She felt Dupree's eyes on her. He was watching her, his head tilted slightly to one side. No, he wasn't watching her, he was *scrutinizing* her as he'd done that morning in his office.

Emerson leaned forward. "I still think there's a flaw in your theory. Sure, all that stuff about disasters determining the place of the crime makes sense. But we still don't have enough to explain how he chose these families."

"I can't explain that," Amaia admitted, locking eyes with Emerson, not so much to challenge him as to escape Dupree's penetrating gaze. "It's too early to answer that question. We can get closer to him once we understand his timing. I'm more interested in figuring out how long he's been murdering families."

Emerson was exasperated. "We've traced him back to February—"

"For the moment," Amaia interrupted him sharply, "we can trace his activities back to Cape May. But I'm certain he started long before that. He's perfected his rite and his method; he knows what he's doing. He knew Belinda Wright played the role of the grandmother, even though she wasn't a blood relation. He's an expert, which strongly suggests experience, practice, and skill. A beginner makes mistakes."

Dupree nodded slowly. "More about that?"

"The Millers in February, the Masons in March, the Jones family in April, and now it's August with the Allens. There's a three-month gap in the timeline. We should look for failures, attacks gone wrong. He can't be scoring a hundred percent."

Tucker nodded and stepped forward to face Amaia. "For example, families with the same composition but where not everybody died. Maybe they weren't all at home when disaster struck."

Amaia smiled, pleased that Tucker was accepting her ideas. Exhilarated, she continued, "It must be hard to control that many people. He forces them to surrender their weapon, ties them up, gets them into a room, and executes them one after another. Belinda Wright got away—others might have as well. I'm sure he had screwups; taking on a family in the wake of a disaster is a risky business. Too many things can go wrong, and something completely unexpected could always occur."

Dupree nodded again and addressed his team. "Look for cases where families with a similar composition complained of a suspicious visitor after a disaster. Let's look for failed attempts, times when the perpetrator had to back off. Maybe a neighbor showed up to help them or outsiders were present; maybe one or several family members were absent. Anything that broke the pattern or complicated his task."

Amaia nodded at each phrase. Dupree turned to her. "What else?"

"I . . . well, if I were in charge . . . I'd want to know everything possible about these families, every detail of their lives. I'm sure their profiles fit the killer's criteria in ways that aren't immediately obvious. It could be some aspect so trivial that we've overlooked it. This type of psychopath doesn't have conventional motivations, but something he finds terribly important is driving him. By understanding the families in depth, we'll have a better chance of figuring out how the killer gets to them. Despite the geographic dispersion of these random disasters, he's managed to identify families that perfectly fit his requirements. How does he do that? We need a better victimology profile."

Emerson leaned close to her and muttered so no one else could hear, "*If* you were running this team."

That was a stupid thing for him to say, but it was enough to distract her for a moment.

"Salazar, what else?" Dupree prompted her.

"The geographic profile," she said, refocusing. "I'd consider a wider area."

"How wide?" Johnson asked.

"Nationwide. Let's look anywhere a natural disaster has struck over the last two years. If nothing turns up, we may have to go farther back."

"That's crazy!" Johnson exclaimed.

Emerson spoke to Johnson as if Amaia weren't present. "I guess she hasn't heard about Canter's Circle."

Amaia struck back. "You can't apply the theory of the geographic locus of a serial killer's action without determining whether additional cases exist."

"I believe what Emerson is referring to," Tucker intervened, "is the killer's reach. He has to be extremely close. Otherwise, in a country as big as the United States, he can't find his victims and track them in such detail that he knows the type and caliber of firearm in the house. Here he even knew that a nonrelative had assumed the role of grandmother. He has to see them first in order to pick them out. And to develop a hatred for them."

Amaia shook her head. "He doesn't hate them—or at least he doesn't hate them for themselves. The important thing is what they represent to him. He prays for their souls, and he wants them to rest in peace. He erases every sign of obvious violence, takes the cord he used to tie them up away with him, spares them any indignity. The fact that he prays for them shows there has to be a rationale, but I don't think it's hatred. He doesn't want anything from them. He doesn't take or remove anything—what could he take from people who just lost everything?

"We live in the information age and the era of exhibitionism. The Internet allows anyone at all into our private space. People post information about their private lives with no thought of who might be reading it. I'm not claiming that's his method, but there are many more ways to track a person or a family than being a voyeur in the shrubbery outside their house."

"Another point," Dupree added. "The killer must be someone who doesn't stick out too much during or after a disaster. He blends in because he's expected to be there."

Tucker opened the small laptop she was carrying, placed it on the hood of the sedan, and called up a collection of company and institutional logos. "At the start, we speculated his job gave him access. We're still checking phone companies, utilities, and Internet providers, hoping to come across a contact the families had in common. Because of the witness, we know that the man looked like someone they could trust. Now we're checking out police officers, firefighters, rescue teams, physicians and paramedics, ambulance crews . . . in a chaotic situation, our killer could masquerade as any of them."

"Some firefighters travel to help out in national disasters," said Johnson. "I know of a canine rescue team that responds to crises all across the country. They even travel abroad to assist after earthquakes and avalanches."

Amaia agreed and upped the ante. "You could include academic researchers, journalists, reporters, and TV camera crews. People who rush toward a crisis everyone else is trying to escape."

Johnson tapped notes into his personal digital assistant. "Including volunteer groups who pitch in for disaster relief."

"Churches, civic groups, and charities," Tucker added.

And Amaia said, "Don't forget storm chasers, pseudoscientists, and nut cases who want to film disasters."

"There's no limit to the number of idiots out there," Johnson said with a grin.

"Or the number of fiends," Dupree said heavily. He looked Amaia directly in the eyes, and this time she met his gaze. Amaia was no stranger to the staring game. She knew men were attracted to her. But Dupree's attention was different. He was evaluating her spirit. The shadows in his dark eyes contained as much curiosity as suspicion.

She was adept in perceiving intentions and hidden attitudes toward her, but Dupree was all white noise. She'd analyzed each of his reactions, his expressions, and his words, and she still couldn't decide if he was friend or foe. But she did know one thing: he paid attention.

"'I've got your back,'" he'd told her. She wasn't depending on that; she was sure of herself and didn't fear for her safety or reputation. Amaia Salazar was used to working solo. But at that moment, in the huddle beside the sedan, she'd felt like part of the unit for the first time that day. She'd felt the connection and the respect of the team.

Maybe she'd been going at this the wrong way.

"We've got our work cut out for us," Dupree said. "The medical examiner promised to do the autopsies right away. The unit will spend the night here. Assistant Inspector Salazar, you go back to Quantico. There's a plane leaving for Virginia in an hour. Trooper Harris from the Texas Highway Patrol will drive you to the airport."

So that's the deal. "This one's for us, not for you." What was I thinking?

The others left quickly and without ceremony. Amaia walked to Harris's cruiser, where the trooper waved in greeting without getting out. Amaia realized Dupree was close behind her and turned to face him.

Herding her to the patrol car, he said, "You've got all the information now. Give me all three profiles. I want them on my desk tomorrow morning by eight o'clock."

Before she got into the vehicle, Amaia turned and confronted him. "Why didn't you greet me?"

Dupree was completely taken aback. He cast out his hands in an involuntary gesture of surprise. Then his features settled into indifference. He didn't reply.

She wasn't about to drop the subject. "You looked at me during your lecture and spoke directly to me several times, but afterward, when I was waiting for you in the hall, you ignored me completely. On purpose. Why?"

Agent Dupree took a deep breath, unzipped his jacket, and placed his hands on his hips. He looked over his shoulder to check the whereabouts of his agents and leaned toward her. "I wanted to avoid influencing your judgment by paying special attention to you. I know all too well how an instructor's interest can have unintended consequences."

She gave him a calculating look. "No, I don't think so. You'd have ignored me from the first if that were it. I saw your interest in me—so did Emerson—but afterward you pretended I didn't exist. You were provoking me on purpose, treating me like I was a presumptuous little shit."

Dupree looked at her. Amaia thought she'd really put her foot in it and he wasn't going to reply, but after a moment he did. "That was no mistake. I needed you to pay close attention during the lecture. And I needed you to take out your anger on the exercise afterward, which is exactly what you did. You were right about one thing: it was no coincidence that I talked about Inspector Sherrington and the hidden victims. For weeks now I've thought we were looking at the same type of case. The revelations of the last few hours have given us new insights and put us on a fresh track."

"Why me?"

Dupree's face hardened. "It's the investigation that counts. You're here today because I thought you could make a contribution."

"That doesn't answer my question."

Dupree turned away, annoyed; he seemed about to stalk off. But then he gave her an incredulous sneer. "You've got to be kidding! You turned in a report that was nothing but a handful of sticky notes. Even Johnson was outraged, and he's usually the world's calmest man. I'm not going to answer your question, Salazar. Maybe someday, but not now. Today you were a tool, that's all, and you provided vital assistance, but there was no need for you to know that in advance. It wouldn't have worked as well if you'd been aware of it. We'd have missed your presumptuous grilling of the medical examiner . . . and your hostility out there in the field by the roof."

"You don't know me!"

"You're right. And that's another reason you're here. I needed to understand how much of you was egotistical posing, and how much was talent and intelligence." He smiled derisively. "Plus, I wanted to get a glimpse of that arrogant look you get when you know you're right."

Amaia scowled.

"Bull's-eye!" Dupree cried triumphantly. "That's the one!"

"Arrogant expression?" She rocked back slightly, dismayed. Now she understood him.

Dupree turned away again and set off toward the group of agents waiting for him outside the farmhouse. "Don't forget," he called back over his shoulder, "your report is due before eight tomorrow morning, Salazar."

8

A Tool

Quantico, Virginia

The hours passed with agonizing slowness. She'd gone over her report so many times she could barely think anymore. She had no appetite for dinner, but she went to the canteen with the other European officers anyway. They arrived as Emerson was on his way out. Amaia greeted him, but a surly Emerson walked right past her.

The afternoon had been taken up first by a class on international crime syndicates, followed by one on international transportation, crime on the high seas, and customs processing of shipping containers. She was no better focused than before, but what really got under her skin was that she'd gotten more and more depressed with each passing hour. She'd started to listen to that persistent little voice inside her head insisting that she'd screwed up, the structure of her report was wrong, and she'd drawn the wrong conclusions. She'd refused to listen when Dupree reproached her for her arrogance, and she was sure she'd proven him right by putting down exactly what she thought. She'd drafted and signed her own expulsion order.

She understood now that they'd toyed with her like cats tormenting a mouse. They'd amused themselves by provoking her. Now they'd abandoned her. Amaia was tired and disoriented, her head full of crime photos, pathology reports, financial information . . . Dupree had been cruelly explicit. "It's the investigation that counts" and "Today you were a tool."

She pushed the food around her plate, smiling dutifully at her colleagues' cheerful talk. She excused herself early and returned to the room she shared with Gertha. She could hardly hold her head up and desperately needed sleep, but the case kept tormenting her. She stared blindly at a book. Gertha was sleeping on her stomach, snoring quietly. Amaia put down the book and turned out the overhead light, certain this was going to be another sleepless night. Moments later she was asleep.

A knocking at the door accompanied by a male voice calling her name interrupted her slumber. Her bedside lamp was still on. She sat up, awake but groggy. She got out of bed and went to the door, turning back for a moment to reassure Gertha, who was peering sleepily at her. "Go back to sleep. It's for me."

Gertha obediently turned on her side and closed her eyes. As Amaia started to open the door, she realized she was in her nightdress. She peeked out, shielding her body with the door.

"Come with me," the man said, indifferent to her attire. "Special Agent Dupree wants to speak with you."

Taking time only to pull on clothes, she followed him. The labyrinthine path to Dupree's office was even more confusing in the dead of night. The midnight calm vanished when the elevator door opened to the basement space. There was little activity at the desks in the open plan of the Behavioral Science Unit. The agent escorted her directly to the office.

Agent Johnson looked as alert as if he'd had a full night's sleep. He rose from the office chair behind Dupree's desk and leaned forward to shake her hand. Johnson settled back into the chair without saying a word. Dupree, in shirtsleeves, was standing to one side before a map. He turned, acknowledged her, and without ceremony, asked, "Salazar, have you been following the weather forecasts over the last few days?"

Amaia didn't see how she could have failed to do so, and not only because of the case. All day long the national newscasts had been obsessed.

"Yes, I saw the news."

"Yesterday, Katrina, a category one hurricane, crossed the tip of Florida. So far, it's left six dead, countless others injured, a wide area blacked out, and highways blocked throughout the state. We have reports of several families who haven't been heard from for at least twenty-four hours. Some of them fit the victimological profile of our killer."

Amaia took in a lungful of air and held it in suspense.

Dupree qualified his narrative. "This may mean nothing. Maybe they evacuated early or went to ride out the storm with family or friends."

"But . . . ," she piped up, unable to contain herself.

"But maybe this is our man at work again."

"You and your team should go there," she suggested, aware she was overstepping her bounds.

"Yes, I agree. I already sent Tucker and Emerson to Florida. We need our people there; we can't afford to have the local authorities miss something. We're hoping they will report back in a few hours."

Amaia looked down and nodded. That was it, then; she was out. Then why had Dupree summoned her? Only to make it clear they had no need for her?

"After she made landfall in Florida, Katrina slowed considerably, but now she's moved out into the Gulf of Mexico. The higher temperatures there have intensified the storm. She's gathering force. The National Hurricane Center currently expects Katrina to make landfall as a category four. Earlier forecasts predicted Katrina would move north across Florida and Georgia, but she's headed west toward Louisiana instead."

A shiver ran up Amaia's spine. She knew most of this already. The newscasts had flashed maps of the hurricane's progress all day long, a huge eye staring down menacingly from above the Gulf of Mexico. She jerked involuntarily, a reaction to the sudden tension she felt.

"Mayor Nagin's staff informed us he's going to decree a mandatory evacuation." The import of his words floated in the air.

"That's where the killer will go," she declared firmly. Her shoulder had stopped quivering.

"That's what I think too. And this time we'll be there waiting for him."

"You will be?"

"*We* will be. Assuming you want to come."

Amaia smiled. "Of course I do."

Dupree offered his hand. "Johnson will accompany you. You have to fill out some security paperwork first, and then they'll give you temporary credentials and a firearm. You don't have much time. We leave for New Orleans in two hours."

Johnson was all smiles as he escorted her to be sworn in as a temporary FBI agent. They gave her clothing, a bulletproof vest, a temporary badge, and a gun.

She went back to the dormitory. Trying not to make noise, she opened the low chest of drawers where she kept her few belongings. She smiled at the thought of choosing appropriate attire for a hurricane. She put a bag on the bed and set out her few things next to it. When she had it ready to go, she checked her watch. Half an hour until departure.

Gertha hadn't budged. She seemed to be sleeping peacefully. Amaia weighed whether to wake her friend.

There was no need.

"Either you will tell me what is going on or I will explode," the German officer said, her eyes still closed. Smiling and drowsy, she listened to Amaia's account, then congratulated her and gave her an affectionate hug. "How do you feel?"

"Fine," Amaia replied, perhaps a little too quickly.

"Natürlich!" her friend said, rolling her eyes. "And now, my little Amaia of the valley, tell your friend Gertie the truth."

Amaia shut her eyes and chewed her lower lip. "Scared, Gertha. I'm scared. This is the real thing, friend, not an exercise. If I make a mistake, people could die. I can't get that out of my mind. It's all very fine to discuss theories in an office, but yesterday, when I saw the horrible wound in that child's head . . . They think I'm out of my depth, and what if they're right?"

Gertha took Amaia's hands in her own. "Listen to me, Amaia. We do not know one another very long, but I see things in you. What makes you strong, what makes you fragile, the questions you always ask yourself—I hope someday you will find the answers to them. You are good, Amaia Salazar, you are strong. But more than that: you are an outstanding police officer. You have the instincts of a born detective. Dupree isn't stupid. He saw it too."

"Yes, but if—"

"No ifs! Go to New Orleans, do a good job. Do not be afraid, and stick to your guns. That is what Dupree wants. He said this yesterday, correct? And don't forget that yes, they are FBI agents, but you are not a cadet. You were the youngest assistant inspector ever in your force. You tracked down a collector, for God's sake! And you did it all by yourself. You hold your head high, Amaia of the valley, and do your job!"

A knock at the door interrupted them. Amaia checked the time. She still had twenty minutes. She opened the door and found a woman in uniform standing in the hall.

"Assistant Inspector Salazar? You have a telephone call from Spain."

She felt a chill. Only one person could be calling, and it could only mean bad news.

Amaia couldn't hide her concern. Gertha frowned, detecting it. Amaia gave her an unconvincing smile and then followed the officer to a room with half a dozen phone booths. She went to the one the woman indicated and picked up the phone.

"Aunt Engrasi, are you all right?"

The calm, beloved voice came to her through the line. "I'm fine, dear, and I didn't want to alarm you. How are you? And how's everything going?"

"I'm fine, Auntie, it's going really well. But what is it? Why are you calling?"

She heard a tense silence at the other end of the line. Amaia could almost see her aunt Engrasi in the big armchair next to the little telephone table. Her hair would be up in a Parisian bun, and the window would be open to let the breezes from the River Baztán in to cool her house.

"Amaia, it's about your father. He's very ill. On Sunday he had another attack, and he's been in the hospital for the past three days. I didn't call before this because I didn't want to worry you, but his condition has gotten much worse in the last few hours."

No, no! Anything but that!

"Auntie . . ."

"The cardiologist says he won't hold out much longer. I am so very sorry, Amaia."

She remembered staring up at her father from the hospital bed all those years ago and making that terrible pledge to him.

She didn't know what to say. She looked down at the little shelf below the telephone, which clearly served as a writing surface. It was marked with dozens, maybe hundreds of scribbles from different pens. In the middle of the chaos, someone had sketched a heart, going over the lines so many times that it stood out from the tangle of random marks and designs that surrounded it. She traced the heart with one finger.

"Amaia. When you were twelve, I swore I'd always tell you the truth. I wish I could lie to you now, but I'm keeping my promise." Engrasi's firm voice broke a little. "Amaia, your father is dying. If you want to say goodbye, you have to come back now."

9

Apex

Elizondo

Amaia thought it was strange that Aunt Engrasi had sent her to bed so early. She was allowed to watch television after dinner—not too much TV, because Engrasi liked to read in the evening, and when Amaia's bedtime came, she usually went to bed as well. So Amaia pretended to be sleeping when she heard the creak of the floorboard outside her room. The door opened just enough to throw a narrow band of white light across the dark wooden floor of her bedroom. That's when someone rang the doorbell and Aunt Engrasi went to see who it was.

Amaia tiptoed across her room, carefully stepped over the squeaky spot in the hall, and went to the top of the stairs. Engrasi's friends often came in the afternoon to visit and play cards, but no one had ever come to their home at this late hour. Engrasi opened the front door.

Amaia's heart leaped with joy when she recognized her father's voice. She was about to fling herself down the stairs and hug him, but his words stopped her cold.

"Your phone call really scared me. I came as soon as I could."

"There are problems, Juan." Her aunt's voice was earnest. "It's Amaia."

The child held her breath, though those words stung her. Problems with her? She didn't understand. She did her best to be a good girl, despite the constant harassment from other children. She waited until her father and aunt had gone into the living room and then she crept down the stairs. She sat in a dark corner and listened, her index finger tracing the fanciful design of the grain in the banister railing. It resembled a heart.

Her father's voice was emphatic. "If you want to talk about sending her to school in Pamplona, I'll refuse again. It's hard enough for me that the girl can't live at home. You know how much we have to do at the bakery, and if she transfers to Pamplona, I'll never get to see her. As long as she's here, at least I see her on her way to and from school."

Amaia was about to turn twelve, and she was a superb student. They'd already had her skip two grades, and she would finish middle school that coming June. She didn't want to go to the local high school. Her classmates already thought it bizarre for her to be finishing eighth grade when other kids her age were only in sixth. One of her teachers had told her about a boarding school in Pamplona, a place where kids even younger than her were doing advanced work. She wouldn't stand out there. Amaia had come back home, pleased and hopeful, carrying a brochure for the school. The idea had disconcerted her aunt a bit at first, but, as always, Engrasi took her side, knowing how cruel the other pupils could be to her. Juan knew it too. He was extremely proud of his daughter, but he wouldn't hear of Amaia going to school away from their town.

"School has nothing to do with it." Engrasi's voice was tense. She was worried. "I'm concerned about something a good deal more delicate."

Juan waited, stubbornly wrapped in deep silence.

"A couple of weeks ago, I was helping Amaia comb out the tangles in her hair. I didn't mean to, but I hurt her when I touched her scar."

Her father held his breath. Crouching on the stairs, Amaia put up her right hand and probed the rough edges of the healed gash under her hair.

"The poor girl grabbed her head and asked me, 'What's this on my head, Auntie?' I told her, 'That's your scar, darling.' And she asked me, 'What scar?' I put down the comb and looked her in the eyes to make sure she wasn't trying to fool me. And I told her, very seriously, 'That's the scar from when you got hit on the head.' Amaia smiled as if it were nothing, and she said, 'I was probably really little, 'cause I don't remember.' I talked to her for a long time, careful not to prompt her, hoping she would work it out for herself. Finally, I said, 'It was in the bakery kitchen, don't you remember?' She just smiled and said, 'I was probably being naughty, 'cause I know I was a real *bitxito* when I was little.' She doesn't remember a thing, Juan. It's completely gone from her memory."

"Well, what should I say, sis? Maybe that's for the best. I wish it hadn't happened. I pray about it all the time."

The pause that followed meant Engrasi must have been glowering at him. When she spoke, her tone was hard. "You're an ostrich, burying your head in the sand. God won't erase what happened, no matter how hard you pray. And no, it is *not* better this way. I don't think you understand the seriousness of what I just said. Amaia suffered a life-threatening head injury. You have no idea how serious, because you didn't take her to the hospital."

Juan didn't reply. That was always his reaction when he was overwhelmed. Amaia could almost see him staring at the floor with his hands jammed in his pockets.

"A head trauma that serious can cause hidden nerve damage. The symptoms can take years to manifest."

"But since she's so clever . . ."

"Neurological damage has nothing to do with intelligence. It's silent, and it can remain hidden for years before coming to light. When it does, the effects can be catastrophic."

Amaia heard nothing at first. Then she made out low sounds. She held her breath, overcome by her father's weeping.

"We have to take her to the doctor," he said through his sobs.

"I already did. Dr. Munguía is one of Spain's best neurologists, and he takes patients at University Clinic in Pamplona. He was my classmate in college. A good man."

Amaia had liked the doctor. They'd had a long conversation.

"He didn't detect any signs of neurological damage, and in fact he told me Amaia's IQ is far above average. But I didn't need a specialist to tell me that."

"That's good news," her father said cautiously. "Isn't it?"

"Sometimes people who've suffered serious trauma develop defenses to block out their suffering. I believe that's what's happening with Amaia. She is suffering."

Her father's next words were stifled, almost inaudible, as if he'd covered his face with his hands. "We've all suffered."

Engrasi's voice took on new force. "Don't you give me that crap!"

That was the first time Amaia had heard Aunt Engrasi use such coarse language.

"Amaia is the one who's suffering, and *you* are responsible. That's why I called you. You have to put an end to this, once and for all."

"An end to what?"

"Amaia has always been quiet and obedient. She loves to read and stay here with me. She's always doing schoolwork, even if it's not assigned. But she hasn't gone out to play or visit friends for months. No matter how much I try, I can't get her to go out. She simply refuses. Last week I sent her to the pharmacy on an errand. That night at bedtime she asked me if she had to live here because she was being punished. Can you imagine how appalled I was? 'Of course not, darling, wherever did you get that idea?' She told me some women recognized her and asked if she was feeling better now. She, poor thing, told them she was. Within her hearing, one of the women told the other that Amaia was living with me because she was ill behaved. She stole, she talked back, she hit her sisters, and she even attacked her own mother. They'd had to punish her. The story was that you'd planned to send her away to boarding school, but Rosario took pity on her, so you sent her to live with me."

A pained silence followed.

"My canasta friends didn't tell me, because they didn't want me to be upset, but they'd all been hearing the same *ttuku-ttuku* for quite a while. I suspect those rumors are the reason Amaia never goes out. It probably wasn't the first time somebody scolded the child. Juan, tell me you didn't know about this!"

Her father's first words were inaudible, then, "I was leaving the kitchens, and I heard Rosario saying something like that to the customers."

"When was that?"

"It's been a while. Maybe a few months ago—"

Engrasi shrieked in anger. "And you dare claim that you're suffering! How can you let your wife go around telling people the child is evil?" She lowered her voice and her tone became gentle. "Do you know what she asked me yesterday? 'Auntie, if I'm a very good girl, do you think they'll let me go back home?'"

Her father was sobbing.

"The poor child has blocked off her pain, walled it off with a barrier so tall and strong that she can't remember what you two did to her. All she wants is to be a normal child. To be loved." Engrasi didn't bother to hide her contempt. "And this extraordinary little girl has to deal with the shame of being pointed out in the street! Amnesia spares her from her painful memories. But it's an abyss, an open hole beneath her feet that one day will gobble her up."

"Don't say that, Engrasi! You know what it's like in a small town: nobody says a word, but they all know everything. I did scold Rosario when I heard her say those things, I really did. What more can I do? She's very sick, Engrasi. She's a model mother to Flora and Rosaura. The doctor says she's not aware of how she's hurting Amaia."

"But you are. You have to put a stop to it."

"But how?" he cried in desperation.

"By telling her it's not true! Forbidding her to say such things!" Engrasi was disgusted. "How could you permit it?"

Juan got up. "And what do you want me to tell them?" He grabbed her by the shoulders and shook her. "That I had to get my daughter out of the house because otherwise she'd be dead by now?"

Sitting in the phone booth at Quantico, Amaia realized she'd been distractedly tracing that heart in the wooden shelf. Her index finger stopped again at the point of that heart, so similar to the one that an eleven-year-old was able to imagine in the grain of a wooden banister.

Her aunt's voice came to her from very far away. "Amaia . . ."

"I'm not leaving here, Auntie."

10

Thermal Conditions

New Orleans, Louisiana
Early morning, Saturday, August 27, 2005

The FBI regional office in New Orleans was located at the edge of Pontchartrain Park, adjacent to the New Orleans Lakefront Airport. Their initial plan had been to land at the small airport, but that proved impossible because it was being evacuated. They'd been put in a holding pattern over Lake Pontchartrain and later directed to Louis Armstrong International Airport in Kenner, exactly what they'd been trying to avoid. As their jet was on approach, they got a radio message that two FBI agents were standing by with vehicles to take them to the regional office.

Their first impression as they deplaned in New Orleans was one of stifling heat. The sun wasn't up yet, though the silvery-gray light of the coming dawn was visible above the horizon. Warm humidity settled on Amaia's skin as soon as she descended the ramp. A thin film of sweat covered her. Two agents in what she had come to see as standard-issue FBI suits—dark jackets and spotless white shirts—awaited them on the tarmac. Resisting the impulse to use the folder in her hand as a fan, she wondered how they could bear to be dressed so formally in the heat.

The agents stepped forward to brief Dupree and the team. "Sir, as you requested, we collected and reviewed all the lists of people arriving in the city, both here at Armstrong and in nearby fields, paying special attention to individuals who rented cars on arrival. We have rental car information from across the state, just in case the suspect arrived elsewhere."

"Do you have census information, voter rolls, any kind of accounting for the citizenry?" Dupree asked.

The agent grimaced and gestured ambiguously. "The city offices have been as helpful as possible, considering the circumstances. We have a team collating information according to your instructions. That will take a few hours more, and I should warn you, it won't be definitive."

They crossed a crowded terminal full of families waiting to evacuate the city. They carried their own bags and sometimes stepped carefully over children who'd stretched out on the floor, exhausted by the hours of waiting. Many were asleep.

"The sun isn't up yet, and look at this crowd," one of the New Orleans FBI agents commented. "They're expecting thousands more from the city over the course of the day. This is the first time in the history of New Orleans that they've ordered a total evacuation."

The sun had broken the horizon while they were in the terminal. It was shining flat and harsh across the black official vehicles. Dupree stopped at the driver's side of the first one. "You men go back to headquarters and make sure they're processing the data as fast as they can. Pay attention to the age profiles we gave you. Send me the results as soon as you can. Agent Johnson and Assistant Inspector Salazar are coming with me."

The more senior New Orleans agent started to protest. "Sir? Our instructions were to get you to the regional office. Director Peterson's waiting for you."

"Tell Peterson I'll catch up with him later." He glanced at his watch. "Right now, I have an appointment with Captain Forneret, commander in District 8. I suspect he won't be too happy to see me in this fucked-up mess, so I don't want to keep him waiting." He held out his hand. The agent reluctantly turned over the keys.

Amaia was amazed to find that Interstate 10 heading toward the city center was deserted. In contrast, the outbound lanes were a virtual parking lot. Close-packed vehicles moved at a snail's pace.

Nevertheless, as they got closer to downtown, the sense of normal city life gradually established itself, and things were unexpectedly orderly when they arrived in the French Quarter. The calm of the neighborhood contrasted vividly with the frenetic activity inside the police station, where it looked like all the city's police officers had been called in.

Team members were relieved to find that despite the bustle, Dupree's prediction about the police commander's mood had been mistaken. Captain Forneret was on the phone but hung up when he saw them. He came around his desk and embraced Dupree like an old friend.

The two broke from their hug, and the commander stood there studying his former companion. "I didn't think I'd see you back here again. To tell the truth, I didn't think they'd let you come back."

"This is not a pleasure trip."

"And it better not be, not with a hurricane bearing down . . ."

"Our man isn't put off by natural disasters."

"And it's nothing to do with Samedi?" The commander watched him closely.

Dupree's expression hardened.

Forneret tried to match his stare but gave up after a couple of seconds. "Don't get offended. I had to ask."

Amaia turned to Johnson but found him looking down at the floor, carefully disengaged. Perhaps he knew what they were talking about.

Dupree felt Amaia's eyes on them, and it appeared to annoy him. "I'll be happy to continue that discussion later on, but right now we have to get to work. And I'm sure you've got plenty on your plate. Do you have what I asked for?"

"I do. I hear y'all are looking for a really bad one. I want you to know it's a real sacrifice to release a man like Jason Bull right now." He lifted a warning finger. "Dupree, I'd have helped you out, even without a call from the big boss, but since you went over my head, I hope you'll mention this station's enthusiastic support and cooperation when you turn in your report afterward."

"You can count on it."

The commander settled in behind his desk, picked up the phone, punched a button. Two men appeared in the doorway to the office. Neither looked older than thirty. One was white, the other African American. Trim and muscular, they wore tight jeans, black T-shirts, and sneakers. Each had a pistol holstered on his belt. If it hadn't been for the bulletproof vests and the New Orleans police badges, Amaia might have taken them for actors.

"Come in, boys," Captain Forneret said. "Let me introduce y'all to FBI special agent Dupree and his team. You'll be working with them for the next few days. Agent Dupree, let me introduce you to the two best assault cops in New Orleans, Detectives Bill Charbou and Jason Bull. Bill and Bull. They're with the Violent Crimes Unit. These fellas have arrested more criminals than all the rest of my officers combined. They know these streets better than anyone." He grinned. "If I had a son, I'd trust them with his life; if I had a daughter, I'd keep her out of their reach."

"Assault cops?" Amaia asked as they shook hands.

Charbou, the African American, gave her a big smile. "That's the New Orleans police term for a team that patrols the underworld. 'Assault' because we're always ready to act. We have every judge in the state on speed dial so we can order up a warrant anytime we need one. Never in uniform, never without our vests; down where we work, keeping your vest on can mean the difference between getting home after work and never coming back."

Amaia raised an eyebrow, not quite buying the macho posturing, and she glanced at Johnson. His phone rang. He excused himself to take the call.

"The boss told us you're planning to move through the city after the storm hits," volunteered Bull, who'd gone to stand next to Dupree.

"That's the plan," Fortenet confirmed without meeting Bull's gaze.

"We're happy to work with you," Charbou said. "This city's complicated enough already, and things are going to be a lot worse after the hurricane. We'll be your guides and protect your asses, but if anything happens on the streets, we're in charge. We decide when to enter, and we'll be the first ones in. And we'll make the call *whether* to enter." He raised a finger. "The streets are ours."

Johnson came back into the office. "Just talked with Emerson and Tucker in Miami. They've gotten office space, but things are a mess. Internet is down, most of the physical data in the census archives and electoral rolls has been destroyed or damaged, and none of it's up to date. They're doing the best they can. Right now, they're trying to find a helicopter to take them into the zone. So far nobody's reported finding a dead family. But our boys here have made a good deal of progress." He lifted his BlackBerry and showed them the screen. "We have a pretty comprehensive list of families that fit the profile, but now we're working on other records, updated ones, to see who is missing. The FBI driver this morning said it would be a long list. He was right. It's longer than I expected, and the families are scattered across the city."

Detective Charbou went to Johnson's side to squint at the screen. "Right. That's no surprise; there are lots of big families in our city. Mama's house is used as the central gathering space, and her family members come and go depending on personal circumstances. Sometimes one leaves and three come back later. That type of stuff won't show up. Fact is, this list ain't going to be much use." He tapped the screen with his index finger. "If you're looking for a family that's gonna try to ride out this hurricane, you should forget the rich parts of town. People there have already cleared out; there's nobody there but hired security guards. If your killer is looking for a family in the city, he won't go to the French Quarter or the Garden District. He'll go to a poor neighborhood."

Amaia nodded. It looked as if Bill and Bull might be useful after all.

"Can you show us the neighborhoods where people are likely to stay?"

"Sure." Bill Charbou walked over to the map of the city displayed on the wall. "This isn't the first hurricane to hit New Orleans. And even though they're getting ready to call for a total evacuation, we know there are people who won't leave. They'd rather risk it." He pointed to an area on the map. "For example, the really poor. And the old folks who have nobody to help them. And the handicapped, folks who don't have a car—lots of those in New Orleans—and some delinquents, who'll be hanging around for the looting afterward. You're gonna wear your vests every moment you're moving around with us." He caught sight of Amaia's backpack beside the door and the FBI regulation vest neatly rolled up behind it. "And—good God! What's this? Kevlar? Spectra? Forget it. You're going to wear Type IV vests like ours, made of Spectra and an aramid, fifteen times more resistant than steel plate, buoyant, impervious to almost everything, including rifle bullets."

Johnson protested. "This is official FBI equipment, made to our standards . . ."

"Maybe you test them with live fire at the FBI, maybe not. But I guarantee you that three out of four drug traffickers carry weapons that'll slice through that vest like a knife through butter. You think those guys are going to clear out and leave business to the competition just because of a hurricane? If you plan to go out in those neighborhoods to knock on doors and flash your FBI badges, it'll be on our terms or not at all."

Dupree ended the debate. "Agreed! Officer Charbou, Officer Bull, I'm sure we'll all get along just fine." He offered them his hand.

Jason Bull gave Dupree's hand a quick, firm shake and accompanied it with that knowing expression of complicity Amaia had noticed earlier. She read it as an unmistakable confirmation of an alliance between them. Jason Bull and Dupree knew each other. She wondered why they'd made such a show during the introduction.

Bill Charbou's dissatisfaction was evident, but he took Dupree's hand anyway. "Bill and Bull. Forget the 'officer this' and 'mister that.'" He was in a sour mood. "That's what they call us here, and that's how they know us out there in the streets."

Amaia again saw Jason Bull give Dupree an apologetic look. *He knew this was coming,* she thought.

"As you like," Dupree agreed. "Bill and Bull."

Pleased by that, the detectives went back to the map.

"Bill and I were discussing the best place to sit out the storm. Probably the fire station near Lake Pontchartrain. Emergency services are headquartered upstairs. Since we need to be on top of any reports of gunshots, that's the place to be. We discussed it with the fire chief and the ops center supervisor there. We've got a top-of-the-line SUV, and the harbor rescue service has reserved a Zodiac for us. If things get complicated—and they will—they have trucks and special vehicles, even their own helicopter. Most of the station's squad cars are out on the streets right now. They'll be able to give us a fairly clear idea of which areas are still populated."

Dupree scanned an incoming text message and interrupted the discussion. "Quantico's going to send us a list of the cases that fit the criteria Salazar suggested—assaults against families like those our man is targeting. Maybe we can identify some failed attempts. Johnson, Captain Forneret will get you an office where you can print it all out. Six cases, lots of documentation and plenty of photos. We'll need high-resolution prints. When you're done with that, Bill and Bull will take you to our hotel. Get to work on those cases. I'll meet you there later." He turned to the New Orleans policemen. "Gentlemen, don't let these two out of your sight when you're on the streets."

Dupree left the office and the police commander trailed him down the hall. When he was sure no one else could hear, Forneret stepped around so he could look Dupree in the eye. "Let's get serious, old friend. What the hell are you doing here?"

"I told you when I called. We're tracking down a killer who targets families. He's struck several times, in widely dispersed locations, but he seems to have a weird attraction to natural disasters."

"And this has nothing to do with Katrina?"

"You don't get it. It has everything to do with the hurricane."

"Look, Dupree, let me be straight with you. When the boss called to tell me y'all were coming, I wasn't pleased. In one room, I have fellas from FEMA planning to send half my officers to close down roads and holding on to the rest to respond to emergencies; in another, the Red Cross is working to set up shelters. And we have to coordinate the whole mess. In the middle of all this, you land with practically no warning. Don't forget that after everything that happened, you're not exactly in my good graces. We're going to have two or three very bad days after the hurricane. Everyone's on edge. The last thing I need is for the shit to hit the fan again. So if you're thinking about digging up old ghosts . . ."

"That was a decade ago," Dupree murmured dryly.

"Ten full years ago, but not a single one of us has forgotten."

"There's no connection. None. I'm not going to go over it again," Dupree said flatly. "My orders come directly from Washington."

The commander put his fists on his hips and studied the floor. He sighed. "Okay. I want to trust you. I want to believe it's got nothing to do with Samedi. You're going to have to stay away from Terrebonne Parish. I want your word on that."

Dupree tightened his lips and said nothing. He gripped the commander's hand and clasped the man's upper arm for a moment, signaling, *That's it, discussion closed.* He walked toward the exit.

Forneret watched Dupree leave. He took out his phone and punched in a number that wasn't in his contacts list. Someone answered. "We may have a problem," the commander said.

11

A Shroud

New Orleans, Louisiana

Agent Dupree walked south for a while, but he changed his mind when he heard a streetcar coming up behind him. He climbed aboard the bright-red trolley for the ride, even though he was only two stops from his destination. The conductor warned him it was the last run of the day. All the cars were returning to the garage.

People were carrying equipment and furnishings out of storefronts to pack them into the vans crowded along the sidewalks. The unlit interiors of some businesses had turned shop windows into mirrors dark as muddy pools, reflecting distorted images of the streetcar as it rolled down one of the city's main streets. Though not deserted, the avenue seemed tired and lifeless.

He left the trolley at Bourbon and walked up that street. The heat was overwhelming. He saw a police cruiser in the distance. The restaurants and bars were shut, but he heard music playing inside some strip joints.

The heat seemed to get worse with every step. Breathing heavily, he looked up and caught sight of an elderly woman and a girl no older than ten who were removing flowerpots from balcony boxes and lining them up against the wall. The woman's tears glinted in the sun. Dupree was surprised by a sudden, intense feeling of alarm. Her eyes met his. She watched his progress and slowly shook her head. She said one word. He read it on her thin, discolored lips.

"Bazagrá."

His back tensed. Refusing to acknowledge her, he walked away, keenly aware of her watery gaze on his back. He quickened his pace. At the nearest corner, he turned left onto Ursulines Avenue, but he couldn't keep himself from glancing over his shoulder for just an instant. The crone raised a small, dry hand that looked like a wrinkled leather glove. She waved at him. Her thin lips smiled and mouthed a word. He felt a sudden stab in his shoulder and a pain deep beneath his old wound. He gasped as memories flooded back, and pressed his palm to a spot just above his heart.

Dupree found himself in a blind alley and had to turn back. He hadn't recognized the shop. He didn't remember the address, and the carved wooden signs usually posted above the sidewalk had been removed so the winds wouldn't carry them away. At last, he spotted the familiar front window. It was boarded over with newly sawn lengths of pine board. He saw the store's familiar dark-maroon doors and ancient shutters.

He grasped the white porcelain doorknob and entered. Inside, a boy and girl, mere teenagers, were packing up merchandise from display cases, wrapping it in sheets of white paper, and carefully stowing the bundles in old fruit crates. Dark hair cascaded almost to their shoulders and long bangs dangled in front of their liquid brown eyes.

"We closed!" they chorused without stopping their work.

Dupree closed the door behind him. "I'm here to see Antoine."

The girl stopped what she was doing and gave him a wary look.

"M'sieur Meire ain't here," she said in a melodious voice, watching him closely for a reaction.

"I'm sure he'll be here for me," Dupree said and reached into the interior pocket of his jacket. The boy put a hand under the counter, ready to grab a weapon if the situation called for it. Dupree smiled. He slowly showed them his two fingers and used them to extract a translucent cellophane envelope containing a banknote from his pocket. He held it so they could see the portrait of the president.

"Y'all tell him Grover Cleveland lookin' for him."

The kids grinned and exchanged a glance. The girl came to him, accepted the envelope, opened one end, tried the quality of the paper between her fingers, nodded, and gave it back. The boy gestured toward the back of the store, inviting him in. "Welcome, Mr. Cleveland; M'sieur Meire gonna see you now."

The boy led him around dozens of cartons heaped high against the walls. In them Dupree saw card trinkets, empty skulls, and crude rag dolls with beads for eyes.

"Phony voodoo," the boy muttered.

"What?"

"Crap for tourists." He gave a little shrug of apology. He showed Dupree to the back and left him at the foot of a steep, narrow staircase, completely unlit, that seemed to stretch up at least two stories. As Dupree climbed into its darkness, he made out a dusky orange light at the far end, as if the third floor were on fire. The irregularly spaced steps echoed hollow beneath his tread.

The top floor was a loft. The stairwell appeared to be the only way to access the room. The air was heavy and still. Shafts of sunlight, insufficient to illuminate the room fully, came through a half dozen small vents. A number of gas lanterns carefully hung from the ceiling produced the strange yellow-orange glow he'd seen from the stairs. At the far end of the loft were two men, one white and the other black, both wearing coveralls, gloves, and surgical masks. They were packing gauze-wrapped objects that looked like dried roots or chunks of tree bark. The smell of earth, talcum powder, and musty flowers filled Dupree's nostrils.

He knew they hadn't noticed him, so he took a moment to watch them work. The black man was Jacques, who'd always been Meire's assistant, as far as Dupree knew. The white man was Meire himself. His deep tan ran right up into his receding hairline, where it contrasted with a bushy white mane combed back in a style that reminded Dupree of Christopher Lee.

Meire's left eye was blind. While playing in a harvested corn field at the age of three, he'd fallen headfirst and a jagged stalk had penetrated that eye. He didn't lose it entirely, but the pupil and the iris were destroyed, their colors mixing to resemble a tiger's-eye marble. Nana always said there are some folks who see too much, so fate maintains balance by depriving them of an eye. Antoine wore tortoiseshell glasses with a magnifying lens for his good eye and a plain lens for the blind one.

Meire and Jacques carried their dusty load to a metal table where a bag lay open. They wrapped the soiled contents in a second layer of gauzelike fabric that resembled a shroud. Dupree looked away and suppressed the urge to gulp for air.

"I'm always tempted to ask how they find 'em." Meire's voice was just as dusty as the brown residue on the surgical mask he pulled off his face with gloved hands.

Meire stood in front of him. That blind eye looked different than Dupree remembered. Its owner, aware of its hypnotic effect, held Dupree's gaze for five seconds before giving him a sly wink. "Show it to me."

Dupree held out the thousand-dollar bill. "The fact is—"

"Not a word!" Meire cautioned him. "I said I'm always tempted, but I never said I give in." He pulled off his gloves, extracted the banknote from the cellophane envelope. With his other hand, he adjusted an overhead lantern and held the bill up against the light. "Grover Cleveland, our twenty-second president. And our twenty-fourth. The only man to occupy the White House in nonconsecutive terms."

"I guarantee it's real," Dupree said.

"I know it's genuine, even though those notes got no stripes or watermarks. Wasn't the custom back in those days. There aren't enough in existence to make counterfeiting worthwhile, and besides, my babies wouldn't have let you up here unless it was real." He smiled.

"Caleb and Emma?" Dupree was surprised. "My God, how the time passes! I remember when . . ."

Meire stepped toward Dupree and raised his glasses to peer into the agent's face. "My, my—if it ain't Andrew Aloisius Dupree!" he muttered. He stepped closer and for an instant seemed about to hug his visitor, but instead he put his glasses back on, took Dupree's hand with both of his own. "Must be somethin' serious. You wouldn't be here otherwise."

Dupree pressed his lips together and looked over his shoulder as if to admire the strange variety of goods that filled the room. He didn't want to look into that eye. He fixed his gaze on the different colors of cascading human hair that hung like a curtain from a rod fixed to the ceiling. On one table, a bowl with a cork lid was full of molars. He saw cardboard boxes of dried animal parts. Silky shrouds, still marked by the reddish-brown outlines of bodies that had lain in them for years, were draped from hangers suspended from the ceiling, as if the souls of their deceased owners still inhabited them.

"What you need?"

Dupree reached into the same inside pocket where he'd carried the banknote and took out a list written in pencil. He gave it to Meire, who bent over to examine it. Two seconds later, he looked up to study Dupree's face. "This ain't for you."

"It's not. It's for Nana."

"Nana," Meire murmured and turned toward the room. "Jacques!" He raised his voice and waved the list at the man working in the back. "I hope you haven't finished packing up *le petit enfant*! Mr. Cleveland here has an order. He's going to need some."

12

Windows

New Orleans, Louisiana

Johnson gave Charbou the keys to the huge black SUV they'd parked in front of the District 8 station. The New Orleans cop gave a whistle of appreciation when he saw the FBI vehicle.

Bill and Bull had taken the front seats without giving them a choice, so Johnson and Amaia buckled themselves into the back. "Is the hotel far from here?"

"Five minutes by car, ten or twelve by foot," Bull answered.

The AC was on full blast against the oppressive heat of the city. Amaia put her forehead against the cool window and watched the passing scenery. Colorfully painted, well-kept houses stood cheek by jowl with decrepit shotgun shacks. On some homes, new-cut pine boards that had been hammered across the windows clashed with the colors of the brilliantly painted walls. There were no cars parked along the street. And they hadn't seen a soul, except in the immediate vicinity of the station. Looking up, Amaia glimpsed the eyes of a woman at a second-story window; she was holding a lace curtain to shield her lower face as she spied on the street below. Amaia was reminded of Calle Santiago in Elizondo and the thousands of times she'd seen women posed in windows in just that way.

"Looks like the evacuation was a success." Johnson's comment brought her out of her musings.

Keeping his hands on the wheel as they advanced, Charbou turned toward Johnson and seemed about to say something. He held back but kept his eyes on

Johnson for so long that Amaia thought it was inevitable he would crash the car. He turned his attention back to the road without comment.

Jason Bull spoke instead. "Let's just say that District 8 is about the sweetest little spot in New Orleans. Close to the tourist area, not too far from Frenchmen Street. Maybe not very elegant, but good enough to give tourists the illusion they're in the real, authentic New Orleans. It's all a con job. We know you got important stuff waiting, but we can't take you out into the streets tomorrow if you go to bed tonight thinking you know the real New Orleans. You can't track down a killer if you don't know where you are, and for that, you need to see more before it gets dark today. For Christ's sake, they've stuck you in rooms in the stinking French Quarter!"

Johnson checked his watch and Amaia thought he'd say they didn't have time. He'd promised Dupree they'd review those cases and have them ready on his return. Everything Amaia had noticed about Johnson confirmed the man was orderly and methodical; disregarding Dupree's instructions, even for just a few minutes, was something he'd probably consider irregular and exceptionally indulgent. But he looked at her for any objection, then nodded to accept the offer.

They got to the end of Simon Bolivar Avenue, which gave them scenes very different from those in District 8. Charbou slowed to a crawl, for many more people were in the streets. Most of the houses were drab or ramshackle, and few showed signs that any effort had been made to protect them against the hurricane. Precautions against the storm seemed limited to hauling the porch furniture inside. Instead of bright pine boards, people in the quarter had used all sorts of materials to protect their windows—plastic sheeting, colored tarps, even dirty lengths of scrap lumber. The empty lots between the houses were piled with garbage. Doors of abandoned automobile carcasses yawned open, and stuffing spilled out from the slashed seats like the guts of roadkill.

Bull turned to Johnson and Amaia. "I have a wife and two little babies; they're in Atlanta with my in-laws, who are delighted to remind my wife that life in New Orleans is a shitty pain in the ass. My mother's with them too. I got my whole family out."

"I didn't," Bill Charbou said. "I've only got an aunt, my mom's little sister. She decided not to go. She's kind of an activist in her neighborhood, and she's still in her house over in the Ninth Ward. Nobody's going to make her leave.

Y'all have to understand there's lots of folks like her, people who aren't leaving even though they could. And then there's others like those who live here. This is their home, the street, and they got nothing else. They've lived in misery all their lives, and this isn't going to be any different. They're not going somewhere else; they're staying right here. Believe me, they're ready to protect their homes and families with their own lives, even from somebody claiming he wants to help."

"But there's a hell of a storm coming," Johnson objected. "I don't think they understand the danger. They could get killed."

"Yeah, yeah, they could get killed," Bill agreed. "They don't care. Johnson, with all due respect, you're an outsider, you drive down the street, and you see their shitty little world and ask yourself, 'Why do they want to risk it?' You don't realize that maybe this is a pile of shit, but it's theirs, it's all they've managed to make for themselves. I learned a long time ago that every arrogant SOB who visits NOLA looks down on these kids."

Provoked, Johnson took a deep breath, but Amaia got in before him in an attempt to calm things down. "And how about you, Mr. Charbou? Are you married?"

The policeman guffawed. "'Mr. Charbou'? Don't call me that ever again. Bill or Charbou, but forget your 'Mr. Charbou'!"

When it became obvious Charbou wasn't going to answer the question, Bull spoke up. "Bill Charbou doesn't have any other family here. His parents, brothers, and sisters live in Baton Rouge. Nobody's left for him here 'cept his old auntie. He's got half a dozen girlfriends, but not one of them likes him well enough to wait out the hurricane with him." He pretended to be pained when his partner punched his shoulder. "Ouch! Guess by now they're all holed up somewhere safe with some other gentleman friend."

"Augh!" Bill Charbou moaned and shook his head, pretending to be offended. His partner laughed.

They turned back toward Simon Bolivar, crossed Marigny and Esplanade, then took Dauphine.

Dauphine Orleans Hotel had an orange façade facing the street of the same name. Bottle-green shutters on the balconies contrasted with the ground floor's white arches. Bill stopped their 4x4 in front of an open archway beside the main entrance and pointed. Despite the evacuation order, the parking lot in the hotel's inner court was full. They went in and found three large black women busy behind the reception desk. The proprietors quickly checked the visitors in and invited Bill and Bull to take a seat in the little bar next to reception. One of them came out to show Amaia to her room. Bill, who'd insisted on carrying Amaia's knapsack for her, escorted them to the elevator but was reluctant to give up her bag. The hotel owner grabbed it out of his hands, brooking no nonsense, but gave him a sweet smile when she told him to wait in the bar.

She turned to Amaia as soon as the elevator doors closed. "Your friend there is a fine-looking man. You know if he's single?"

Amaia smiled. "Yes, I think he is."

The woman looked at her, intrigued. "Well, seems to me he likes you."

"He likes me"—Amaia smiled—"he likes you, he likes the women he sees walking down the street . . ."

The woman laughed. "Don't worry, your 'boyfriend' gonna be fine in May Bailey's; it's the hotel bar now but used to be one of the city's best whorehouses." She gave Amaia a wink. "That has to be one of the most witchified places in the Big Easy."

Amaia grinned. "You mean there are ghost prostitutes?"

"Fallen ladies, they call 'em here. We got a ghost, but not exactly a prostitute one. The sister of May Bailey, the madam, didn't like life here, she dreamed about getting away. Met a young soldier who proposed to her and promised to take her away, but on the very day of the wedding, he died in a gunfight. They say it broke her heart and drove her out of her mind. Never did get away from here. Some of the clients say they seen her in her white-lace gown, crying her heart out in the garden or up on the balconies."

The elevator doors opened, and the woman took Amaia to the first room on the right. Amaia smiled to herself as her new friend unlocked the door, wondering how many times she'd told that story to her customers.

The woman turned to her and resumed her tale. "But you don't have to worry your head 'bout that. She appears only to men." She shrugged. "Maybe still looking for her fiancé."

She opened the door and stood back to let Amaia pass. Everything in the room—furniture, bed, walls, ceiling, carpet—was of a satiny cream color, the epitome of French style. The bathroom with a claw-foot tub was to one side, and the exterior wall was dominated by huge southern-style guillotine windows hung with venetian blinds. The woman tugged the cord to raise the blinds so they could see the building across the street.

"I'm sorry we can't give you a better room, but it was last minute, and the hotel was mostly booked."

"I noticed. I thought that with the evacuation . . ."

"Lots of folks decided not to leave. Want to stay to protect their property from looting after the storm, so they took rooms with us 'cause they know the French Quarter never gets flooded. Never has, since New Orleans was founded, and little ol' Katrina won't be any different." She opened the window. Music came into the room; a brass band was passing. Amaia poked her head out, and despite the angle, she caught a glimpse of a large group of musicians marching smartly in formation.

"Musicians!" she commented, coming back inside. "I thought they'd all have left."

"Two kinds of folks never leave New Orleans: musicians and ghosts."

The hotel owner paused to switch on the television and turn to a news channel. The inescapable image of the hurricane out over the Gulf appeared on the screen. She nodded in satisfaction and went to the door. When it opened, she found herself face to face with Agent Johnson.

He nodded, let her pass, and stepped inside. Tucked under his arm were the half dozen folders of case material they'd printed out at the station. Amaia pointed without a word to the large desk by the window. She took one of the folders and settled on the corner of the bed, leaving the desk to Johnson. He raised the blinds all the way to let in light from outside and then settled down to work.

It took her twenty minutes to rule out the first two of the three cases she'd picked up. In the first one, men with gas company credentials got into a family dwelling where service had been interrupted by an earthquake. They tied up the father and mother, then tortured the elderly grandmother until she gave them the code for a safe. The second case was a late-night assault by a group of hooded thugs who tied up a whole family. The intruders took valuables, but they also forced the husband to watch them rape the women. The children were kept in another room.

The third case was a murder-suicide. Eight months earlier in Galveston, Texas, in December of the previous year, Joseph Andrews, forty-eight, shot his wife and his two children, a girl of sixteen and a boy of twelve, before taking his own life. He'd been transferred from Sacramento for work only a month earlier.

His wife was a well-known decorator with a popular blog, as well as a dedicated theatre enthusiast. The image of their teenage daughter had been lifted from a group photo taken at her new school in Galveston. The case file noted that Andrews hadn't shown up at work on the day of the murders. A neighbor went by to check on them and found the bodies. The father's gun lay at his side.

Amaia spread the half dozen crime scene photos across the bed for closer examination. The bodies were stretched out on the floor with the heads aligned in the same direction. There was no way of knowing which direction that was, and the ink-rich photo print made it impossible for her to discern any signs that they had been tied up. Most telling for Amaia was the general scene. The case report didn't comment on it, but disorder prevailed. All the furniture in the living room had been overturned. Flowerpots were tipped over. Pictures hung askew. It wasn't as evocative as the aftermath of a tornado, but . . .

She decided on an order for the six photographs, laid them out that way, and added the four individual portrait photos of the family members.

"Johnson, take a look at this."

Johnson put a file back onto the pile and crossed the room.

"The assumption is that the father stayed home that day because he was planning to murder his family. He shot each one in the head, then put a bullet through his brain. But look at how these bodies are arranged; I know there are only four, and I don't see any ligature marks, but that could be due to the quality of the print. The file says he fired four bullets from the pistol found beside him. It was registered to him."

Johnson picked up one of the photos and took it to the window, where the light was better. "Does the reporting officer say there were family members who weren't home that day?"

"Yes. An older son, which would fit the family profile we're looking for. The police gave him extra attention because he inherited two houses and a ton of money, but they never seriously considered him a suspect. He was living in Sacramento, and they confirmed he was there on the day of the murders. Looks as if he's been stirring up the press, telling anyone who'll listen that his family was murdered by an intruder, even though the police are convinced his father did it. He claims the investigation was mishandled."

Johnson took the report and turned to the back page to check the name of the investigating officer. He called the Galveston number and learned that

Detective Nelson had resigned and moved away. Smiling, he pressed the speakerphone button for his next call. Agent Tucker's slightly nasal voice came through loud and clear.

"Tucker, I have Salazar with me on speakerphone. Are you still at Miami police headquarters?"

"Yes, we're waiting for transport to the disaster zone, but it's still cut off. Meanwhile, we're monitoring reports for any mention of homicides or accidental deaths during the storm. Not expecting too much for a while; most of the phone lines are down and even the working phones are unreliable. They've gotten several reports of shots fired, but those we were able to verify didn't match what we're looking for. We do have a couple of missing families that fit the profile. Problem is, even if the Composer has struck, we might not hear about it for hours."

"We've been reviewing the case files sent this morning, and Salazar found a murder-suicide eight months ago in Galveston. A husband who killed his wife and two children, then used his own pistol to kill himself. Nothing that really catches the eye there, but there's more: an older son wasn't home, so that's one step closer to the profile we're looking for. In the crime scene photos we have here, the bodies are close together and side by side. There's no way to tell if they're oriented toward the north. Can't see any marks around the wrists. Ballistics report is sketchy; just says there's gunpowder residue on the father's hands and the bullets extracted postmortem match his pistol, a twenty-two. The gun was found on the floor beside him."

"You think our man might be behind it?"

"That's what we're trying to establish. But we urgently need to talk to the investigating officer. Report's signed by a Brad Nelson, homicide detective in Galveston."

"And?"

"Turns out Detective Nelson moved to Tampa. Seems his wife is there, and Nelson now works for the Tampa police."

"We're on it. You can imagine the chaos here at headquarters, but we'll track him down. Let's have a conference call in fifteen minutes. I'll give you the number."

In the interval, Amaia went to the bathroom, turned on the faucet, and put her wrists under the gush of cold water. She sensed the intense heat was bringing on a headache. She wet a towel and wiped her neck.

"Salazar!" Johnson poked his head through the doorway, startling her. "It's time."

Tucker took over. "Agent Johnson, Assistant Inspector Salazar—Agent Emerson is here with me. We've learned that Detective Brad Nelson went out with the first batch of volunteers dispatched to the disaster zone, and he's not likely to be back any time soon. I spoke to him by radio. Here's what I have so far: the gun was a Smith & Wesson twenty-two-caliber revolver, and bullets of the same caliber were taken from the bodies. The detective thinks the son's refusal to accept the police's conclusion is simply the boy's inability to accept what his father did and the consequences for his family. The young man's a student at Tulane in New Orleans. The case is closed. The boy still telephones Nelson practically every week, insisting it has to be reopened. Most recent call was yesterday, from New Orleans. He hasn't evacuated, so maybe you can find him and talk to him. Name is Joseph Andrews, same as his father."

Johnson watched Amaia for a reaction. She pressed her lips together, shook her head, and shrugged slightly. This didn't really add much to what they'd already found in the file. Sure, they could interview the boy, but if Nelson was right, he was a grieving youth who refused to accept a horrible reality.

Tucker's voice vibrated over the phone line. "I asked him about the mess in the house too."

Amaia held her breath.

"A tropical storm hit Galveston that day. Not a bad one; there were no deaths or injuries, mostly fallen trees and minor property damage. The father didn't go to work because his firm told all their employees to stay home. The family was new to the city, and they'd never been through a coastal storm. The mess in the house was caused by violent gusts through the broken windows. The detective thinks that at some point during the storm, they opened a window, and the sudden change in pressure blew out several more. There were no cuts on the bodies, no injuries from flying glass. There were marks on the father's wrists, but the police concluded that they were self-inflicted, tentative attempts at suicide. No sign at the scene of any kind of bindings. They left that out of the report; considered it irrelevant. He says that without rereading the report, he can't be absolutely sure how the bodies were oriented, but he's practically certain the heads were aligned toward the north."

“For Christ’s sake!” Amaia couldn’t contain herself. “Is Agent Dupree going to think this one matches close enough to investigate?”

Johnson said goodbye to Tucker and called Dupree, though not on speakerphone. He outlined the new information and listened intently. Amaia watched Johnson’s face, trying to guess what would come next.

“He told us to go to the campus, but he insisted Bill and Bull go with us.”

“Do you think they’re still downstairs?”

“Sure,” Johnson said as he collected the photos and returned them to the file. “And I suspect they’re having a good time. The hotel owner told me that for years the bar was the reception room for May Bailey’s brothel.”

Amaia nodded with a smile. She’d guessed right. The owners did tell that story to all their clients.

13

Misery, Deaf and Mute

Elizondo

Annoyed, Engrasi raised a hand and pushed the remains of an old spiderweb away from her face. She'd been kneeling in the most cramped section of the attic, looking for Christmas ornaments. As usual, she'd found everything except what she was looking for. Boxes of clothes she'd worn only on the streets of Paris, tons of handwritten notes in French from her days as a psychology student, cartons of books that had filled the shelves of the house she'd shared with the man she loved. These things had once meant the world to her, but now she saw them only through a haze of nostalgia: emblems of a bygone life, as remote and unattainable as if she'd been reborn into a completely different existence. She closed a box and leaned to one side so the light from the open attic door fell across the dial of her watch. She'd lost track of time. Amaia should have been home already.

She crawled back toward the stairs and noticed, close to the doorway, a little wooden chest she'd brought back from Paris. She heaved a sigh, knowing exactly what was in it. She stopped at the door, one foot on the first step, and before leaving the attic, she raised the chest's lid just enough to slip a hand inside, extract a sheaf of papers, and tuck them beneath her jacket. She quickly descended, having made a mental note that the boxes of garlands and tinsel she had been looking for were at the far end of the attic. She called out to Amaia in hopes that the girl had scurried into the house like a timid little mouse while Engrasi was in the attic.

She saw her own reflection in the window, for it was already dark outside. Her hair was unruly, her brow was furrowed with worry, and the bulky folder was obvious under her jacket. She had to deal with the documents first. She fished in her blouse for the tiny gold-colored key that always hung from a delicate chain around her neck. She used it to open the only locked drawer in her wardrobe, deposited the folder, closed the drawer, and dropped the key back inside her blouse. She picked up the phone from the little table by the sofa and dialed a number from memory. The call went through. She shaded her eyes to peer through the window at the street.

The warm voice of her brother responded on the other end. "Hello! Mantecadas Salazar."

Normally Engrasi would have smiled, but tonight she was worried. Her brother had always answered the phone with an unobliging grunt; he'd changed his ways recently, no doubt under the tutelage of his ambitious wife.

"Juan, is Amaia with you?"

"No, she's not."

"It's just . . . she's not home yet, and I'm worried."

"She's probably talking with some friend from school. The days are shorter now, so it seems later. It's only six thirty."

"Juan, I already told you the child always comes directly home to me unless she stops off to see you. I thought she might be there playing with her sisters. Are you sure she's not out on the patio behind the bakery?"

"No, Rosario and the girls went home early to decorate for Christmas."

Engrasi hung up without another word. She put on a heavy coat, went outside, locked the door, and hurried down the street.

Juan was right. The early dark did make it seem later. The autumn had been long and mild, and the first frosts took the valley folk by surprise, prompting them to hole up at home. She saw the lights of vehicles in the distance crossing the bridge to Calle Santiago, but not a soul on the street. Gas lamps on houses cast their glow across the wet ground and created shifting orange patterns on the pavement. She couldn't see the river, but she sensed it rushing through the darkness, cold but alive. She had to watch her step because sometimes the Baztán caused the pavement to buckle. She put one hand to her chest, fingered the tiny key, pursed her lips, and quickened her pace. She needed to locate the child; she hoped the girl wouldn't be where Engrasi expected to find her.

Her brother's house was on one of the finest streets in Elizondo. An archway gave direct access from the street to the front yard, where the previous owner had planted two weeping willows, one on either side of the walk. The willows had flourished and grown until their branches hung all the way to the ground.

Standing beneath the archway, Engrasi saw warm yellow light from the living room spilling through the window and illuminating part of the garden.

She didn't see the child at first, which was a relief, though she was still worried. But once her eyes adjusted to the dim light, she made out an odd shape against the dark trunk of one of the trees. As she entered the yard, she realized the shape was really a girl embracing the willow trunk. Engrasi bent over and saw her little face through the dark branches that fell like cascades of tears. The girl was weeping too.

Engrasi stooped under the branches, went around the trunk, and covered the child's hand with her own. She was surprised to find that it was warm despite the chill in the air. Engrasi now saw the scene from Amaia's perspective.

Rosario had left the curtains wide open, so from the shelter of the willow, they had a clear view into the room. Behind the broad picture window, Amaia's mother and sisters were decorating the Christmas tree. Engrasi remained by Amaia's side, bearing silent, patient witness to the girl's pain and trying to think of what to say. After a few seconds Amaia let go of the tree, pulled her sweater down over her hands, and wiped the tears from her face. She stepped back from their hiding place, held out a hand to her aunt, and asked, almost pleading, "Can we go home now?"

Engrasi didn't say anything. She couldn't. She kissed the little girl, nodded, and took her tiny hand to guide her on the short journey home.

Engrasi looked back before they stepped out of the cover of the willow. Rosario was watching them from the window. Her face was half obscured by the darkness of the night, but the twinkling Christmas tree lights were sufficient to reveal for an instant a broad wink and a delighted smile.

Engrasi held Amaia's hand tighter and pulled her toward the street. The tenderness that had overwhelmed her an instant before had been transmuted into rage.

And, she had to admit, into fear.

14

The House of Many Colors

New Orleans, Louisiana
Late afternoon, Saturday, August 27, 2005

After he left the store, Dupree went up Ursulines toward Treme, then took a detour so he could pass by Saint Louis Cemetery. He knew he was too pressed for time to linger. Despite all the years that had passed, the impulse that directed him there was the same one that had guided his steps as a child. His internal compass was fixed forever on his parents' graves.

Two cemetery employees were up on ladders at either side of the gate, taking down the canvas banner advertising guided tours. One of them noticed the man observing them. "We're closing, *mon ami*!"

He was sure they'd mistaken him for a laggard tourist. "Just for a minute. Want to make sure the family tomb's going to stand up to the storm."

The employee brushed off his uniform and gave Dupree a suspicious look. "What family that?"

"*Famille* Dupree-Sabrier," he said calmly.

"Oh! Of course, monsieur." The man stepped aside.

Dupree went left and all the way to the back. The cemetery was strangely different from his childhood memories of it. Even so, he felt the same familiar dejection as he passed along the rows of stucco-covered tombs. Many had settled into the marshy ground and now were well below street level. He could hardly make out the names of those sealed inside. He cast about at the back wall and eventually located the family tomb.

The sight left him desolate. He remembered a white edifice five feet high with a marble plaque bearing the names of his parents. The side walls of the structure were now in such disrepair that brown brickwork showed through the stucco coating. Their broken plaque was propped against the front corner of the niche. Damp rising from the ground had stained the walls with mold. Filth covered every surface, and moss obscured the names, making them illegible to an outsider. He rubbed his fingertips along the grooved letters. He stood contemplating those names in silence, as if they were indeed indecipherable—even though they meant the world to him.

The cemetery employee rattled the heavy metal chain against the iron gate to remind him it was closing time. Having nothing else to offer, Dupree squatted, picked up a gray stone fragment that had fallen from the mausoleum itself, and placed it beneath his parents' names. He hurried to the gate and thanked the employees on his way out.

Dupree walked past a succession of multicolored houses on his way to the lower part of the Treme quarter. Night was falling and streetlamps were coming on, but most of the windows along the streets were dark. Archways had been stripped of hanging ferns, potted vines, and the metal supports that had held them up. Chains and padlocks secured shutters where inhabitants hadn't nailed boards across the windows. He saw people making last-minute escapes, their cars loaded with the things they couldn't bear to leave behind.

That's when he got to her house, one of the most eye-catching on the street. The place looked much smaller now than when he was a child. Nana had kept it carefully maintained. The walls were yellow, the window frames bright white, and the shutters were dark green. The two-storied house had four broad windows that looked out onto a narrow porch not much deeper than a balcony in the French Quarter. The space had been dedicated to a little front garden bordered by a low white picket fence. He pushed open the gate, marveling at the strings of Mardi Gras beads hung between the fence posts and swaying in the breeze. Nana preferred green, gold, and purple beads, representing the justice, wealth, and faith of her city.

He went up the steps onto the narrow porch, empty now of flowerpots and furniture. He saw no light inside, and when he tried to pull open the shutters across the front door, he found someone had nailed them shut. He crossed the front yard and took the alley to the back. He walked toward the kitchen, feeling the damp earth spongy beneath his feet. When he reached the back door, he heard a low wooden rumble, almost inaudible, followed by a distinct creak. Then another. He recognized the sound of furniture being dragged across the floor. He carefully put down the sack Meire had prepared for him and took out his pistol. He eased off the safety, slowly turned the copper doorknob, and felt the door give way. Someone yanked it from the inside and it flew open.

"Mon cher petit cœur!" she exclaimed and flung out her arms.

"Nana!"

"Al! I knew it was you, my Al. Ever since you were little you liked to come around to the kitchen instead of to the front."

Dupree smiled. No one else ever called him Al.

He hugged her, feeling how fragile she was. She'd gotten much thinner. Her clothes hung loose from her angular frame. Dupree held her tight and closed his eyes. When had she gotten so small? He remembered her being as tall as he was, but now her frizzy locks of white hair hardly grazed his chin. He leaned down and planted a long kiss on the top of her head.

"You here, you here, my baby boy," she murmured through tears.

It broke his heart to see her weep. He held her tighter and pressed his own lips together to keep from blubbering. "Nana, I'm sorry. I'm so sorry."

"Why that, *mon cher*?"

"Because I didn't get here earlier."

The old woman leaned back enough to look him in the eye. "Don't you talk nonsense to me now. We both know you not s'posed to come back, but you were going to, anyhow, sooner or later, and now that you here, I don't know if that good or bad."

"I don't know either."

She motioned toward the pistol in his hand. "You better put that away before somebody round here get hurt."

"It's your fault," he answered with a smile as he holstered his gun. "For a minute there I thought somebody was looting your place. I heard you hurt your hip. You shouldn't be moving furniture."

"Your Nana stronger than you think. You think a broken hip gonna finish me off?" she said, giving him a defiant look. "My hip just fine. It my chest where the hurt won't ever get better. Just like yours."

She took his hand and guided him across the unlit kitchen to the living room. Her uncertain steps gave the lie to her confident declarations about her hip. He started to say something, but was struck dumb when they entered the living room.

"I had to move some of the furniture 'cause I needed the space . . ."

Every piece of furniture in the room was pushed against the walls or the windows. Dozens of lit candles were placed on the tables and the upturned chairs. The blurry faces in old photos of their deceased ancestors peered at him, their eyes brought to life by the gently flickering candlelight. Next to the wall was a little altar where saints and skeletons contemplated death amid scattered coins that were no longer legal tender. The feeble flames cast an uncertain light, and for a moment, he feared they might ignite the silken garlands decorating the *loas*.

"Only important thing is having you here, darling. That got to mean something." She gave him a concerned look. "You think the storm gonna be bad as they say?"

"Yes."

"Bad enough to lure him out?"

He sighed deeply but said nothing. He nodded, his heart heavy. She came to him and ran her hands up his arms, across his shoulders, and over his chest. She lifted her right hand as if to bless him but instead placed two fingers directly over Dupree's heart. His old wound burned beneath his shirt as if new and raw. She took his hands, cupped them, and placed a tiny cloth sack in his palms. Dupree took it and felt a dry, earthy substance inside. He closed his eyes, both relieved and deeply moved, and slipped it into his pocket. When he opened his eyes again, she was watching him calmly.

"Finish him. Bring my girls home."

He nodded. "I'll do everything I can, Nana."

"Swear it to me. Even if they dead. Even dead, you bring my girls home."

Dupree's eyes filled with tears. "I swear it to you, Nana." He stepped back in an effort to master his emotions. "But we need to make a deal. You have to promise me you'll leave the city soon as you finish here. They're still running evacuation buses. I'll pay for a hotel room in Baton Rouge, in Dallas, wherever you want."

She shook her head. "You can't ask that. You know I can't leave. But don't you worry 'bout me. People here in the quarter watching out. You remember the Davis family?"

Dupree nodded. He recalled Nana's neighbor, the one with two husbands and five kids.

"They still here too. Seletha been a widow for a while now; she had a stroke and been laid up for three solid years. Her boy Bobby, the littlest, a good boy, take care of her. Got an old car that won't take us far, but he promised he gonna get us out if things go bad. They sayin' the city gonna open that Superdome for emergency shelter."

"Oh, Nana!" objected Dupree. "The stadium?"

"Only if they have to. Bobby's daddy, bless his departed soul, worked there when they buildin' it. Bobby says it's high, above the water, good and strong, made with concrete and rerod. Says the space under the stands good as any bunker." She smiled and gestured toward the altar. "Anyhow, you know I always been faithful to the *Santos.*"

Dupree tried to smile back, but he wasn't very convincing. His concern was plain. He went to the door, still ajar, and retrieved the sack he'd left on the porch. He held it out. "I thought you'd need this."

She closed the door, took out the package, put it on the kitchen table, and used a butcher knife to cut the fabric Meire had wrapped it in. She studied the contents. She looked into the silk bags, examined the labels Meire had laboriously prepared in his backward-leaning handwriting, and held the vials and powder tubes to the candlelight. She turned to Dupree.

"I got just one question. What you want to do with all this, *mon cher*—drive away that hurricane or call it here?"

15

Pain

New Orleans, Louisiana

Joseph Andrews Jr. wore jeans and an olive-green Tulane University sweatshirt. His long hair dangled over his blue eyes and stood out against the pallor of his face. He slouched in a chair in the dean's conference room with a book on the table before him. He wasn't reading. Amaia observed him from the hall, listening to the dean's whispered comments.

"He's an amazing young man and a brilliant student. We try to do everything we can for him, especially since the tragedy. He lives on campus and never leaves the university. When the evacuation order was given, we knew some students wouldn't leave. We set up a shelter in the main building, and I was sure Joseph would be one of those who would stay."

"Is that wise?"

"The main building has weathered hurricanes before."

It wasn't much of a guarantee.

Joseph Jr. straightened up when they went in. His attitude changed as well; he tensed and hunched his shoulders. He was slim, but his impressive biceps were visible through his cotton sweatshirt. Joseph stared at them through that dark curtain of hair. They held out their credentials; he glanced at them, not particularly interested. Johnson gave the boy their names and said nothing more. He'd told Amaia to take the lead, guessing that a young male student would be more likely to open up to a woman closer to his age.

"Good afternoon, Mr. Andrews," she said. "Amaia Salazar, I'm from the FBI. I'd like to ask you some questions. May I call you Joseph?"

"You're no FBI agent," he countered. "Your badge says 'temporary.' How old are you? Twenty-two?"

Johnson crossed his arms and stepped back to give Amaia room to work. He'd guessed right. Despite the hostile tone, Joseph was willing to talk to her.

"Twenty-five, actually. You're right, I'm not an FBI agent. I'm a police officer, temporarily with the Bureau." She jerked a thumb at Johnson. "But that guy is the real deal. We're in the middle of an investigation, and we'd like to talk to you about what happened to your family."

The young man smiled bitterly. "What happened to my family? Nothing *happened* to my family. Disease happens, accidents happen. Disasters too. My family was murdered. I've been trying to get somebody to listen to me for eight months. Why is the FBI taking notice all of a sudden?"

Johnson spoke, careful to keep his tone neutral. "We just want to clear some things up." He didn't want the boy to think they were reopening the case, as no official decision had been made. "Detective Nelson tells us you believe your family was killed by a stranger. We want to understand why you think this."

"I saw my father's body. His face was bruised and bloody. Like he'd been in a fight."

Johnson gave Amaia a doubtful look.

"And I knew my dad," the boy added. "He'd never have hurt any of us."

Johnson nodded. He'd heard that before.

Joseph knew what he was thinking. "You don't understand. My parents loved us, and they were like lovebirds to one another. We were always making fun of them for all their kissing and hugging. My father was a good man who adored us. Nothing anyone says will ever make me believe he was a murderer."

"Sometimes a life event like relocation for work can destabilize a family," Amaia commented. "Moving from California to Texas must have been a big change."

"Dad's career was going great, and Mom traveled all over the country for her work. They'd been getting ready for this for months. And as for big changes, Sacramento's not such an amazing place, and our Galveston house was right on the Gulf. Moving to Galveston was perfect. My sister had new friends, and Mom was really pleased to be there."

"Okay, but not everybody was happy. I heard your little brother was having problems."

"He was twelve! He was just a kid! It was hard for him, changing schools and leaving his friends behind. He threw a tantrum like a two-year-old, stomped through our neighbor's flower bed. The neighbor hadn't even met us. He called the cops because he thought some punk did it. My parents apologized and hired a professional landscaper to fix it. The man was okay with that, so he dropped his complaint. In fact, after that, he was one of our closest family friends. He's the same neighbor who went to check on them after the storm, the one who . . . found them . . ."

Amaia knew Joseph couldn't bring himself to say it. They were discussing murders, but that word—"dead"—was too much for him.

"Did you live with your parents in Sacramento?"

"Yes."

"Seems kind of strange that they moved and left you behind."

Two fierce points of light flashed in Joseph's blue eyes. He exhaled sharply and took a deep breath. She saw this young man was capable of real anger.

"They didn't leave me behind! My grandmother fell and broke her hip two months before our move. She had an operation and was recovering, but she still had another month of physical therapy left when it was time to move to Texas. Dad tried to negotiate it with the insurance company, but they said she'd lose her coverage if she moved out of state. I was going to be free until my classes started in the fall, so we decided I'd stay with her in Sacramento until she finished her physical therapy. After that, we'd go to Galveston."

"You were all going to live in Galveston together?"

"That was the plan."

Amaia glanced swiftly at Johnson. "Your grandmother too?"

"Sure," the young man said. "After her accident, my parents decided she should stay with us, just like in California."

"Who knew you were going to move?"

Joseph shrugged. "Well . . . lots of people, I guess. Neighbors, friends, everybody at Dad's firm, of course. People who worked with Mom. Mom's theatre group, the principals and teachers at our schools, the health insurance people . . . Like I said, it was all set up months in advance."

"Detective Nelson told us you decided not to live in the Galveston house, and the dean says you don't leave campus. You're even going to stay here despite the hurricane."

His eyes drifted off toward some far, indistinct point. "I don't have anywhere to go." His voice was low and anguished.

"How about your grandmother?"

Joseph looked at his hands, and she thought he was shutting down and they wouldn't get another word out of him. But they did, and his answer surprised them. "You ever hear the expression 'to die of a broken heart'?"

Amaia nodded.

"That's what the doctor said. He told me she died of a broken heart. She'd been getting better after the operation, but after the . . . murders . . . she got terribly depressed. She died six months ago, two months after the rest of my family."

Amaia saw his expression change. Joseph's eyes were retreating into that hazy infinity of loss. He was taking refuge somewhere far away. She was certain he was spending more and more time there. Young Joseph was a potential suicide risk.

"I need to understand your reasoning!" she said sharply to jar him out of his distraction.

"My reasoning?" he echoed with indifference, as if awakening from a dream.

"The reason you think your family was murdered. I need more to go on than the infantile faith that your father wouldn't have done it." Amaia leaned toward him, emphasizing the urgency of her questions. "What's wrong with that picture? You knew them better than anyone, Joseph. You've got a gut feeling about what happened. Tell me now. I know it had to be something, something Detective Nelson couldn't see. Some feeling even an army of detectives would have missed. They couldn't see it because it was hidden from their eyes, but you could. What was it?"

Joseph looked at her, shaken. His breathing had become fast and shallow. She was sure he was about to deliver a revelation, but she sensed how deeply unhappy he was, mired in a state of despair where nothing mattered anymore. For a moment she was afraid they would lose him; he was perilously close to collapsing into himself and retreating into silence. He looked away, but then his eyes returned to hers.

"The violin," he said firmly. "A violin, but without a bow. And afterward it disappeared."

Joseph Andrews Jr. told everyone who would listen to him that he didn't believe for a second his father had murdered the family. His conviction gradually began to weaken as Detective Nelson interviewed him. The policeman was doing his best to sound sympathetic, but the man's tone betrayed him, and Joseph could tell that the cop didn't buy his assertions. The detective wasn't sympathetic; what the man was feeling was pity. Joseph had an innate ability to read other people's emotions. The cop's pity undermined Joseph's certainty, because Nelson's attitude suggested the police might know something they weren't telling him.

Joseph had been steeling himself for what he'd face when he entered his parents' home. Nelson had described the condition of the house, the disorder, the broken windows. Joseph couldn't help imagining the bodies of his family in the living room. Standing on the street, he knew he wasn't ready. Seeing the scene of the murders was going to change his life forever, but this was his destiny, whether he was ready or not.

The neighbor, the same one who'd complained about his kid brother, had called in specialists to clean everything up and nail plywood panels across the broken windows. The neighbor was trying to explain all this as he accompanied Joseph up the front walk.

Joseph had prepared himself for overwhelming terror, but there was none. Even as he listened to his neighbor, he became increasingly bewildered. He looked for reminders of what had occurred, but he found nothing. Horror had left no trace. He saw his little brother's backpack leaning against the coat rack in the entry hall. Marveling, he breathed in the delicate perfume of the white orchids his mom had placed all about the living room. The abstract painting in shades of blue that his sister had done in her Sacramento art class the year before stood out against the brilliant white living-room wall. There was the enormous flat-screen television Dad had bought so they could watch Tulane football games together. Those memories crowded in upon him. It was as if everyone had gone out to the movies or the mall, and they'd walk in the front door any moment.

Joseph was terribly tired. He walked the good neighbor to the front door and ushered him out. Shutting the door against him, he suddenly felt stronger, as if latent energy from his family members was bolstering him. This was his house; he would stay here with the souls of his family. It all made sense. He'd transfer to Texas A&M's Galveston campus, he'd bring his grandmother from California, and they'd live here together.

When someone dies, those left behind frequently ask themselves what that person would have wanted them to do. But death changes everything. Would they have wanted their son, their brother, to stay here after what had happened? The unknown answer suddenly became moot. Because that was when he saw the violin, a dark, shining instrument, both innocent and incongruous. Someone had leaned it against the steel chiminea, the decorative metal fireplace his mom had filled with stout white candles. The presence of that violin was as revealing as if the murderer had scrawled the names of his victims across the wall in their own blood.

Joseph couldn't take his eyes off the violin. He backed away, still focused on the instrument. He reached the front door and opened it. The breeze from the Gulf did nothing to lessen the sensation that he was trapped inside a mausoleum. Joseph was trembling from head to foot.

He'd been mistaken. This wasn't his home anymore. His parents were never coming back, because someone had murdered them.

16

Caressing the Beast

New Orleans, Louisiana

Officer Jason Bull drove through the increasingly deserted streets, engaged in lively conversation with his partner, while in the back seat, Johnson and Amaia stared silently through the side windows. Jason could tell they'd had an argument; that was obvious. Or maybe just a difference of opinion. Johnson had caught up with Amaia next to the vehicle and had said something sharp and emphatic, and she'd replied with impressive serenity. Those Washington folks were so refined they didn't shout even when they had reason to. The two had exchanged no more than a few words all the way from Tulane to the Dauphine Orleans Hotel.

Johnson saw Bull studying him via the rearview mirror. He looked away, annoyed. Johnson considered himself a good man. He tolerated differences, could talk easily with almost anyone, and fully appreciated outside talent. He understood why Dupree had brought Salazar on to the team. He could even understand Emerson's poorly concealed jealousy. The difference between Johnson and Emerson was simple: Emerson was a loser. Johnson had been in this job long enough to know that the good of a unit is far more important than the personal qualities of any of its members. That's why Emerson was in Florida with Tucker, and Johnson was with Dupree in New Orleans.

He'd tried to call Dupree while walking across the university campus at Salazar's side. No one picked up. He ended the call and glanced unhappily at his colleague. God knows he was doing his best, but he just didn't understand her.

Before they'd arrived at the dean's office, Johnson had thought that Joseph Jr. would be more likely to open up to Salazar than to him. And he'd been right. He'd stepped back and given her plenty of room to carry out the interview. And Salazar was skillful. She'd displayed an extraordinarily sensual mixture of strength and fragility that clearly attracted young Joe.

When the crucial moment came, Johnson thought the boy was going to clam up for good. Joseph had doubled over, elbows on his knees and head in his hands, looking like he was going to vomit. Salazar had inched her chair forward until their knees almost touched. She'd mirrored his position, leaning forward until they were almost cheek to cheek. That's when the kid opened up. About how he'd gone back to the family home, how he'd found the violin, how he'd known at that moment the killer had left it there deliberately. And how Detective Nelson hadn't believed him but instead had dismissed it completely.

The boy was exhausted by the time he finished his account.

Johnson came forward, close behind Amaia, leaned over, and whispered in her ear. "Listen, I think Nelson was right. A violin?"

She swiveled and glowered at him. She was ferocious. "I saw a violin at the Allens' farmhouse."

Johnson searched for a response. "Okay, but that's not so unusual—"

Amaia was on her feet in an instant, moving on Johnson and pushing him back where the boy couldn't hear them. "And I'm certain there was one in the photos I saw of the Mason murders in Texas, in the same room as the bodies."

"Seriously? First we have a composer and now we have a violin?" He realized he'd raised his voice.

Their exchange caught Joseph's attention. He looked up at Johnson, faint hope dawning in his eyes.

She warned him with a gesture toward the boy. "I wasn't the one who chose that stupid name!" she hissed.

Johnson looked away from Salazar and tried to summon up the images of the room where the Masons had been murdered. He didn't recall a violin in that chaos, but he couldn't dismiss the possibility either. He just wasn't sure. He gave Salazar a look of consternation. "If that's so . . ."

"I'm sure of it. Phone Dupree. We have to go back to the hotel right away. Someone has to talk to Detective Nelson and review the photos." She checked her watch. "A Texas state trooper told me the contents of the Allen farmhouse would be held in a state-controlled warehouse. If we're quick about it, maybe we can catch the warehouse staff before they close for the day."

Before they left the dean's office, Johnson had leaned on the table where Joseph sat motionless. "Evacuation buses are still leaving the city. You can get on one if you hurry. It's going to be pretty dangerous around here."

"What's the worst that could happen?" Joseph replied with complete indifference. "I could die?"

Johnson had no reply to that.

Amaia turned to Joseph. "*You're not allowed to die.* You're going to help us track down your family's murderer."

Joseph inhaled sharply. The limp doll before them was suddenly infused with life. He nodded slowly, almost as if bowing.

"I won't die," he told her.

"Give me a number where I can reach you," Johnson said, "and then get out of town."

Johnson tried Dupree's number again. It kept ringing. He glanced at Salazar, who seemed not the least affected by their disagreement, unlike him. Her face was relaxed; the shadow of a smile played across her lips as she gazed out at the passing scenery. Sitting like that, she seemed younger, practically a teenager. She blinked several times, and he realized she had been dozing off. It occurred to him that she'd gotten very little sleep over the past couple of days.

He shook his head. This woman was getting on his nerves, but he had to get over it. Johnson was used to taking orders; he was an experienced field operative. But she had an unusually arrogant self-assurance that exasperated him.

"Salazar, encouraging that boy was a mistake. I was moved by his despair too, and that's why I encouraged him to leave the city, but you . . ." His grimace pulled down his mustache. "You lied to the kid. You can't say things like that. We're not sure the Composer was behind his family's death, and you saw how he reacted. He'll cling to anything to keep from accepting the truth. That boy's a potential suicide risk."

She straightened up, turned toward him, and said, "Agent Johnson, the only effective way to escape death is *to try not to die today*. And that's not always possible."

"Oh, really? And what'll happen tomorrow if you have to tell him you were wrong? That it wasn't a serial killer who did away with the family, but his own father?"

"In that case, he'll have lived one more day. Another day of opportunities, of meeting people along the way, of learning, of surviving. A person learns to survive by living. She won't have another chance after she's dead."

Johnson fell silent. He'd heard that pronoun: "she" wouldn't have another chance. He was certain it wasn't a slip of the tongue. She wasn't talking about the boy.

17

Before Dying

Elizondo

Amaia warded off the threat by going to bed immediately. She wanted to sleep, because she was safe then; if she was sleeping when the menace arrived, she wouldn't be terrified by it. She wouldn't know, and if she didn't know, she wouldn't suffer. One evening she'd fallen asleep without trying, it had just happened. She couldn't believe her good fortune when she awoke the next morning. She'd slept and hadn't been afraid!

She hadn't managed that feat since, but she'd tried her best. She was always the first to go to bed; she brushed her teeth to make sure forgetting her end-of-day health ritual couldn't be used as a reason to drag her out of bed, and she peed so she wouldn't be awakened during the night by the need to go. She put her school things in order, selected her clothes and laid them out, got into bed, and closed her eyes, doing her best to conjure slumber, longing for its silence and amnesia.

Go to sleep! she commanded herself.

She turned toward the wall and tried to ignore the whispered confidences exchanged by her sisters in their adjacent beds.

Go to sleep!

She heard her father come into the room and kiss her sisters goodnight. She sensed him come to her bed, lean over, and hesitate. Sometimes he caressed the hair at the nape of her neck; usually, though, he refrained because he didn't want to wake her. He tucked her in to make sure she'd be warm.

Go to sleep!

The greatest sacrifice was her father's warm kiss. Amaia gave it up because she wanted to avoid delaying sleep's arrival.

Go to sleep. This is your last chance!

The room was cloaked in a silence interrupted only by an occasional swish as Flora turned a page, until twenty minutes later, their mother called from the hall that it was time to turn out the light.

If she hadn't gotten to sleep by then, any chance of escape was lost.

You didn't go to sleep, and now she's going to come get you.

From that moment on, the minutes and hours dragged by.

Never sleep on your back!

If she waited in that position, she'd be aware not only of the hot breath, but also the closeness of those lips, the hanging hair that brushed her cheek, microscopic drops of warm saliva exhaled across her face . . . and she couldn't stand that.

Never on your back!

She didn't look at the door either, because if she did, she'd have to open her eyes to keep watch.

No, don't look at the door!

For a long time, she'd made sure to turn her back and face the wall. When she heard the creak of the hall floorboard, she closed her eyes, huddled motionless, and prayed silently. *Our Father, our Father, ourFather ourFather ourFather ourFather . . .*

Never on her back, never facing the door. Turned toward the wall, she was less vulnerable, but that position displayed an impudence that offended her mother. Rosario found it both upsetting and provocative. She was confident in her power and enjoyed inflicting terror, but she saw that something had changed the first time Amaia dared to lie there turned to the wall.

Amaia heard her come into the room and approach the bed, and felt that malevolent, calculating gaze on her back. She pretended to sleep, but her eyes were so tightly shut that any fool could see she was acting.

The girl heard the watery smack of saliva, the bony click of teeth. She sensed the tensed muscles of that neck and leering face, and she was out of her mind with terror.

Amaia felt hot breath in her ear and on her cheek; she sensed the approach of those feverish lips. Rosario opened her mouth—close, closer—and exhaled so profoundly that her breath stirred the girl's soft locks. Her lips clamped shut upon them. She snorted and trembled in frustration as if tempted to say something. She straightened up abruptly, the girl's hair slipping wetly from her mouth. The malevolence fed on the child's terror as it whispered, "Sleep tight, little vixen. *Ama* isn't going to eat you up tonight." She backed slowly toward the bedroom door and stood observing the child for a long, long time. Amaia prayed, her eyes now wide open in the darkness.

Our Father, our Father, our Father . . .

18

Archway

New Orleans, Louisiana
Nightfall, Saturday, August 27, 2005

Amaia opened her eyes. Had she been asleep?

"Salazar," Johnson murmured. "Dupree is calling."

Dupree's voice was deafening inside their vehicle. She was feeling dizzy. She focused, trying to follow him.

"An entire family was found dead in their house in Miami. Emerson and Tucker are on the scene now. We've conferenced them in. Agent Tucker, go ahead, we're listening."

Tucker's voice was almost unrecognizable over the static. Amaia fought to clear her head. She had difficulty understanding Tucker's accent through the poor connection.

Tucker was ticking off points that matched the profile. "The family's name is Samuels, and I swear it's like being right back in Texas. There's practically no deviation from any of the previous murders. Father, mother, three children, two boys and a girl, and a grandmother. Same cord marks on the wrists, twenty-two-caliber shots to the head from the father's gun, bodies laid out south-to-north. All the ages match as well."

"We got it wrong," Johnson said unhappily. "It wasn't New Orleans. He went to Florida."

"We got nothing wrong," Dupree replied. "We have half our team there."

Only half, Johnson thought, resigned to half a failure.

Dupree made the executive decisions. "Agents Emerson and Tucker will stay with the investigation, take charge of the bodies and the crime scene. They'll attend the autopsies. We stay here. His pace is accelerating. He killed the Allens only four days ago. No one knows what's motivating him, but he's going full speed ahead. I'm sure he's coming here. He doesn't want to waste an opportunity."

Amaia spoke. "Agent Tucker, this is Salazar. Are you at the murder scene right now?"

Tucker's answer rattled on the line like the voice of a robot. "Yeah. We're with the medical examiner."

"Check to see if there's a violin anywhere near the bodies. It's bound to be located somewhere close to their heads."

Two seconds later, Tucker confirmed it. "There's a violin here all right, on the floor, kind of between the mother's head and the older son's. How the hell did you know?"

Dupree spoke. "Salazar, explain."

Amaia closed her eyes and leaned her head against the window. She motioned to Johnson to reply.

And because Johnson was a good man, he forgot his resentment for Salazar and ran interference. "Agent Dupree, we've just arrived. Detective Bull's parking the vehicle in the hotel courtyard. We'll see you in a moment. Agent Tucker, it's important to look for the bow. If this is the Composer's work, there won't be one."

Dupree listened as they briefed him on their conversation with Joseph, all the while studying photos of the crime scenes. He concurred with Amaia that the photo from the Masons' living room showed part of the chin rest of an instrument that was almost certainly a violin.

Johnson glanced at Amaia. "Assistant Inspector Salazar says a state trooper told her they inventory the contents of a house and hold them in a state warehouse pending disposition."

"All right," Dupree said and checked his watch. "We'll get on that as soon as we finish with Detective Nelson. He's calling us in two minutes. Agents Emerson and Tucker will join us on the line from Miami."

Brad Nelson came on the line as scheduled. Dupree summarized the situation. "The Andrews family murders in Galveston appear to fit the profile of a series of murders we're investigating. The FBI is treating this as kidnapping and murder. Your former chief, Captain Reed, sent us the case files and offered Galveston's cooperation; we hope you'll give us a hand. It goes without saying that this conversation must remain absolutely confidential."

"Fine, y'all go ahead and do whatever you want!" Nelson's response dripped with scorn. "It's none of my business anymore. Hasn't been for months, in fact."

"Detective, this is Assistant Inspector Salazar."

Nelson answered her questions in a bored tone: Yes, that goddamned violin. He saw it right away, part of the interior decoration. Trivial. CSI teams don't go around impounding violins as evidence. No traces of an intruder were found, no hairs, no prints, nothing at all to suggest somebody else had been in the house.

"Detective Nelson, this is Agent Johnson. Were you aware Mrs. Andrews was an interior decorator and had done the work on their new house herself?"

"Pleased to speak with you, Johnson. Yeah, Joseph explained all that, and he claimed his mother wouldn't have used a violin. Said it would clash with the 'aesthetic sensibility' of the room. Said violin lessons were the last thing in the world that'd interest his little brother . . . But the thing could have gotten there any number of ways. Remember, Junior wasn't living in Galveston at the time. Any other family member could have brought it home. His mother was volunteering with the repertory theatre."

"The fact that a family member insisted it didn't belong in the house should have rung a bell," Johnson commented, applying a little pressure. "Okay, he wasn't living there, but he knew them better than anyone else."

"It did raise doubts. I sent a crime tech to dust the thing down for prints a second time. It was clean. I even considered examining it a third time, but it was stolen."

Dupree's voice was steely. "This was *after* you authorized the professional cleanup of the crime scene."

Amaia glanced at him, impressed. *He comes across as a gentleman, but don't let that fool you.*

Nelson sighed into the phone. It rattled like thunder. "Look, I know what y'all are up to. I'm sorry for the boy, I understand what he's going through, and it's a shame. That's why I kept taking his calls. But I've seen plenty of cases like this. He's got survivor's guilt. On one hand, he wasn't with them; on the other, he wants to deny it happened at all. He's grasping at straws. That's why I sent my tech over there. Not because I thought our work was shoddy, but so I could give Junior a definite answer once and for all. But there was nothing—nothing at all—to suggest that any person outside the family had been in that house. The gun was inches from the father's hand, and he had powder residue on that same hand. Ballistics confirmed his pistol had fired the shots. It was an open-and-shut case."

"What kind of violin was it?" Amaia asked.

Nelson's reply was less aggrieved now that he'd made his case. "That I can tell you. Because of the boy's complaints about the violin, I didn't just order it dusted for prints; I had a full report drawn up. It was an ordinary violin, the kind used for teaching, the type anybody might buy for a teenager who is taking lessons. Made in the USA, available in any music store for about seventy bucks."

Amaia probed further. "Detective, did you find the bow?"

The question obviously took Nelson aback. "The bow?"

"It's a long, thin piece of wood, slightly curved, with strings along the length, used to stroke the violin and produce the sounds."

"I'm perfectly aware what a bow is," he growled.

"Well, then? Did the team find one?"

Another of those thunderous sighs into the phone. "No. No, we didn't find one. But I hardly think that means anything . . ."

She kept at it. "Tell me how the violin disappeared."

"It didn't disappear, it was stolen!" he exclaimed. "And that was after the lab examined it a second time, so if you're trying to make that out to be important, you're completely off track. They nailed the windows shut after the storm, and I guess they did a shit job of it. A few days later, some guys in a squad car noticed the plywood across one window was hanging loose. Nothing of value was missing, not even the expensive computers. Someone left a package of cookies open on the kitchen counter. The only inventoried items missing were a crystal decanter, the crystal bowl where they left their keys, and the violin. We think it was some neighborhood kid who walked off with a few souvenirs, nothing more than—"

"Detective Nelson?" Johnson interrupted him. "Mr. Andrews insisted on viewing his family's bodies. We know the authorities tried to dissuade him. Joseph told us that his dad worked out every day and claimed he would have tried to take on an intruder. He also told us there were cuts and abrasions on his father's face, signs of a fight. He remembers a broken fingernail. I have the autopsy reports here in front of me. The other victims showed no defensive injuries. What's your explanation for Mr. Andrews's facial injuries?"

"You think it was an intruder? Maybe when you picked apart the ME's report you forgot to compare it with mine. There was no indication of forced entry, no signs of a struggle. The fella just lost his head! We think the injuries were self-inflicted. The pistol butt had his DNA on it. I've seen it before, a suicidal person working himself into a frenzy before pulling the trigger. He's out of his mind, he hits himself to overcome his panic. Physical pain helps him focus."

Amaia changed the subject. "Detective, there are some things in the ballistics report I don't understand. A comparison was made between a bullet fired in the lab and a twenty-two-caliber slug taken from the younger son."

"That's right."

"Why did the lab compare only one bullet?" Johnson asked.

Amaia answered that. "I see here they tried to recover bullets from the wife and the daughter, but the bullets fragmented when entering the skull. The medical examiner was able to extract an undamaged bullet only from the boy."

"Like she says," Nelson agreed. "They couldn't match those bullets, but they confirmed the shots were of the same caliber."

"How about the father?" Amaia challenged him.

"Well . . ." Nelson seemed to be searching for words.

"They didn't compare that bullet," Amaia declared.

"They already knew that it was a twenty-two because the residue is less extensive than that left by higher caliber firearms. The lab subjected the swabs from his hand to exhaustive analysis. They tested for lead, barium, and antimony. Positive results for all three, and on the left hand; the man was a lefty. How could an unknown attacker know that? The father fired the gun."

"And the bullet?" she insisted.

"We didn't recover the bullet."

Dupree interjected, "It couldn't be found at the crime scene?"

Amaia knew the answer. "It's still inside the father's skull."

"For God's sake! It wasn't needed. We have the residue, the bullet from the kid's head was whole, and we had the shattered bullets from the wife and daughter. The slug in the father's head must have been just as fragmented."

"It isn't," Amaia stated flatly. "We just received the autopsy report. The X-ray of the man's skull shows the bullet's intact."

They waited for Nelson's response. Several long seconds passed.

"That changes nothing. He fired the gun, he killed his whole family. All the evidence supports that conclusion. I'm starting to get the feeling you want to accuse me of sloppy work. I'm a professional, an experienced homicide detective. We investigated that case just as thoroughly as any other."

Amaia's inquiry was quiet, almost offhand. "Detective Nelson. Could you answer one last question?"

"If it's the last one, you bet I can!"

"There was another bullet recovered at the crime scene . . ."

"From the door frame, yes. It was undamaged. A twenty-two-caliber slug fired from the same gun."

"I'm looking at a close-up photo. I can't make out the height of the impact, but I'm guessing it's just inches above the floor."

"Yeah. How'd you know?" Nelson's astonishment was mirrored in Johnson's and Dupree's faces.

Amaia tapped a button and put Nelson on hold. "Everything went wrong for the Composer. The storm turned out to be less destructive than expected; not all the family were on site; and the father resisted. But either our man decided to proceed as planned, or for some reason he couldn't stop what he'd started. We've speculated that the Composer murders other family members but leaves the father till last. But Andrews fought him, and the Composer had to shoot him to get the twenty-two. The killer had to have been carrying a different gun. Maybe he didn't need it for the other murders, but he had to be prepared in case things went wrong. In this case they did. He killed the father with his own gun and then murdered the others with the father's gun."

"What about the bullet in the door frame? You think Andrews managed to get off a shot?"

"It's from Andrews's pistol, but I think it was fired after the father was dead. Suicides typically shoot themselves in the head or, in rare cases, in the heart. No one intending to kill himself would be able to shoot himself twice. If he had two bullets in his skull, that would literally have been a dead giveaway. The killer had to place the twenty-two in the father's hand and fire it to leave powder traces, but Andrews was dead and lying on the floor. That's why the trajectory was low."

Johnson inhaled deeply and let out a long, slow sigh. "And the Composer had seen he was left-handed."

Dupree punched the call button. "I want an exhumation order for Andrews Sr. If I can convince the judge it's urgent, we might get it by tonight."

Amaia muttered, "I need to tell Joseph Jr."

Dupree rejected that idea. "Salazar, we don't need the boy's permission. We know from experience that sometimes it's better for the families not to know until it actually happens. They suffer less that way."

"Salazar's right," Johnson said. "It may be painful to young Andrews, but it's the closest thing to a victory he's had in a long time."

19

Mary Ward

Cape May, New Jersey

The ring of the telephone broke the quiet of the Ward Funeral Home. It startled Mary and made her look up, half-annoyed and half-amused. She'd been in the profession for forty years, and she still jumped like a scalded cat at any sudden noise. She preferred to work in silence. That's how her father had done it, and she'd followed his example, at least until the day Ben, her son, decided to accept tradition and dedicate himself to mortuary work. She was happy to work with Ben, but their conflicts over the heavy metal music he blasted at work had come close to wrecking their relationship and ruining the family business.

They'd negotiated a compromise. Ben could stay with the firm, but he'd have to listen to his music through headphones only. There was one disadvantage to having him wear headphones all day long, though: he couldn't hear anything else. The problem with all this was that someone might call requesting services and he wouldn't hear the phone ring. Ben had solved that problem by installing a commercial-grade notification system like they had down at the firehouse. Whenever the phone rang, loudspeakers blasted the sound throughout the building. Ben heard it despite his headphones, and Mary practically went through the roof.

Mary gestured to her son to keep on working. She picked up the phone and smiled when she heard a young woman identifying herself as an FBI agent. How things had changed! Mary was a bit disappointed, because she doubted they'd be able to help. After the storm killed the Miller family, Cape May's city government had declared their place a ruin and ordered it bulldozed as a safety measure. Nothing from the house had been preserved. But her son and several of their employees had removed and transported the bodies after the judge released them. Her Ben had taken violin lessons from age five. He had poor coordination and a terrible ear, so he finally gave up at age ten. But his memory was excellent; if there'd been a violin in the room, he wouldn't have missed it.

Mary put down the phone with a little grin. He was working with his back to her, that infernal music blasting in his ears. She crept up on him and ran her chilly hand down his neck.

20

Preacher

New Orleans, Louisiana
10:00 p.m., Saturday, August 27, 2005

They hadn't eaten a proper meal all day; they'd scarcely touched the snack the owners of the hotel had brought up while they were studying the case files. The team went downstairs together.

Distant music from the street complemented the bar's quiet piano medley. They passed through the bar to an indoor patio where sand-colored walls were lit by candles in hurricane lamps.

"That's the original 1930s paint job," Bull said. "They say a New Orleans mayor owned the place before it became a bordello."

Amaia wound up sharing one of the small tables with Dupree, feeling that the team had somehow maneuvered her there. They ordered oysters Bienville and crawfish, which were delicious. "You need to come back in the spring," Bull said. "Practically every house has a kettle of crawfish boil going over a fire in the yard then."

They'd been pleased that the judge had authorized the exhumation of the body of Joseph Andrews Sr. They couldn't do much more until the Galveston police communicated the medical examiner's results.

Afterward, they set out on a walk through the French Quarter. During their windshield tour of the city earlier that day, Amaia had thought the evacuation orders had cleared out much of the city's population, but the lengthy stroll on

Dauphine Street to Frenchmen proved her wrong. Amaia was astonished by the crowds of beer drinkers lining the streets. They seemed to be celebrating the arrival of the hurricane.

Along Bourbon Street, the usual boozy stink was mixed with cooking smells from the few restaurants still open. The brief illusion of calm that Dupree had seen at noon was swept away by crowds bustling in both directions. Some of the tourists wore party hats.

Maybe two yards away, a ragged man standing on an overturned bucket in the middle of the street howled to the skies and berated the tourists milling in front of a strip joint. "*Repent, sinners!* The end is near. The Lord is sending his wrath upon you; you devote yourselves to the pleasures of the flesh today, but tomorrow you will cry like babes, and tomorrow it will be too late."

Amaia gave Dupree a shrug and an ironic glance. It wasn't the first time she'd seen a street preacher or heard warnings about the end of days, but the scene seemed particularly bizarre in a city battening down before the approach of a hurricane.

Bull stepped to Dupree's side, whispered something, and pointed to a balcony. Dupree looked up at the balcony, the same one from which the crone had addressed him that morning.

The street preacher jumped down from his perch, took two swift strides to Dupree, and jabbed an accusing finger into his chest. Johnson and Amaia were alarmed. Dupree's stifled groan was followed by a wheeze and a gasp for air. He fumbled in his pocket for the gris-gris Nana had given him, but he'd left it behind when he changed his jacket. Bill Charbou instantly grabbed the preacher's wrist, twisted his arm up behind his back, and put him in a choke hold. Bill snarled into the man's ear, "Hands to yourself, buddy! Shout all you want, but keep your hands to yourself!"

God's self-appointed apostle immediately went limp. Bill pushed him away. "Most of 'em are harmless, but sometimes they get a little carried away with their apocalypse thing. I guess the hurricane has really riled them. Did he hurt you?"

Dupree shook his head. "A twinge in an old wound. It's been bothering me all day. Probably because of the humidity."

Amaia lowered her gaze. It wasn't physical pain she'd seen reflected in Dupree's eyes. She knew all too well what he'd felt. Without a word, she lifted a hand to her scalp and touched the rough edge of an almost invisible scar. She immediately regretted her reaction. She forgot that hidden scar for months at a time, but her aunt's phone call and Dupree's pained expression had awakened and inflamed her own mark.

Bill and Bull suggested a stop for dessert.

Sitting at a café table and spooning up outstanding fig ice cream, Amaia felt her scar still throbbing like an open wound. She again lifted a hand and traced the hidden trail of stitches with her index finger.

Dupree seemed unusually relaxed. "I wasn't so sure about Bull and Charbou at first."

Amaia awoke from her reverie. "Sorry?"

"Bill and Bull." Dupree jerked his thumb toward the bar, where the New Orleans cops were engaged in a lively discussion with Johnson and the bartender. "Those boys have a completely different style and approach. But I'm beginning to see they're going to be a big help."

Bill Charbou was urging the barkeeper to raise the volume of the television. The screen displayed the now familiar satellite image of Katrina revolving relentlessly above the Gulf of Mexico. Charbou raised a hand and barked something that silenced everyone in the bar.

The voice of an off-screen commentator accompanied the image of the advancing storm. "Gale-force winds subsided temporarily, but in recent hours, Katrina has doubled in size, and she's entering a phase of accelerating intensity."

A murmur of sharp disappointment went through the bar, but that was all. The music resumed. No one made for the door. Charbou and Bull went back to their conversation with Johnson and the bartender.

She nodded pensively, watching them.

Dupree called her out of her musings. "You dream of the dead, Assistant Inspector Salazar?"

She looked at him, bewildered, thinking her ears had deceived her. "I didn't catch that."

"Let me try again. Are you haunted by visions of the dead at the foot of your bed, Salazar?"

She moved her lips as if to answer him, but nothing came out. *What was this? Some kind of joke?*

As if reading her thoughts, he responded, "It's no joke. I do; I dream of the dead. They follow me and try to tell me things I can't quite catch. The nightmares don't go away until I finally manage to understand what they're trying to say."

Amaia's eyes opened wide. "Uh, okay, well, I . . ."

"Oh, I understand. It's not the sort of thing a person wants to go around talking about, and certainly not to a person in my position. You don't need to tell me; I know you see them. I read a summary of your report about the kidnapper you tracked down in Spain. I was impressed by your stubborn dedication to the victims. And that explanation you gave. You called it—"

"A hunch," she completed his sentence.

Dupree nodded slowly. "I've known lots of law enforcement agents over the years. I can tell when someone has the gift. And you do."

Amaia pressed her lips shut. This kind of talk made her uncomfortable.

"You know, lots of people will think you're odd. They'll call your hunches some sort of sixth sense. But you can't fool me. I know where a sixth sense comes from. It develops in those who've lived through the kinds of things that would destroy other people. But some of them, rare birds like Sherrington, learn from the experience. He was capable of seeing beyond, intuiting the evil lurking out there in the world, alive and real, disguised by a thin mask of human skin. A disguise like that hides its malevolence from most of us, but not from you."

"I'm not so sure that's true . . ."

Dupree was suddenly annoyed. "This is no time for false modesty. It doesn't matter whether you're conscious of it or not. The vital thing is to recognize where that hunch comes from. The process doesn't seem logical in most cases, certainly not to the minds of ordinary people, those who haven't explored the dark well of evil. But you've been there. You mentioned latent variables when Emerson asked how you evaluated the probabilities. Anyone can put together the obvious bits of evidence to suggest a coherent hypothesis. I've lectured on that a thousand times. But there's a special talent endowed to only a few, and they all have one thing in common." He looked deep into her eyes. "They've all lived through hell."

She glanced down for a moment, even though she knew she shouldn't, because it was an admission his insight was accurate. She lifted her gaze and detected in Dupree's always-controlled facial expression the satisfaction of being proved right. She couldn't help wondering why this was so important to him.

"That's why you have the ability to see things hidden away in some blind corner, invisible to others. It's the gift of second sight, which is required to monitor a demon. You have to know the demon intimately to maintain your safe distance, all the while keeping your eye on the fiend."

Dupree crossed his arms on the table and leaned in close. "*You* can do that. You paid a high price for that ability. I want to know where it comes from. When you found the old woman's body under the roof out on the farm, you said the situation reminded you of a place. Tell me about that."

Her boss searched her face, silently testing her defenses and probing for weakness.

Amaia overrode her urge to look down submissively again. She chose to present a more confident front. She met and mastered his challenge. "I have no idea where that came from. I'm not tied to that place, I have no roots there, and I'd never thought about those old stories. I suppose somebody told me those legends when I was little. It was a simple logical deduction. Some synapse clicked and hauled that reference out of my subconscious."

He shook his head impatiently. "It's no use trying to explain it away. The place where we were born and grew up shapes us forever. Our origins determine our character and how we see, hear, learn, and draw conclusions."

"Agent Dupree, I've lived as long in the United States as I did in the town of my birth. I came here as a child."

"But you went back."

"I went to a city in Spain, a place that has nothing to do with where I was born. I never particularly cared for my birthplace. I didn't much dislike it either. It's an ordinary, run-of-the-mill little town."

"Elizondo."

She reeled as if he'd struck her.

He wouldn't leave it alone. "A place you never mention, known for folkloric traditions so powerful they enabled you to explain why the Composer found nothing grotesque about shoving a grandmother's corpse under the roof of a farmhouse."

"I remember those stories, but not the details. I thought they were foolish."

"Are you sure you always felt that way?"

"Yes. Always."

"You don't recall a time when you really did believe them, maybe just for an instant? No need to feel ashamed. It's a basic tenet of anthropology that the motivations and rationales determining human behavior all across the planet are fed by identical needs, anxieties, and fears. Those apprehensions shape people's understandings of their place in the world. Your knowledge and mastery of the mythology give you the privilege of the damned. Sherrington had it, and so do you."

She kept shaking her head, denying it.

He appeared to give up. He checked his watch. "It's getting late. We have a tough day ahead, so we need to hit the hay." Dupree got up and went to the bar to call the others.

Amaia sighed, relieved to have escaped his interrogation. Dupree returned and put a generous tip on the table. "There's a reason why some people cut off all ties with the places where they were born and grew up. It's always an unpaid debt. Be careful about unpaid debts, Salazar. They come due sooner or later."

Amaia had to restrain herself from touching her scalp, where the scar under her hair was burning.

21

Premonition

Elizondo

Engrasi's theory was that premonition was essentially a manifestation of the survival instinct, a capacity formed over centuries of human evolution but now mostly masked by the commercial abundance of developed economies. Premonition was the innate sensitivity to signs we used to be able to read in the air—all those changes constantly evolving at a level below consciousness that can signal an approaching storm, an upcoming birth, the menace of a predator, the outbreak of an epidemic, and even imminent death.

She believed in first impressions. In her view, that first encounter was the moment when the senses, the receptors of perception, were still fresh enough to read a situation accurately. Our perceptions advise us without the extraneous information that only misleads and misinforms us.

The knock on the door at eleven o'clock in the morning was completely out of the ordinary. She bristled. Engrasi wasn't expecting visitors, and it was too early for Amaia to be back from school. She put down the book she'd been reading, went to the door, and was surprised to find Juan, her brother. He was usually hard at work this time of day. His appearance alarmed her. He was always dressed in his baker's whites during the work week. Today he was outfitted in a sober marine-blue suit she'd seen him wear only in church on Sundays. She was even more alarmed by the fact he hadn't called to let her know he was coming. Over the previous three years, Juan had come to her house only when summoned. Engrasi's heart began to pound. *Something must be wrong.*

Later, when it was all over, she thought back on that first impression. She sensed the alarm bells, felt the surprise and amazement. She suspected, intuited, perceived . . . and yet she decided to hear him out because, after all, he was her brother.

She gave Juan a hug and a kiss, took his hand, and led him to the living room. He was reluctant to take the chair she offered; he stood in the middle of the room and gave her a broad smile. He began rambling on about how well the bakery was doing, the investments he was making in new equipment, how Rosario's initiatives had brought in a lot of new business . . .

Engrasi refused to put up with his blather. "Why are you here, Juan?"

"It's something good, Engrasi, something really good that'll please you." He sat down at last but was still as stiff as a board.

She went around the table and took the seat opposite him. The concentration in his face and the way he was rubbing the fingers of one hand with those of the other made it obvious he was mentally rehearsing a prepared presentation. It took him a few seconds to find his opening point. "Engrasi, I was very worried after our conversation about our little girl."

Engrasi just nodded and waited.

"I was very hurt by what you told me, sis. I don't want you to think I dislike Amaia, because I love her more than life itself . . ."

Engrasi studied his expression.

"I talked with Rosario. It was very difficult for me, but I told her what you said about the horrible things people say about Amaia. Engrasi, Rosario broke down in tears." Juan seemed about to do the same. He resisted the quiver in his lips by clamping them shut, closing his eyes, and reaching out for Engrasi. She took his hands in hers. "Engrasi, the drugs make her feel strange. Nauseated, you know? Sick and angry. Dr. Martínez said those side effects are common, and they will last until he gets the dosage right . . . and sometimes that takes years. Rosario admitted that there were times she didn't take her pills at all, and that's when she said those things. But now it's all better." He shrugged, an involuntary sign that even he didn't believe what he was saying. "It looks like the doctor found exactly the right mix of drugs. She's been a lot better for quite a while now. She's her true self again, the way she was when I met her. You can't imagine how much she regrets what happened. She asked me to apologize to you."

Engrasi sat up warily, abruptly removing her hands from her brother's. He seemed not to realize that she'd withdrawn her confidence in him at the same time.

He kept talking. "People can be really nasty, and this is a tiny little town. Rosario realizes how something like this can hurt the family."

Engrasi heard him clearly. He'd said "hurt the family," not "hurt the child." She responded with great caution. "I'm glad she sees that. That both of you see it."

"That's why she thought, why we both thought, that it would be best for Amaia to come home."

There it was. Engrasi couldn't believe her ears. And she hadn't seen it coming. "What?"

"Rosario has been terribly unhappy being separated from her daughter. Those comments, the horrible things she said, they were just her way of defending herself. She felt people were criticizing her for not having her daughter living at home. Normally people would expect a girl as young as Amaia to be living with her family."

Engrasi looked at her brother, but she was no longer listening to what he said. She realized how carefully this had been staged. His best suit, his unexpected appearance at her door, the elaborate prologue Engrasi knew was impossible for him to have prepared alone.

She looked again at her brother and saw him for what he was: An emissary. A puppet. Engrasi hadn't spoken to Rosario for years, but Engrasi didn't need any contact with Rosario to see the truth. Her studies in the psychology department seemed a thousand years ago now, but she recognized the characteristics of a psychopath. She was astonished at herself; she couldn't believe she'd been so obtuse as to miss what was happening. Engrasi had underestimated that neurotic, malevolent woman, her power, her influence, and her ability to project her psychoses upon those around her.

Engrasi pressed her hand to her breast, trying to calm the acid roiling her gut. Her growing unease was so great she could hardly breathe. Not a single word about Amaia, no mention of the suffering the child had endured, or the banishment of a child now almost twelve years old, who'd been excluded from her home for nearly three years. Engrasi's hands were trembling, so she hid them in her lap and admonished herself to regain her calm and analyze this. She sat mute and grave as she regarded her brother.

He eventually broke the silence. "Aren't you going to say anything?"

"I'm still processing this," she replied as mildly as she could.

He seemed disappointed. "I thought you'd be glad, and I honestly can't understand why you aren't. The other day when we spoke, you were really hard on me, and I appreciate that. I discussed it with Rosario, and now I see things the way they really are."

"The way she says they are."

He continued as if he hadn't heard. "I thought this was what you wanted."

Engrasi shook her head in disbelief. "The only thing I want is to keep the child safe."

Juan got up and came around the table. He leaned over and placed a conciliatory hand on her shoulder. "Sister, I'll never be able to thank you enough for taking care of Amaia while Rosario was in such delicate health, but *now my wife is healthy again*." His emphasis was borne of conviction.

Engrasi pushed his hand away and got to her feet. They stood face to face, almost touching. "No, Juan! Rosario is not healthy. Rosario will not be healthy as long as she lives."

What happened next shouldn't have surprised her, but it did. Juan's face twisted in bitter triumph, as if he'd just confirmed something. He stepped back, not bothering to hide his anger. "Just as I expected!"

"What do you mean, Juan?" she asked, offended. "What were you expecting?"

"That's exactly what Rosario told me you'd say."

Engrasi shook her head. Her brother was an ass. She stepped forward the same two paces and confronted him anew. "And what exactly did she predict?"

He stumbled backward, intimidated. "Nothing . . ."

"No, no. Tell me!" she demanded. "I want to know what she's thinking."

Juan looked up. "She believes you've gotten too attached to the child . . ."

"Too attached? You mean more than is normal?" She pressed him with grim determination. "Are you really trying to say you think it's possible to love this child too much?"

"You're acting like you're her mother . . . because you never had children of your own."

Engrasi's jaw dropped in astonishment.

"But you're not her mother, and it seems to me like you've forgotten that."

Engrasi looked at her brother as if he were a complete stranger. "She certainly coached you well." Her voice dripped with contempt. "And you parrot every word."

"Engrasi, you'd better just get used to the idea. The girl's mother wants the child to come back home, and so do I."

She got right in his face to make sure he couldn't miss her determination. "No!"

He nodded spitefully, as if he'd been expecting that answer. "Rosario told me you'd refuse. She's already consulted a lawyer. There's nothing you can do. If you keep making things difficult, you'll only end up wasting your time and money. The girl is our daughter and should be living at home."

"*This* is her home," Engrasi replied, "and it looks like you've forgotten why she's living with me and what happened to make you bring her here."

Juan answered without hesitation, "Any judge will understand that an ill mother couldn't care for her daughter. We are making this difficult decision for the child's own good. You knew the terms; you agreed that Amaia would live with you until Rosario was well again."

Engrasi's face tensed in fury. "No! You didn't bring her to me because Rosario was sick. She'd been abusing her, humiliating her, and terrorizing her for months."

"Rosario was in poor health," he repeated, as if citing a mantra.

"And you, brother, didn't do a damn thing about it. Nothing when Rosario forced her to wear that dead child's clothes, and nothing when you saw her get up at night to go to the girl's bed and threaten her. You did absolutely nothing when she chopped off the child's hair with blunt scissors."

Juan exploded. "Rosario was ill!" he shouted.

Engrasi refused to be intimidated. "You did nothing, because you thought it was better not to see. You chose to wait, to wait until it was too late. Until she was just about to—"

"It was an accident!" he yelled.

"It was not!" she shouted with all the strength she could muster.

Juan closed his eyes and shut his mouth. When he finally spoke, his voice was stifled by desperation. "Yes, it was, Engrasi. I've thought about it a lot, and it had to have been an accident."

Engrasi stalked to him and poked her finger in his chest. "That is *not* what you told me that night, when you carried Amaia here. No, Juan. An 'accident' is what you said it was when the people saw you come out of the bakery carrying an unconscious child. You said the girl slipped, fell in the mixing bin, and hit her head. That's the stinking lie you had to make up, and you've finally convinced yourself it was the truth." She accompanied every word with a fierce jab of her finger. "But when you brought the child here, you sat right there." She pointed to the staircase. "And you confessed! You told me what had been going on. You may have forgotten, but I haven't."

He broke into tears.

"I took that baby in, and I saw the state she was in. She was barely alive and she was terrified. It was months before she could sleep alone and not wake up screaming in the middle of the night. You can go on telling that shitty lie to anyone you want, but *not* to me!"

Juan's face lost its color, and he looked like he was about to be violently ill. "The girl has forgotten all that," he whispered, wiping away snot with the back of his hand. "Rosario doesn't remember. Why can't you forget too?"

Engrasi's smile was bitter. "I know you, Juan. You're not a bad man, but you're a coward. That's not a crime in itself, but you let yourself be manipulated by your wife. You let her drag you down into a morass of evil. Think about that."

Juan wiped off his tears with the sleeve of his Sunday best suit. "I don't want to talk about this." He turned to go.

"Just a minute. I have something for you." Engrasi pulled out the little key she wore on the chain about her neck. She leaned over and inserted it into the lock of the drawer. She took out a thick envelope and tossed onto the table an X-ray image of a human skull. A child's skull.

He came back. "What's that?"

"When you brought the girl here, she could scarcely speak. She was deeply disturbed. I was afraid she might have internal bleeding. I took her to a neurologist, as I told you, but I also took her to a physician friend of mine, a pathologist. He drew up a detailed diagnosis of the girl's trauma." She pointed to a thin white line on the X-ray. "Here, on the side of her head. That's where the first blow from a blunt object struck her. I also have the X-ray of the fingers of her right hand, fractured when she tried to protect herself. And look here, at the second blow. She didn't defend herself, because she was unconscious on the floor. The identical downward trajectory. It started from the same place and was delivered with a great deal more force. This is where the edge of the steel rolling pin fractured her skull." She fixed Juan with a ferocious, accusing glare. "It was meant to kill her, and it almost did."

Juan gaped at the X-ray as if about to have a heart attack.

Engrasi dumped out the rest of the contents of the envelope: X-rays, photos, and a thick typewritten report. "The girl also had an abrasion around her neck, produced when Rosario seized the cord that the child wore to carry her bakery key. A lesion caused when she was yanked back and forth with tremendous force. The scrapes on her calves, her rear, and her elbows occurred as Amaia was crawling across the floor trying to escape."

"You had those reports prepared so you could . . ."

She gave him a disgusted look. "Don't be absurd. I took the child to the doctor to make sure she would heal, but yes, I kept the results. And now I see I was right to do so."

"If you go waving that around now, you'll be sorry!" Her brother's threat took her breath away.

"The difference between you and me, brother, is that I am ready to do anything at all to protect the girl, no matter what the cost."

Witless and speechless, Juan stared at the pile of documents.

"Go on, take them. I have copies safely stowed with a friend."

He looked up in alarm.

"Tell your wife to show them to that lawyer of yours to get an idea of what the judge will think of them, because the conclusion will be obvious to anyone. It wasn't an accident; it was attempted murder."

Juan went toward the door, and Engrasi pursued him with the documents in hand. "This was premeditated. Rosario followed the girl to the bakery when she knew there'd be nobody around. She could have confronted the child at home, but she waited until she could corner Amaia without witnesses. Rosario lied to you about where she was going when she left the house; she followed Amaia to the bakery to make sure no one would stop her from murdering the girl. She hit her with tremendous force, and the only reason she stopped was that she thought she was dead. She buried her in the flour bin and went back home. She thought she'd finally accomplished what she'd been planning since the day Amaia was born."

Juan had already opened the front door. He looked back and cried out in a panic, "How could you possibly tell people that? I shouldn't have told you. Rosario was depressed after Amaia's birth. It happens with lots of women."

"Rosario has no friends. Did you know she doesn't even talk to Elena Ochoa anymore? Elena was her best friend. Maybe you should do yourself a favor, Juan, and go see Elena. I ran into her daughter in the street and asked why I hadn't seen Elena in such a long time. She said her mother was very ill, so I went to visit. She's not ill, Juan, she's scared. I don't know what your wife has gotten herself involved in, but ever since they stopped seeing one another, Elena stays home behind locked doors and surrounds herself with saints and crucifixes. She's terrified. She doesn't want to hear a word about Rosario. She said your wife sold her soul. What do you think she means by that?"

"It's envy, that's all. The women in this town have always been jealous of her."

"Does she still go out at night without telling you where?"

Fear showed on his face. Engrasi knew she'd guessed right. Even so, Juan tried to brave it out. "I can't believe this. Are you going to use what I told you in confidence to attack my wife?"

Disgusted, she glared at him. "Juan, you don't *want* to understand. This has nothing to do with Rosario; it's about Amaia. It's always been about her. You're a lost cause; you can go on and keep justifying and rationalizing Rosario's behavior all you want. But if you think there's any way in the world I'll deliver Amaia to the woman who's been trying to murder her since the day she was born, you're a fool."

22

The Charbou Method

New Orleans, Louisiana
Sunday, August 28, 2005

Amaia woke early. After showering and dressing, she made the bed and watched the six o'clock newscast.

The news was reporting that the authorities were using all available means to warn the public that Katrina would have a devastating effect on the entire Gulf Coast. The prospects for New Orleans weren't encouraging. Parts of the city were as much as ten feet below sea level, and with Lake Pontchartrain to the north and the Mississippi River snaking through the heart of the city, the threat was real. A hurricane tide was almost inevitable. The National Hurricane Center was predicting a category five, meaning winds of 280 miles an hour and gusts of more than 320. New Orleans had never experienced a category five storm. In 1965, category three Hurricane Betsy had worked her way up the Mississippi Delta and rolled over New Orleans, killing eighty-one people and causing untold millions of dollars of damage. The television was now alternating weather forecasts for Katrina with streams of alarming images from Billion Dollar Betsy.

Unwilling to watch any more, Amaia turned off the set and went out into the hall. She caught a glimpse of Dupree, who was on his way down the stairs. She quickened her pace, intending to catch him. The wide opening of the stairwell amplified her boss's voice as he spoke into his cell phone. "Okay, right, I'm on my way downstairs. Wait for me in the car."

Curious, she went back to her room and looked through the window that opened onto a narrow balcony. She went out there, walked along above the arches, and peered down. Their official vehicle was parked immediately beneath her. Jason Bull sat behind the wheel and Dupree was in the shotgun seat. There was no sign of Charbou.

She gave up and went back inside. She was ready for breakfast.

Reports from the National Weather Service crackled loudly from the old transistor radio the Dauphine owners must have fished out of storage. They'd placed it beneath the television screen, on which could be seen the inevitable image of the hurricane's advance.

Crossing the hotel patio to the glassed-in café corner, Amaia felt a warm, gentle breeze ruffle her hair, almost as if someone were blowing discreetly in her ear. She paused, pulled an elastic from her wrist, and put her hair up.

Bill Charbou watched her with a smile as he helped position a sandbag atop the half dozen already piled against the door. "Good morning, Assistant Inspector."

"Good morning, Detective." She glanced toward the street entrance. "Why are you here?" Dupree was alone with Detective Bull. She wondered if Charbou knew it.

He gave her a charming smile. "I was hoping you'd have breakfast with me."

She nodded to the Dauphine proprietor and stepped around the pile of sandbags, ignoring the woman's knowing smile.

She served herself scrambled eggs and coffee. She took her time at the toaster, hoping Johnson or Dupree would turn up, but at last she couldn't put it off any longer. She went to the table. "Your partner's not here this morning?"

"Sure, he's in the car, on the phone with his family. He really loves his kids."

"Of course." She saw Charbou believed what he was saying.

"And his wife," the detective added with a smile.

She made no comment.

"Sometimes I really envy him," the detective added pensively.

Amaia took a big bite of toast, determined not to make it easy for him.

"Having a wife, I mean. You know, someone to share things with."

She acknowledged that with an ambiguous nod. So that was going to be his approach. She'd heard of men who brought up the subject of marriage during their first encounter with a woman, but she'd never had to deal with one.

They—and Charbou—were about as interested in getting married as in having a root canal.

She chewed slowly, watching him. Today Charbou wasn't wearing the bulletproof vest he claimed never to be without. He must have left it in the vehicle. Instead, he was wearing a snug-fitting T-shirt that showed off his muscular chest and arms. His big brown eyes radiated sincerity. He was handsome and he knew it.

He leaned over the table as if to confess. It was so obvious that she couldn't help smiling, and that put him momentarily off his stride. "I know from experience it's hard to find someone who'll put up with our schedules, the way we live . . ." He looked down and then up again to project heartfelt sincerity. "The way it winds up affecting everything we do."

Amaia grinned. She was entertained, despite herself. Bill Charbou took her reaction as an invitation to continue.

"Assistant Inspector—can I call you Amaia? I noticed you're not wearing a wedding ring. Are you married?"

Her colleagues appeared in the doorway. She waved and beckoned to them.

"Salazar," she said.

Charbou looked a bit confused.

"You may address me as Assistant Inspector Salazar."

One of the proprietors of the Dauphine came running through the café toward the back, holding the TV remote control high above her head. When she got close enough, she pressed the volume button so hard that her fingertip went pale. It was just before nine in the morning, and Mayor Ray Nagin was about to hold a press conference to declare the mandatory evacuation of New Orleans.

The plan Dupree and the police commander Forneret had worked out, Operation Cage, was to go into effect as soon as Katrina passed. They would establish tight control of the main traffic arteries, the train stations, buses, and airports, and keep a close eye on all persons arriving or departing by air, including by military aircraft. They'd also monitor emergency personnel. They aimed to identify the Composer, whether he arrived alone or as part of a team.

They were placing their faith in the witness's conviction that he'd been wearing a badge of some sort. Keeping that in mind, as soon as they received any report of a crime that fit the parameters, they would keep it out of radio crosstalk, maybe even impose strict radio silence to avoid signaling their own movements. They'd do their best to keep him bottled up in the city.

Dupree was certain the man they were looking for was already holed up somewhere close by, waiting for the weather to wreak havoc. The FBI was holed up too. They'd chosen the emergency operations center on the third floor of a building close to the lake as their shelter from the storm. The firefighters occupied the lower two floors. The administrator had given the team a disused conference room. He'd provided everything the FBI required, including whiteboards, computers, landline connections, and half a dozen camp cots, since they'd be spending the night. The building was a massive edifice of reinforced concrete that had withstood previous storms. The third-floor operations center next door had thirty workstations, only a third of which were currently occupied. Each had a computer screen and a multiline phone console. A huge screen with a computer-generated map of the city dominated one wall; the software was capable of marking the map with points of concern of all sorts, from traffic jams to bar fights, from electrical system failures to buildings on fire.

Dupree and the team spent time briefing each of the operators about what kinds of reports to relay immediately to the FBI agents next door: a series of gunshots, four, five, or more in rapid succession; all members of a single family killed by gunshots inside their residence; or all bodies grouped in one room.

They'd have to be prepared for anything after the call came in: flooded streets, blocked doors, fallen trees, and downed electric lines. They'd count on the firefighters for transport if the streets proved impassable for ordinary traffic.

In the early afternoon, Dupree suggested to Amaia that they make a tour of the city, escorted by Bill and Bull. They were enveloped in unexpected quiet as they crossed the parking lot. Rain began to fall. The shower was surprisingly gentle, considering the threatening gusts that had gathered force in the course of the morning. The interior of the vehicle was silent except for radio reports updating the command center on earlier incidents. Out in the city, they found that the cars previously parked on both sides of the streets had disappeared overnight. From the vantage point of Poydras Street, they saw crowds streaming toward the Superdome's access ramps. Many were senior citizens on crutches or in wheelchairs. Some in the crowd carried infants, and others had arms full of blankets and pillows to spend the night in the stadium.

Dupree was dismayed by the crowding outside the entrances. He wondered if Nana was out there. He said nothing, but the others noticed his worried look.

"They started arriving last night," Jason Bull explained. "Officers in the stadium report there are ten thousand inside already, and more keep coming."

No one said anything. Bull switched on a commercial radio station, perhaps to break the silence.

Interstate 10 had cleared up somewhat, and traffic was moving. There'd been few police control points the previous evening, but now they were in place all across the city. Officers were insisting that everyone either leave the city or go to designated shelters. The streets had to be completely empty by the six thirty curfew. They made it clear that everyone outside after that would be detained for their own safety.

The radio warned that Katrina's leading edge was approaching. Amaia watched as curtains of rain lashed across the city from east to west. A phone rang. Bull lowered the radio volume, and Dupree answered the call. He listened intently and then ended it.

"Detective Bull," he said to the driver before turning to the others, "we're going back to the operations center. They have the bullet from Andrews, the father. It's not the same as those that killed the others. The techs found it was old, manufactured decades back, and when they put it in the system, all kinds of alarms went off. The ballistics match the weapon used to murder a family in Madison, Wisconsin, eighteen years ago.

"Madison and Quantico are sending everything they have to us. We have a conference call with Tucker and Emerson in twenty minutes."

23

Evil

New Orleans, Louisiana

Martin Lenx, his wife, two sons aged twelve and sixteen, and a daughter of fifteen lived in a big house in a small community outside Madison, Wisconsin, with Alma, Martin's elderly mother. Martin had no siblings, and he'd inherited the house after the death of his father, a stern Lutheran pastor. Reverend Lenx had escaped from Austria to the United States during the Second World War. Alma's inherited wealth had allowed them to live well. After her husband's death, Alma moved into a separate suite on an upper floor. The family's bodies were found in a state of advanced decomposition, after neighbors began to wonder why the Lenxes hadn't returned from visiting relatives.

They'd been dead for a month.

The house was unheated, but even so, the stink was appalling. The pealing bells of the fifth movement of Berlioz's *Symphonie fantastique* incessantly sounded their warning knell as a counterpart to the hideous dark brown trail of blood leading to the mansion's music room. There, laid in a line with their heads oriented toward the north, were the bodies of the entire family—except for the father, a devout Christian, a corporate branch office manager with a good reputation in the community.

Martin Lenx had disappeared. In his office, the police found a letter addressed to his pastor, in which he explained he'd been obliged to take action because his family had strayed from the godly path. He found his wife's devotion to makeup and modern aesthetics inappropriate; his teenage daughter's recent declaration that she wanted to be a singer and his sons' increasingly "depraved" musical tastes were offenses to God. Martin had seen them slipping away, and he'd refused to accept their fall. As head of the family, he'd recognized his responsibility and known he had to act. He'd prayed a great deal, and he'd concluded they had to die. He would save their souls before they were too depraved to be redeemed.

In the weeks after the bodies were found, the police discovered that Martin Lenx had serious financial problems. A few weeks before the murders, he'd been unusually happy, optimistic about his chances for a management position at a local bank, but that hadn't panned out. The investigators found he'd filed an application for a gun permit the day after he received the rejection letter. The gun shop's records were a perfect match to the .22-caliber revolver used to kill the Lenxes. The huge house inherited from his father was encumbered with two mortgages, and Lenx was facing foreclosure.

A month later, Martin's car was found abandoned in a parking lot at Chicago's O'Hare Airport, though there was no record of him in the passenger lists of departing flights. His pistol was never found. Martin Lenx had been listed as missing, possibly armed and dangerous, for eighteen years. Forensic psychologists thought there was a chance he had committed suicide.

Amaia Salazar didn't for a second believe Martin Lenx had ever entertained the idea of killing himself.

Johnson read to them the letter Martin had left for his minister. Amaia weighed each word, knowing she had to pay attention both to the explicit message and to what lay behind it, for only a deeper reading could throw light upon the man's state of mind and intentions. She scribbled her impressions about stylistic variations and the odd thread of Lenx's narrative, transcribing entire sentences verbatim in her own private shorthand.

He used apocalyptic metaphors several times. "The sun darkened, and the moon no longer gave its light." His prophesizing was nothing more than an attempt to justify his act; he presented it as impossible to avoid, for it was the destiny to which he'd been condemned.

"The stars will fall from the sky, and the powers of the heavens will be moved." Martin had accumulated decades of resentment; his letter described failures, perceived slights, frustrations, and trivial humiliations. Despite all he had suffered, he knew he was special; he lived on a higher plane, looking down on the rest of the family.

Amaia knew that people with Lenx's obsessions usually found an excuse to blame their failures on the women in their lives. Martin blamed his mother above all. She'd been terribly strict with him when he was growing up, but now she'd been encouraging her granddaughter's absurd ambitions, tolerating her youthful impetuosity, and mocking Martin's discomfort. He dismissed his wife as a timid, fearful creature who'd spoiled his offspring rotten. She'd failed so completely that he no longer recognized the charming children who'd once filled him with pride.

Amaia held her breath when she heard the part of the letter that concerned the daughter. Martin was obsessed with her. The child who'd been the apple of his eye, his tiny princess, lost his favor as she grew up and revealed herself to be a wanton, hell-bent on besmirching the family name. He wrote of failed attempts to correct her and bring her back to the path of truth and righteousness. Nothing had worked. Martin had seen his little angel mutate before his eyes.

Some nights he got up and visited their bedrooms one after another. He studied them as they slept, heedless of how damned they were. He'd loved those innocent faces. Imagining himself as Lot, the pious patriarch who fled Sodom and Gomorrah, Lenx had hovered over them for hours, seeking some feeling, any feeling, within himself. The last visit was always to his daughter's bedroom. Her abundant red hair lay spread across her white pillow like a fiery halo. She'd always been his favorite. He'd placed his greatest hope in her, and she was his greatest disappointment.

The time for pity was past. Martin was exhausted; he'd used the last reserves of energy trying repeatedly to bring them to the light. He'd done all he could, God knows; he'd worked, prayed, and sacrificed in the struggle to preserve his home and family. It was too much for any man to bear.

Each of those nights, he'd leaned over before going back to bed and whispered his promise to her. "I'll save you. Daddy will save you."

As Amaia listened to Johnson read Lenx's crazed letter, its powerful threats and weighty words of condemnation echoed in her mind. Without intending to do so, she released a long, stifled groan that made them all turn to look at her.

She felt the floor open beneath her feet, casting her into a dark, terrifying, and all-too-familiar hell.

Tucker's voice seemed to come from very far away. "Assistant Inspector Salazar was right." A moment passed. "That letter makes it crystal clear this is an evangelical murderer who sees himself on a mission from God. As soon as we got a copy of the text, Emerson identified the Bible quotes. As we suspected, most are from the New Testament, specifically from Mark, chapter 13, where he gives his vision of Judgment Day. I've sent you a copy of the texts. Of particular interest is the part where Lenx refers to the powers of heaven being shaken. I'm pretty sure he interpreted that to mean hurricanes, thunderstorms, and tornados. This is a causal relationship for him: those acts of God show the Composer who deserves to die. Emerson thinks this might be just a coincidence, but my feeling is that these words from twenty years ago probably still apply to the crimes we're investigating now."

"Emerson?" Dupree invited his comment.

"I think we're really making progress," came the enthusiastic reply. "But before we use what we've learned about Martin Lenx to alter the profile of our target, we have to establish beyond doubt that Lenx and the Composer are one and the same."

"The bullet in Joseph Andrews's head matches the gun Lenx used on his family eighteen years ago," Johnson reminded him.

"This could be a copycat killer, maybe even a disciple," Emerson argued. "But if he's a disciple, he'd also be an evangelical killer."

Dupree directed the discussion. "Let's list the points that suggest the recent killings could be the work of Martin Lenx."

"Okay," Johnson began. "First, the ages correspond. Martin Lenx was thirty-seven when the murders were committed, and that was eighteen years ago. If he's not dead, he's fifty-five. A man of that age who's active and has taken care of himself can be in excellent health. Still, he wouldn't fit the typical age bracket of serial killers. We don't know what he's been doing for the last eighteen years, but maybe with age he's gotten calmer, more careful, meticulous. That would fit the modus operandi of the Composer."

"Don't forget the gun," Tucker added. "The fact that he didn't leave it at the murder scene in Madison is a sign he intended to keep it, maybe as a souvenir, but also just in case he wanted to use it again."

Emerson refused to get on board. "The profiles of the other families are similar to those of the Lenx murders. The ages aren't exactly the same, but they're very close. But there's a contradiction: The Composer kills the fathers. If Martin Lenx is the Composer, obviously he never killed himself. In a perfect match, the fathers would be absent or be spared."

Dupree spoke. "I assume everybody noticed the fact that Martin Lenx dragged the bodies through the house to assemble them in what the Madison police file called 'the music room.' I just spoke with Officer Carter, head of the homicide squad there. He was just a boy at the time, but it turns out his father was police chief. Carter said his dad often told the story of those crimes. The building was eventually torn down, but Carter remembered that the Lenx family had a small performance hall in the house, with a piano and a number of musical instruments. Maybe this leads us back to the violins we've now confirmed were at five of the crime scenes. The presence of a violin isn't necessarily unusual enough to consider it a signature, but still, he could be using it as a prop to evoke his scenario. What do you think, Salazar?"

Amaia, who'd been watching Dupree closely during this exposition, stared fixedly at the telephone console. "Emerson's right," she said, causing Johnson to swivel toward her and hunch his shoulders. "I agree with what's been said, but first we have to establish whether Lenx really is the Composer."

Dupree couldn't believe his ears. "I don't understand. Martin Lenx is a perfect fit for the profile you've been building!"

"I don't yet have sufficient evidence to confirm that," she replied, avoiding his challenge.

"This is incredible," Johnson muttered loud enough for Dupree to hear his dissatisfaction.

Frowning and annoyed, Dupree studied her.

"My opinion?" she responded, looking at the attachment from Tucker matching passages from the Lenx letter to Bible verses. "I grant you this could be Lenx. There's another verse that says, 'Seest thou these great buildings? There shall not be left one stone upon another, that shall not be thrown down.' One of many characteristics of an evangelical killer is an obsession with scripture, or with mysterious messages thought to be from some kind of sacred source. In his confession, Lenx mentioned how he had to strive to maintain the household and how crushed he felt. Killing a family after their home is destroyed by a catastrophe symbolizes the perdition of his own family. He selects families he thinks are as sinful as his own. He saves them from damnation, just as he redeemed his own family—by sending them straight to heaven."

Johnson and Dupree had nodded along with her reasoning. Tucker's voice rattled from the speaker. "So, Assistant Inspector Salazar, are you trying to tell me you have problems with your own theory? What bothers you?"

"The problem is that Martin Lenx killed his family, his own people." She enumerated them. "His wife, his own mother, his sons, his daughter. He's a textbook annihilator. The four categories characteristic of family annihilators are belief in one's own moral superiority, anomie or alienation, deception, and paranoia. He fits at least two of those. Four out of five killers of this type commit suicide afterward; the exceptions are those convinced of their superiority. That would be Lenx. But even though he remained alive, what would trigger him, eighteen years later, to set out on this murder spree? Granted, the families share some characteristics with the Lenx family, but why those exact families? They're different from one another, in different parts of the country, with no apparent links between them.

"And the big question is, what has Martin Lenx been doing for the last eighteen years? The murder of an entire family is striking enough for someone, especially the press, to notice, even if it occurred in the remotest region of the country. But no; there was no word of a murder of this type until eight months ago. Two possibilities: Martin Lenx murdered his family, fled, and has nothing to do with the Composer's murders, or he's the Composer. In which case, how could he have controlled such powerful impulses for so long? If there's one thing I'm sure of, it's that when a lunatic is convinced that God, or the devil, or whatever, is telling him what to do, he has to be tracked down because he'll never stop. So how did Martin Lenx go underground and suppress those urges for so long?"

Tucker went down the list. "Typical reasons for the interruption of serial killings are death, a long illness, absence abroad, or imprisonment for some other crime. If we start by assuming he's alive, it's hard to believe someone who suffered from an illness that kept him sidelined for eighteen years would be physically able to confront and kill whole families. Repeatedly. And let's not forget some of the fathers were strong, as were some of the teenage sons.

"Martin Lenx, who presented himself as a model citizen, probably wouldn't have wound up in jail, and his fingerprints haven't been connected to another crime.

"At first, the idea that he left the country might seem plausible, but—and I don't know why—I just can't imagine Martin Lenx living abroad. His exalted opinion of himself doesn't square with a fugitive's life. The original investigating team decided the car being abandoned at the airport was a ploy, though they looked into the possibility he might have gone back to his parents' place of origin. It turned out Lenx had no remaining family in Austria. My bet is that he set himself up somewhere else in the United States with a new identity and a different way of life. That's hard, but not impossible. It's what he'd aspired to do, and what, in his opinion, his family was preventing him from doing."

Dupree watched Amaia during Tucker's analysis. He saw her mouth twitch discontentedly. She clearly didn't agree with Tucker, but she said nothing.

"Let's recap," Johnson said, losing patience. "Lots of elements fit: the way Martin Lenx murdered his family, the families' profiles, the positioning of the bodies, the room in the house, ballistic evidence establishing that the same gun was used both in Madison and Galveston. But despite all that, Salazar is suggesting we suspend judgment because she doesn't know what he's been doing for the last eighteen years."

Amaia bowed her head.

"Respond, Salazar!" Dupree commanded.

"Until I have a better understanding of what could have set him in motion, I can't categorically state that Martin Lenx is the Composer."

An uncomfortable silence prevailed, interrupted only by the static on the telephone line.

Dupree spoke at last. "All right, fine. Everybody get back to work. We'll hit it on two fronts: on one hand we'll continue working on the Composer as an independent agent, and on the other, we'll renew the nationwide search for Martin Lenx and keep developing a profile for him. We're looking for a connection between the Lenxes and the other families. Let's review everything known about Lenx and take a closer look at his personal relationships outside the home. Maybe he had some kind of ministry or mentor relationship. Try to locate former acquaintances at work, people at his church."

Emerson spoke again, triumph in his voice. "Hey! It'd be a good idea to remember he could have been leading a double life, with another girlfriend or wife, children out of wedlock, homosexual relationships, who knows? The kinds of things that a man who wants to be above reproach feels guilt over. Maybe something like that recurred and set him off. Maybe we could identify somebody who served as his disciple."

Dupree got up, indicating the conference was over. "Salazar, come with me."

He left the room and went toward the interior staircase, the only place they couldn't be overheard. Dupree didn't beat around the bush. "What the hell just happened in there?"

She shrugged, somewhat annoyed. "I don't know what you're talking about."

"You don't know? I'm talking about your changing your mind. Again! You pull a rabbit out of your hat and a second later you agree with Emerson. Why? I didn't bring you here to play nice or pretend you don't know something's wrong!" He was remembering her facial expression when she heard Tucker's analysis. "One moment you stand up to defend your own interpretation. You get in our faces, make us hear you out and take you seriously. Then when corroborating evidence turns up and everything seems to fit your thesis, you retreat."

"I shared my opinion . . . but I respect what others have to say . . ."

He sized her up. "It's because of the Lenx family, right? You find it easier to accept the idea of a serial killer targeting families of strangers than the fact that Martin Lenx murdered his own flesh and blood." Dupree saw it now, and he nodded. "The bastards who hurt their own, especially their own children, are the hardest to take. Those things he wrote about his daughter—" Dupree broke off, suddenly intuiting a new connection. As he paused to think about it, she silently prayed he wouldn't try to dig any deeper.

But he did. "You have to face it. You have to factor it in. God knows that's not the same as understanding it, nobody could, unless . . ."

He fell silent.

She half closed her eyes and breathed deeply, trying to cope with her violent reaction to Lenx, the man who'd murdered his own mother. The dark forces pushing a parent to kill a family member or massacre an entire family were far more horrific than mere murder; they were demonic. The very nature of Lenx's crime, the execution of his own flesh and blood, was beyond comprehension.

She was especially shaken because if Martin Lenx and the Composer were one and the same, the team wasn't after an evangelical killer rooting out sin or an annihilator avenging himself for childhood abuse. If they were the same person, the killer was conducting rehearsals in preparation for his big finale.

Yes, she'd been there in that scorched and smoking part of hell. She knew the nature of the demon who draws power from the fact that no one believes it can exist. Dupree's expression told her he'd figure her out sooner or later. She knew he wouldn't give up. The allure of that secret was the reason he'd recruited her.

"Why are you so determined to pass yourself off as hay?"

She gave him a baffled look.

"Hay, in the haystack! I know agents, men and women, who'd give their right arms to be considered the needle in the haystack. Lots of them pretend they are, every time they get the chance. But you really are the needle in the haystack. Brilliant, sharp, and piercing. You, Salazar, are condemned to stand out; you'll never blend in."

She had no idea what to say.

"Something doesn't fit, Salazar, and I'll bet my life it never has. It's just not normal to take a twelve-year-old girl away from home and pack her off to a boarding school on the other side of the world. You want to try to convince me I'm wrong?"

Angered by his harsh insistence, she clamped her mouth shut and refused to look at him.

"It doesn't fit, and there's only one thing you can do: use it in your favor."

She stood still as a statue for several seconds. At last she turned, looked him in the eye, and nodded.

He nodded back, pleased, and stepped forward so his face was only inches from hers. "Joseph Andrews was right. His father fought back, and the killer had to shoot him with the gun he brought to the house. With the same damn weapon and ammunition he used on his own family eighteen years earlier. Those are facts. You told us to look in the past; you said it wasn't the first time he'd killed. That's how we got Lenx. So tell me: Is Martin Lenx the Composer?"

"I can't understand how he dropped completely out of sight for eighteen years. And I can't see what would convert a family annihilator into an evangelical serial killer all these years later. But yes, I do think the Composer is Lenx."

Dupree nodded, satisfied. "I saw you disagree when Tucker was speculating about his life in hiding."

"I haven't wrapped my mind around Martin Lenx yet. I have to understand him before I can try to guess what kind of life he's living today."

"But—"

"One thing at a time!" she cut him off. "I'm not going to speculate!"

Dupree's approval turned to disdain. There it was again, that flash of imperial haughtiness. "Tell me, Salazar, you think you can get into the head of this son of a bitch?"

She nodded.

"Then get to work on him. Forget the Composer. Concentrate on Lenx." He was issuing an order.

She looked relieved as she pushed open the heavy door of the stairwell on the way back to the third floor. Dupree stayed behind on the landing, deep in thought. Some minutes later, he appeared at the conference room door, signaled to Johnson, and stepped outside to await him.

Dupree heard the door open and shut. He turned on his heel and came face to face with his deputy. "You mentioned that Salazar got a phone call after she signed on for New Orleans."

"Right. I told admin she was coming with us and any urgent calls should be patched through to the jet or routed to my mobile, because we didn't have a phone for her yet."

"Do you know who called?"

Johnson nodded. "I told them to advise Salazar and route the call to a booth, but first the operator passed the caller to me. Her aunt in Spain was trying to reach her. The aunt must've thought she had to justify the call, so she told me that Salazar's father was seriously ill. The doctors said he had maybe forty-eight hours left to live."

Dupree took this in, looked at him, but didn't comment.

Johnson didn't know what to make of his silence. "Guess I should've told you. Frankly, I was surprised she didn't head back home."

"Don't worry about it," Dupree said. "You did the right thing."

24

Old Photographs

Superdome, New Orleans

Nana looked into the sky above the Superdome. The clouds that had spread across the noonday sky had a greenhouse effect, and the temperature had risen rapidly. Rain had started a few hours earlier, but it was gentle, like the spray of a sprinkler. Most of the people in the crowd outside the stadium didn't bother to cover their heads.

Nana had thought the greatest challenge would be getting through the main entrance, but once inside, the crowd pushed forward into the concrete tunnels giving access to the stands. She nearly fell several times as people elbowed their way past her. Bobby grabbed her arm and pulled her in front of him between the handles of his mother's wheelchair, so he could shield her with his body.

An announcement over the PA system welcomed them to the Superdome and urged them to find seats. The passages were jammed and there were lots more people waiting outside in the rain. Nana sighed.

Cheering erupted from all sides. Confused, she looked up at Bobby.

"They said the city gonna deliver food for our dinner," he explained with a smile. "We gonna be okay, Nana, don't you worry."

She tried to smile back.

Bobby had come to her back door at noon. "Nana, Mayor Nagin says everybody has to leave, and the national weather folks talking 'bout a category five storm. The TV been showing old pictures of Betsy all day long, Nana, and they awful scary. I know you say we oughta stay home, but I think it's gonna be better to leave."

Nana had nodded unhappily. Behind her the TV set showed Katrina rolling across the Gulf of Mexico. "Betsy was category three," she said beneath her breath.

"We can spend the night in the Superdome, lots of folks already gone there. They sayin' they'll be doctors and ambulances in case things get bad. I'm hopin' Cousin Gabriel gonna come and help get Mama there. I got water, sandwiches, and some covers; you take your medicine and anything you think you gonna need."

Nana had closed the door and gone to the big kitchen cabinet. She pushed its sliding door open and took out a photo album with heavy blue covers. She pressed it to her chest with one hand. The rise in humidity had made her hip creak like an old wooden board. She put the album on the table, opened it, and sat down.

The album was a collection of the old newspaper clippings she had kept under the bed linens for years. The time they'd been tucked away there had discolored the photos and deteriorated the newsprint so much that the headlines had faded and the clippings had become almost transparent in some places. Almost all of them were from the *Times-Picayune*, New Orleans's oldest paper.

Nana ran a fingertip across the plastic sheet, even though she knew the words by heart. She leaned forward to read them anyway.

> THOUSANDS FLEE FLOOD THREAT AS HURRICANE SLAMS INTO N.O.
>
> Nearly Half Million People Beat Betsy to Safe Areas
>
> MAYOR VIC SCHIRO URGES NEIGHBORS TO KEEP AN AX IN THE ATTIC
>
> Because the storm struck New Orleans in the middle of the night, countless residents awoke to find their houses flooded. Seeking to escape the rising waters, many climbed into their attics, where they were trapped and drowned.

'BILLION-DOLLAR BETSY' THE MOST EXPENSIVE HURRICANE IN U.S. HISTORY

Betsy carried off the dubious honor of being the first billion-dollar hurricane in the history of the United States.

Nana lightly rubbed her palm across the next article.

SEARCH CONTINUES FOR SIX GIRLS WHO DISAPPEARED DURING STORM

The girls are among two dozen persons who went missing as Betsy passed over the city, but the police do not consider them victims of the hurricane.

BODIES OF DR. DUPREE AND HIS WIFE FOUND UNDER DEBRIS OF COLLAPSED BUILDING

Dr. John Dupree was returning from an emergency call, and his wife, Marion, a nurse, was with him.

Both were still in their automobile. It had literally been flattened by a building toppled by the storm. The bodies were found in an advanced state of decomposition, attributed to the high temperatures that have plagued New Orleans throughout the week since Betsy lashed the city.

DISAPPEARANCE OF SIX GIRLS FROM TREME TO BE INVESTIGATED AS A KIDNAPPING

A group alleging to be a rescue team took six young girls from the home of their babysitter during the hurricane, and nothing has been heard of them since. The girls, all minors, were sheltering from the storm. The babysitter's daughter and niece

> are among the missing. The woman and her nephew, related to two of the missing girls, were the only witnesses. The police are taking their statements today.
>
> NO MORE 'BETSY' IN THE LIST OF HURRICANES
>
> A year after the disappearances of "the six girls from Treme," the authorities have closed the investigation and declared them victims of Hurricane Betsy. Their names join those of 47 other persons still missing and now officially declared dead.

Nana turned several of the thick pages and got to one with a photograph of a teenage girl smiling into the camera. Her abundant dark curly hair cascaded down to her shoulders. This was the photo they'd used for the posters after she vanished. The police had returned it in fairly bad condition. The intervening years had yellowed the creased photo but hadn't reduced the brilliant sparkle of those dark eyes. Nana had resisted putting it into a plastic protector. She needed to be able to touch it, to feel she was communicating with her child. She hadn't buried the girl, and she didn't intend to treat the photo like a funeral urn or immortalize the child behind picture glass.

Nana looked around. She'd promised herself that she'd wait in her little house as long as it took for her baby to return, but the city was forcing her to leave. Her blue purse on the kitchen shelf contained her ID, a little money, and her pills. She stared down at the photo as if about to sweep it up in her arms like a living child, then picked it up with both hands, pressed it to her chest, and closed the album. Nana left the photo book on the table but slipped the picture of her daughter into her blouse, snug against her heart. She picked up her cane and blue purse. She locked the door behind her when she left the house.

25

A Needle

New Orleans, Louisiana

Amaia studied the photographs in the case file. School yearbook pictures showed the boys. There was a studio portrait of the father. The only time the wife appeared was with the rest of the family. Amaia paid particular attention to the carefully posed family portrait. Martin was a characterless little gray man. Everything about him, from the tight knot of his tie to the stiffly starched collar of his spotless white dress shirt, suggested meticulous attention to detail. His horn-rimmed glasses would have suited a college professor. Amaia perceived him as a man obsessed with control. His posture, carefully combed hair, and short-trimmed nails cried out that this insecure man was used to being dominated by his beady-eyed mother. Lenx hadn't been permitted to live with his own family in a separate home; they all had to stay under his mother's roof. Amaia was certain he'd found that humiliating. She was convinced Lenx had never managed to escape his mother. Perhaps in an effort to dominate a woman for a change, he'd married the mousey little woman peering back at the camera.

The boys were entirely different. They smiled, carefree and sincere. They looked happy. Lenx's daughter wore her cascade of red hair tousled and spread carelessly over her shoulders; her smile was warm and confident. Amaia noticed a modest but slightly provocative touch of red lipstick, in contrast to the sober, undistinguished dress, undoubtedly worn only for the photo session. The Lenx family stood close together, looking directly into the camera. Except for Martin, who stood to one side in three-quarter profile.

Amaia picked up the solo portrait. Martin was wearing the same suit and tie, so the photograph was probably taken the same day. She noted that his pose was exactly the same as in the group photo—the way he held his hands, the tilt of his chin, his shoulders up and slightly back. The only difference between the poses was Lenx's mouth. In the family photo, there was an icy cut to his lips, while in the solo image, his lips were relaxed, almost smiling. She zoomed in. With a bit of effort, she deciphered the legend stamped at the bottom: Clayton Gray Photography, with a telephone number.

The fixed line they'd used scarcely an hour earlier to talk with Emerson and Tucker was wired into the station's emergency equipment. It had been ringing regularly for the past few minutes, so they'd stopped using it for outgoing calls. Wondering if Gray was still active, she tapped the number into the cell phone Dupree had provided her after they arrived in New Orleans.

Clayton Gray was alive and well. More importantly, he remembered the Lenx family.

Amaia asked him if anything had caught his attention at the time.

"My wife tells me I chose the wrong career. Instead of going into photography, I should have been a psychologist. I can look at the way a young couple poses in their wedding photos and tell you with just about a hundred percent accuracy if they'll still be together two years later!" He chuckled. "Has something to do with the way they stand for the photo, what they do with their hands, and especially their mouths. More than the eyes. People claim the eyes are the mirrors of the soul, but I read a lot more in the way you hold your mouth."

Amaia smiled. "It's what they call nonverbal language. Do you remember taking that photo?"

"Well, most of the time I can remember more or less how things went, and if I need to be sure, I check my photo logs. But when it comes to the Lenx family and what happened, I've gone over everything related to them again and again. The details are impossible to forget, practically burned into my memory. He came to my studio about two months before the . . . the . . . you know. The father, Martin, visited us three times before he made up his mind. Really demanding fellow. We show all our potential customers an album with samples of our best work. But that wasn't enough for Lenx. He insisted on inspecting the studio itself, the backdrops we had, even got me to show him the various types of lighting. By the time he brought his family in, he'd decided everything, down to where to place each member of the family."

"He sounds like someone who really likes to be in control."

"Yes, well, it didn't do him much good that day. Everything started off just fine. They went to their places and I took a few trial shots. But Mr. Lenx wasn't satisfied. He repositioned them maybe eight times. The boys seemed to enjoy it, but it was too much for the wife. Then Mr. Lenx decided I should take the photo without the younger boy. Mrs. Lenx said that was a ridiculous idea. She was a timid little thing, but when she got going, she put a stop to it. The final picture, the one that ended up in all the papers, was the very first one I took. I didn't keep the rest of the proofs. But in that photo—I have it in front of me right now, by the way—there's lots of information, at least as I see it."

"All right, Mr. Gray," she replied in an admiring tone, "tell me what you see in that portrait."

"Pay attention to Lenx's mouth. It looks like a gash made by a hatchet."

She murmured her agreement. That was exactly the impression she'd had.

"I've seen that a lot in my forty years as a professional photographer. It's what I call the Wet Bride Syndrome."

Amaia zoomed in on Martin Lenx. She studied it and ran her finger along the man's lips.

"The wet bride? Explain that to me."

"Fortunately, things have changed over the years. Getting married isn't young folks' main objective in life anymore, and I think that's an improvement. But it used to be, for a long time, for most women and many men. These days a formal wedding ceremony is just kind of a pleasant celebration. But I've known some cases where the women, it's usually the women, were so in love with the idea of a formal wedding that it got to be absurd. I call it the Wet Bride Syndrome because it's more common among young women, girls who've been dreaming about their wedding day their whole lives." He laughed aloud. "Not dreaming about falling in love, mind you, but fantasizing about getting married. They visualize that day, plan the ceremony and reception, and imagine every little detail."

She nodded. "I know what you mean."

Gray continued enthusiastically. “But then reality steps in. The hard truth is that it rains a lot in Wisconsin. Those young brides get up that morning, ready for the most important day of their lives, and when they see it’s raining, they want to postpone everything. That’s when that sour expression appears, obvious on the faces of some brides, nearly invisible on others, but there’s no mistaking the resentment.

“That’s the nasty look you see there on Martin Lenx’s face. He’s a wet bride. He wants to give up because things didn’t go the way he planned. And look at his wife’s face, it’s almost as obvious there. She’s upset, she knows something’s going wrong, she realizes that her husband’s resentment is only the tip of the iceberg, and they’re headed for disaster. But just then she’s too overwhelmed to admit it, she pretends nothing’s wrong and she poses for the photo . . . I’ve seen that a fair number of times.”

“Do you think Lenx was deciding right then what he was going to do?”

“That day, I don’t know. He told me, and later it was in the papers, that he expected to be hired to manage a local bank, but they turned him down just a few days later. Something was going on during the photo session, though; just look at the way he kept repositioning the children. It almost got to be a game of musical chairs, where he tried to eliminate one of them . . .”

A fierce gust of wind hit the building. Amaia heard the crash of a shattering window somewhere, a couple of yells, and some loud swearing.

“What was that?” Clayton Gray asked. He’d heard the noise through the line.

“A hurricane, Mr. Gray. I’m calling from New Orleans.”

“From Katrina? What on earth are you doing there, my dear?”

Amaia exhaled slowly as she put her thoughts in order. “I also have a photo of Martin Lenx here, a solo portrait, maybe you took it on that same day,” she said, steering the conversation back to the subject of her call.

“I understand why you might think that, since he was wearing the same clothes, but I actually took that one two days later. Martin Lenx turned up at the studio and told me he wanted a photo of himself alone. Quickest portrait I ever did in my life. He came in, struck his pose, and I clicked the shutter once. Martin didn’t even let me take a backup shot. He told me that was how he wanted it, and he was sure it was perfect.”

Amaia ran her pencil across the eighteen-year-old calendar that Johnson had found for them. Two days after the family photo. On the same day he got the bank's rejection notice, the day before he applied for a gun permit, Martin Lenx had his image preserved in a perfect photo, all alone.

She thanked Clayton and said goodbye, just before all the sirens at the fire station erupted in a sustained howl. She looked up. Other alarms were going off on the street outside. Johnson leaped to his feet. She looked at him, perplexed. He tapped the face of his watch and mouthed "curfew." She nodded, looked down again, and went back to her study of the photo of Lenx.

She zoomed in closer. Lenx's lips appeared slightly pursed, clear evidence of tension in the zygomaticus major and minor, the muscles that control the movements of the mouth. There was no doubt the man was suppressing a smile, as if pleased by some secret knowledge.

There are many types of smiles. Most are fake. For example, the smile someone assumes when posing for a photo; or the slightly pained look someone gets in response to an inappropriate joke; that seductive smile that spreads across your face when someone attracts you sexually; or the sarcastic smile so typical of politicians when asked a difficult question. And then there's the authentic smile, the smile of real happiness. She remembered that when she was little and felt sad, she would try to smile to conceal it from her aunt, but in vain: "You're not fooling me, Amaia. Your eyes aren't smiling."

Amaia enlarged the image once more and focused on the eyes. Even through the lenses of his heavy-framed glasses, Amaia detected the signs. The tension of the orbiculares oculi stretches the skin above the cheekbones taut to form subtle wrinkles around the eyes. Psychopathic individuals learn to imitate ordinary human emotions, but she'd never known of a psycho who could control the autonomic response of the orbiculares. To her mind, those smiling eyes established his profile beyond any doubt. He had been happy when it was taken. Inexpressibly happy.

26

Her Winner's Smile

Elizondo

Engrasi took the Mendinueta bridge across the Baztán, turned onto Calle Braulio Iriarte, and walked downstream. The house where she'd lived since returning from Paris was midway down the street. The walls of massive stone block protected it from the damp of the river, though Engrasi could swear she sometimes felt the Baztán flowing under her feet.

She wasn't paying too much attention to her surroundings as she enjoyed the brilliance of the sun reflected in the roiling river. Sunbeams caressed her through her clothing and infused her with warmth. That's why she didn't see Rosario at first. The woman was dressed in an elegantly tailored suit. Her jacket was beige. She wore shoes with medium heels and carried a brown purse dangling from a short strap, her left hand pressing it to her hip in a gesture that appeared casual but was carefully calculated. The mahogany highlights in her impeccably combed chestnut hair glinted in the brilliant sunlight. She was standing at Engrasi's front door, waiting.

Rosario smiled when she saw Engrasi approaching. Hers was a full, beatific smile. She removed her sunglasses to reveal her eyes, almost as if to force her smile upon Engrasi. The cheerful crinkle about her eyes showed her expression was one of complete happiness.

Engrasi stopped short. She wasn't afraid of Rosario, but her sister-in-law's triumphant smile made her uneasy. Engrasi didn't doubt its authenticity for a moment. She'd remained perpetually on her guard since the night her brother had turned up at her house unexpectedly. Engrasi trusted her intuition, and it warned her that Rosario had prepared some kind of ambush.

"Why are you here, Rosario?"

"Aren't you happy to see me, sister-in-law?"

"No." Engrasi didn't bother to say more than that.

Rosario put her sunglasses back on. "Well, there's no need to be rude. It's been a long time since we talked, you and I. I thought it was time for a little chat."

Engrasi didn't move. Her stare was unforgiving. "What do you want, Rosario? Why are you here?"

Rosario's smile seemed to widen, if that was even possible. "Juan told me about the little talk you two had . . ."

Engrasi said nothing.

"Just between us, my dear sister-in-law, I have to admit I underestimated you. Not on purpose, don't misinterpret me. It's just that I don't know much about the cute games psychiatrists and psychologists play. To tell you the truth, they always seemed like idiots and navel gazers." She shrugged and made a pouting grimace that in other circumstances might have appeared coquettish. "So I apologize, little sister-in-law. You really were quite clever."

Engrasi tilted her head and pursed her lips. Her expression hardened. The affectations and poisoned politeness didn't fool her; Rosario's apparent amiability was charged with venom. She stood her ground and refused to flinch when Rosario stepped close and patted her arm in a confiding manner.

"I'm not reproaching you, Engrasi, for I know it's partly my fault. I made it easy for you. But even so, I have to admit you were clever. You saw the opportunity and you took it."

"I don't know what you mean. There was no opportunity. A man came to my door with an injured child in his arms."

Rosario smiled again as if none of that was important. "I told you already, little sister-in-law, there's no need to be rude. I really thought it would be easier to talk with a psychologist." Her leer suggested the comment was supposed to be witty. "I wasn't healthy back then, Engrasi, so I wasn't responsible for my actions. But that's changed now. I'm taking my medicines; the treatment has done me a world of good." Another satisfied smile was followed by a feigned confidence:

"Don't think I was always like this. At first, I was reluctant to take medical advice. The drugs made me feel terrible—sleepy, slow, even a bit stupid. I hated that, sister-in-law, because if there's one thing I definitely am not, it's stupid. I was frightened, panicked even, because I thought those pills had warped my personality; after all, a woman is defined by her personality."

Engrasi crossed her arms over her chest and continued to stare. She was beginning to tire of this performance, but she needed to know where Rosario was headed.

A magnificent smile spread across Rosario's face. "But that's all in the past now! Dr. Martínez finally came up with the right combination of drugs. I feel really good, Engrasi, on top of the world. Taking the right medication makes all the difference." She slid her sunglasses down her nose and peered at Engrasi over them. "And they don't change my personality a bit! I'm still the same person I was before."

The she-wolf was showing her fangs.

Now it was Engrasi's turn to step in close. She placed her right hand on Rosario's shoulder. "Well, I'm very happy for you, dear sister-in-law," she mimicked Rosario's mocking tone, "but I don't care if you take your pills or flush them down the toilet. It doesn't make a damn bit of difference to me."

Rosario's smile vanished, but she placed her right hand over Engrasi's. "Oh, no! They change everything. As I said, I know my behavior was irrational. Don't get me wrong; I've always known that I had a mission, but I couldn't decide how to go about it. The difference is that now I know what I should do every moment of the day." She seized Engrasi's hand and squeezed it hard. "And if there's one thing I've known since the day that girl was born, it's that we all have a destiny, Engrasi. She'll fulfill her destiny just as I must fulfill mine."

Engrasi recoiled, pulling her hand free as if struck by pure evil. She gasped. "You're fucking insane!"

Rosario feigned disappointment. "Oh, dear God! I might have expected that sort of talk from any other woman, Engrasi, but from you? A psychologist?"

Engrasi's hands were shaking so violently that she had to clasp them to hide her consternation from Rosario. "The girl will not go back to your house. I won't give her to the two of you! I will do whatever's necessary, and if you want to take it to court . . ."

Rosario was smiling again, amused. "Nobody's going to court. That doesn't suit us, you know that." She looked around the street. "That would cause a big scandal. You can't imagine! And especially not now that I've finally managed to really make something of your lousy bakery. No, no, we don't want anything like that."

Engrasi was disconcerted. "So?"

Rosario stepped past her and started down the street. Then she paused, turned, and favored Engrasi with a winner's smile. "I told you I'm thinking clearly now. Now I know what I should do every moment of the day."

Engrasi stood speechless in the middle of the street until Rosario disappeared from view. She thanked God Rosario wasn't watching, for she dropped her housekeys twice before she could get the front door unlocked. She went inside, shut the door, and leaned back against it, as if barricading it with her body. Never in her life had she been so frightened.

27

Scrapes and Scratches

New Orleans, Louisiana
Dusk, Sunday, August 28, 2005

Dupree came into the conference room, accompanied by two uniformed officers none of the team recognized.

"Johnson, Salazar, these are Officers Elliott and Case from the Galveston police," he said. The visitors nodded. "They just drove more than six hours to bring us prints and negatives of the Andrews crime scene photos and the forensic report on the violin." He held up a medium-sized cardboard box.

"Good God," Johnson exclaimed. "You drove all that way into the hurricane? The curfew sirens went off an hour ago."

The Galveston cops exchanged a glance. "We weren't expecting it to be this bad. We thought we could beat the storm here. Captain Reed said it was urgent."

"It *is* urgent . . . It's just that we weren't expecting you'd risk heading into the storm."

"We really appreciate it," Dupree interrupted him. "But we can't allow you to leave. You'll have to stay here until the hurricane passes."

"No problem. The news is saying it'll be a hell of a storm."

Dupree nodded. "Check in with the ops center and ask them to find a place for you to bed down."

The officers nodded and left.

Johnson flipped on the recorder and spoke for the record. "Five types of experts are required for a full analysis of any crime scene: a photographer, a draftsman to draw up a plan of the scene, an evidence technician, a medical examiner, and a specialist to take swabs and analyze chemical traces." He paced back and forth as Bill Charbou and Jason Bull helped Amaia lay out more than two hundred photos on the conference room surfaces. "Ample photographic evidence shows that the team at the Andrews family crime scene included all the necessary specialists."

All the overhead lights were on, and Dupree had commandeered a few high-intensity desk lamps from elsewhere in the building. Brilliant light illuminated the grisly images that entirely covered the huge conference table. The team's workspace had suddenly been converted into a crowded autopsy room.

Amaia wasn't the only one who felt queasy at the sight. Charbou and Bull were also unusually quiet. Amaia was sure they'd seen worse, but they were visibly disturbed by the photos. Most of the prints were extreme close-ups of wounds, bloodstains, textile fibers, and dusted fingerprints. The rulers in each image gave the close-ups a cold, technical aspect deprived of humanity. But the wider perspectives that showed the victims aligned in the rubble and bathed in pools of blood . . . those were something else entirely. And the close-ups of the dead faces were horrific.

Dupree was right. Any normal human being forced to look into this killer's mind saw hell itself open up. She felt the cops' pain; she knew they'd never forget this. It would change their view of others and alter their understanding of themselves. The evidence that a person had been capable of such savagery put them face to face with the worst of human nature.

Amaia took a folder from the box and went to the table. "Here," she said, offering Bull the bulky file. At first he didn't look up. "Detective?"

He met her eyes. She knew that look. It was the somber, distant gaze of someone struggling to comprehend the unthinkable.

"These are the photos they took of the violin. At the request of Joseph Jr." She pointed toward the back of the room. "Can you lay them out on the other table?"

He nodded, took the folder without a word, and began to place the photographs on the table beside the whiteboard.

Amaia studied a cluster of images devoted to blood—drops, spatters, smears, and reddish-black pools. They were individually numbered. A ruler appeared next to each stain.

"They appear to have followed standard operating procedure to identify evidence, preserve it, and maintain the chain of custody," Johnson commented. "Each sample was photographed, sealed in an envelope, and labeled."

Johnson pointed to another group of photos. Odd shapes glowed against dark backgrounds.

"What are we looking at?" Charbou asked.

"Our Galveston friends were thorough. They used luminol reagents and a black light to search for hidden blood stains. Results were negative; there were no signs of an attempt to scrub away blood or any other substances."

Amaia looked through photos of fingerprints and scanned the accompanying summary. "Every fingerprint they found was from a family member. They were meticulous about collecting and preserving textile fibers. All were later matched to the victims' clothing."

Dupree crossed the room and stood next to Johnson and Amaia. "In sum, this crime scene was professionally analyzed right down to the last detail. There's nothing we can take exception to, as far as technique is concerned."

"I can't fault the work," Amaia said.

"Okay, then," Dupree said, "but why?"

Johnson and Amaia looked at one another. Johnson responded, "Why what?"

"The Galveston police already emailed us a copy of this stuff. We had the reports and digitized photos. We asked for photos of the violin. Why did the chief send two officers in a squad car to bring us the originals . . . with the hurricane bearing down?"

"I don't know," Johnson said. "Do you?"

"I have no idea," Dupree admitted. "But *something* must have made Brad Nelson's boss think it was urgent for us to have them."

"Might be he knows what young Andrews has been going through," Johnson suggested. "He could be having some regrets now that he's heard we might reopen the case."

Amaia took another slant. "Maybe he doesn't entirely trust Detective Nelson's claim that the job was done correctly."

Johnson shrugged and gestured toward the material spread over every work surface. "As far as I can see, their methodology was above reproach."

"And the violin?" Dupree went to the table where Jason Bull was standing. They followed.

"Same detail, same technically correct work," Johnson reported. "Granted, a cleaning team had mopped things up by the time they examined the violin the second time, but the instrument's clearly visible in the general views and the overheads. The photos show no marks, stains, or any dried liquids on its surface. We can make enlargements from the negatives, but honestly, given the quality of the work, I doubt the technicians overlooked anything."

Jason Bull cleared his throat.

"Yes?" Amaia invited him to comment.

"Well, maybe it's nothing at all. I'm no expert or anything, but . . ."

"Bull, did you see something?" Dupree pressed him.

"Maybe it's nothing," he said, pointing to one of the photos. "But this right here looks like writing."

They leaned close and examined the photo, a shot of the violin lying on its side. They saw a curved line where the varnish appeared to have peeled away from the wood under the chin rest.

"Looks like a scratch," Johnson said. "Like it was scraped against a harder surface."

Dupree took the photo into his gloved hands and peered at it. "Could be it continues beyond the curve of the sound box. Is there a better view?"

They went through the images of the violin one by one, but none showed whether the mark extended beyond the curved surface.

Dupree sighed, annoyed.

"Let's check the images of the full room, where the violin is leaning against the chiminea," suggested Amaia. She led them back to the larger table. She went through those photos and chose two of them. "These capture the side of the instrument, but I can't see how far the mark extends. We have the film negatives; we can make enlargements to see if we can get a clearer image."

"Go ahead," Dupree authorized her. "Do it."

28

Hidden in Plain Sight

New Orleans, Louisiana

The rain had gotten heavier. Billowing sheets of falling water, ever more forceful, battered the windows so hard it sounded like an enraged madman was pelting them with fistfuls of rock. The wind howled. The National Hurricane Center reported that the storm covered the entire Gulf of Mexico and the eye of the hurricane was thirty miles across. Katrina was advancing inexorably toward New Orleans.

Surprised by the fury of the rain lashing against the windows, Amaia looked up and wondered if the brown paper and duct tape the firefighters had used to cover the glass would protect them if the windows imploded.

Loading the negative had taken just a few minutes, and she'd spent only a little longer with a program that isolated and identified the marks. It yielded a cryptic image.

The program evaluated parameters of continuity, morphology, constancy, and dimension. All suggested that the marks might correspond to writing or some kind of inscription. The mark could still be only a random scrape, as Johnson had guessed, but it could be more. Amaia thought it looked like a truncated inscription, or perhaps there was a space between this scribble and something that followed. She shook her head, regretting the lack of clarity, and felt defeated. "Maybe it's a scratch after all."

They telephoned Emerson and Tucker. Dupree indicated that Amaia should take the lead.

"I found very little on record concerning Martin Lenx's activities before he murdered his family. He didn't serve in the military, and few students took personality tests back in the sixties and seventies when he was in high school and college. No record that he was ever treated by a psychologist or psychiatrist. Employer records aren't particularly revealing. Regular medical checkups, nothing really of note. The psychological profile we have was drawn up after the murders, largely from witness statements, since by that point he'd disappeared. Experts' opinions differ. Some think he probably killed himself after the murders. But I find nothing to substantiate a contention he was suffering from guilt, despite the confession he wrote to his pastor. His character, as far as we can understand it, seems consistent with the assumption that he made a new life for himself after the murders. He was a perfectionist. Starting over and building a new, unblemished life would be the approach of an obsessive-compulsive personality. I suspect Martin Lenx and the Composer may be the same person."

Tucker strongly agreed. "We definitely have to keep that in mind."

Dupree encouraged Amaia to continue.

"Okay then," she said. "If Lenx is indeed our man, I have a different idea of what he might have been doing for those eighteen years. Agent Tucker, you said he could have radically changed his life, his image, his appearance. But if the Composer is the same man who had himself photographed with his family just days before murdering every one of them, his fundamental character won't have changed. The way he set up that group portrait gives us a clue to his thinking. He moved them and rearranged them over and over, and he even tried to remove the youngest son altogether. Only when he saw that his wife was surprised by his erratic behavior did he agree to accept the initial pose. Two days later, he came back for a solo portrait—one for which he didn't change his clothing, his appearance, the way he combed his hair, or his glasses. He even struck an identical pose. The solo portrait looks as if he'd just eliminated everyone else from the group portrait. The only difference is that in the solo portrait, he's smiling."

"I don't see where you're going with this," Tucker objected.

"Martin Lenx did away with his family because they didn't conform to his ideal. He had no awareness of his own faults or shortcomings and no concept of evil. He saw nothing in himself that needed correcting or changing. Martin Lenx considered himself perfect in every way. If Martin Lenx has made a new life for himself, he'll have done his best to control his surroundings. He won't tolerate imperfections."

She expected Tucker to contradict her, but the reply from Florida was positive, thoughtful, and analytic. "So you're thinking our Composer will be a man of about fifty-five, the age Lenx would be now . . . married, conservative, and traditional. Is he likely to have the same number of children?"

"Probably. A conservative type like Lenx would try to re-create his family, but this time without flaws. And, remember, he assumes no personal responsibility for any of his own shortcomings."

Johnson took it one step further. "Following that reasoning, you'd assume his wife wouldn't stand out, and neither would his car. He'd have a middle-class house and a middle-management job, and he'd still be religious. Lenx went to church several times a week, insisted his children attend confirmation classes, and did a lot of volunteer work for the congregation. He seemed dull on the outside, but in fact he was a zealot. His letter makes that clear. He justified the murders by claiming that his family had deviated from the path of righteousness."

Dupree nodded, looking down at the phone console.

"Well, then, what we have found here is going to please you," Tucker said excitedly. Amaia heard a smile in her voice. "Emerson and I have been looking into something from the conversation with Nelson that bothered me. Nelson denied any negligence this afternoon, but he was evasive. Agent Johnson sent us the case summary of the Andrews murders, and it sounds like the investigation was done properly. So I had to ask myself, *Why was Nelson so defensive?* Remember, when we called to interview him, he was in Miami with a rescue team just after the most recent family murders. And he was in Galveston when the Andrews family was killed."

"He's a homicide detective!" Johnson interrupted her. "And he lived in Galveston before he moved to Florida. I don't see what—"

"And as soon as Joseph Andrews Jr. raised the alarm about the violin, the evidence disappeared."

"Agent Tucker, let me remind you that the violin disappeared after the forensics team's *second* visit," Johnson said. "Nelson himself authorized the reexamination of the violin when the son insisted it was important."

"I'm sure whoever placed it there wiped it down; a killer like the Composer wouldn't fail to do that. There's not a single unknown fingerprint anywhere at the scene, remember, and it's pretty easy to fake a burglary. Especially if you're a police officer."

Johnson wasn't buying it. "If there was a reason to lose the violin, wouldn't it be logical to have done that before the crime techs took a second look?"

"I think it would have been too obvious for it to vanish as soon as Joseph Andrews drew attention to it; but after the lab checked it out, the disappearance would mean nothing. Maybe the violin could suggest a different approach. It might be a clue, but not in a way that the technicians could detect. Maybe its mere presence has a significance. Andrews certainly thought so."

Dupree took charge. "Agent Tucker, we studied the photos of the violin and found a mark along one side. Assistant Inspector Salazar is almost certain that something was inscribed there. We asked for assistance from Quantico in deciphering it, but we sent you a copy too."

They heard the faint sound of computer keys clicking on the other end of the line. "Yeah, I have it. It actually does look like some sort of inscription, like someone tried to mark the instrument. That's the sort of evidence I was talking about, something that could be easily overlooked because it seemed like a scratch or accidental damage. Do you think it could be used to identify the person who left it there? Maybe whoever placed it at the scene wasn't aware of the mark. Or he could have noticed it for the first time in the photos, the way you did."

"Are you suggesting Detective Brad Nelson should be a suspect?" Dupree asked.

"How should I know?" said Tucker, sounding a bit hassled. "I've been trying to get in contact with him for a follow-up, but they say he went to New Orleans to help with Katrina."

"Shit!" Amaia exclaimed. Johnson and Dupree looked at her, fully realizing the import of that information. "He's hiding in plain sight! Agent Tucker, does Brad Nelson have children?"

"Two boys and a girl, ages twelve, fifteen, and sixteen. And there's more. Nelson and his wife are separated. They haven't filed for divorce, but they've been living apart since she came to Florida. She moved out eight months ago, not long before the Andrews family was murdered, and he followed her to the state three months later, when he landed a job in Tampa."

"She left him, so he sent out his résumé?" Dupree commented.

"That's what I think," Tucker replied. "He followed them to Florida, so he's enough of a family man not to want a divorce. He's a midlevel officer of no particular distinction. He drives a family car, a four-year-old Crown Victoria. In the photo I found, he's wearing the kind of suit and tie you could buy off the rack in any department store. Nelson fits the profile."

"He's conservative, like millions of other Americans," Johnson objected. "As for following his family, well, why wouldn't he? You said they haven't filed for divorce."

"And on top of that," Tucker said with a certain flourish, "he joined a rescue team only fifteen days after the Andrews murders in Galveston. It's a nonprofit called Rescue Me that puts together teams of firefighters, police officers, and specialists from all over the country to help at disaster sites. Anywhere in the United States. I'm scheduled to talk to the administrator in half an hour. I'm going to get the details of Nelson's participation, especially dates and places."

"Sounds like a good guy," Johnson said.

"Agent Tucker," Amaia interjected, "I have a good photo of Lenx and a facial recognition program. It can compare images and detect similarities even when the individual's features have been altered by plastic surgery. I'm going to need a headshot of Detective Nelson."

"I sent you one by email, but I don't know if it'll be of much use."

"In fact, I'll need photos of his whole family. And their names."

"Emerson will take care of that."

Dupree took command, speaking into the console but keeping his eyes on Johnson. "We urgently need to establish beyond a doubt whether Nelson was at any of the disasters where other families were killed. A volunteer quick-response team would be a perfect cover to travel anywhere in the country, but whatever we find will be circumstantial at best. There's lots more work to do, but maybe this explains why Captain Reed sent us the original file on the Andrews killings. I think we need to have a chat with him. Good work, Agent Tucker, Agent Emerson. I'll call you as soon as we have news. You do the same."

Johnson held up a hand. "Agent Tucker, you didn't say anything about Nelson's religion. Martin Lenx was deeply religious. We all agree that his bizarre concept of sin drove him to murder his family. Does Brad Nelson go to church?"

Tucker didn't answer immediately. "We're still working on that, haven't had the time. But everything I've seen suggests that he doesn't."

After they hung up, Amaia was convinced she saw a smile hiding behind Johnson's bushy mustache.

Special Agent Stella Tucker used her ballpoint pen to underline the names of each locality the Rescue Me administrator dictated over the phone. She was comparing them with the list of Nelson's leave requests she'd obtained from HR.

"Brooksville, Oklahoma; Texas, in a crossroads near Alvord; Miami, Florida; New Orleans, Louisiana," she recapped. "And you're sure, absolutely sure, that Nelson was at every one of those places?"

"We make up our teams from volunteers in the vicinity, but if necessary, we'll move people all the way across the country. Nelson just put in for New Orleans. Our team leader there is Michael Meigs, a great guy, firefighter from Boston."

"Right, Detective Nelson's personnel officer told me he'd left for there, but we do need to consult with him. It's not terribly pressing," she lied. "And if he's doing urgent rescue work, we don't want to bother him. I just wanted to confirm he actually is in New Orleans."

"Well, I won't know until I can talk with the chief. I can confirm that Nelson accepted the invitation, but something could have come up. I can give you Meigs's number. The last we heard, they were in Kenner at the fire station at Armstrong Airport. They were scheduled to move from there to Charity Hospital."

Tucker thanked the administrator and took down the team leader's number. She hung up and tried to reach him.

"The number you have dialed is not in service at this time."

"Goddamn hurricane," she muttered.

Tucker drew circles around Cape May, New Jersey, and Killeen, Texas, on the map. She had no confirmation Nelson had been in those locations in February and March. He was still on the Galveston police force at the time, as he had been in December when the Andrews family was killed. Dupree had mentioned needing to talk to the Galveston police chief; if she contacted Galveston, there'd be a risk that someone would pass it up the line and the chief would tell Dupree. Tucker was pretty sure the Galveston force would wonder what was up if the FBI called twice in the same day, but it was equally risky not to give it a try.

She knew the others' opinion of her, but she didn't care. She'd learned long ago that the only unforgiveable errors she'd ever made had come from failing to follow her own convictions. She was intelligent, which had given her insight into two things early on: first, an institution like the FBI wasn't particularly willing to mentor a woman, especially an African American; second, the only way to ever change that was by showing *results*.

Agent Tucker tried Meigs's number again but ended the call as soon as she heard the recorded message. She stared at the office telephone for several seconds as if it were an alien object.

Emerson watched her, his hands hovering above the keyboard. In the months he'd worked for Tucker, he'd learned to be especially vigilant during her moments of inaction, for that capable, ambitious woman never slowed down except to weigh the facts before taking action. She would sit motionless for several seconds, scarcely blinking as she looked about the room, her gaze jumping sightlessly from one random object to another. And when she came back, she'd have decided what to do.

Finally, she looked up. Emerson took that opportunity to speak. "Agent Tucker, I have the photos of the Nelson family that Salazar requested. Most are from the school yearbooks or official records. They're not high res, but . . ."

Tucker came over and Emerson pushed back his swivel chair to give her a better view. She took the mouse and clicked one by one on the photos he'd attached to the draft email. Emerson had already spent some time studying them.

Mrs. Nelson was good looking, maybe a bit too striking to fit Lenx's profile, and the boys strongly resembled the mother. The girl was different. She was a bit sullen; she didn't look comfortable being photographed.

Tucker released the mouse, turned, and perched on the edge of the desk to look at Emerson. He waited for her instructions the way a cat pauses in expectation of a bowl of cream.

"I talked with the coordinator of the rescue organization and compared his information with the HR list of Nelson's leave requests since last April. They matched from April in Brooksville to three days ago in Miami. He was in Galveston when the Andrews family died, and I'm pretty certain he's in New Orleans now."

"He's our man."

"That's what I think. I'm trying to contact Chief Meigs, their team leader in New Orleans, for more info, but we haven't linked Nelson to Cape May in February or Killeen in March."

Emerson took the bait. "Nelson was with the Galveston police department then. I could call their admin offices and ask." He checked his watch. "It's Sunday. I don't know if they're staffed on weekends."

She didn't answer, so there would be no record of her telling Emerson to make a call that might overlap with Dupree's. She turned back to the desk, giving him room while he tapped the number.

Emerson was grinning when he hung up soon afterward. "He took leave on those dates to go out with the rescue team."

Agent Tucker leaned over the desk, a fist under her chin. She was looking in Emerson's direction but not at him. Her eyes were far away as she made one of her almost interminable pauses for reflection. "What do you think—does Mrs. Nelson go to bed early?"

Emerson said nothing. That was another thing he'd learned: a question from Tucker didn't necessarily mean she was expecting an answer. He rose and put on his jacket. He hesitated a moment, looking at the unsent email with the attached images. He hadn't added the new information about Nelson's leave requests.

Tucker was already at the door. She looked back and answered as if Emerson had asked about the email out loud. "Everything in its time. Let's get to work."

After she turned away, he sent it anyway, just as it was.

Amaia logged on and the symbol immediately filled the screen:

She found herself speculating if it might be an *N* followed by an *E*. The truncated line could be an *L*.

"Looks like a kid wrote it," she heard from behind her. She looked around to see Detective Bull carrying two paper cups.

"I took a coffee break; thought you might like one." He held it out.

Amaia gave him a grateful smile, accepted it, and picked up on his comment. "You said it looked like a child's writing?" She gestured to the chair next to hers.

The detective settled there with a smile, pleased to contribute. "I have a six-year-old boy and a girl who's ten. That's how they write. They never use capital letters."

Amaia looked at the marks in a different light. Maybe they were, in fact, made by a child.

"But maybe it's from some adult who writes a lot with a pen or pencil."

Amaia turned to him with renewed interest. "Explain that."

"Addison's handwriting was really good from the start. But Liam, the little fella, well, let's just say it's not so easy for him. Your handwriting reflects your personality, and my little guy has a lot of that. But Liam's teacher doesn't think the way I do, so she's always marking up Liam's work with comments about his handwriting and the way he holds his pencil."

Amaia nodded, inviting him to continue.

"Last week my son's teacher put another of those notes at the bottom of an exercise he'd written. I'd seen her comments before, and I'd noticed the way other teachers write. But that note really annoyed me. I took a closer look and saw she didn't close off her *s*'s or her *a*'s, and in fact she inverted the curves on her *m*'s and *n*'s. I do the same thing. The thing is, if an adult writes like that, it's acceptable, just a quirky little peculiarity, but a kid gets told off for sloppy handwriting. She wrote something like, 'Liam needs to improve his penmanship, because it's hard for me to understand.' I wrote a reply: 'Excuse me, teacher, but I can't decipher your handwriting.'"

Amaia laughed aloud. "How did she take it?"

"Oh, really well, actually; she thought it was funny. That afternoon when Liam got home from school, I saw she'd written back: 'Touché, but Liam still needs to improve his penmanship.'"

Smiling, Amaia studied the scrawl shown on the monitor. She turned back to Bull and fired a shot across his bow. "How did you and Agent Dupree get to know one another?"

The detective was taken aback for a second or two but quickly regained his composure. "You were there yesterday morning when they introduced Bill and me."

She smiled and clicked her tongue, tilting her head to one side to signal her disappointment at his evasiveness.

A ping from the computer announced an incoming email. It was a message from Tucker with attached files. Amaia glanced at Bull, who took the opportunity to get to his feet.

"I'll let you work."

"You didn't answer my question!" she said sharply to his retreating back.

When the image came up on the screen, she understood why Agent Tucker had said Nelson's headshot might not be of much use.

Brad Nelson matched Martin Lenx in terms of height, complexion, age, and hair and eye color, but his face was terribly scarred. She zoomed in for a closer look, knowing already that her facial recognition program would be of no use. The scars were from burns, third and maybe even fourth degree, undoubtedly from a fire. Thick scars ran from his forehead to his chin. His nose and left cheek were disfigured. He must have had several skin grafts. Suture marks had altered his hairline. She could tell that the scars were old, for they were dead white. Brad Nelson had been burned many years earlier. He wore wire-rimmed glasses so light they were almost invisible, and he was smiling. His zygomatic muscle had been injured, so she wouldn't be able to read from the lines around the eyes whether that smile was real. Scar tissue to the right of his mouth pulled it slightly downward and distorted his smile. But in this headshot, he looked relaxed and confident, a man who loved his job.

She opened the other attachments. Tucker and Emerson hadn't found a Nelson family portrait. The children's pictures were taken from school yearbooks, and the wife's picture was probably from her driver's license. Despite the mediocre quality of the image, it was obvious that Sarah Nelson was good looking. She was meticulously made up, and her carefully brushed hair had a gentle wave. She smiled directly into the camera. Anyone who was that particular about her appearance at the DMV would surely take good care of herself all the time. Except for her obvious interest in grooming and makeup, she was the polar opposite of Martin Lenx's spouse.

The two boys, Dylan and Jackson, resembled their mother. They were both handsome, with dark hair and large eyes. The older boy was grinning, the younger one had an earnest expression. The girl, Isabella, looked nothing like the rest of the family. Her hair was a curly chestnut mop with reddish highlights. Amaia wondered if Isabella's features came from her father or somewhere further back in the family line. She duplicated the picture of the girl, planning to compare her features with those in the Lenx family portrait, even though she knew the program wasn't designed to detect inherited characteristics. Lenx's sons had had the chestnut hair of their mother, and the Lenx girl had had a rich, curly red mane fit for an Irish princess.

She compared the two girls. Isabella's curls were more obvious and untamed, and the color was quite different from the flamingo tint flaunted by Martin Lenx's daughter. They were teenagers of different eras, with as many differences as similarities. This was getting Amaia nowhere.

She positioned the photo of Brad Nelson on the screen next to the portrait of Martin Lenx. Would Lenx have deliberately disfigured himself in order to escape arrest? She thought he might have. Martin Lenx's high opinion of himself wasn't based on his looks but his conviction of his innate superiority and strong moral values. He would have considered physical appearance superficial, no hinderance to his striving for moral perfection.

In Galveston at ten o'clock in the evening, a cheerful feminine voice answered the phone. "Reed residence!" Music and chatter filled the background.

"Good evening, ma'am. Sorry to bother you so late. This is Agent Dupree of the FBI. I was hoping to speak with Captain Reed."

"Oh. Just a second, I'll let him know," she replied, sounding slightly put out by the intrusion.

For a time, Dupree could hear only music and the lively chatter of a social gathering, but then a man came on the line. "This is Captain Reed."

"Captain, this is Agent Dupree of the FBI. Your headquarters gave me your private number. I hope I'm not bothering you—sounds like I'm interrupting a party—but it's extremely important."

"We're celebrating my wife's birthday. But never mind that, I know it's important." The background noise ceased abruptly, probably because Reed had closed a door. The captain's voice was tense when he came back. "Someone from your team called our admin office this evening and wanted to compare some dates with Nelson's leave requests. I don't see what that could have to do with anything."

Dupree gave Johnson a surprised glance. His deputy mouthed, "Tucker!" and threw up his hands in a gesture of disgust.

Dupree closed his eyes for a moment and exhaled sharply. "Captain, I have you on the speaker now, and I've got Agent Johnson and Assistant Inspector Salazar with me. We need to hear your thoughts on Detective Brad Nelson and the Andrews case."

The captain sounded troubled when he spoke after a lengthy pause. "Shoot. What do you need?"

Dupree didn't beat around the bush. "How long have you known Brad Nelson?"

"Twelve years."

"What's your opinion of his professional ability?"

"He's a good officer, but I have an even better opinion of him as a man. Nelson is good-hearted and generous. It's rare to have a career officer who hasn't been beaten down and dehumanized by his work. He's empathetic; he suffers along with the victims."

"Can you explain what happened to his face?"

"Sure. It was a long time ago, before I met him. Maybe that's where his empathy is rooted . . . The landlord of the old apartment block in Boston where he was living set fire to the building to collect the insurance money. Ten people died in the fire. Nelson doesn't like to talk about it. A fireman pulled him out. Once he was released from the hospital and was pretty much back on his feet, he applied to join the fire department. He couldn't meet the physical requirements because of his injuries. But the Boston police accepted him. He met his wife Sarah, they married, they had children, they moved to Galveston. That's about all I can tell you, since as I said, he doesn't like to talk about it."

"Do you have any reason to believe the handling of the Andrews case was flawed?"

"No, none at all. I think we did everything possible. But policemen are human beings, and no one is a hundred percent all the time."

"What are you suggesting?"

"There's always talk about how the stress of police work affects the officer's private life, but it works the opposite way as well. We're talking about people, individuals, and when an officer has problems at home, that can reduce his effectiveness on the job. I'm not saying that was the case, but Nelson was having a pretty hard time at home during that investigation."

"You mean Nelson and his wife were talking about separating?"

Captain Reed's reply was drowned out by static on the line.

"Captain, we're calling you from New Orleans, and it sounds like the hurricane might be interfering with the line. We didn't hear what you just said. Could you please repeat it?"

"I said I don't think 'separating' was the issue. How much do you know?"

"The wife moved to Florida with the children, and Nelson followed them three months later. But they're not living together."

"Listen, I admire Nelson. Not that we're close friends or anything, but we've always gotten along. Family meals together, barbecues, that kind of thing. He never said he was having problems with his marriage; never even hinted at it. After they moved away, my wife told me Sarah used to complain about how strict Brad was with the youngsters. Maybe too demanding, too rigid with their schedules, their choice of friends, you know . . . Anyhow, that's not so unusual. Lots of police officers are like that with their kids. It's probably an attempt to protect them from all we know, what we see every day. But from what my wife said, it sounds like Nelson got carried away."

"Did he hit them?"

"Not that I know of."

"But?"

"Well, a couple of weeks before the Andrews case, his neighbors reported screaming coming from the Nelsons' house. The kids weren't home. Sarah had given them permission to sleep over at friends' houses. The parents argued, it became louder and louder, and then their domestic disturbance got a little out of hand. We sent a patrol car over. When the officers got into the house, they found that Sarah had locked herself in the bedroom. Nelson hadn't laid a finger on her, but he'd gone on a rampage. Smashed the furniture to bits. Even so, she declined to make a statement or file a complaint. The patrol officers called me and I invited him down to the station, where he slept on a sofa. He'd calmed down by the next morning, and I drove him back home. I couldn't believe it when he opened the front door. Looked like a tornado had hit the place. Turns out it wasn't the first time they'd fought like that, but he'd never been that destructive before. Sarah was flat-out gone. She'd loaded up the children and left for Florida, where she's from. Told him she wasn't coming back. Nelson gave notice the same day, told me he wanted to join his family. I tried to convince him to let things settle down a bit, but he said he loved her and was going to change his ways. Then, bang, the storm hit and the Andrews family turned up dead. Then that poor boy kept insisting the violin didn't belong to his family and shouldn't have been in the house. Claimed the investigation had been completely mishandled."

"Do you think Nelson could have had something, anything at all, to do with the case?"

"What? What are you thinking? Of course not!" The captain sounded deeply offended. "Nelson wasn't focused, that's all; all he could think of was finding a job in Florida. He flew there whenever he had time off. He was obsessed with convincing Sarah they should get back together. His behavior *had* changed; he had a totally different attitude."

"And one of those changes was his decision to join the team that helped out after disasters?"

"Yes. He went with them several times when he lived here in Galveston."

"Can you be more precise? Could you tell us how many times he did that and when?"

"Well, I understand that our admin already gave that information to the FBI."

Johnson gave Dupree a fierce glare, as if he'd only just remembered how furious he was with Tucker.

"I don't have that information here," the captain went on. "And the admin office is closed at this hour. I can send it to you early tomorrow morning. Off the top of my head, I seem to recall he went out twice: once in February, and another time in mid-March, just a few days before he left for Florida. I remember that one because it was in Texas. They were helping with rescue and cleanup after a whole series of tornados up by Killeen."

"Captain Reed, this is Assistant Inspector Salazar. You've known Detective Nelson for twelve years. Is he religious?"

The question was simple, but Reed was silent for quite a long time, so long that Amaia thought they might have lost the connection.

"Did you hear my question, Captain?"

"Roger that, loud and clear . . . It's just that, well, if you'd asked me a year ago, I'd have laughed my head off. Nelson's a good man, sincere, generous, lots of virtues, but he swears like a sailor. A good man, but not the sort that goes to church."

"What changed?"

"A while back, after Sarah left with the kids, I saw Nelson downtown one afternoon. I lowered the window to ask him why he was out so far from his neighborhood, but then I saw him go into a church. Didn't get the chance to make contact, so I raised the window and left. And I didn't mention it later."

"Are you sure? Do you remember the name of the church?"

"Sure, it's right in the center of the city. Guardian Angel Catholic Church."

"Did you ask him about it?"

"No. No, I didn't. Seemed obvious he didn't want anybody to know. He looked up and down the street before he went in, like he was afraid someone might see him. If he wanted to keep his faith to himself, it was none of my business, right? And I wasn't going to tell anyone. I guess a man like Nelson could think that going to church is a sign of weakness."

Amaia shook her head and waved Dupree off. Whether from friendship or from allegiance to the force, Reed wasn't going to tell them anything more. "Thanks for your time, Captain. You've been a big help." They ended the call.

Johnson was doubtful. "You think he was being honest?"

Just then the door opened. Detective Bull beckoned Dupree to join him in the hall. Dupree raised a finger to hold Bull there. "I think he was straight with us, but I don't know if he was straight with himself. What do you think?" He looked at Johnson.

"The captain said Nelson was very strict with his children, like Lenx; two boys and a girl, like Lenx. And there's this business about church that he seems to be trying to keep secret. If he's religious in private, that could link him to our man."

Amaia had been busy with her computer. "That struck me as well, and that's why I asked for the name of the church. Guardian Angel Catholic Church. We know Lenx has his own twisted interpretation of his faith, but I have trouble believing a devout Lutheran would ever change denominations. And I don't believe he'd fail to educate his children in his cradle faith. If you ask me, it doesn't fit at all."

"And that story about the fire?"

"I believe Lenx was capable of setting one," Amaia replied. "You have to admit that an apartment building fire that disfigures someone would be a good cover for a new beginning. A new face maybe helped him wrangle a new identity. I think Lenx was so sure of himself spiritually he'd have had no problem sacrificing himself physically."

"There aren't going to be many apartment fires in Boston that are close to the date of Lenx's disappearance. Especially considering the deaths." Johnson's fingers flew across his keyboard. "Here it is. Fire in an apartment building. Death toll of ten, two slightly injured, one seriously hurt—a man who escaped by himself but passed out as he exited the front door. Firemen had just enough time to pull him clear before the building collapsed. Bodies inside were all badly burned, some impossible to identify, speculation that several were undocumented immigrants. Assuming the identity of someone who died in a fire wouldn't be terribly difficult. He could have approached the building when the fire was out of control, gone inside, gotten burned, and staggered out just in time to be rescued. Sounds horrific, but, as Salazar says, a man like Lenx would have been capable of it. And a lot more, besides."

Detective Bull looked through the doorway, silently entreating Dupree. Neither said a word to the other. The boss held up that finger again, ordering Bull to wait. Bull leaned against the doorframe.

"Go ahead, Johnson. What else?"

"All this reminds me of something Joseph Andrews said. The boy had the feeling Nelson thought he'd have been better off if he'd died with the rest of his family. Joseph gave us no specifics; it was just an impression he had. I do remember Nelson saying something like that when we talked with him."

"I disagree," Amaia said. "Nelson was stating the obvious. The boy was depressed, and he was going to wind up dead if things didn't change."

"And then there's the fact that he decided to volunteer for these rescue teams, starting eight months ago," Johnson went on. "Just when the massacres began and his family was coming apart. That could have plunged him back into the same cycle as before. Reed mentioned a trip with the team in February; maybe that was New Jersey. He confirmed Nelson was in Killeen, where the Masons were murdered. We don't have the dates. Tucker should have sent them to us. But you have to admit, it at least looks like it matches up. Rescue team members wear badges. Any kind of badged official, say a policeman, a fireman, a rescue team member, would be welcomed with open arms." Johnson looked at Amaia. "Even someone with a face as scarred as Nelson's."

"He could even be canny enough to use it as a way to build a connection with the family," she commented. "Think about it—a family's hurt, their house is destroyed, they're in a truly vulnerable position, and then someone arrives with a face that shows he's suffered too. If he's a clever enough actor, that face could project compassion. It could be a means of creating a bond and establishing trust long enough to disarm them, first psychologically and then physically. Still, we shouldn't be too hasty. We don't know if he was in New Jersey. And even that would be no more than circumstantial evidence. We have to locate his rescue team, but discreetly, so Nelson doesn't realize we're watching him. We need to know how and when they arrived and where they're waiting out the hurricane. I'm guessing it's someplace like this."

"Agent Dupree!" Bull called insistently from the doorway.

"The rest of you keep at it," Dupree said. He got up and went out with Bull.

Amaia remained seated, her eyes on the two men in the hall. They stood very close to one another. Bull was explaining something intently as Dupree nodded, his expression grave. Dupree looked up at her, and their eyes locked. Dupree abruptly gestured to Bull, and they moved out of her sight.

Charbou came in with a plate of sandwiches. He'd walked past the conversation in the hall and hadn't seemed to find it unusual.

Johnson rubbed his eyes, bookmarked his place in the pile of loose pages in the case folder, and closed it. He took one of the sandwiches and settled, like Charbou, on the edge of a camp cot. He saw Amaia watching the door to the corridor. "You should try to get some rest. It's late, and tomorrow's going to be a tough day."

"I think I'll try to locate Nelson's rescue team," she replied despite her deep fatigue.

"Agents Tucker and Emerson are taking care of that," Johnson commented sourly. "They'll give us a call once they have something."

"How about you?" She waved at the pile of thick folders on the table in front of him. "Find anything?"

Johnson shook his head, his expression grim. "Nothing that stands out. These were ordinary families with ordinary problems. The Millers had filed for divorce a year before the murders but were going to counseling and had put the divorce on hold. The Masons were in financial difficulties and had just taken out a second mortgage on the farm. The Allens had their share of challenges too. The wife was diagnosed with breast cancer and had surgery to remove the tumor. Went through chemotherapy and seemed to be on the mend, but her illness affected the children's schoolwork and behavior. The boys went joyriding with a neighbor's tractor and turned it over. One of them was trapped underneath. Broke his leg and had to have an operation, but he recovered.

"I just got the info they collected on the Samuels family in Miami, and it's more of the same. Another ordinary family, with completely normal problems. The girl was caught shoplifting lipstick from Walgreens, that's all.

"What else? Let's see: as Joseph Jr. told us, the Andrews family's grandmother wasn't in Galveston, but that doesn't exclude the possibility of the Composer, since the killer might have assumed she'd be there; she was due in just a couple of days.

"It's worth noting that there's no grandmother in the Nelson family. His parents died when he was twenty, and he was an only child. We'll have hit the jackpot if he really is Martin Lenx masquerading as Nelson. The mother of Sarah Nelson, née Rosenblatt, died when Sarah was just a child; her father raised her and her brothers in Florida. And get this: her father is Stephen Rosenblatt, a Republican senator from Florida."

Bill Charbou whistled and grinned.

Johnson smiled behind his mustache but went on as if he hadn't heard. He gestured with his sandwich. "I'm trying to find some pattern of offenses the Composer maybe thought deserved capital punishment, but I'm still baffled." He took a big bite of his sandwich to signal the end of his presentation.

Charbou piped up. "Do you think things like a divorce, financial troubles, a tractor accident, or stealing a lipstick could be why the Composer killed them? Look, I'm a street cop; I'm no stranger to how dealers, whores, and pimps behave. But I'm a zero when it comes to psychopaths and the weird games they play. By those standards, nine out of ten families in this country would be facing the death penalty."

Amaia stared intently at Charbou as she thought that over. "I think you're right. None of those offenses seems particularly serious or deserving of punishment. According to the textbooks, psychopaths like Lenx murder to prove to themselves they're not failures. They take out the frustrations of their failures on others."

"That could be an argument for why Lenx started killing again," Johnson added. "For more than a decade and a half, the new life apparently satisfied him. I suspect that eventually things fell apart."

Amaia sighed. "A psychopath's reasoning isn't necessarily logical, calculated, or even based on facts. It's enough that his victims annoyed him. We should imagine Lenx as the director and protagonist of his own play. One of his supporting actors screws up, so Lenx gets rid of him and substitutes someone else. No regrets. Just like a Broadway director drops an actress who can't remember her lines."

Charbou looked at her wide eyed. "You're smart as a whip, Salazar. God, that turns me on!" He quickly put up his hands to fend her off. "Forget I said that! I mean, your mind really impresses me. It's your mind that's sexy."

She stared him down, deliberating whether to react. She'd had her fill of the Charbou approach, but she was too exhausted to respond.

"How about me, Bill?" Johnson's jocular comment settled the matter. "My mind's not attractive? I came up with half of the analysis. Salazar shouldn't get all the credit!"

Charbou waved in surrender, still smiling. Amaia was amused but did her best not to show it.

The wind outside had risen to a fever pitch. Air whistled under the windows and rattled their flimsy frames each time someone opened a door to the stairwell.

"Take a break, Salazar," Johnson said, picking up a sandwich from the platter and offering it to her. "Have something to eat. Try to sleep."

"I couldn't sleep a wink with all this noise."

He smiled. “Go ahead, surprise yourself. You managed to doze off in the car yesterday.”

Charbou nodded. “He’s right. If you can’t sleep, you should at least lie down.”

She nodded and gave in. She unwrapped the sandwich and settled on a cot, her back against the wall.

“Want us to turn off the lights?” Charbou asked.

Before she could reply, the entire building was plunged into darkness. The ringing of the 911 emergency line suddenly ceased. A deafening silence descended inside the building. The hurricane howled, and a blast of thunder shook the windows.

“There, you see? Folks in New Orleans don’t mess around!” Johnson joked in the darkness. “When they turn off the lights, they turn ’em off!”

A brilliant flash of lightning silhouetted Amaia against the window. She’d pulled back a corner of the brown paper and was peering through the glass. “The power’s out. Lights are off as far as I can see.”

“Don’t worry, everybody!” someone bellowed in the hall. “Emergency generator’s about to kick in!”

Darkness always disconcerted Amaia Salazar. For as long as she could remember, she’d left a light on while she slept, ensuring there was just enough illumination for her to recognize her surroundings if she woke. That way she’d know she was safe and nobody was going to lean over and threaten to devour her soul. She couldn’t sleep easy unless she was sure she wouldn’t awake in pitch darkness. She rarely slept with anyone else. Her excuse wasn’t strictly accurate, but it was sincere: “I have nightmares.” She claimed they were caused by the grim things she’d seen at work. No one had ever questioned that excuse. She wondered what they’d have said if she’d confessed that in darkness, a ghost from her past materialized and threatened to eat her alive.

Nervous in this unexpected blackout, she suddenly felt the need to chat. “Agent Johnson, what’s up with Tucker?”

“Yeah,” Charbou, clearly entertained, took up the subject. “What the hell’s with Tucker? She dropped out three or four times during the conference call. And you sounded pretty damn pissed off at her.”

Johnson harrumphed like Yosemite Sam. “I can’t stand the woman!”

His declaration was so sincere and unexpected that both Amaia and Charbou burst out laughing.

Amaia still couldn't see the others' faces. The darkness was no longer complete, for the emergency exit signs in the hallway now cast a feeble red light.

"Now, hold on," Charbou gasped, once he'd finally gotten his mirth under control. "You mean you can't stand the sound of her voice, say, or the way she slurps her coffee? Or do you really detest her?"

Johnson took a couple of seconds. "I'd like to think that I don't really detest anyone—though I do, actually. Pedophiles, for example, and serial killers." A pause. "I can't stand Tucker because she's disloyal."

Amaia considered that. "Loyalty's something abstract for me, at least in the way you're putting it. I understand devotion to family, to friends, but this is the first time I've worked on a team like this. I understand how important it is to be absolutely honest and keep your word, but I've never felt compelled to identify unconditionally with a group."

Johnson responded, "You think you don't know much about it, but in the few hours you've been in this unit, you've shown more loyalty than Tucker has in her whole life. She phoned Galveston, remember, even though Dupree told her he was going to call the police chief after our conference call." He snorted. "*Tucker!* Believe me, if the guys over at the National Hurricane Center knew her, they'd have named this one after her. She's as unstoppable and just as destructive. That sort of disloyalty undermines an investigation; she gets out ahead of the group so she can scoop up the credit.

"Her meddling in Galveston got to Captain Reed and made him suspicious. When we called, he was already on the defensive, which maybe made him less forthright than he would have been. When it comes right down to it, I just can't stand her! She waited until the end of the conference call to say Nelson's behavior had raised her suspicions—why didn't she share that earlier, so the whole group could look into it? I know she's smart. Everything she does is deliberate; there's a calculation behind every move she makes. Tucker's an unprincipled schemer, and I can tell you right now, the carefully drafted report she's going to turn in will emphasize which ideas, discoveries, and suggestions came from her. She's disloyal to Dupree, and she has no allegiance to the unit."

Amaia nodded, thinking. "And Emerson?"

She heard Johnson exhale loudly. She was sure he was shaking his head. "Emerson's a slimeball and not too bright, but at least he knows how to work on a team. Knows he's not as smart as Tucker and that unless he follows her line, he'll be in over his head. That's why he does her dirty work. Emerson's a follower. He's not particularly original or insightful, but at least he's loyal."

Amaia considered that. "You know Dupree. Why does he keep her on the team?"

"All Dupree cares about is the investigation, and Tucker is really talented, in her own way. He doesn't give a shit about her character." Johnson paused and then added woefully, "Tucker's planning to walk right over him, and he doesn't seem to give a damn."

"You think Tucker wants to take Dupree's job?"

Johnson's laugh was more of a growl, low and bitter. "What she *wants* is one thing; what she's capable of doing is another. Tucker is a superb investigator, but she doesn't compare to Dupree. He's a needle in the haystack. You run into an agent like Dupree once every fifteen, maybe twenty years. He's on a different level. Don't get me wrong, Salazar, I know I'm no needle. But I'm not a brown-noser either."

Amaia accepted that. Under cover of the deeply disquieting darkness, she pushed further. "What do you think the boss is up to now? You should have seen him and Bull conspiring when they thought nobody was looking."

"Assistant Inspector Salazar, there's one thing you need to know about Dupree: he's constantly thinking about the big picture. He's one step ahead, maybe a whole day ahead. That's why he always seems worried and distracted. He's Atlas with the fucking world on his shoulders."

"He doesn't smile much," Charbou acknowledged. "That's for sure."

"He's the serious kind, but I will admit he's been particularly remote since we got here."

Amaia looked toward Charbou, still cloaked in darkness. "And you, Bill? Do you know what your partner's up to? Maybe I'm wrong, but when they were introduced at the police station, I had the distinct impression they knew one another."

"Oh, no, Assistant Inspector, don't go there," he said with a chuckle. "I, for one, sure know about being loyal."

"I thought loyalty and sincerity went hand in hand," she insisted. "Doesn't it bother you that your partner's hiding things?"

"We're Bill and Bull, not Tom and Jerry. Loyalty doesn't mean sharing everything. It means sharing whatever needs to be shared."

Amaia gave Charbou a big, invisible smile. She'd never have done so if he could see her.

29

Maudit

Superdome, New Orleans
3:00 a.m., Monday, August 29, 2005

Nana hadn't taken her sleeping pill. She'd been convinced that without it, she'd stay awake, but she dozed off anyhow. She roused to the constant murmur of ten thousand people breathing and whispering and the constant moan of the wind against the stadium's dome. She looked up. They'd finally stopped broadcasting music through the PA system, and someone had dowsed the glaring stadium lights. Children who'd been playing on the track earlier in the day now lay across their parents' laps or curled up like kittens on the ground.

Nana felt a distinctly uncomfortable pressure in her abdomen. She needed to pee. She'd gone to the bathroom before leaving home, but she hadn't dared leave her seat, for fear someone would steal it. They'd taken the first two seats on the aisle, next to the passageway. Bobby had Seletha's wheelchair parked in the aisle seat next to him.

More and more people had arrived throughout the afternoon, an ongoing human stream that let up only after the curfew was sounded.

It was hot inside. Nana had drunk all the water in the little bottle she'd received with dinner, and now her bladder was about to pop. She got to her feet, carefully supporting herself with her cane. She'd been sitting for a long time. She was expecting her rheumatic hip to give her trouble, but her knees were worse. Seletha was sleeping with her head dangling. Nana heard her friend's rattling breath over the constant whine of the wind and the ongoing chatter of those still awake. Bobby was stretched out, his face muffled in the hood of his sweatshirt, hugging their knapsack to his chest. Nana tried to step across his legs, but she stumbled a bit. Bobby opened his eyes.

"Where you going, Nana? You need to stay with us!"

The man in the row behind them watched them without interest. He had three small children in two stadium seats and another asleep in his arms.

Nana blushed. Her kidneys hurt. She leaned over to whisper into Bobby's ear. "Baby, I have to go to the bathroom."

Bobby straightened up, alarmed, and looked from his sleeping mother to the passageway where a sign showed the direction to the restrooms. "My God, Nana! What am I gonna do? I can't leave Seletha, and we can't all three of us go, because people gonna take our places."

"Of course not, baby. Don't you worry, I can go by myself."

It wasn't her lucky day. The sign for the restrooms directed her to an entirely different section. Few people were in the passages; most folks had opted for the limited comfort of the stadium seats over the oven-like heat under the stands. The humid air in the tunnel moved sluggishly. There was a line outside the men's room. She thanked the Lord when she saw there was no line outside the ladies'.

She started to enter, but a woman burst out and almost knocked her over. "Don't go in there, ma'am!" the woman shouted over her shoulder and ran down the tunnel.

Nana turned to look after her. She didn't doubt for a minute that there was a disgusting mess inside by now. Did it matter how bad it was? Her bladder was about to explode. This was an emergency, and she'd seen plenty of horrors in her life. She pushed the door open and went inside.

It didn't stink, or at least not too bad. The place was deserted. Then she heard a panting, a stifled voice, a struggle, thrashing, and choking. She hobbled past the line of sinks, careful to avoid putting her cane in the wet spots on the floor, and she looked around the corner into the long room with stall doors to either side. At the back, in the last stall, two young men were standing in front of an open door. A woman's long legs were stretched out on the floor, her feet in sandals with narrow red straps. For a moment, Nana thought she was giving birth and the sounds were those of a woman in labor—until she saw a man get up from between the girl's long legs, hauling up his pants while the next man in line undid his belt buckle and dropped his trousers.

A wave of hot indignation struck her. Her breathing accelerated, and her eyes filled with tears of pure fury. "What you doing?!" she yelled as loud as she could.

The three men looked around, surprised at first and then amused. "Get your ass out of here, old woman," one of them called with a sneer. He grabbed his crotch and shook it at her. "Or maybe you want some too?"

Nana shook violently. Without stopping to think, she advanced on them. Feeling her cane slipping and unsteady in her trembling hands, she still went for them, staggering and driven by a fury and hatred she'd felt only once before, during that other hurricane.

One of them came out, laughing and mocking, to receive her. He stretched out his arms as if to hug her. Nana clenched her right hand into a fist and threw it with all her strength at the man's chest. He intercepted it, grabbed her wrists, and effortlessly moved her backward toward the sinks, almost as if leading her in a waltz. Nana wept her hatred. Her tears burned, poisoned by guilt and impotence as she struggled against him. He chuckled and pushed her back with delicate motions as if trying to avoid hurting her, which just humiliated her even more. Once he'd moved her all the way back to the door, as if to counteract his attitude, he said, "Get out of here, old lady, I don't wanna hurt you. You remind me of my granny."

Nana was spent. Her arms ached from the struggle, her legs shook with fright, his tight grip about her wrists had hurt her hands. From the back of the restroom, she heard the moans, twice as loud now, of the woman whose face she hadn't even seen. Their sobs united them, sisters in misery. Nana could do no more. She hated her old woman's body, her sluggish, useless body filled with rage and hatred. She looked up to see her assailant watching her with obvious indifference, maybe even a touch of sympathy. All that anger and resentment rose up and burst forth from her mouth with the force of a fury from hell. "Damn you! I curse you and those dogs, in the name of your grandmother, your mother, and in the names of all the women buried in your family graves!" she screamed, jabbing her finger at him. "May you be damned for eternity and never see the light, may your semen rot your guts, may you never find peace!"

His face darkened as Nana heaped her maledictions upon him. All amusement disappeared. He pursed his lips and started shaking his head. He was confused. "What you saying, you damn old witch?"

"I curse you!" Nana continued, her contempt doubling as she distilled into words all her rage and pain, her disgust growing in measure with his cowardly alarm.

"Shut yo' mouth!" he almost pleaded.

She filled her lungs, raised her chin, and looked deep into his eyes. *"Maudit!"* she answered, knowing it was so.

He panicked. His breathing was fast and labored. His eyes bulged from the surge of adrenaline. He raised one immense fist and aimed it at Nana's face.

The lights went out everywhere in the Superdome.

Nana sensed the speed of the punch, felt the displacement of air, and heard the tremendous bang just beside her ear as his fist slammed into the wall. Her legs gave way. She slid to the floor. On all fours she groped numbly for the door. She pushed it and kept crawling until the humidity and heat told her she was back in the tunnel. The only illumination was from the emergency lights pointing the way to the exits. She dragged herself to the wall and somehow found handholds that let her get back to her feet. Leaning against the concrete block wall, she took one step after another, wondering how she could still hear the stifled sobbing of that poor woman before finally realizing she was the one making those agonized sounds. She stopped and forced herself to breathe deeply and steadily. There was a draft in the passage, and it built to a steady blast, as if she were standing in a wind tunnel instead of sheltering in a stadium passage. She felt a spreading wetness below her waist. She knew what it was, but even so, her hand went between her legs to verify her shame.

The lights came back on and Nana began to scream.

30

Not Tonight

New Orleans, Louisiana
Early morning, Monday, August 29, 2005

Amaia came awake slowly and listened carefully. She made out rhythmic breathing. Johnson and Charbou were sound asleep despite the roar of the storm and the constant ringing of telephones in the command center next door, which was only slightly muted by the walls. She assumed Dupree and Bull were still busy somewhere else in the fire station. Checking her watch, she found it was almost five in the morning. Dawn would arrive soon, though as yet the covered window admitted no light.

From the cot she could see some of the crime scene photos they'd sorted spread out across the conference table. Disorder, destruction, and chaos ruled each scene. Her impressions were jumbled. She was absolutely certain crucial clues were to be found at the crime scenes, and she hadn't been able to get them out of her head. The answer lay in the killer's staging, again and again, a desired outcome. Was it some sort of macabre therapy in which he took out his bitterness upon others? Or were these just rehearsals for an upcoming final act? If so, what was he waiting for, what permission did he need before murdering his entire family a second time? How many more times would he be driven to rehearse his final solution?

She closed her eyes and called up images—Lenx, alone, smiling at the photographer; Brad Nelson in a group of policemen at a party; the Lenx daughter and Nelson's, both redheads; Lenx's wife with her prudish, fearful expression; Nelson's Sarah, confident and smiling. The two women were so different! Amaia wondered if this was the sort of adjustment a psychopath would be capable of making. Would he seek out a good-looking, independent wife? That didn't fit Lenx as Amaia understood him. Captain Reed had tried to convince them the Nelsons' domestic disturbance hadn't been terribly serious, yet he'd acknowledged it wasn't the first time Nelson had gotten carried away. Brad Nelson had tried to force his wife to accept his way of thinking and return to the fold.

Sarah Nelson's smile on her driver's license looked carefree, but Amaia knew that meant little. Could she have been enduring abuse? Violence, even? And then there was the business about Nelson sneaking into a church. It would have been interesting to have photos of the Nelson home before and after the domestic dispute that brought the police into the picture. Nelson's wife left him after that and took the children almost a thousand miles away. What would Lenx do in that situation? Resolve it the way he had eighteen years earlier? He'd go after them, certainly. But if he was a policeman now, he couldn't just go running off to kill them all.

Someone opened the door at the end of the hall. The clamor of dozens of telephones ringing simultaneously burst across her like an ocean wave, then lowered abruptly when the door swung shut. She had the impression that the incoming calls in the operations center had intensified over the last hour. She needed to think, but as her mind grappled with the information she'd received over the last twenty-four hours, she realized she was going in circles, a sure sign that sleep was about to overpower her. She could choose to resist it or give in. Falling asleep wasn't deliberate, and sleep wasn't something she willingly yielded to. It stole up on her like a thief in the night. It kidnapped her consciousness while she struggled and resisted. She'd always been that way.

And . . .

She's very tired, but she knows she mustn't sleep, so she forces herself to open her eyes, sit up, and leave the bed. She feels the warmth of the waxed floorboards beneath her. She looks down at her little feet, tiny and pale, shuffling across the dark floor to stand between her sisters' beds. Ros's eyes are closed, and she looks like she's sleeping, her long, dark hair in an intricate braid stark against her pillow.

Flora, also with her hair in a braid, is reading by the light of the little bronze lamp with the mermaid base. Flora becomes aware of her sister's presence and puts down the book with an annoyed expression. "You again? Now what's wrong?"

Amaia takes a deep breath and exhales before answering. "I'm scared, Flora. Let me sleep with you."

"I already said no. You better go back to bed before Ama *finds out."*

Ros opens her eyes and pushes herself up on one elbow. She heard everything, but she repeats the question anyway. That's just how Rosaura is. "Amaia, what's wrong? Why aren't you asleep?" She regards Amaia with infinite patience.

"Ros, I'm really, really scared. Let me sleep next to you." Her voice breaks. She's about to cry, but she wills herself not to, because Flora makes fun of her whenever she weeps.

"Amaia, there's nothing to be afraid of." As usual, Ros speaks slowly to her, as if Amaia is just a baby. "Flora's bed is by the door, and I'm here too. We'll protect you."

"Not me!" Flora contradicts her. "I don't protect anybody at night. All I do is sleep. And you two had better do that too. I'm going to turn off the light."

Amaia is terribly tired, and she feels everything slipping away. "No, no, no, don't turn out the light, don't do that, don't turn it off, don't turn out the light!"

Despite the chill in their bedroom, Amaia is sweating in terror, her eyes squeezed shut. She's sinking fast. She tries opening her eyes wide, but that triggers the first tears, and after that, they flow freely down her cheeks, a torrent of fear and anguish.

"Please!" she begs in a whisper, so exhausted she's almost inaudible.

Moved by her weeping, Ros opens the covers and makes room. "Come on. Get in."

Amaia curls up tight against her sister, making herself as tiny as possible. Ros is talking to her from somewhere far away. "But you'll have to go back to your own bed before Ama *comes to get us up, because she'll get mad if she sees you here. Amaia? Are you listening?"*

Amaia doesn't hear her. Safe now, she's sleeping deeply.

Then . . .

Her eyes fly open. Instead of the deep silence she expects, there is a loud pealing in her head. The bells continue, reverberating, ding-dong. She sits up and looks at her sisters, amazed that the deafening clamor hasn't awakened them. She realizes that behind the tolling, there's a furious roaring, like gusting wind or a house on fire. She senses something close by; she turns to look at the doorway and glimpses the pearly silk of her mother's robe, billowing as she walks down the hall. Amaia slips out of bed, and her bare feet encounter the floor, now cold; the house is freezing. She peeks out and sees the amber-colored light reflected from the living room. Her mother is still visible, far away, her back turned to Amaia. The rear hem of the robe floats after her, a ghostly wake. Ding-dong! Amaia tells herself that it has to be a dream. No one in this house, no one in all of Elizondo, could sleep through this tolling.

The ominous insistence of the bells shocks her. She puts her hands over her ears, trying to shut out the sound, and she becomes aware of an evil portent—a loud, dreadful breathing that fills the intervals between the peals. She stares about her. Blood streams from the bedrooms, pooling in the living room. Shaking with cold and fright, she goes slowly down the hall.

She finds an entire family laid out on the floor, first the adults, then the children from oldest to youngest. The littlest one is her own age. Ding-dong! The horrid, deafening tolling erupts from the walls of the music room in an evocation of Judgment Day. Amaia is shaking violently from the cold. The arms of the dead lie lax along their bodies; she avoids looking at their hands. Each head in that precisely laid-out line is oriented toward the river that Amaia knows is north of them. Small-caliber bullets have left a dark circular mark in each forehead. She's terrified because she knows their wounds are impossibly deep. The hair of the littlest boy, the one closest to her, is tousled and tangled as if he'd squirmed and thrashed under the covers in his sleep. Blood from his broken skull has gushed out and soaked his hair, turning it into a dark, sticky mass that looks like molasses. The blood puddles next to him, slowly oozing toward Amaia. Her heart breaks. She feels an irresistible urge to stanch the flow with her own hands, even though she knows she shouldn't.

She opens her eyes and sees that Rosario's face is inches from her own. Her mother's expression is one of absolute disdain.

"Maybe you think it doesn't matter when? One night is the same as another?" Rosario asks with contempt written across her face. "You think none of this matters?" Rosario makes a grand gesture, her arms encompassing the living room, the bodies, the music. She comes closer, so terrifyingly close that her hot, sour breath stirs Amaia's hair across her brow. "Maybe you think I'm crazy? No . . . Ama *isn't going to gobble you up tonight! Go to sleep, you little vixen."*

Amaia bolted upright as if erupting through the surface of a frozen lake. Trembling in terror, she was drenched in perspiration and cold dread. She fought for breath and looked around, hoping she hadn't screamed, knowing she hadn't slept, certain she'd closed her eyes for only a few seconds.

Do the dead stand at the foot of your bed, Salazar? Dupree's voice berated her in her mind. *It's a goddamn hallucination, for fuck's sake! Stress, fatigue, worry, and a half-waking dream. Just a goddamn hallucination.*

"The dead are . . . just dead. That's all," she whispered, trying to convince herself. She realized she'd said that aloud, and she whipped around to make sure the other team members were still asleep.

They were.

Groggy, she got up and fumbled her way to the door. In her confusion she thought that maybe the roar of the storm would help fend off her nightmare. *Maybe you think I'm crazy?*

Almost instantly, the wind seemed to double in strength. It became a howl almost human. Amaia pressed a hand to her chest, shaken suddenly by an obscure shudder, and she followed her instinct to seek the light. There had to be distinctions; it wasn't true that one night was the same as another. There was no such thing as chance, and when her mother came gliding silently to her bed, it wasn't to grant her another night's sleep. *Ama* wasn't sparing her life; she was confirming a death sentence. Just as Martin Lenx had done.

The operations center was boiling hot, even though the air-conditioning was turned up high. In the blue glow of a dozen flat screens hung from the ceiling, Amaia saw images from traffic cameras. Rain and wind swept along deserted streets. The furious blast propelled branches, signs, plastic sheeting, boards ripped from windows, and gutters torn away from roofs by the impact of the hurricane. More than half the screens showed nothing, for the storm shaking the cameras reduced the images to gray, unfocused blobs.

The high temperature was due both to the lack of windows and to the combined body heat of all the people in the room. Thirty operators sat at computer screens, and a dozen assistants moved from workstation to workstation. The supervisor stood at the central desk next to his deputy, the woman they'd briefed about how to identify an attack by the Composer. She beckoned to Amaia. She poured iced coffee into a paper cup and gave it to Amaia. She didn't get up; instead, she pulled another chair close to her workstation so Amaia could join her.

"Sit here, sweetie. This place is a madhouse." She pointed overhead to one of the monitors showing surging gray sheets of rain whipping through the darkness. "Katrina's in Louisiana; she came ashore over Buras, in the western Mississippi Delta. That's a traffic camera out on the interstate. That's all we have. All the other lines are down. The hurricane center's talking about a twenty-eight-foot hurricane tide."

Amaia stared at her, impressed. "Twenty-eight feet, that is . . ."

"Honey, it just *is*."

Amaia saw that the woman was terrified.

"We have no way to confirm the reports. Most of what we've got is rumors passed along from 911. Communications are down all along the coast. They say Gulfport and Biloxi are underwater." She took a shuddering breath. "I have friends down there."

Amaia saw the glint of tears in the woman's eyes.

"And here in the city?" Amaia asked, wanting information but wanting just as much to change the subject.

"Some places have been without power since it went down this morning. Lucky for us, the phones are still working. What we're really worried about is that when the power came back on, some of the pumps along the main drains failed. They're dead. The hurricane center says the flood tide is going to push water from Lake Pontchartrain toward the coast. It's already over the banks and flooding the nearest houses. In fact, it's right downstairs, outside this building."

Amaia found that incredible.

"But it's not the lake we're worried about. Those floodwaters won't move very fast. This has happened before. But if the hurricane winds push the Mississippi waters upstream, like with Hurricane Betsy, they might crest above the levees. In some spots, the city's six feet or more below sea level, so if those pumps don't start, the streets'll fill up. And it's going to keep raining. Central City has just started to flood, but water's flowing in torrents out on Highway 90."

The power cut off again as she was speaking, leaving the operators' monitors and the overhead screens dark. A disappointed groan went through the room.

"Y'all relax, the generator's going to start in a minute!" the supervisor shouted to make himself heard above the growing din of complaints. "Let's take it easy until the power's back on."

Dupree appeared in the doorway, silhouetted by the emergency lighting, and gestured insistently to Amaia. Outside she found Johnson and the New Orleans detectives on the landing. They set off down the stairs as soon as they saw her.

"Agent Tucker has located Nelson and his group. They're at the Charity Hospital emergency room. We can't get through by phone, but the fire chief has a radio link to Charity's emergency operations. He got to Chief Meigs, in charge of Nelson's group. We're due to talk to him in two minutes."

"What about radio silence?" asked Bull. They'd decided to avoid unencrypted communications because the killer might be monitoring them.

"It's not on the official frequency; we're using a standby channel. Even if he's monitoring, he probably won't be sweeping all the channels. And besides, we have no other choice."

The firefighters occupied the bottom two floors of the building. The ground-floor garage was flooded. The glassed-in reception area was located at the front of the building, halfway between the garage level and the floor with offices and crew space. Three large sofas sat around a blank television. The radio console stood behind a partition.

The water outside was surging across the steps that led up to the reception space. Several men huddled together at the picture window, peering out at the darkness and talking energetically. They'd didn't seem to feel the least threatened by the rising water. A turtle the size of a man's hand struck the glass, propelled by the surge. Surprised and delighted, the men cheered. Amaia had observed similar excitement in a weather forecaster on a Kenner television station, emotional agitation that verged on exhilaration. The firefighters were venting it with jokes and laughter, though she detected repressed concern in their expressions. For the following five minutes, they were entertained as one of them, suited up with protective gear and clutching a shovel, carefully made his way down the exterior steps into hip-deep water, scooped up the turtle, and deposited it safely on the top step. His colleagues cheered his spectacular accomplishment.

A minute later, the fire chief signaled that their radio call was ready. He brought the group into the little glassed-in radio dispatch booth; the operator greeted them and pointed to the microphone with the red button set up on the table. "It's really simple. Press to talk, release to listen. Remember to say 'over' after each transmission, so the others know you're done."

He leaned over and pressed the button. Dupree had dialed in Tucker and Emerson; he set his cell phone by the loudspeaker so they could hear the conversation.

"Attention, Charity, this is the fire station at Lake Pontchartrain. I'm giving you the FBI. Over."

"This is Chief Meigs at Charity Hospital in the ambulance garage. Over."

Dupree motioned for Johnson to sit in front of the microphone.

"Chief Meigs, this is FBI special agent Ambrose Johnson. We're investigating a case, and we need to confirm the presence of one of your team members on several of the missions you've carried out in recent months. His name is Brad Nelson. Over."

"Happy to help you guys. What do you need to know? Over."

"Was Nelson on the mission to Cape May, New Jersey, last February? Over."

"He was. That was his first outing with the team, but it turned out there wasn't much for us to do. The damage didn't extend too far beyond the shoreline, and they had things pretty much in hand by the time we arrived. Over."

"How about March fifteenth in Killeen, Texas? Over."

"Yes, Nelson was with us. Over."

"Next is Brooksville, Oklahoma, on April twenty-sixth. Over."

"Yes . . . hold on, now, I'm not sure. I know he went out there with us, but he didn't ship out at the same time afterward. He was called back by some sort of emergency. I wasn't there when he left. His partner will know more than I do. Sometimes we have to break into smaller units. The smallest is the buddy team. Over."

"Can you give me the name of his partner that time? Is that team member with you now? Can we talk to him? Over."

"He was with Phil Lorenzo. Phil's here, but he's been sent out already. The hurricane blew off part of the Superdome's roof, and there's rain pouring in on the people there. Word came in about twenty minutes ago, and we were dispatched because our team was closest to the scene. I was just about to leave when they said you needed to speak to me. If it's urgent, I can get Phil to a radio as soon as possible, but it could be several hours from now. Over."

"We understand the difficult circumstances, but we wouldn't be troubling you if it weren't vital. We'd appreciate it if you could put Phil Lorenzo in contact with us as soon as possible. Just a couple more questions. Did Nelson go with you to Alvord, Texas, last week? Over."

"Yeah, he was there, but not the whole time. He couldn't get away immediately. He arrived a few hours after we did. Over."

"How much later? Over."

"Hmm . . . seems to me we got there around noon, and he came in that night. Over."

"Was he with you in Miami three days ago? Over."

"Right. He went there on his own because he was close to the scene. Drove to Miami in his personal vehicle, so he was waiting for us at the airport. Over."

"And he traveled to New Orleans as part of the group? Over."

"No, Nelson isn't here; he had to work. He let us know at the last minute that he couldn't come. Over."

Johnson turned to look at Dupree and Amaia.

"He made a leave request in Tampa," Dupree said under his breath.

Johnson turned back to the mic and pressed the red button. "Chief Meigs, this is very important: Can you confirm that Brad Nelson didn't travel to New Orleans? Maybe he's going to join you later? We understand he requested leave for that reason. Over."

"Hundred percent sure. Happens all the time. Remember, these guys are police officers, firefighters, paramedics—emergencies happen, and they have to cancel at the last minute. Over."

Johnson thanked the chief, signed off, and turned to his colleagues. "Where is Nelson?"

Charbou answered. "I'll tell you where he is: here in New Orleans. You heard Meigs. Nelson was on location everywhere the murders occurred. Any alibi he might pretend to have is blown by the fact his timing is sometimes erratic. It shows he had ample unsupervised time to commit the murders when he was working with the teams. We can't eliminate him as a suspect."

"I agree," Tucker said via telephone. "Traveling solo gives him options. He has the authorization both from his employers and from the rescue group. He's a cop, he has a badge and rescue credentials. That's all he needs to circulate in a disaster zone. If anyone spots him, he explains he's getting there at the last minute and comes across as a hero."

Dupree listened, analyzing Tucker's contentions, head tilted in thought. "What do you think, Johnson?"

"We're getting ahead of ourselves. First thing to do would be to check whether there really was an emergency, something that kept him from traveling. Some things still don't fit. But when it comes to opportunity, I have to admit he could be the one."

"Yes," Dupree conceded. "At first it seemed unlikely, but arriving as part of a rescue team justifies his presence in each place. It also means he's being watched and supervised. At first glance, that suggests he'd have trouble getting away long enough to commit the crimes, but what we've just heard shows it might've been easier than I thought. Maybe he claimed he was busy somewhere else or dispatched to a different area. They're under local command, so if the team splits up, I doubt anyone but his buddy could vouch for him. And Meigs confirmed that the team does get divided. For example, how difficult would it be for Phil Lorenzo, traveling right now between Charity Hospital and the Superdome, to get away from the team for, let's see . . . How long do you think it would take him to locate pre-identified targets, round them up, kill them, and rejoin the team?"

Tucker's voice was a metallic rattle that dropped out briefly but came back again. "For the actual murders, between twenty and thirty minutes. So an hour and a half max, assuming he's got it planned. The witness told us he's quick. He goes to do the job, carries it out, then leaves. Fits the profile of the perp; everything is prepared in advance. He's not there to enjoy himself. That wouldn't be characteristic of someone conducting a rite of purification and then disguising his targets as victims of the storm. Travel time is another question entirely. Moving around in a disaster zone has to be difficult, and we've got to keep in mind that in every case, he got to the families before any other rescue personnel. And that was with communications cut and roads impassable. But it seems to me that the real problem is that we have no idea how he chooses his victims."

Dupree kept his eyes on Amaia as she was hearing the others out; she hadn't joined the discussion. He'd seen a change in her over the past few hours, and it wasn't just fatigue. She was withdrawn, and her face had the look of someone beginning to intuit a harrowing insight; he took this as a sign she'd deciphered something the others hadn't grasped. Her colleagues were debating among themselves while she stood motionless, her eyes on the floor, as if saving her energy to deal with some thought that was draining her spirit.

Dupree called on her. "Salazar?"

She took a step forward. Her voice, in contrast to the anguish in her face, was clear and firm. "We've agreed that the Composer and Martin Lenx are probably the same person."

They nodded.

"I seriously doubt those identities can be reconciled in Nelson." They started to protest, but she stopped them. "Yes, I know he fits the timeline, but the evidence is all circumstantial. We have a lot on Lenx: the crime scene details, the photos, and the letter he left for his pastor. All we have for the Composer is his obsession with re-creating this ritual presentation. That's all the evidence we can rely on to catch this killer. From the Composer's staging of the scene, we've deduced how he presents himself and behaves to take in his victims, and that has to be the basis of the investigation. We have six crime scenes spread out across the eastern half of the country to compare against Martin Lenx's murder of his family in Wisconsin eighteen years ago. The comparisons are complicated by the force of the natural disasters, but when we filter out those elements, each crime scene is just as orderly and unspoiled as the original one in the music room in Madison."

"We've all accepted that," Tucker declared, annoyed. "What are you trying to get at?"

Amaia ignored Tucker's sharp tone. "What I'm trying to get at is that Nelson, enraged by a difference of opinion with his wife over their children, smashed up their living room. His chief in Galveston said the place looked like a tornado had hit it."

"It was like that in the other cases," Charbou pointed out.

She shook her head decisively. "No, it wasn't, and that's what's confusing us. Nelson smashed his living room furniture when he flew into a rage, and that wasn't the first time he had done it. Nelson is choleric; when he gets angry, he loses control. It happened often enough to make his wife want to pack up and leave with the kids. Martin Lenx, on the other hand, put up with years of frustration, years of disappointment when nothing went as he'd hoped. And then, on top of all that, there was the children's disobedience and his wife's indulgence of them.

"His finances were a disaster. He'd taken out loans with the house as collateral. His world was falling apart. And in all the months leading up to the murders, he never gave a sign he was even the least bit upset—not to his family or the people at work, not to the other members of his congregation. In fact, in all those interviews, and there were plenty, everyone talked about his controlled character, his discretion, his excellent manners. Martin Lenx never lost his calm.

"Lenx ended it all in one bloody day. From his first murder, his mother, to his last, his older son, Lenx stayed unperturbed. He had more than enough time to feel guilty, to regret what he'd done, but he didn't. When he finished, he went to the kitchen, where he'd put writing paper and a fountain pen. He took the time to write a three-page letter to his minister. The lines were straight and perfectly spaced. The graphologists tell us he was completely calm when he wrote it. You know the rest.

"Not a single one of Martin Lenx's actions was unconsidered, impulsive, or taken on the spur of the moment. Nothing in the man was hasty or spontaneous.

And in each of the six mass murders over the last eight months, he repeated that pattern down to the tiniest detail."

Maybe you think I'm crazy? Rosario's voice echoed in Amaia's mind. She closed her eyes for a moment and concentrated on blocking out the image of her mother bending close above her. "One night is not the same as another."

She immediately regretted saying that but couldn't take it back.

Dupree had hunkered down into that pensive posture of his, studying her. He knew she was speaking of her own experience. "What are you talking about, Salazar? Lenx murdered his family in the daytime."

She shut her eyes. "I meant to say that no day is the same as another. And no moment. The chosen moment is what counts. Not one of those six mass murders, scrupulously compared with that of his original family, can be seen as a separate action. They were rehearsals for the real thing. Every time he kills, he confirms death sentences he's already passed on his true intended victims, his current family."

Dupree prompted her calmly, as if he already knew the answer. "And why hasn't he carried them out?"

Amaia again had a vision of her mother leaning close, night after night, throughout her childhood. She looked around. "Because one night isn't the same as another. He was waiting for a sign. The sign is essential. It constituted part of the ritual."

"'*Was* waiting'?" Tucker sounded confused on the other end of the line. "'Constituted'?"

"I meant to say 'constitutes,'" Amaia corrected herself, coming back to the subject, momentarily squeezing her eyes to push the image away. "The sword of Damocles he has hanging over his victims makes him feel powerful, but it requires him to wait for just the right moment to let it drop. That gives us a clear picture of his mental state. He's not tormented or enraged. Not a single piece of evidence suggests he's capable of the kind of fury that drove Brad Nelson to smash up his house during the argument with his wife."

"Are you saying that the destruction in every one of those crime scenes isn't an expression of uncontrolled rage? I thought that's exactly what we concluded from Lenx's referencing destruction in the Bible," Tucker asserted across the line. Static and the poor connection gave her tone a malevolent edge.

"Destruction, yes," Amaia asserted, "but the Composer left the destruction in God's hands. Divine retribution rendered via natural disaster, a judgment Lenx didn't dictate but did accept. Moreover, Johnson and I both find it hard to believe that a man with Lenx's fervent moral and religious convictions would manifest no sign of them in his new identity."

"Don't forget that the Galveston police chief saw him sneaking into a church," Dupree reminded her. "Maybe he decided to hide his religious zeal in his new life."

Amaia didn't accept that. "I do find that strange, but I think it really unlikely a fervent Lutheran like Lenx would switch to Catholicism. He relies on faith to justify the killings. That's a profoundly Lutheran view, in stark contrast to the Catholic doctrine that good works offer redemption even for those who lack faith. Martin Lenx wasn't going to pardon anyone's trespasses. His victims were offending God, and Martin saw himself as God's appointed avenger."

She motioned to Johnson, who took up the thread. "And then there's the grandmother. We've confirmed there was a grandmother, or at least a surrogate, in each case. He considers that important. But Nelson's parents died a long time ago. His wife was still a child when her mother died. His children are older, and the Nelsons have never had a servant or nanny who could be considered a grandmother stand-in."

Emerson spoke up for the first time. "Okay, I understand the assistant inspector's reasoning, but it's possible that this time he couldn't exactly match all the patterns of his previous life. If, as Salazar suggests, he sees his current existence as a new, improved version, he could have modified some things. Changing religion could have been a deliberate tactic to make sure he'd never come face to face with anyone from his former parish, even by chance."

Amaia snorted. "Of course I don't believe he was trying to reproduce the errors of his previous life, but his Lutheran faith was vital to him, more important than anything else, and the grandmother role was so crucial that he included it in each mass murder. So much so that at the Allens' farm he ran her down in a field and stuffed her body under the roof. He might have been trying to correct errors from his previous life, but I think he's fated to repeat them. After all, he's striving to realize an impossible ideal. The everyday lives of these families have more in common than appears at first sight. They were going through the same sorts of conflicts that inevitably occur as children grow up."

"And if they weren't, you'd have to wonder why," Johnson added. "He probably kept them under his thumb when they were younger, but kids usually try to exert their independence as soon as they hit their teenage years. Things tend to get tense, the way they did with the Lenxes. And if his current spouse declined to back up his inflexible demands, maybe her opposition triggered a reversion to previous behavior patterns. No new family could ever live up to his expectations, I guarantee you that."

Tucker tried to comment, but her voice was garbled through the static. It cut out, came back, then dropped out entirely.

Dupree called her back. "Sorry, Agent Tucker," he said when she picked up. "I'm afraid we're about to lose our connection. The Internet is still up, so we can resort to email if we have to. Go ahead with what you were saying." He put his mobile on speaker phone.

"Right. I don't agree with your analysis, Assistant Inspector Salazar. I think Nelson's our man. Sounds to me like every objection you're making just confirms it. Emerson thinks so too. Johnson, how about you?"

"I'm with Salazar. I don't think Nelson fits the profile at all. There are enough similarities for us to maintain him as a person of interest, and obviously we should keep tabs on him to see what he gets up to if he's here in the city. First step would be to verify whether he's riding out the storm at home."

"What do you want on your pizza?" Tucker asked.

"Double servings of anchovies and olives," Johnson replied.

Bill and Bull gaped at the cell phone and at Johnson's broad grin.

"It's a little trick we like to use to check whether someone's at home. One of our agents disguised as a pizza delivery person turns up with an order." Johnson smiled again. "Anyone will open the door to a pizza delivery man, even if no one placed an order."

The cell phone screen went dark. Their connection was gone. Dupree tried to call Tucker again but couldn't get through.

31

Eternal Sleep

Superdome, New Orleans
8:45 a.m., Monday, August 29, 2005

Nana pushed a sedative tablet between her lips and swallowed it without water, her own saliva forcing it down to the ball of anxiety inside her. She leaned against the wall, trying to ease the pressure on her right hip. Intense pain shot up her leg from heel to waist, and agonizing cramps threatened to throw her off balance. She closed her eyes, focused on waiting for the sedative effects of the pill to kick in, and tried to convince herself relief was on the way.

She'd taken refuge in the Superdome passageway almost three hours earlier. At six o'clock in the morning, a furious gust of wind had ripped open the roof above their heads and heavy rain had burst into the stadium. Soaked and panicked, the three of them first sought shelter in the access tunnel, but the surge of frantic bodies pushed them farther and farther beneath the stands. Bobby jammed his mother's wheelchair against the wall and helped Nana find a place alongside it, her pillow on the concrete floor. Nana had slumped against the wall, overcome. She rested her head against Seletha's chair and dully watched the pushing, milling crowd look for places to deposit their possessions. The heat was intense. Her hair was drenched, but at least the pee stain on her skirt had dried and left only a whitish circle. Nana rubbed it in disgust but saw a worried Bobby watching her.

"It's okay, Nana. It ain't important, and besides, you don't hardly see it anymore."

She closed her eyes.

When she'd staggered out from the restroom where those men were raping that woman, her screams attracted the attention of a group of youngsters hanging out by the stairs; she told them what was happening. They stopped the game they were playing and stared in consternation at the door to the women's restroom. A girl said she'd seen a policeman at the nearest gate, and a couple of boys ran there for help. It took forever. In the meantime, Nana saw three men leave the restroom and disappear into the crowd. A bedraggled woman tottered out not long afterward, fumbling at her torn clothing.

By the time the boys got back with two cops, she was nowhere to be seen.

"They were raping a woman," Nana cried. "Three men, but now they gone!"

The officers looked at one another and went into the restroom. They came out almost immediately. "Nobody there," declared one, his hand resting on his nightstick.

"I told you already, they gone!" Nana said. "Three of them, I couldn't do nothing."

One officer noticed the stain on her skirt. "Ma'am, are you here with someone? You better stay somewhere safe. And please stay out of the restrooms. They're dangerous."

Two of the girls retrieved her cane and helped her back to her seat. And that was that. No one did anything, because there was nothing to be done. Nana, Bobby, and Seletha had stayed in place all night. Nana said nothing, but she brooded on those shitty goings-on until the Superdome roof flew off and they had to seek shelter elsewhere in the stadium.

She stared down unhappily at the spreading brown puddle approaching her. Because the hurricane tide and rising waters had backed up the toilets, watery human waste was flowing out of the restrooms. Superdome toilets and sinks had begun to vomit forth warm geysers of turbid water contaminated with human feces. She was so exhausted, she hadn't even noticed the nasty flow was about to soak the cushion she was sitting on. Bobby helped her get up, apologizing profusely as if he were somehow to blame for the shit erupting from the toilets. He grabbed Nana's pillow, pulled off the stained cover, and gave back the pillow, which now had only a little yellow-brownish stain at one corner.

Bobby put his palm across his mother's damp forehead. "I think she got fever."

"Really hot in here," Nana commented, resolved to minimize the seriousness of their plight.

"Mama, wake up! Mama? Mama!" Bobby put his ear to her mouth, trying to detect breathing. He lifted her eyelids to check her pupils; they were of different sizes and didn't respond to the light. He took her hand and entreated her. "Mama, wake up, Mama, please wake up!" He was desperate.

Bobby grabbed one of her fingers and pressed the base of the nail. He applied so much force he broke the skin and a trickle of blood appeared. Seletha did not react.

Bobby turned, terrified, to Nana. "Nana, I think my mama is dying!"

32

Anchovies and Olives

Tampa, Florida

Through the tinted windows of the surveillance van, Agent Tucker made out a couple of billowing clouds sailing across Tampa's blue sky. Her view of the door to Brad Nelson's rental was partly blocked by the townhouse next door.

They'd been watching the place for almost an hour in the eighty-five-degree heat. The air-conditioning wasn't on, so the interior of the van was stifling. Tucker was doing her best to concentrate on the briefing memo Amaia had sent. She sighed and glanced behind her into the body of the van. The body heat and reek of sweat from the three men back there was just about more than she could stand. They'd tapped into Brad Nelson's phone line as one of their officers, pretending to be an operator, rang his number until the answering machine came on. That didn't prove he wasn't home; he might have checked caller ID and decided not to pick up. They masked their number to match that of Nelson's cell phone service provider and tried to reach him via his mobile.

"The number you have called is not responding or is out of coverage at this time."

She was relieved when she saw the scooter with the pizza carrier on the rear. She rolled up the report she'd been reading and signaled to the tech to check the radio frequency and verify that the agent outside could hear them clearly. Her man gave her a thumbs-up, and the operation commenced. The young officer parked his scooter at the curb, crossed the graveled space past the untended plants in Nelson's small front yard, and approached the door.

"Go!" Tucker told him by radio.

He pressed the doorbell. Nothing. A second time. Still nothing.

"Ring again," Tucker insisted.

No response.

Tucker let a few more seconds pass as she studied the tableau from her vantage point in the van. "Try one more time to be sure, then you can snake the camera under the door."

The officer rang a couple of times. The next-door neighbor, a man in his seventies wearing pajamas with an unbuttoned top, opened his front door. He leaned on the railing of his front steps and stared at the pizza man. "Son, I don't much think my neighbor ordered your pizza."

"Don't break character," Tucker radioed. She knew from experience that neighbors could be a rich source of information.

The officer pretended to consult his notebook. "Well, sir, I have an order for a family-size pizza with double olives, double anchovies, and double capers for a Brad Nelson, 556B Tivoli Avenue. Did I get anything wrong?"

"Yeah, that's here, and Brad Nelson is my neighbor, but it looks like someone's playing a practical joke on you. I saw Nelson putting luggage in his SUV, and he told me he was taking a trip."

The pizza man sighed in disgust. "Yeah, I guess that's it. There's a bunch of kids making phony orders. We should have known. Not many people want anchovies for breakfast." He went down the steps as if returning to his scooter, then stopped. "Maybe you know when Mr. Nelson's coming back? He's a good customer. I got the pizza here, if he's coming back soon, maybe I could just leave it on the porch."

"Don't bet on it, son. He said he'd be away for a couple of days, maybe more. But if you want to leave the pizza with me . . ."

Snickers filled the van. The agents exchanged exaggerated grimaces of disgust.

Tucker got out of the van and walked to her rental car, her sweat-soaked shirt plastered to her back. She tapped her hip with the rolled-up report from Salazar. *Fuck, don't those jerks know they need to wear deodorant?* She urgently wanted a shower to get rid of the stench, but first she had to do something more important. She opened the car door and settled into the passenger seat.

"Okay," Emerson said as he pulled into the street, "we've confirmed Nelson's not in town, so he's probably on his way to New Orleans. Or he's already there. You going to call Agent Dupree?"

"Phone lines and cell service have been down since this morning, and they evacuated the FBI office. It's going to be complicated to get back in touch. And impossible once they leave the ops center."

Emerson lapsed into a pensive silence. For a moment, Tucker thought he was reflecting on what she'd just said, but to her surprise he volunteered an opinion. "Salazar is wrong. Nelson is the Composer."

Tucker's head swiveled. She regarded him with interest. "Oh, yeah? Just what did she get wrong?"

Emerson looked at Tucker until she gestured, warning him to keep his eyes on the road. He stammered a bit as he presented his thesis. "Well, uh, she's just wrong . . . there in her analysis." He pointed to the report in Tucker's hand. "She thinks Martin Lenx is the Composer, but she doesn't agree Lenx could have assumed Nelson's identity."

"You think she's off base?"

He glanced at her again, confused. He was trying to insinuate himself, to show that he was on her side, but she was being particularly unreceptive. "Well, I just think we're right and she's wrong."

"She gave a brilliant analysis; the woman is practically clairvoyant. We're fortunate to have her on the team. You'd do well, Agent Emerson, to take a few lessons from her. If you want to make a career in the FBI, remember not to doubt what a woman says just because she's a woman. Think twice before opening your mouth."

Emerson emitted an anguished whimper. "I don't understand! You don't agree with her either."

"The difference is that I respect her. You can brownnose all you want, but if you think I'm going to gang up with you to criticize a woman who's worth two of you, you have another think coming."

Emerson released a stream of air through his nose and chose to remain silent, uncertain how to respond to her criticism.

Tucker smiled again. She took out her mobile, looked up a contact, and pressed a button. “No reason to be down in the mouth, Emerson. Maybe Nelson’s in New Orleans. And who knows, Salazar may even be right.” She waved the rolled-up report at him. “But believe me, you and I are in the right place at the right time.”

33

Pieces of Silver

Washington, DC
Monday, August 29, 2005

Director Wilson looked down on the slow traffic along Pennsylvania Avenue, typical of a Monday in August. He was relaxed and disengaged, his hands in the pockets of his slacks, the bright sunshine illuminating his ruddy face. That attitude was somewhat belied by the tough set of his mouth and the slight frown above his wire-rimmed glasses.

"Am I the only one who sees this as a knife in the back?" Michael Verdon asked him from behind the desk.

Wilson turned and gave him a sympathetic but resigned look. "A badass is going to be a badass."

"And we all know that's how Stella Tucker operates."

"Right. She may be a loose cannon, but she's a smart operator too. I've seen enough of life to know that sometimes you need to pin a medal on a shit like Tucker to keep her from destroying someone you respect."

Verdon nodded in disgust, but he went ahead and picked up the phone. He told his assistant to put the call through. He put it on speaker so Wilson could listen.

"Michael?" Dupree's voice was clear, but Verdon, who knew him well, detected a wary tone.

"Aloisius, Jim Wilson's here with me. It's a beautiful day in Washington, though I guess you can't say the same where you are. The television images we're getting are dreadful. Things are going to get worse over the coming hours, and we think Operation Cage is in real trouble."

Dupree replied prudently, for he knew that none of what Verdon had said so far was important enough to reach out to him during the storm. "Michael, Jim, what's going on?"

"Dupree, we've had to make some decisions due to the weather conditions, the fact that your unit is divided and working two different regions, and the magnitude of the disaster that has cut off New Orleans."

Dupree said nothing. The static on the line was the only sign that the connection was still live.

"We decided we needed to brief you," Verdon added, doing his best to sound supportive. "We've been following your progress. Agent Tucker has informed us—"

"Am I hearing you right?" Dupree interrupted him. "Tucker contacted you directly?"

"Aloisius, please, take it easy and just listen!" Wilson raised his voice. "We're your friends!"

Verdon patiently resumed. "As I was telling you, Agent Tucker has informed us that you've confirmed the presence of a Tampa policeman, Brad Nelson, in geographical proximity to all the family murders. She also informed us that Assistant Inspector Salazar has identified significant similarities between these murders and the murder of another family eighteen years ago."

Dupree's reply was swift. "Right, then, I guess Tucker neglected to tell you that although Nelson was on rescue teams in several of those locations, he came back early from Brooksville and he's not officially in New Orleans right now. And she didn't mention that even though Salazar believes the Composer could be a man named Martin Lenx, who killed his family eighteen years ago, Salazar also says Nelson doesn't fit the profile."

"I understood that Nelson was your principal suspect."

"And are you asking me or swallowing the line Agent Tucker fed you?"

"Aloisius, for God's sake!" the CJIS director exclaimed.

"Nelson is definitely a person of interest, but the evidence is circumstantial at best; we're doing what we can to get hold of his partner on the rescue team and follow up. Earlier this morning, I asked Tucker to verify specific pieces of information. I still don't have her report, but evidently you do."

"Tucker tried to contact you, but she said it was impossible."

"What else?" The question was sharp and impatient.

Wilson nodded, looking at Verdon. Dupree smelled what was coming. It wouldn't do any good to try to hide it.

"Agent Tucker spoke with Nelson's wife."

"What?!" Dupree wasn't asking how she'd managed it; he was too incensed she'd dared to do so without his authorization.

Verdon understood. "Given the information she'd gathered, she thought it was the right thing to do."

"And why didn't she ask me first?" Dupree snapped.

"Listen, Dupree, I know you're upset, but comms are down. Cell phones don't work in New Orleans. It took us almost an hour to set up this call, and no one has better resources than we do."

Dupree ignored Verdon's excuses. "When did you get confirmation that Nelson isn't in Tampa?"

"A couple of hours ago."

"Why didn't you let us know? The phone lines may be down, but I specifically ordered her to inform me of any new developments by email."

"It wasn't much more than you already had, and she figured that interviewing the wife would help advance the investigation."

"When was that?"

"Dupree . . ."

"What time did she interview Nelson's wife?"

"We don't have that information," Wilson lied.

Verdon tried to smooth things over. "You told us you were having comms problems because of the hurricane and the blackout."

"I'm at the emergency ops center, with a generator and thirty operators taking phone calls. I find it hard to believe that she wasn't able to get in contact." His voice was bitter and sarcastic. "Interesting—now that you have something to tell me, you managed to establish communication."

"Aloisius . . ." Verdon was trying his best to sound a conciliatory note.

"Aloisius," Director Wilson went on, "here's the deal. Nelson's wife confirmed aspects of his behavior that caught our attention. He turned up at her house the day before yesterday. She said he was unusually calm, but acting mysterious and evasive. He'd completely changed his attitude from before. Here's what he said, according to her, and I quote: 'Everything that happened was my fault. I know I got everything wrong, but I'm going to find a solution. Right now I have to go, because I have something I can't postpone, but when I get back, I'll be ready to fix all the mistakes.'"

"Did he say '*the* mistakes' or '*my* mistakes'?"

"The report says 'the mistakes.'"

"That could be the promise of a man trying to fix things, but it could also mean he's preparing for something big, something he's been expecting," Dupree mused. "'*The* mistakes' suggests he doesn't see them as his fault, but he does feel the responsibility to correct them. Salazar thinks our man has been postponing the murder of his own family, waiting for the right moment. He's watching for some kind of sign, and we're trying to figure out what it is." Dupree paused, and when he spoke again, the indignation had returned. "Do you two understand the importance of what you just told me? This information is crucial, and Agent Tucker deliberately held it back. She wasn't thinking! She could have put the whole investigation in jeopardy. If Nelson does turn out to be our man and calls his wife, she could inadvertently tip him off."

"That's why we're calling, Dupree," Verdon explained. "I've authorized measures to protect the Nelson family, and I asked Tucker to head the Tampa team."

Dupree remained stubbornly silent.

"Aloisius," Wilson appealed to him. "Just understand and accept it."

"Are you seriously telling me you're so blind you don't see what Tucker's up to?"

Michael Verdon's heavy sigh was clear across the line. "Aloisius, I appreciate you, I really do, but you can't blame us for this one. After what happened in New Orleans the last time you were there, you know we're going to have some misgivings . . . I'm not going to offend you by asking if this has anything to do with Samedi. I hope to God it doesn't."

"I'm not going to comment on that." Dupree's voice was unforgiving. "That was completely uncalled for."

"A professional with your experience should have recognized there are factors in this investigation you should have reported up the chain of command."

"I have no idea what you're talking about."

"There's at least one thing you forgot to mention, and it's in the briefing Salazar sent to Tucker. Sarah Nelson's maiden name was Rosenblatt. She's the daughter of a US senator from Florida."

"I can't believe it!" Dupree's tone made it clear he wasn't kidding. "You're seriously telling me this whole circus is because Nelson's father-in-law is a senator?"

"For God's sake, Dupree! Why are you surprised?" Wilson exclaimed. "You know damn well how that complicates things!"

Verdon intervened, calmly but just as firmly as before. "I don't think you understand the seriousness of the situation, Aloisius. The naval air station has reported that our New Orleans headquarters has been completely destroyed. The National Guard is doing their best to get the agents and their families out. When the storm's over and you go out on the streets, you'll be all alone. If Operation Cage fails and this guy Nelson turns out to be the killer—and if the senator finds out that his daughter and grandchildren were in danger because we failed to protect them—then heads will roll. And I don't need to tell you that ours will be the first."

Verdon had more to add. "One thing more, Dupree. We know you feel we're interfering, but I want to stress we have full confidence in you. I have information concerning Assistant Inspector Salazar, but I'm leaving it entirely up to you how to use it if you think she can advance the investigation. This is an exceptional case and it deserves exceptional treatment. If you decide to keep this information confidential, we'll do the best we can to follow your lead."

34

Insomnia

New Orleans, Louisiana
10:00 a.m., Monday, August 29, 2005

Amaia put her eye to the slit someone had cut in the brown paper taped across the window. The windowpane mirrored her peering eye. Shading her face to reduce the reflection, she tried to see outside. The city was a leaden gray; the day had begun hours earlier, but the dark skies were as opaque as a bottomless lake. Flames caused by gas explosions flickered low against the horizon.

Several cars floated slowly down the street, bobbing in the water like dead turtles.

After they'd quizzed the rescue team chief by radio, she went back to reviewing the Galveston files. She paid particular attention to a statement by the younger Joseph Andrews, the crime scene analysis, Nelson's own accounts, and Captain Reed's summary. She and Johnson had searched archives and databases all the way back to 1982 but found no earlier case that matched the Lenx murders. Everything suggested the serial killer's spree had begun with the Andrews family.

"Murder was the alpha and will be the omega," Amaia whispered aloud, praying for insight.

The racket from the operations center made it hard for her to stay focused.

Johnson and the New Orleans cops appeared in the doorway. She shut her laptop and followed them.

The phone lines were jammed. The instant an operator ended a call, another came in. Amaia went to the deputy who'd spoken to her the previous day. The operator raised a finger in acknowledgment as she dealt with a caller. Her voice remained calm and professional throughout the call, though tension was evident in her face.

The supervisor put the calls on speaker phone.

> Sobs. *"Please help me, my house is off the foundation, I'm here with two little babies, and the water is pouring in!"*
>
> *"Ma'am, we can't do anything; I can't send anybody right now, the police can't get into the streets until the storm's over."*

> A man, desperate. *"Please help us! We here in the attic, they's no way out, the water's all the way up to the ceiling down there. Come get us out!"*
>
> *"Sir, we had to take our officers off the streets; it's too dangerous out there. I can take your names and address."*
>
> *"What you mean, 'your names'? So you know who we are when you find us here dead?"*

"All our calls are like that."

The supervisor placed an encouraging hand on the deputy's shoulder. She didn't react; she put her headset on and went back to work.

"People call us for help, and all we can do is put their names on a waiting list."

"What's it like out there right now?" Johnson asked.

Suddenly incensed, the supervisor waved a hand toward the monitors suspended from the ceiling. All of them looked up.

"In one word? Chaos. The city's without power. High-tension lines are down; cell phones aren't working. It's raining into the Superdome where people are massed in the interior passages, human waste is gushing out of the toilets and flooding the place. We've received reports of assaults, rapes, and fights, both at the Superdome and the convention center. Reports of several fatal stabbings, rumors of more. Houses are on fire because gas lines broke when the foundations shifted." He fixed his eyes on the monitor before him. "And as if we didn't have enough to deal with already, now we're getting reports of tornados and water-spouts. Bodies are floating in the streets and houses have washed away. As for your successive gunshots, you can forget about them. We have nothing so far."

Johnson took offense. He stepped in close, so only the supervisor's console stood between them. Johnson glanced at the man's nameplate on the front of the desk.

"Listen to me closely, Mr. Ante."

"Antée," the supervisor corrected him automatically without looking up.

"Look at me, Antée," Johnson insisted.

The supervisor did. The aggressive lift of his chin emphasized his foul mood. "What is it now?"

Without visible emotion, Johnson leaned over and whispered into his ear. "We are here to help; we're looking for a killer. He's going to murder, in their own home, some luckless family who managed to survive this catastrophe. And yes, there will be a series of gunshots, because he'll blow their heads off. One after another, including the children, forcing the others to watch. I know you're not having a good day, but don't you dare think we are. Those are not *my* gunshots; unless we can prevent them, they'll come from the execution of a family guilty of nothing but surviving this disaster."

Antée's expression changed. He looked up at Johnson, nodded, and said nothing more.

35

Beauty

New Orleans, Louisiana

Martin chose this hotel because the bathrooms had no windows. They'd been designed as separate little rooms off the hallway between the bedroom and the door to the hotel corridor, and their only connection to the exterior was a grated air shaft. He'd blocked it with towels so he wouldn't have to listen to the threatening low moan as the wind made the metal vibrate. In the late morning, he finally decided to step out of his refuge. The windows to the balcony had disappeared, as had every bit of furniture, even the bed. The headboard, bolted to the wall, was still in place. Ceiling panels had been ravaged, and the yellow electrical conduits for overhead lights dangled like wild vines. The worst of the hurricane was past, even though the wind was still blowing hard. Stepping over the debris, he approached the gaping opening where the window had been. The balcony railing was still in place, though it was battered and badly bent. Martin decided not to risk stepping outside. He leaned out to survey the scene. The sky in the east, still dark, was beginning to clear; the rain had let up, and the flood was starting to subside.

He'd been listening to the radio chatter as the Coast Guard's Sikorsky helicopter pilots prepared to sortie. He had to hurry. He went back to the bathroom, clicked on his flashlight, and checked his appearance in the mirror. He peeled off his cotton shirt. He turned the handle of the faucet but got nothing but a gurgle and empty hissing sounds. Early that morning, the taps had disgorged a brownish, muddy trickle, but even that minimal flow had ceased. He used bottled water from his briefcase to brush his teeth, wash his face, and slick down his military-style crew cut. He put on a clean shirt, carefully starched and ironed, tucked it in, and buckled his belt. He checked himself in the mirror again and pinned his badge onto his breast pocket so the logo was clearly visible. He picked up his briefcase.

He grinned as he traversed what had been the reception area. The water was up to his knees. The downstairs was empty, as if a gigantic vacuum cleaner had sucked everything up.

No doors, no windows, no revolving door, no lights. All the ceiling panels were gone, and silvery sheets of insulation hung down like Christmas tinsel.

He left the hotel and made his way across the submerged sidewalk to the middle of the deserted street, carefully avoiding the splintered remains of advertising signs that hung perilously from building fronts. The rain had all but stopped. He waded down the flooded street. Several of the big trees nearby hadn't survived the storm, including the immense live oak that had sheltered the local café. Swarms of mosquitoes hovered just inches above the surface of the water. Martin knew that when the sun came out, the marshy stink would be asphyxiating. He looked at his city map. He'd marked his route the night before.

In the distance, people were poking their heads out of windows and emerging into the flooded street. Their movements were sluggish and inhibited. It was like waking to a shared hangover; bewildered, they shrugged, exchanging those dismayed expressions Martin knew so well. He ignored calls for help from some of the people who were beginning to get over the initial shock.

"Hey, buddy! Give us a hand over here?"

He strode purposefully and pretended he hadn't heard.

He kept wading through the streets, avoiding debris, mattresses, collapsed walls, and fallen trees. A couple of times he was forced to deviate from his planned route to get around fallen power lines. Reports on the radio had said the power was out in most of the city, but some fallen cables were buzzing ominously and generating showers of sparks when they brushed against walls.

It took him more than an hour to get to his destination. The edifice stood on a solid cement foundation, and perhaps that was why its inhabitants had decided to wait out the hurricane there. Access to the apartments was via a side staircase to a balcony passage that ran along the front of the second floor. He climbed eight steps, sat down, and dumped the water out of his boots. He gazed down in distaste at the thick black stain that discolored his trousers almost up to his waist. Glancing toward the end of the street, he was surprised to see turbulent water surging toward his location. That made no sense. The flood was rising, when by all rights it should have already begun to drain. He used his handkerchief in an effort to wipe the slime from his shirt, but all he managed to do was ruin the handkerchief. He folded it carefully and tucked it away in his back pocket.

The pervasive filth that surrounded him was even more disgusting than the discomfort of the damp heat and his wet clothes. Martin was a clean and meticulous person, and he knew that in moments of chaos and loss, when everything around them was covered with mud and dirt, his crisp appearance would project polite concern to his victims. That, along with the detailed advice he gave them, would assuage their initial misgivings and persuade them to give themselves freely into his care.

He pressed the doorbell to make sure the electricity wasn't working. The result was a dry click under his finger, nothing more. Martin took a deep breath and let it out slowly, an actor preparing his entrance. He rapped his knuckles against the door and heard a distinct echo inside. The almost immediate response to his knock was the murmuring of stifled voices. Their voices were a mixture of both hope and fear. The door started to open but scraped the floor and jammed. A pistol barrel was thrust through the crack.

Martin used a sales technique he'd once found in a 1950s manual written by a traveling salesman. He stepped back just as the door opened. He remained absolutely still when a man's face poked out. The man scrutinized him suspiciously. Martin smiled and tapped the badge on his mostly clean white shirt to draw the man's attention. "Sabine family?"

He waited the full three seconds recommended by the manual and was greeted by an exclamation of relief. "Oh, my God! Thank heavens! It's wonderful you got here so fast!"

Martin stayed where he was. The man hauled at the jammed door and eventually forced it open enough to admit him. Part of the rear wall and roof had been ripped away by the force of the winds, and rain had soaked almost everything inside the apartment.

"Is everyone all right?" asked Martin.

He really did want to know.

"Yes, thank God. We're all fine, just a few scrapes and scratches, though I think Jana's wrist may be broken." He waved his hand toward a teenage girl seated on the floor, huddled under a blanket and shaking with chills. "But the house! Our home is wrecked," he exclaimed as he kicked a tree branch that had made its way into the middle of the living room. He looked at Martin, who hadn't moved from his place outside. Martin gave him a rueful, inquiring look; the man looked down and saw he was still carrying the gun. "Oh, of course. Sorry!" He looked around for some place to put it, found a low table littered with debris, swept it off, and left his gun there.

Martin stepped inside. Serious and confident, he looked from one family member to another, all of them congregated as if summoned by a divine apparition. With the tip of one shoe, he pushed aside enough splintered wood to clear a space for his briefcase. He leaned down, deposited it, and in a smooth continuation of the same motion, he picked up the man's gun.

"This is the Smith & Wesson you bought in 2000. No other weapons in the apartment, correct?"

"No others," the man replied. There might have been a note of worry in his voice.

Martin smiled.

36

Dependency

New Orleans, Louisiana

Dupree left the fire chief's office and took the interior stairs two at a time. His mind echoed with Michael Verdon's offer to withhold information, as if granting a special concession. His Washington bosses apparently considered Tucker's betrayal the most efficient way to proceed and thought he could be convinced to accept it. He went to the conference room they'd commandeered. No one was there. That meant the team was in the ops center.

Amaia, seated next to the supervisor and his deputy, was listening to incoming calls through headphones and watching the call log scrolling down the monitor. Dupree had to go up to her and wave a finger in front of the screen to attract her attention. "Salazar, come with me!" He turned and went to the door.

Dupree crossed to the conference room, where he started ripping down the brown paper that covered the windows. Amaia closed the door behind her and stood watching as her boss worked.

He turned. She could see from his expression he was serious. He was bottling up a lot of anger. "Salazar, I think you need to sit down for this."

She stood where she was, staring at him. Maybe to encourage her, he went to the table, pulled out a couple of chairs, took one, and gestured toward the other. Amaia settled in across from him.

"You were in the ops center; I don't have to tell you the hurricane was a lot more destructive than we expected. Most of the city has no power and no potable water. The eye of the hurricane passed to the east, sparing New Orleans from total destruction, but we know the water along the coast will go up almost twenty feet. The Coast Guard helicopters are back in the air, and imaging from the crews shows nothing but desolation. The French Quarter came through okay, but other parts of the city were flattened. The West End is flooded. Operation Cage, at least as we planned it, is a no-go. In the face of all this, I need everyone on the team to be totally committed." He paused and looked down for a moment. "Salazar, Washington told me that your aunt called from Spain. I'm sorry to have to give you the news: your father died yesterday morning."

Amaia took a deep breath. She needed all the air in the room, all the air in the world. Dupree went back to the now-exposed window, worked at the latch, and got it to open. He pushed, and the sash of the tall, narrow window rose with a ripping sound as it pulled duct tape off the casement.

The humid, smelly air surged in. The sudden draft swept all the photographs off the tables onto the floor in total confusion. Amaia stared down at them.

Dupree studied her expression for a moment, then started toward the door. "I'm going to be with the rest of the team in the ops center. If things go as we expect, it won't be long before the call comes in. It's up to you. If you decide to leave, I'll try to get you transportation back to the naval air station. The last I heard, they were bringing in a Marine Corps aviation team to evacuate the remaining FBI personnel. Once you get away from the storm, you can book a plane ticket to Spain."

Amaia sensed his presence as he started past her and then paused for an instant. He extended his hand as if to touch her shoulder but dropped it instead. She heard him quietly close the door behind him.

She bent over to pick up the photo that had landed closest to her. She studied it for a few seconds, folded it in half and then in quarters, and tucked it inside her blouse.

37

Our Father

Elizondo

Amaia inhaled the rich aroma of melted butter. She liked it better than that of caramelized sugar, which the least moment of inattention could convert into a smell as acrid as burned embers, or the smell of flour, a coarse, primal odor that was deceptively mild but as suffocating as dirt from a grave.

She watched her father working heavy sheets of pastry dough. Her heartbeat accelerated. A Strauss waltz wafted from the radio he kept on while he worked. He smiled when he saw her, and she tried to reciprocate, but couldn't. *How can you tell someone you love something that you know will make him terribly unhappy?* She seemed to observe herself from above, a nine-year-old girl standing hesitant behind him, searching for words that by all rights she shouldn't know at all. She loved him so, so much . . .

She listened to the impetuously accelerating waltz on the radio, imperial and elegant and completely inappropriate for talking about her fears. She pressed her lips together in a determined expression. She knew then that she wasn't going to tell him, because if she did, he'd stop smiling, he'd turn off the radio, and the waltz would disappear into the ether, to be replaced by the crackling sound of hot ovens and the relentless drip of water from the faulty faucet at the deep steel sink.

It cost her to hold back. Her chest constricted. A deep pain forced her to close her eyes. She couldn't look at him. Her lids squeezed out a single tear, silent and heavy. It slid down her cheek just as her father turned to smile at her.

"May I have this dance, Princess?"

His smile vanished instantly. He knelt before her and traced his finger along the track the tear had left on her cheek. "What's wrong, darling?"

Amaia kept her lips pressed tightly together as she looked at him and struggled, agonized, against her inevitable fate. She threw her arms around his neck and pressed herself to his chest so she wouldn't have to look in his eyes.

Juan hugged her, deeply distressed.

"Amaia?" he called in a worried voice. He picked her up and seated her on the edge of his steel worktable so that they were face to face. He released her long enough to switch off the radio, then took her hands and kissed them. "Tell me what's happening, dearest."

The waltz was gone forever. She heard the crackling of the lit ovens, the constant drip of that faucet. The sensation of déjà vu was so overpowering that it almost made her ill as she feared the outcome of her confession. From this moment on, that place and those sounds would bring to her mind the dark recollections of a night, of death, spurring in her a survival instinct that bid her to flee as fast as possible.

She opened her mouth and described the horror.

"Ama," she managed to say through sudden sobs. "She scares me . . . she makes me really afraid. At night, when you're asleep, she comes to my bed." The terror of it replaced her desperate shame, and her eyes opened wide. "*Ama* wants to eat me, she really does! She says she's going to gobble me up, and if you don't stop her, she will!"

Juan looked away from his daughter's pleading eyes and, vacantly, into the middle distance.

> *In his mind he hears the swish of the bedclothes. The floorboards creak beneath the light tread of his wife's feet as she crosses the room in the dark. Juan sits up, turns to his left to peer toward the door, opens his eyes wide in the dark as if somehow that will help him hear better. The girls' room is directly across the hall. Rosario takes two steps or maybe three to get from one door to the other. He hears her move and sometimes makes out a low murmur of words that he doesn't manage—or want—to understand. Only a minute passes, a tiny minute during which all his senses are intensely focused as*

he holds his breath and prays this will not last any longer than that agonizing eternal minute. He senses his wife's return. Juan lies back, careful not to make noise, and pretends to be sleeping. She lies down at his side. Even without touching her, he knows the chill in the house has penetrated her body. Her heart is beating wildly. It's over, it's done, and she won't get up again tonight. But he doesn't dare relax until he's sure that she's sleeping.

Juan released his daughter just for an instant. He reached to click on the radio. A melancholy piano piece had replaced the waltz.

"Lots of children have nightmares. That's normal at your age. You have a lively imagination, and you read a lot. That gets you excited. Don't you worry, those are just dreams. They can't hurt you."

She couldn't believe what he was saying. "But, *Aita* . . ."

"You dreamed it, Amaia. Dreams aren't real, even though sometimes they seem to be." He lowered her to the floor. The girl wept, intense and forlorn, her eyes squeezed shut. Juan was convinced she was refusing to look at him. He again gazed out toward that faraway point beyond the wall, this time in shame. Regretting his response, but unable to look at her, he bent down and kissed the top of her head. "But any time your nightmares scare you a lot, you can call me." He turned back to his worktable.

Amaia wept for a long time without opening her eyes. When at last she did, her father was back at his work, and the notes from a new waltz floated in the air, mixed with the buttery scent of baking pastry. He continued rolling out the dough, his back to her, though he no longer seemed to have his heart in it. Amaia picked up her school bag and shuffled slowly to the door, giving him time to stop her, to call her back. But that call never came. She turned at the door to look at him, a condemned prisoner hoping for a last-minute reprieve.

At that moment, the door of the bakery workshop and that of the conference room on the other side of the world were one and the same. Amaia was simultaneously the girl who couldn't stop crying and the woman who couldn't weep at all. They both turned and looked at their father.

"Agur, Aita," they say.

"Agur, maitia," he says from the far side of the room.

Amaia entered the ops center just as Charbou started waving frantically to attract the others' attention. "Series of gunshots on Maine Street, in Jefferson! The woman who called it in heard five shots, fairly close together."

"We have records of several families living in that area," Johnson said, spreading out a map and locating the house.

"We got a problem," Bull interrupted. "We don't know why yet, but for the last half hour, all the information coming in says the water is rising, even in places that weren't flooded before or where it'd started to go down. It's rising fast, all over the place. There's a rumor going round that the levee has broken at Seventeenth Street. No confirmation yet, but someone just called to say the water is waist deep on Poydras Street."

"All right," Amaia said, "Jefferson Parish was already flooded anyway. I assume you weren't expecting to come back with dry pants. Right? So what are we waiting for?"

Dupree studied her. He got up, went toward the door, ordered them to check their equipment—supplies, batteries, flashlights—and mentally adjusted his plan. He gave her a nod as he passed, a sign of respect more than anything, for her ability to make the decision.

"Do you want me to have them send an acknowledgment to Spain?"

"No. My aunt already knows. But . . ."

"What?"

"Could you let Inspector Gertha Schneider know? She's a German officer in the Europol group in Quantico. Tell her mountain folk are strong. She'll understand."

PART TWO

What the caterpillar calls the end, the rest of the world calls the butterfly.

—*Attributed To Lao Tzu*

On the afternoon of Monday, August 29, 2005, Hurricane Katrina moved inland and began to break up. It devastated the coast but passed just east of New Orleans, sparing the city from total destruction.

This is the story of what happened after that.

38

AFTER THE STORM

New Orleans, Louisiana
Monday, August 29, 2005

They left the fire station in their inflatable flat-bottomed Zodiac. It was as if they'd landed on another planet. Gone were the frantic calls to the ops center for help. As were the weather reports, blurry video from traffic cameras, calls from patrol cars, and excited outbursts from newscasters reacting to the disaster. But one thing was undeniable: nothing they'd heard about the horror and desperation could have prepared them for what they encountered.

Dupree leaned on the armrest and looked around to study the faces of his team. When they'd set out from the base, he'd expected to be concerned about Amaia. He knew the risk he was running by including someone who'd so recently received such terrible news. It was clear to him that when Wilson and Verdon had given him that information, they'd been granting him the discretion to decide whether to keep her on the team or put her on a plane back to Spain. Something told him she'd do just fine.

In Texas, when he'd sent her back to Quantico, she'd asked him, "Why me?" He'd ducked the question by stressing the need to use individuals as tools. Investigators were part of the mechanism, vital cogs to keep it targeted and on track.

He'd been lying.

He knew Amaia was a searcher, one of those exceptional beings naturally gifted with the ability to detect and track evil. A dubious distinction, certainly, and one that was a lasting effect of enduring her own personal hell. Salazar was as arrogant and temperamental as you might expect of an officer who'd already achieved star status at the age of twenty-five; but at the same time, she was so calm and divorced from her emotions that he had to ask himself if that was a defense mechanism or a gift she didn't fully understand. If the latter, she was truly extraordinary. She was a rare bird in any case, and if things went as he expected, she'd soon be put to the test.

But his immediate concern was for Bill and Bull.

Amaia and Johnson had exchanged only a couple of murmured phrases during the voyage upriver. They were affected by what they saw, but their reactions were contained, in contrast to those of Bull and Charbou. His FBI team members knew their own emotional responses were nothing in comparison to what the two cops must be feeling at the sight of their destroyed city. The extent of the devastation overwhelmed Bill and Bull and they quickly lapsed into a stupor.

Amaia, on the other hand, remained serene. She concentrated on breathing deeply, taking the warm, humid air in through her nostrils and releasing it very slowly from her mouth.

The building at 428 Maine Street was the only two-story structure in the area. It was run down and probably hadn't looked that good before the storm hit. Fortunately, the apartments were all upstairs. Access to the apartments was via a second-story balcony that ran above the street. The succession of apartment doors was visible from below.

Just past the intersection of Highway 90 and Maine Street, they killed the motor so as not to betray their presence. The Zodiac's momentum carried them the rest of the way, but just as their craft bumped against the steps, a strong new current began pushing them northward again. They glanced at one another, perplexed, grabbed paddles, and fought their way back to the stairs. Water had almost reached the eaves of most of the houses along the street. The lowest dwellings had disappeared beneath the flood.

They tied up to the stair railing. It tilted dangerously outward, and its base was completely submerged, like the foundation of a riverside pier. Dupree estimated that at least ten of the concrete steps were underwater.

Securing their ballistic vests, they followed Bill and Bull, who were driven by a new energy—no more dismayed contemplation. The cops swiftly mounted the stairs, silently signaling caution where lengths of balcony rail were missing. They passed two doors marked with orange paint from spray cans like those in their own kits. The large *X* on each door was the verification code established by the Federal Emergency Management Agency (FEMA) for urban search and rescue.

Bill and Bull took positions on either side of the apartment door and glanced back at Dupree. An orange *X* had been sprayed across this door as well, showing someone had checked the apartment. The FEMA code required all four interstices of the *X* to be filled: above, the date and time of the visit; to the right, the status of the structure; below, the number of victims inside; and to the left, the rescue team's own ID number.

Bill read the codes in a whisper: "Nobody inside, structure damaged, stay out."

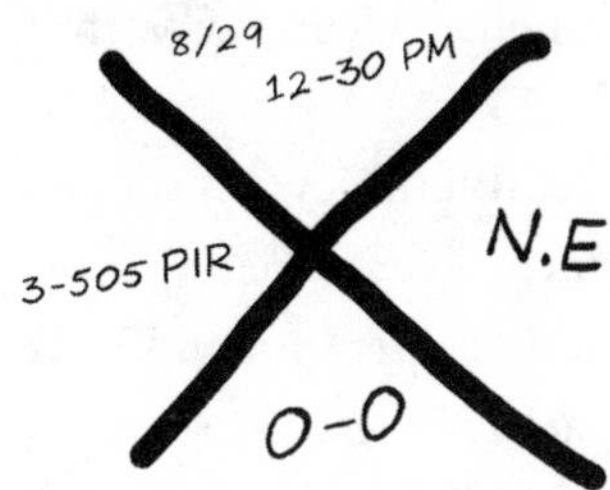

Charbou tapped the date and time with his pistol barrel. The record at the top of the *X* indicated August 29 at twelve thirty p.m. He held up his own wristwatch.

Dupree checked the time and understood instantly. Given the indicated time, the rescue team should have still been on site or at least nearby, checking other residences along the street. He moved a couple of steps back along the balcony to check the *X*'s they'd passed. The notations hadn't been completely filled out.

Johnson was the one who settled the matter in a whisper. "The 3-505 PIR is the Eighty-Second Airborne Division. I'm sure they're coming, but they haven't had time to get here yet."

Dupree silently sent Charbou to check the next apartment. Charbou was quick. He returned immediately, shaking his head.

Dupree nodded. The Composer had covered his escape route, making sure that no one would challenge him if they should arrive while he was still there, but he hadn't bothered to extend the masquerade. Dupree signaled for them to go in but gestured a warning that the murderer might still be inside.

Charbou rattled the door handle. "New Orleans police! Open up!" he shouted from his stance tight against the wall. They listened closely.

No response.

Bull was the next to yell. "New Orleans police! Stand back! We're coming in!"

But they didn't. Charbou fired point blank at the lock and jerked back as the metal housing, blown loose, swung wildly around one of the remaining screws, sending splinters flying. The air was full of the smell of gunpowder and burned wood. The gunshot echoed dully in the flooded street. The door swung slowly open about six inches or so and then jammed against the floor.

Bull called, "This is the police. Get away from the door! We're armed and we're going to shoot."

They didn't do that either. Bull threw his shoulder against the flimsy door, which yielded some but stuck before opening completely; he went low and covered his partner as Bill leaped over him and landed in a kneeling position, pistol ready, surveying the interior.

The reek of death overwhelmed the stink of gunpowder. The hot iron-and-ammonia tang of spilled blood and urine evoked the last gasps of the dying. Beneath it all was the penetrating smell of feces that follows violent death. Salty drops of sweat and tears had dried in white tracks on the faces of the dead.

The cops took only a few seconds to confirm that they themselves were the only ones alive in the small apartment. The team went in.

The rear wall of the living room was mostly gone. All the furniture was piled in a corner. Perhaps they'd been trying to barricade the opening in the back wall, but Dupree's bet was that the Composer had moved it. The apartment was cramped and must have been crowded with furniture. He'd simply needed more floor space to lay out his victims. The family members were stretched side by side just inside the front door, heads toward Lake Pontchartrain to the north and feet toward the Mississippi.

Amaia stood there, unable to move. For a brief moment, she had an eerie vision of herself as a little girl with bare feet on the chilly floor of a dance studio. She looked down to make sure she wasn't standing in a puddle of sticky black blood. The ominous tolling of the bells resounded in her mind.

The apartment was so small that the closest corpse, that of a boy, was only two steps from the door. She was sure he was eleven or twelve years old, the Composer's target, but he was small and could have passed for nine or ten. He wore a black-and-gold New Orleans Saints T-shirt. He'd wept copiously. The traces of snot and tears on his face were obvious, and his half-open eyes were inflamed and rimmed with red.

This boy isn't much older than I was. Amaia closed her eyes and squeezed them tight as she tried to wipe that absurd thought from her mind. When she looked down at the little body, she saw that the gunshot wound in the crown of his head had released a gush of blood that had pooled almost to where she was standing.

The smell of suffering was so intense that even Johnson was moved. He stepped back, stood with his eyes fixed on the victims, and shook his head angrily. "We just missed the bastard. They're still warm."

Bill and Bull checked the other apartments. Dupree had Johnson take the first set of photos, and then they began to remove the objects lying over the victims, mostly the contents of a wooden sideboard, including a shattered set of antique dishware. The team took blood samples, labeled them, and stored them carefully, knowing they couldn't be sent for analysis until much later. Johnson found the violin positioned close to the victims' heads. The Composer had tried to make it blend in with the general disorder, but it shone with the polished brilliance of a coffin lid. The sight of it angered Dupree. He was careful to contain this emotion, clenching his jaws and tightening his lips in an expression Amaia now recognized as characteristic of him.

This had to have been the humblest home the Composer had ever visited. The front door opened directly from the balcony into the cramped living room which ran from the front of the building to the back. Doors to the kitchen and a master bedroom were on one side. A single door on the opposite wall opened on a narrow hallway leading to a tiny bathroom and two minuscule bedrooms, one obviously for the boys and the other shared by the girl and the grandmother. One of the walls in that room was plastered with posters of rock bands; the other side had a simple shelf with a prayer book and a cross on a wooden base. Amaia searched the bedrooms, which were made even more claustrophobic by all the furniture taking up available space.

In the kitchen, they had a large table against one wall, with a couple of chairs behind it and others stored beneath or on either side. Amaia assumed that they moved the table to the center of the room at mealtimes. The sink was empty and stained by muddy tap water. She checked the refrigerator and found the interior relatively cool. There was enough to eat, and the food was well packaged and organized.

The bathroom door was off its hinges because the blast of the winds had dislodged the top of the doorframe. The bathtub was almost completely full of reasonably clean water, probably a provision against an expected outage, and next to it was a full plastic bucket of the sort children take to the beach. A single pump container of liquid soap and another of shampoo stood at one corner. The battered window above the tub hadn't stood up to the storm. Forced inward, it had shed wood splinters and flecks of mold across the water. Lifting the toilet lid, she caught the sharp smell of urine. Her flashlight beam lit up an object behind the toilet that glimmered like glass. She bent, picked it up, and found that it was only a plastic wrapper for a large gauze pad.

She felt a tug at her calf as she left the bathroom. A nasty-looking nail protruded about two inches from the splintered doorframe. She squatted to check the damage and was surprised to see she hadn't been gashed, even though the nail had ripped the leg of her boot-cut jeans. She shined the flashlight beam at the nail and found blood on it. And not only on the nail; looking closer, she found spots on the varnish of the dark wood frame. She went back to the main room, where Johnson and Dupree were examining the corpses.

"Are any of them injured on the leg? Just above the ankle or maybe on the calf? It'll be a deep cut that bled a lot and required a bandage."

They cleared enough debris to examine the victims' legs. The women wore summer dresses, and it was immediately obvious their legs weren't injured. Dupree and Johnson looked at her, shook their heads, and waited for an explanation.

"The hurricane blew in the bathroom window. It tore the door right out of its frame and left a nail poking out. Someone cut himself on it, and that someone applied a bandage and took the time to wipe up blood from the floor." She took them into the narrow hallway.

Johnson swabbed the dried blood and sealed the sample in a plastic bag. His face was serious when he looked at Amaia. "You understand the importance of this?"

Amaia thought for a moment. She wasn't as convinced as Johnson. "I'm not sure . . ."

"What do you mean? It's the killer's DNA!"

"Probably," she admitted. "But he's started to do weird things, and that worries me."

"'Weird things'?" Johnson repeated. "What kind of weird things?"

"For instance, it was more important to him to set up his exact scenario with the bodies than to hide his presence. That's just the opposite of the previous cases. He piled the furniture in a corner to make space for the bodies. He spray-painted FEMA search and rescue codes. We haven't seen anything like that before, even though the other murders also took place right after disasters."

"None of those disasters was as vast as Katrina; and this one's in a city," Dupree pointed out. "It's the first family with neighbors in adjoining apartments. The others were in fairly isolated single-family homes. He probably changed his methodology because he wanted to make sure he wouldn't be interrupted while he was dealing with this family."

Amaia directed her flashlight beam along the hall. "I think he killed them and then went to the bathroom. I smelled urine in the toilet; the tank was dry. The family had a bathtub full of water and a plastic bucket to scoop it with, but he must not have thought of that. I'm sure that the pee's not from anyone here. These people were poor, but they kept the place clean and tidy. I think the killer cut himself on the way out of the bathroom. He wiped up the blood, but he was in a hurry, so he made do with a quick swipe with whatever he found at hand. I don't think he paid much attention to it or even really cared. Of course, he didn't want to leave obvious bloodstains, but in a dark hallway with no electricity, nobody would be likely to notice a faint stain on the floor outside the bathroom."

"You're not going to suggest he's hoping to be caught, are you?" Johnson challenged her. "If so, you should forget it. He's doing everything he can to avoid detection and arrest."

Amaia saw a smile playing around Dupree's lips. The boss was an adamant advocate of the theory that the Composer wasn't just avoiding capture, he believed no one even knew he existed. She thought the same. "No, he's not going to allow himself to be trapped, but in this storm and in this city . . . You saw it in Bill's face on the way here and on Bull's as well. This is like the end of the world. Just imagine the mentality of someone who seeks out this kind of devastation. What I meant when I said he didn't care is that I believe he's nearing a climax. The grand realization of his destructive work is at hand. In my opinion, Katrina isn't just a sign," Amaia argued, "for him, this storm is his direct channel to God. 'There shall not be left one stone upon another, that shall not be thrown down.' He's accelerated his rhythm, and he's not going to stop. New Orleans is his revelation. I believe that, somehow, he doesn't really care what happens next."

Johnson studied the stain on the floorboards. "He wiped up most of it, but there's still a lot here. Any normal person with an injury like that would try to get to a hospital. You think it'll help to notify the emergency rooms?"

"He bandaged it himself. A pressure wrap would be good enough, unless the nail hit an artery. Besides, remember what it's like out there—there's mud everywhere, nobody can see the bottom, and there'll be lots of injuries to feet and legs as time goes on."

"He'll stay in the city," Johnson replied.

"I'm sure he will."

"So am I," Dupree said. "The only thing we can be sure of is that he's facing the same difficulties we are. Operation Cage, as we planned it, is cancelled. I just radioed Captain Forneret, and they're overwhelmed. They stood down the roadblocks because they need every officer. The 911 center can't handle all the incoming calls. They're talking about leaks in the levees, maybe even breaches. And that's what they're really scared of: if the levees give way, that'll create a massive surge, and New Orleans will disappear." Dupree raised a hand and pinched the sides of his nose, trying to forestall a developing migraine. He smiled, but his expression was bitter. "Listen, I radioed the District 8 police station to see if we could get someone to evacuate these bodies. Never got the chance to ask. After he gave me that information dump, I didn't even bring it up. We'll seal the door and mark it with crime scene tape. That's all we can do. We had a taste of the storm damage on our way here, but it was enough to show us things are only going to go from bad to worse as the day goes on."

Amaia heard the churning sound of an approaching outboard motor and went to the front door just as Bill and Bull returned from their tour of the building.

"Police launch just got here with a rescue team, a real one, all of them state troopers. We talked with them. The old lady next door phoned in about the gunshots. She has an old landline. Nobody else in the building. Took us a damn long time to convince her to open up, and when she did, she told us she'd been hiding under her bed since she heard the shots. She couldn't tell us much more than what we heard from the ops center. She heard five or six shots, one after another, maybe four or five seconds apart. And, worse, she heard people screaming. She said whoever it was tried to open her front door and stood out there for a while, but she didn't see a thing. She was paralyzed with fear, and that saved her life. The troopers are going to evacuate her, unless you want to talk with her first."

Johnson sprayed over the fake rescue sign with the correct information, according to the FEMA protocol. Dupree went to the old woman, whom two troopers were carrying out on a stretcher. She was deathly pale and terribly upset. He leaned close, intending to ask her the same questions she'd heard from Bull and Charbou. She smiled weakly, and Dupree realized he really had no desire to bother her.

She reached out a thin arm and took his hand. "God bless y'all! You so good to me. I was scared to death, the devil come to get me, but y'all my Good Samaritans." The troopers quickly carried her down to the launch.

Dupree stood on the balcony for a long time, watching them advance to the next building while a crew member called through a megaphone. He was again struck by the bizarre way sound traveled along the water.

Bull waved the walkie-talkie to bring him out of his trance. "Several shots, rapid succession, Ninth Ward. Can't identify the address, but it's somewhere near North Galvez Street."

Dupree responded instantly. "If we cut through between Claiborne and I-10, we can get there right away. Maybe we'll get lucky."

Charbou looked at Bull as if astonished to hear the boss raving. "Right! And why don't we go by Simon Bolivar with our Zodiac full of white faces while we're at it and get our damn asses shot off?"

Dupree started to reply, but Bull got there first. "The agreement was that we're in charge of security, that was the condition for our cooperation. We can cross Mid-City instead and then maybe Saint Bernard Avenue, if it's passable, and that goes to North Galvez. If not, we'll find some other secure route."

Johnson and Dupree looked at Amaia. She nodded. "Lots of work ahead."

39

Oceanetta

New Orleans, Louisiana

The sky remained heavily overcast. The persistent gusts of the morning had died away, and the dark, heavy clouds moved almost imperceptibly. Off on the horizon, there was a suggestion of clear skies. The temperature was rising.

The Ninth Ward, the most extensive of the city's seventeen wards, comprised the easternmost part of the city. It was bordered by the Mississippi on one side and the lake on the other. To the southeast it was contiguous with Saint Bernard Parish and the canal. It was a scene of utter devastation. Water was chest deep along North Galvez. Automobiles were floating with only their roofs visible, and along more than one street they had to skirt downed electrical wires and uprooted trees. They didn't have a specific address, but soon they heard shots in the distance and steered toward them. The weapon sounded like a rifle, and it was being fired every couple of minutes, obviously outside a building.

They saw quite a few people looking down at them from the rooftops and upper balconies of apartment buildings. Most were young. As they advanced in the Zodiac, people would call out and wave improvised banners. Dupree was a reluctant witness to the increasing distress in the faces of his New Orleans colleagues as the team passed their citizens without being able to help. A couple of times, Charbou took up the megaphone to say help was on the way, but after a while he gave up. He knew full well he was lying. He had no idea if help was coming, and he had no way of finding out.

At the top of Clouet Street they came across three African American teens distributing supplies from a rowboat. One was down in the water, his red T-shirt so soaked he looked like he was covered in blood. He was wading toward a house and holding a bundle high to keep it out of the water. He grinned when he saw them.

"Hey, y'all! We ain't up to nothing bad!"

"What you sellin' those folks?" Bill Charbou called out.

"Sellin'? Hey, man, we ain't sellin' nothing, we givin' it away! Bud Light and cigarettes." He struck an attitude. "Robin Hood of the ghetto, man!" Two men in the window responded with cheers, but his friends in the rowboat just eyed the FBI team. "Robin Hood of the damn ghetto, folks! Red Cross got nothing for you, brothers, but we sure enough do!"

Charbou grinned. "You're a prince, buddy!"

The boy beamed.

One of his friends was surly. "If we had to wait for help from y'all . . ."

Charbou responded cheerfully. "Hey, shithead, I'm blacker than you are!"

The boy nodded, reluctantly acknowledging that. "Yeah, man. That make you our brother cop, huh?"

Bull took charge of the exchange. "Listen, y'all, they told us someone round here been firing a gun. We heard shots a long way off, but we don't know where he's at. Y'all seen anything?"

"Oh, man, I can't fucking believe it! Check it out: water keeps rising round here and y'all don't give a shit, but that crazy ass old man up on the roof shoots at the sky a couple times and you turn up with the Feds before a brother can say, 'Bless me!'"

"Listen, smart-ass, he could kill somebody by mistake." Charbou jerked his thumb at the boy in the red T-shirt. "Robin Hood here, for example. And then who you gonna call?"

Bull interrupted. "You say he's on a roof?"

"That's Jim Leger," the third boy spoke up.

"Why you tellin' them?" his buddy complained.

"I don't like it none neither. That crazy motherfucker always coming out and wavin' that rifle soon as you step on the sidewalk. Lives close by, right over there." The boy waved toward the main street.

Charbou gave him a little salute of thanks. Before setting a course toward the intersection, he called out, "Y'all know if lots of people still down there?"

The boy who'd named the shooter was the only one to reply. "We don't know. Things ain't so bad right here, but they sayin' the lower part of the Ninth disappeared. Storm knocked the houses right off they foundations. Most of the folks living down there is old as hell, so I hope they holed up ahead of time in the Superdome."

Dupree felt a sharp pang at the mention of the Superdome.

"Nobody thought anything like this could ever happen," Charbou said unhappily.

"Bullshit!" the second youngster in the rowboat answered. "For sure we thought it could, 'cause what happened is the white folks opened up the floodgates."

Bull couldn't let that pass. "What kind of crap you talkin'?"

"What I said: those sons of bitches up north, they be high and dry, but our city underwater now; those white folks opened up the gates to save they nice houses, never mind worrying about us down here. Everybody here saying that!"

"That's not true," Dupree intervened. "Water is rising everywhere, in the north too; they still don't know why."

"They don't know? Well, I sure do!" the boy insisted. "That's how things always been here in this town. Soon as the water rises, they blow up the levees to save the goddamn French Quarter."

Charbou shook his head as they moved away. "Y'all take care."

"You folks is the ones that needs to take care," the boy replied. His words might have been parting advice, but they could just as easily have been a threat.

Charbou kept shaking his head. He looked at Amaia, his lips grimly pursed. She smiled, admiring his patience. Bull steered them toward a cross street, and after a while they again emerged onto North Galvez.

Charbou got to his feet and steadied himself against Bull's shoulder as he scanned the distance. He burst into laughter and pointed to a rooftop where an African American woman was sitting at ease beneath a yellow-and-white-striped umbrella, patiently awaiting assistance.

He cupped his hands into a megaphone. "Oceanetta! You awright?"

She waved both hands. "Awright, baby!" She raised a can of beer. Maybe Robin Hood of the ghetto had already passed her way.

Bull explained. "That's Oceanetta Charbou, Bill's aunt. We couldn't get her to leave the city, no matter how hard we tried."

Oceanetta Charbou never married, and she'd always lived in the house where she and her four siblings were born. She was the youngest sister of Bill's mom and looked to be in her midfifties, maybe a bit older. Wiry and alert, she was just as decisive, able, and attractive as her nephew. From her perch on the roof, she tossed down two plastic shopping bags full of candy, granola bars, and little bottles of water. She slid on her bottom down to the edge of the roof, where the two cops caught her. Once they'd settled her in the Zodiac, she introduced herself to each of the FBI agents in turn. This lady wasn't about to be intimidated by a hurricane.

Charbou glanced up at the umbrella abandoned on the rooftop. "I didn't know you had a hatch in the attic to get on the roof."

"And indeed I didn't, baby, not before today. Don't you 'member what old Vic Schiro told people to do?"

"Hey, give me a break," Charbou said. "Of course! I'm from NOLA too, remember."

"But I'm not!" Amaia spoke up.

"Vic was mayor of New Orleans when Betsy smashed us up back in 1965. He died a while back," Dupree explained. "Lots of our folks drowned when they got trapped in their attics as the water rose. Vic Schiro said everybody in New Orleans ought to keep an ax in the attic." He bent over and took Oceanetta's hands. Her palms were covered with blisters.

Johnson was astonished. "You chopped a hole in the roof?"

Oceanetta didn't reply. She was entirely focused on Dupree. "You from New Orleans, and you was here when Betsy smashed us up. You musta been just a little fella back then." She peered into his face the way some women do when trying to guess age, family, and parentage. "What they call you, darlin'?"

Amaia was entertained. Perceptive and direct, Oceanetta reminded her of Aunt Engrasi.

Charbou made the introductions.

"Dupree," she said, savoring the name. "You a pretty light-skinned fella for a Haitian. They lots of black folks from Haitian families in this area, I know the names."

Dupree smiled. "I'm not upset, but my family is Creole, not Haitian. It's a French name."

"Maybe it is and maybe it ain't. Lots of slaves changed they names when they got free, and Dupree sounds a lot like Dipré from down there in Haiti. Anyhow, your name familiar to me somehow, and I'm gonna remember why. Got a fine memory."

That remark was casual, but it had an unexpected effect. Amaia and Oceanetta saw Dupree close up immediately.

She turned to her nephew. "No way you came all this way just looking for me! You gonna tell me what you doin' here?"

"Oh, it's just 'cause one of your neighbors is shooting at the sky. We want to make sure he doesn't kill somebody. A boy up the street told us his name's Jim Leger."

"Oh, dear Lord, that old crazy man! I heard the shots. It's a semiautomatic, he don't have anything else. Usually keeps it locked up. Must be upset 'cause of the hurricane."

Amaia was surprised. "He's a friend of yours?"

"Well, he's a client. Took out all his insurance policies with me."

"You know where he lives?"

"Sure. Just go down this street and take a right."

Her directions quickly became unnecessary, for the sharp crack of a rifle confirmed them. Bull kept the Zodiac idling a prudent distance back from the corner. Jim Leger had posted himself on his roof near an attic window. Before they could discuss a plan of action, Oceanetta cupped her hands and shouted. "Hey! Jim, this here is Oceanetta Charbou talkin' to you! You gonna tell me what the *hell* you think you doing?"

"Hey there, Oceanetta!" came his polite reply. "Glad to see you okay. Defendin' my house here; not gonna let those sonsabitches steal everything I worked all my life to get."

Oceanetta rolled her eyes. "But what they gonna steal, Jim? You take a look around? We done lost everything, and all you doin' is scaring folks. Look here, the police is come looking for you, and they got a whole heap of better things to do, I tell you. Stop acting like a fool and get down from there before somebody get hurt!"

It took a while, but Jim came down from the roof and leaned out of a second-story window. His bushy white hair framed a face creased with age, but his tank top didn't hide his bulging muscles. Amaia guessed Leger was about seventy-five. He seemed dismayed to find that his actions had brought the police down on him.

Jason Bull was less conciliatory than Oceanetta. "Mr. Leger, we got a report that gunshots are alarming the few neighbors you got left round here. Have you been firing your gun, sir?"

"Well, that is, uh," Leger stammered, "uh-huh, but I was shootin' in the air. Just to keep 'em away, warn 'em I'm still here."

"All right, then, sir, but you need to stop doing that. Nobody's been hurt, but they could be. So no more shooting. You understand what I'm telling you?"

The man nodded and looked toward Oceanetta.

"You're lucky Miz Charbou spoke up for you, and that's why we're not going to report you. But if I hear you get to firing your gun again, if you make me come back, I'll arrest you. Do you understand me, sir?"

Leger, abashed, nodded his head. "Thank you, Oceanetta," he murmured.

She appealed to her nephew. "We can't just leave him here. I know you on duty. I don't think the FBI came all this way because this old crazy man shootin' at the sky. Just take us somewhere dry we can walk out of."

Charbou checked silently with Dupree, who nodded. "Listen, throw some things together—ID, any medicines, just the most basic stuff—and we'll take you and Miz Charbou someplace out of the flood."

Leger turned to Oceanetta. He seemed to feel he owed her an explanation. "I'm gonna stay, Oceanetta. Can't leave my house with nobody in it."

She waved in exasperation, dismissing him as impossible. "You gonna be all right here?"

"Water gonna go down soon. This ain't my first hurricane. Got good water and food, and my house got a solid foundation. But you know that already."

Oceanetta turned to her nephew. "Let's go. I know ol' Jim Leger from way back, and not even the army gonna be able to get him out of there."

They headed down the flooded street and left Leger to his fate, which turned out to be a rescue by the National Guard two weeks later.

Earlier in the morning, it had looked as if the hurricane might come howling down again at any moment. But now the sun was out and threw the devastation into sharp relief. The hurricane had indeed passed. The horrors that remained, anchored in the undeniable reality of the bright light of day, were proof of that.

A stifled, despairing moan brought Amaia out of her musings. She looked behind her. Oceanetta had given in to grief at last, her big eyes filled with fright and rage. She looked around, both hands clasped before her chest.

"You should have listened to us, Auntie, you should have left!" her nephew scolded her, but his heart wasn't in it. "You are such a hardheaded old thing!"

"Had to be here to help my people. Who ever thought things was gonna get this bad?"

"Don't you worry. You got lots of work ahead of you, weeks of it, and lots of people to help."

"Oceanetta," Amaia interjected, "you said something a minute ago that surprised me. Maybe you can help me?"

"Sure."

"You knew Jim Leger had a gun, that it was a semiautomatic, and that he kept it locked up in a gun cabinet."

"I'm an insurance agent, and he bought a bunch of different policies off of me. Life insurance, one on the house, crazy man even got burial insurance to pay for his funeral!"

They laughed.

"Don't y'all laugh! That's my number-one product. More and more people want to make sure the funeral and burial are paid for. But owning a weapon comes with some specific conditions for my company. They don't insure anybody with a gun if they don't keep it locked up in a safe or gun cabinet."

Amaia glanced at Dupree and delved further. "And insurance agents are required to ask that?"

"Not just ask it, baby, they got to document it. Write a report and send photos to prove it."

"So you know everything that's in a house?"

"Long as I was the one who insured it, yes."

"You know how many people live there? And their ages?"

"Of course! If they covered by my policy, I have to know all that."

"Would you know, say, if they've been sick or they've had problems with the law? For example, if the children vandalized things at school or a neighbor's house, or they damaged private property, things like that?"

"Most home insurance—for owners and renters—has liability. These days lots of people have liability insurance, not so much for children as for pets. Fact is, they worry more about damage by the animals."

Amaia gave Dupree an expectant look, but he shook his head. "We already checked the insurance companies," he said. "There's no overlap at all. We looked into the possibility some agent might have changed employers, maybe represented more than one company, but nothing matched up. The insurance agents didn't know one another. Most of the time, they were local reps like Oceanetta, working with different companies. The only thing our cases had in common was that all the properties were insured. That's not surprising, considering they all lived in high-risk areas, and some had previously been affected by storms or tornados."

Amaia stared intently at Oceanetta, as if seeking to divine from the woman's alert, intelligent face the clue that would unlock the case.

Oceanetta returned the gaze. "Of course, if . . ."

"Yes?"

"If those folks you talkin' 'bout was affected before, for example, by a tornado, that information gonna be on record with the AIA."

Jason Bull prompted her. "And so insurance is going to cover the reconstruction of this whole area?"

"Probably the folks who come out of it the best—and it ain't good—gonna be those poor people the banks forced to insure the property when they took out the mortgage. You know, one of those crazy policies that covers everything—right down to volcano damage, even when the closest volcano is all the way on the other side of the country. The kind of policy you got a snowball's chance in hell of ever collecting on."

Johnson looked around. "This looks to me like a clear case for compensation."

"Don't you be so sure," she said with a skeptical look. "Where you think all this water coming from? You sure it's from the hurricane? Why the water keep rising, when the rain finished before eleven o'clock this morning?"

Johnson had been monitoring the radio. "Right now, the Coast Guard's priority is search and rescue, but they're checking the levees from the air. It'll be hours yet before we have any better idea of what happened. It's all speculation at the moment."

"I hope you right," Oceanetta declared heavily, "'cause insurance policies don't cover failures of man-made waterways."

"But that can't be," protested Johnson. "If the canal fails, that's obviously caused by the hurricane!"

"Obvious to you and obvious to me, but not so clear to insurance companies. In sixty-five when Betsy came through, the levees collapsed 'cause people built them with bad quality material. Rainfall that night raised the floodwater two feet, and it stayed like that for hours. Then it went up a foot or more in about fifteen minutes, and kept going, on and on, till it got as high as right now, halfway up the second floor of most buildings. I been up on my roof since eleven o'clock this morning, watching my neighbors' houses break up and float away. The current is so strong and fast it had to be running from east to west—from the streets along the canal toward the far edge of the neighborhood. If it was the levee that caved in and flooded the canal, we gonna get the same thing as back then: pretty words and nothing more."

"Surely you're not telling me the same story those kids did—that the white folks opened the levees to save the French Quarter?"

"The white folks responsible for this mess didn't have to come down to blow up levees or open the gates; they got it all set up long ago, like a time bomb. After Betsy, they rebuilt the levees with crappy material. Second-rate construction to protect second-rate Americans."

Johnson didn't like what he was hearing, because he didn't believe it. He was used to hearing complaints from prisoners—drug dealers, tax cheats, rapists, the whole lot—all of whom had their rants against the system. At the same time, he was bothered, because he liked Oceanetta; she was intelligent and direct. A good woman, devoted to her neighbors, and knowledgeable, she didn't fit the profile of a complainer.

"Wait a minute, Oceanetta," Amaia bid for her attention. "That association must have access to the same information as the insurance companies."

"The AIA insure some on its own, but most of its business is reinsurance and handling reserves. Every state has different laws on insurance, but the AIA has norms for the whole country. They got four divisions: Northeast, Southeast, Midwest, and West."

Amaia took a deep breath, again glancing at Dupree and Johnson. "Let's see, let me get this straight; when someone takes out a new policy to insure a client here in New Orleans, that customer's house, his job, the people who live with him, his pet dog, all that information, with written reports and photos, goes not only to the insurance company . . ."

"They pass it along to the American Insurance Association," Oceanetta confirmed.

"That's for all the insurance companies in the country?"

"Yes, ma'am."

Amaia exhaled and looked around their craft. Despite the surrounding desolation, the glimmer of a smile brightened her face and matched the gleam of satisfaction in her eyes.

40

White Cat

New Orleans, Louisiana

By late afternoon, the heat accumulated during the day and the humidity from evaporating floodwaters had rendered the air all but unbreathable. The most reliable news the team received was via Coast Guard radio, though even that feed wasn't officially confirmed. An hour or so earlier, the guard had reported breaches at London Avenue and Industrial Avenue and verified that the levee at the Seventeenth Street Canal had broken. The first breach had been in the lower section in the far west of the city, sending a flood surge inward from the Old Hammond Highway Bridge. Several search and rescue teams had seen the barrier wall give way before the waters reached the top. More than two hundred feet of levee disappeared beneath a flood that took possession of the area as if it had always owned the place.

Overnight and early in the morning, there'd been reports of cracks in the levees in at least fifteen locations. More rumors and alarms came in throughout the day. Some of the highways that were clear in the middle of the day were now underwater, and the waters kept rising.

At around six thirty p.m., they managed to get Oceanetta on a state police launch that was headed for Charity Hospital with several injured aboard. As soon as she set foot in the other craft, she began handing out snacks and bottles of water to her fellow passengers. Her nephew watched, shaking his head in disbelief, proud but also worried that she'd have nothing left by the time she got to the hospital.

The two vessels parted ways, and Oceanetta turned to wave. At that exact moment she remembered why the name Dupree had seemed so familiar. She gasped, opened her eyes in alarm, and shouted to her nephew. He blew her a kiss and seemed to understand her despite the roar of the motors. Frightened, Oceanetta closed her hand as if catching her nephew's affection out of the air, made a fist, covered it with her other hand, and drew it to her heart. Hoping her message would reach him, she mouthed one single word. Not a sound escaped her lips. The two craft tore off in different directions, but she thought she saw alarm in her nephew's face. She prayed her eyes hadn't deceived her.

They'd kept listening for any reports of serial gunshots. The only news was of single shots, mostly from people on rooftops trying to attract the attention of rescuers. Dupree decided it was time to find a place to hole up for the night. Navigating in circles was a waste of fuel, an increasingly precious commodity, and fruitless wandering would take a toll on their morale. Keeping his team out in the difficult conditions could not only sap them of their energy but also undermine their belief in the assignment. And all the devastation around them—the destroyed houses and ruined vehicles, the desperate cries for help from the rooftops—would overwhelm their sense of purpose.

The unceasing cries of distress brought Amaia to a boiling frustration. She checked for cell service every couple of minutes, but her phone showed no bars at all. She asked Johnson to see whether emails were still working.

"Our Internet service is via satellite, so in theory, it should still connect. Of course, if ground-level repeaters are out, the messages might be stuck in outboxes. The Internet is very slow, but it does seem to be functioning in some parts of the city. Write a message and try to send it. If we happen to connect with a service, it'll go out. But there's no guarantee we'll be able to receive incoming emails."

Amaia drafted a message to the AIA's admin office, addressed to the personnel officer. She gave it to Dupree to review. It identified her as an FBI representative and requested information about the responsibilities of insurance adjustors, their access to personal data, and especially what kind of field assignments they handled for areas struck by disasters. She requested a list of the adjustors between fifty and sixty years of age who had three children. With his approval, she hit send.

What finally pushed Dupree to make a decision was an outburst from Charbou. The detective had remained stubbornly mute since they'd transferred his aunt to the launch. His dull eyes were fixed on the horizon, and he'd only responded in monosyllables. Churning slowly forward, they passed the floating corpse of a white cat just off their bow. Someone had tied a blue ribbon around its neck. And despite everything Charbou had seen that day, the dead white cat with its blue ribbon was the last straw.

He exhaled an enormous gust and turned to them in a rage. "We're not going to catch him. It's impossible! It's taken us hours to get here from Jefferson, and in normal conditions we could have covered that distance in fifteen minutes. The Composer could be in Lakeview or Kenner! How long will it take us to get there? Half the damn highways that were open this morning are underwater now. And that's not even counting the fallen trees, the downed power lines, the cars floating down the streets, or the shit we can't even see, because it's underwater!"

Dupree didn't raise his voice, but he did bend forward, obliging the others to do the same to hear him over the racket of the outboard motor. "I think the Composer's got the same problems we do. He'd need to have some sort of boat, and I don't think he does. When he got to Jefferson, he could still wade, and we're almost sure that's what he did. Circumstances have changed for all of us. I think he's going to choose victims in places where he can easily escape. He can't take the risk of a rescue team turning up while he's busy killing them."

Johnson was seated in the middle of the Zodiac with a city map spread across his knees. "We've been overwhelmed by events, but so has he. If he had a plan, he has to change it now, however difficult that may be. If he selects some family in the city who survived the storm, they'll have to fit his profile. Even if he's got a whole list of families in Kenner, he can't get out there, but the central city is still accessible. No matter how much our murderer wants to kill, he faces the same constraints we do. And remember, he's injured." Johnson placed a finger on the map and moved it from zone to zone. "I believe he'll stay in the French Quarter, around Frenchmen Street, close to the outside edge of Treme, somewhere around Canal Street or Magazine or Jackson Square. That'll be his home base. He needs somewhere to stay. If he doesn't already have shelter, he'll have to find some, just as we will."

"I don't know," Charbou said. "This is total chaos. No power, no clean water, and we're going to need more fuel before long. By nightfall this place will be back in the Stone Age. I think we should be rescuing people instead of maintaining a holding pattern and waiting for reports of gunfire."

Dupree had been dreading this moment all day. He'd been well aware of the cops' anger as their craft passed along the fronts of flooded houses where once-treasured possessions bobbed in the filthy water. He'd seen them clench their jaws when a group of women carrying infants shouted pleas for help from the bridges over the interstate. He knew they were boiling inside.

Bull answered his partner. "You accepted the mission. It's important, and we're responsible for seeing it through. Others are attending to the rescues. Help will be arriving soon."

Charbou looked around wildly. "Oh, yeah? And where are the fucking rescuers?" He was yelling. "All I hear is people shouting for help, help that isn't coming, but we're right here, right now. This isn't why I joined the force!"

Amaia hadn't said anything. She moved to sit across from Charbou in the Zodiac, then reached out and touched his hand. His dark skin shone with brilliant drops of sweat, in contrast to her pale touch.

The effect of her gentle approach was immediate. His angry fist yielded and opened to receive her hand. His jaw relaxed and his anger drained away. Dupree was sure Charbou was about to say something, but whatever the words may have been, he swallowed them and then sat silent with his eyes on Amaia. His cry of revolt had wafted away with the wind.

Her voice was firm. "Nobody who lives through the storm should be forced to surrender to a murderer. Everyone who survives this day is a child of the hurricane. Katrina couldn't kill them, so no one else has the right to. We can't allow him to turn New Orleans into a killer's private theme park."

Dupree nodded, seeing she'd prevailed. He knew she'd done so with her touch, not just with her words. When reason fails, when instructions lose all meaning, when fatigue overwhelms bodies and souls, when it comes down to the decision to continue or give up, no force is more redemptive than the touch of skin on skin.

Sunset was forecast for 7:25 p.m. The light took a sudden flight westward in the last half hour of the day and colored the sky pink and purple. It painted a sunset so glorious and incongruous that not one of them would ever forget it.

Charbou's prediction came true. As light died on the horizon, the city of music reverted to the Stone Age.

They needed to find shelter as soon as possible. Most of the reference points along the flooded streets would soon be invisible. Though they'd originally planned to get to Florida Avenue, they chose a closer street that might have been Dorgenois or Rocheblave. Bull, at the helm, sounded the air horn. Its blast rolled through the dark as they slid up to a two-story house that was completely flooded downstairs. The structure looked stable, and the second-story windows were accessible from the boat. He steered along the side to make sure the house was uninhabited, sweeping their spotlight across the upper windows in search of signs of life. Bull had begun to turn the boat when Johnson called an alert. "There! I saw something. I think there's someone inside."

Bull corrected course and sent their craft back in the direction Johnson was pointing. They all focused their lights there.

The back door downstairs, barely visible in the water, stood open an inch or two. A hand clutched the top of the door.

"Someone's trapped inside!"

They maneuvered the Zodiac close to the house. Johnson and Charbou grabbed the top of the door and yanked. Stuck underwater in the mud, it didn't budge. Dupree joined them. The three pulled with all their might. The door grudgingly gave way just a little, then a bit more, and at last they managed to pull it open. The hand dropped, the Zodiac rebounded sluggishly, and a corpse floated out of the opening. Caught by the strong current, it glided past their craft along the wall of the house. Amaia could tell the man was elderly, because of his white hair and beard. His skin, softened and bleached by the water, gave no clue to his actual age. He'd probably died the previous night during the worst of the storm. Bacteria in the water and the elevated daytime temperature had done the rest. Bare feet, colorless as gelatin, brushed against the siding. He was in jeans. His white T-shirt had bunched up and left exposed the lower part of a pale belly already mottled with the lividity of decomposition. Red letters across his T-shirt proclaimed him "World's Greatest Dad."

Amaia's scream turned into an agonized moan. All eyes turned to her. She was covering her mouth with both hands as if trying to fend off the pain and menacing darkness. Face contorted, eyes filled with horror, she watched, devastated, as the sluggish current moved the body along. Without stopping to think, she plunged overboard so quickly that no one could stop her. As her team members shouted and called her back, she treaded water, blinded by tears and mud-laden water. She swam across the back yard to the street behind the row of houses, conscious she was fortunate to be wearing the buoyant ballistic vest of the New Orleans police, not the FBI issue.

Bull maneuvered the Zodiac in an attempt to reach her, but the sharp points atop the fence between the back yards were too much of a risk to the boat. He reversed course, retreated a couple of yards, and navigated along the far side of the fence to the street.

Dupree stopped Charbou from going overboard after her. "Wait!"

"What? But . . ."

"Just wait."

Amaia reached the floating body and grabbed it by one hand. He'd been a big man. Strong. Even afloat, the body was heavier than she could manage; she couldn't move it back toward the house. Desperate, she looked about her.

"Amaia!" Charbou shouted from the Zodiac. "There's nothing you can do! He's dead!"

But she wasn't listening. Her eyes, filled with tears, fixed once more on the T-shirt. *Was this man the world's greatest dad?* She heard her own voice as a child of twelve, answering from far, far away. *He was. For someone, he was, and that was enough.*

She unbuckled his belt and pulled it free of his jeans. She ran it through the two rear loops, then took the other end and towed the body sluggishly to the metal post of a traffic signal. Finding footing on the cement base, she used the belt to tie the body fast. If that man had been a good father, a child would come to grieve at his graveside; it was only fair to give that child the chance. She was determined to keep the flood from washing him away. She floated there beside the corpse, absolutely still. She sought the words for a prayer. "Our Father, our Father, *ourFather ourFather* . . ."

"What the holy hell is she doing?" Charbou exclaimed, transfixed.

Dupree was going to tell him, but Johnson spoke first. "She's mourning her own father."

Bull and Charbou turned to look at him.

"Salazar's father died yesterday. Half an hour before we left Quantico, they telephoned to call her back to Spain. This morning they let us know he'd died."

"I can't believe it! Why didn't you send her home? Just look at her!"

"She chose to stay. And not one of us has the right to judge her. We all make tough choices, promises that are hard to keep. You were about to give up a little while ago. I'm in awe of the way she's been handling it, but a person can be taken by surprise. By a drowned pet, for example. Or the words on a T-shirt. Sometimes it's just too much."

Charbou accepted that reminder with a nod. Turning away to give Amaia her privacy, he said, "Don't you think we should go get her?"

"Yes," said Dupree. "We should. But give her another minute."

They chose a fairly large house two streets farther west, announced their presence loudly, and shined the searchlight beam into the windows before concluding the place was empty. Then they forced a second-floor window open and crawled inside. Straightening up, they experienced the odd sensation of being able to stand erect and take steps across a firm surface after the long hours in the Zodiac. The staircase to the lower floor was flooded right up to the top. The second floor had three bedrooms in good shape and a bathroom where toilet overflow had left a foul and stinking mess. Johnson closed the bathroom door while Bill and Bull surveyed the rooms and checked a low, windowless attic crammed with junk.

The air inside was hot and heavy and humid and reeked of slime. Even so, they were grateful they could stretch out, take off their protective equipment, and settle down. In tacit accord, they avoided the beds. Taking shelter under an unknown stranger's roof was one thing, but sleeping in unmade beds with outlines left in the bedclothes by the former inhabitants was another. Instead, the team gathered cushions and pillows, placed them along the wall, and sat together on the floor of the room they'd first entered.

The darkness outside was absolute, a black void with not a star in sight. Now that the helicopters had returned to base, the only sounds were their breathing and the creaks of swelling wood and timbers absorbing the foul water. They'd eaten nothing but granola bars since their hasty breakfast at the fire station. They parceled out the night's rations and ate. Their spirits were lifted for the first time that day; they even smiled a bit in the eerie light of their electric lamps.

Johnson spoke to Amaia. "I was trying to think all day long why your hometown sounded so familiar, and I finally remembered. Early in my career, I was assigned to a unit that tracked fanatical religious sects; that was before I got into behavioral analysis. The literature frequently referred to the Pyrenees, especially the border region where Spain meets France. Lots of stories about witchcraft, rites, and covens of witches. Zugarramurdi and those other places must be fairly close to your town. You're from Elizondo, right?"

She nodded reluctantly. "Yes, I am. And they're not far away."

"Come to think of it, wasn't Elizondo one of the places the Inquisition went looking for the devil?"

Amaia said nothing.

Johnson's eyes sparkled. He was into the subject. "Yes, that was Elizondo," he said, pleased he'd remembered the story. "And the attorney for the Inquisition had your name, Salazar." His revelation made the others look up. "Alonso de Salazar Frías!"

"The Inquisition were like the guys at the Salem witch trials, weren't they?" Charbou asked. "You related to them, Salazar? Maybe he was an ancestor?"

"I doubt it," she said grimly. "My family name comes from a river near where I was born."

"But did you ever look into it?" Johnson insisted, rubbing a palm across his bushy mustache. "I think it'd be really interesting. I know a researcher who's good at genealogical research; she can track a family name back hundreds of years."

Dupree, who'd been watching Amaia closely during this exchange, intervened. "Johnson, seems to me Salazar's not interested."

"But why not?" Bull asked. He was surprised. "If it were me, I'd sure want to know all about it."

Johnson didn't give up. "If your family has always lived in that region, it seems likely that sometime or other they could have attended the Inquisition's trials. As witnesses, maybe; maybe even as defendants. I'm remembering now that when Salazar the investigator was sent to look for the devil, he received thousands of denunciations. Must've affected the entire population in one way or another."

"How many people live in your town now?" Charbou asked.

"About three thousand."

"There you go!" Johnson exclaimed. "Every single soul probably either denounced someone or was accused by his neighbors!"

"Exactly!" she replied bitterly.

Dupree addressed Amaia. "I have the impression that bothers you. Why?"

Amaia didn't answer.

Johnson tried to be helpful. "Assistant Inspector, that happened hundreds of years ago. If it'd been in the United States, by now the town would have six haunted hotels, three walking tours to the witches' houses, and a dozen souvenir shops."

"I see two possible explanations for that," Amaia replied. "Either Americans don't believe a word of your haunted history, or you have a healthier approach to the magic that exists in the world."

Dupree refused to let her off the hook. "You're saying the way of life in Baztán isn't healthy?"

Bull was intrigued. "What's Baztán?"

Amaia exhaled loudly. "Baztán is the valley where my town is located. As far as I'm concerned, the world would be better off without that kind of fake spirituality. Cult beliefs may seem amusing, even ridiculous, but they embrace primitive superstitions. They promote social stigma, exclusion, and suffering."

Bull was loving this. "You trying to say they still believe in witches back in Baztán?"

Johnson answered. "The real question is: Are there still witches in Baztán today?"

Once they'd eaten, they became aware of the immense physical and emotional cost of their long day. Bull volunteered to man the radio for first watch. The rest gathered pillows and cushions and chose rooms where they could curl up.

Amaia settled close to the open window, the only access to the outside. She appreciated the movement of air into the room, however sluggish. She detested the darkness. She adjusted her flashlight to point to the floor, where it projected a light that was insufficient to illuminate the room but just enough to keep the night creatures away.

She glanced at the window and realized she hadn't thought of the *gauekoak* since her childhood. *Gauekoak* were the dark ones, the spirits of the night. Those homeless wanderers sought out a dark corner of your soul where they could hide forever. She recalled seeing an old woman crawl beneath her bed, as frightened as a child, in an effort to escape the *gauekoak*.

The Composer floated into her mind. She was convinced that at exactly that moment, he, too, was staring into the darkness somewhere in the city. The difference between them was plain: he was already in thrall to the night. Darkness dwelt within him. He carried the *gauekoak* in his core, because he'd become one with them. She shuddered, surprised by the force of memory and by the realization that her background gave her insight into the Composer.

"Gaueko," she whispered to fend off the darkness. That ancient, menacing Euskara word for the lord of darkness, spoken so far from Baztán, brought to mind so many other words and phrases. Some were obscure and insidious; others were as beloved and as warm and welcoming as a hug.

"Are you feeling better now?" Dupree's voice brought her back to the present. He'd just entered the room.

She let out a strangled sigh. "I'm sorry, I was totally out of line. I wasn't thinking."

"Never mind. It's just that the water out there is full of bacteria. If you have any open wounds, make sure they're clean and disinfected. Otherwise you're likely to get gangrene."

She tried to smile but her grimace was that of a woeful clown. "I wasn't referring to the water."

Dupree nodded. He wasn't referring to the water either. The problem was that he didn't know how to approach Amaia. She was an enigma, one of the most complicated people he'd ever met. He decided to forget subtleties and take a direct approach.

"My parents died during Hurricane Betsy. Father was a doctor and Mother was his nurse. They'd been called to help a woman in labor, and they were trapped on Grand Isle when the storm hit. People found them a week later, dead inside their car."

"I'm sorry," Amaia told him, watching his face. "Katrina must be awakening terrible memories."

"I was very young, just a little kid. The only memories I have of them are from photographs. Nana, my father's cousin, brought me up."

"Do you have brothers or sisters?"

Dupree looked away. "I have a sister. How about you?" The speed of that response was revealing. He didn't want to talk about his family.

"Two sisters, both older. But we're not close. Like you, my aunt brought me up."

Dupree regarded her but didn't ask more. Two older sisters she wasn't close to, she'd gone to schools in the United States since she was twelve, and she'd chosen not to go back to see her dying father.

"I saw you praying for that man. You did a good thing."

She stared at him for several seconds as if she hadn't understood his remark or was weighing its implications. She stared for another ten seconds at the floorboards faintly illuminated by her flashlight. When she did speak, her voice almost startled them both.

"When I was little, I prayed the Lord's Prayer. Do you know it?"

"Of course. I'm not particularly devout, but I am Catholic."

He saw she hadn't heard his answer, for she was speaking as if in a trance. "I prayed each night, every night."

She hadn't listened for his response because her mind was far away. Her posture was revealing. She was pressing her back against the wall, her knees slightly bent, and she was staring at the floor as if hypnotized by the little circle of light projected by her flashlight. "I repeated every word, every phrase of it, but especially the first one: 'Our Father.'" She spoke slowly and quietly. "I wasn't praying to God, though. I was pleading with my own father. He was in the next room, but he always pretended he hadn't heard."

She paused. Then she smiled faintly. "All these years, I never realized that. I saw it today when I was trying to pray for that man's soul."

Dupree was mesmerized. Questions crowded his mind, but he pushed them away. Her father was in the adjacent room, but what had frightened her? Was she pleading with him? Dupree took in what she'd said and what her body language betrayed. He absorbed every syllable. She had just had a true revelation, and as he listened, he knew his intuition had been correct. And he knew this woman was a mystery.

"I was calling for my father. Like this whole city, I was crying for help from the rooftops." Again, Dupree saw Amaia realizing the truth of the words as she spoke them. "You think you're part of a family, and you pray because you think your father's listening. He didn't listen until I died. I waited and waited, and at the last moment, he pulled me out of the grave."

She looked up at Dupree. He silently begged her not to stop. He prayed his expression wouldn't alert Amaia to how much of herself she was revealing.

"For years I thought he picked me up from where I was lying because he loved me. But the truth was that he was ashamed. That's what motivated him: shame. Shame stopped his ears, and shame made him pick me up and take me away. But only because everyone was going to find out. Because if he hadn't moved me, things would have been even worse for him. I was as devastated as this city, but the reason he rescued me was that he didn't want to be humiliated before the whole town."

Dupree watched the young woman as she slept. She'd slipped into sleep almost instantly: one moment she'd been speaking, the next moment she was curled up into a fetal position below the open window. She left him so quickly that he wondered whether she'd actually been aware of what she'd been saying. Maybe he'd witnessed somnambulistic free association brought on by stress and exhaustion. The flashlight beam aimed at the floor painted sinister shadows on her face. He was sure they mirrored the darkness that haunted her dreams.

Amaia was his needle in a haystack, a human capable of brilliant logical reasoning yet keenly aware of the invisible universe. She analyzed the world from two eternally contentious perspectives. Dupree brushed his fingers across the scars on his chest and counted the raised knots along the edge of the injury. Five of them. He'd been honest with her. He didn't remember that distant night his parents had died; that night had belonged to Samedi. That night had plunged the city into chaos. He looked down at the unconscious young woman, fearing and yet at the same time urgently desiring a crisis that would push her to her limits. That crisis would come when Baron Samedi appeared again to reinstate his reign of anarchy and death.

41

The Heart of a Roebuck

Elizondo

Ignacio Aldecoa didn't care for Elizondo. His wife, Joxepi, claimed he spent so much time up in the mountains that he was getting as rough and antisocial as his sheep. She used to tell her women friends that for Ignacio, walking through Elizondo was like being caught up in a mill wheel, because when he got back to their house, he seemed as confused and disoriented as if he'd gotten a toss and a dunking. Ignacio didn't mind. He knew his wife loved him just as he was. She respected his silence and need for his own space, and she was happy raising their children at his side in that remote little hovel her sisters claimed no woman in her right mind would ever put up with.

Ignacio knew that in return, he had to accompany his wife to town, usually once a week. They'd order a coffee, enjoy a snack from the pastry shop, run a few errands, and do some window shopping.

They'd been standing for a while on Calle Santiago in front of the church. His wife was chatting with Engrasi, whom she'd known since their childhood together. Ignacio nodded from time to time without following their conversation as he watched Engrasi's little niece playing nearby. The girl was thin and tall for her age, which was maybe ten or twelve. She hopped, avoiding the cracks between the stone sidewalk tiles that glistened after the afternoon rain and presented an almost invisible hopscotch pattern. From time to time, Amaia raised her head, glanced at her aunt, and then continued her silent, solitary game.

Ignacio appreciated Amaia. He didn't usually care for children other than his own. Most were noisy, wild, and demanding. But this delicate little creature was different. Once he said as much to Joxepi, and she explained, "The poor little thing has suffered a lot. Her mother is sick in the head, and nobody's been able to cure the woman. She has three daughters, but she's rejected this one since the day the child was born."

Ignacio had been raised in the countryside, so he understood entirely. Among animals both wild and domesticated, sometimes a mother rejected an offspring for no apparent reason. She left it to die from hunger, cold, and neglect. And those babies simply accepted that extraordinary cruelty from a mother entirely devoted to her other offspring.

Ignacio was aware he felt an affinity for Amaia because she resembled him in some way. Quiet and watchful, she greeted people shyly and then withdrew a few steps to play in silence, always keeping close to her aunt. Amaia didn't care for Elizondo either. She moved like a roebuck caught in traffic, cocking an ear at every sound. He had the impression that her little heart quivered at every fleeting intuition.

The child continued playing her game of invisible hopscotch. Ignacio glanced at the sky. It had darkened, but he hadn't noticed, because the streetlamps had been lit for a while. He checked his watch and was surprised, realizing once again how much Elizondo's artificial urban illumination distorted his sense of time. He looked back at the girl, lit by the orange-tinted gleam of gas lamps on the church front. He felt a sudden stir of alarm.

At first he wasn't sure what caused it. Long before this moment, he'd developed a reliable sixth sense while protecting and caring for his flock—that's what happens when you go out on the mountainside every day with sheep as tasty to predators as candy is to children. He stepped away from the women without a word and went to keep a closer eye on the girl. Nothing at all unusual happened during the following five minutes. The child continued her game of hidden hopscotch.

Engrasi and Joxepi chatted cheerfully. At one point, Ignacio heard his wife call out for corroboration. "Isn't that right, Ignacio?" He nodded automatically without taking his eyes off the girl. A car pulled up next to the sidewalk. Raindrops on the chassis shone like blisters from countless burns. The orange illumination of the streetlights was mirrored in its high sheen. He instantly recognized it as the car with French plates that had idled past a few minutes earlier on the way downhill. Later that night, as he tossed and turned in bed unable to sleep, he would become almost certain that wasn't the second but instead the third time he'd seen the car. A few minutes earlier he'd wondered why that vehicle with tinted windows was creeping along so slowly.

Amaia stopped her game. Her instinct, acute as that of a roebuck, made her step back. She stuck her hands into the pockets of her overcoat. *Good girl,* Ignacio thought as he focused on the car.

The town's proximity to the French border had provided it with many things throughout its long history, both good and bad. Relations with the neighbors on the other side were generally very good. For centuries, men and women from the two sides had coexisted, exchanging friendship, language, love, black-market goods, and livestock, nimbly avoiding the customs regulations rigorously applied at official crossing points. French neighbors were one thing, but French tourists were something quite different. Given the exchange rate between the franc and the peseta, it suited them to cross the border to send mail, to buy tobacco, alcohol, and food, or just to have a good time. More and more frequently, the town was full of tourists, some of whom had been celebrating so hard they couldn't find their way home.

French visitors lost and looking for the border crossing, a voice of reason told him. His instinct raised a red flag. Logic told him the window on the passenger side would lower so someone could ask for directions to get back home. But no—the rear door opened instead.

Ignacio took a big step in that direction. A pale white feminine hand and a sleeve in billowing sheer fabric emerged and beckoned to the girl. There was something seductive and spellbinding in that gesture, as elegant as the choreographed move of a ballerina. The small pale hand hovered in the air like the head of a serpent.

Amaia stepped toward the car and Ignacio hurled himself in her direction. Engrasi and Joxepi broke off their conversation, astonished at his bizarre behavior, and turned to watch as he ran. His racing figure blocked their view of the vehicle. Thinking of it later, Ignacio had the impression that everything had happened very quickly but also with terrible slowness, simultaneously at full speed and in slow motion. He shouted to the girl, but his throat closed up and no words came out, only a wheeze as desperate as a dying breath.

But the girl with the roebuck's distrustful heart had learned to stay alert. Amaia's head swiveled toward him, and her eyes registered the shepherd's frantic alarm. She froze. She gasped, petrified by the menace and yet entranced and lured toward the car. Ignacio had almost reached her on the sidewalk, but the distance still seemed immense. He had to go faster, because he was as close to the child as she was to the car. Amaia didn't budge, apparently hypnotized by the death angel's white hand reaching out to possess her. Engrasi and Joxepi screamed hysterically behind him, for they'd just seen the car and now understood what was happening.

He reached out, almost there. His fingers brushed the fur around the hood of Amaia's coat just as a leg clad in dark trousers and a high-heeled boot came out of the back seat and planted itself at the edge of the sidewalk. The head of the woman with that pale hand was covered by the cowl of her cloak, and her face was screened by a profusion of dark hair. The color and texture of that skin was burned into Ignacio's mind, forever remembered as that of a wolf. Her elegant hand darted through the air, seized Amaia's arm, and pulled the girl off balance with a powerful yank. Ignacio had no plan; he wrapped his arms around the child's waist and pulled with all his might. Amaia's body rose above the sidewalk as she was jerked off her feet. The white hand on her arm couldn't maintain its grip, and its nails made a long tearing sound as they were dragged the full length of the girl's gabardine coat sleeve. The clutching hand didn't relax its grip even when it reached Amaia's bare hand, where its nails slashed deep red furrows. That hand held on to the very last, until Ignacio's second frantic heave pulled the girl free of those claws.

Everything happened incredibly quickly after that. The woman leaped back into the car and slammed the door. The car roared off. Engrasi and Joxepi came running. Ignacio gasped for air, holding Amaia so close he could feel the wildly fluttering beat of her little roebuck heart. He put the girl down, but he didn't release her. He stepped back only when Engrasi and Joxepi gathered her up, their voices a simultaneous confusion. "My God!" and "Thank God!" rang out as they caressed her head and clothing, demanding to know what had happened. Engrasi shrieked when she saw that the child was bleeding. Ignacio bent over and took the girl's hand. The rip along the sleeve was deep and clean, as if it had been torn not with fingernails but with the sharp tines of a carving fork. The red furrows he'd seen across the back of her hand were bordered by torn whitish shreds of skin that exposed the girl's pink, oozing flesh to the night air.

"It's nothing," Amaia whispered, catching his gaze. "It hardly hurts at all."

She couldn't fool Ignacio, for he heard the quaver of panic in her voice as she tried to reassure them. His heart nearly burst when he heard that. *It hardly hurts at all,* he thought as he fought to catch his breath, but he wasn't reassured, not at all, far from it. He'd give it time and calm down, because, after all, his wife and the girl's aunt kept insisting he'd saved her. Maybe he'd have accepted that if he hadn't glimpsed that fury's eyes, if only for an instant. They were completely empty. No hatred, resentment, or madness; as he defied her, determined not to release the child, she was amused. She showed him her row of sharp tiny yellow baby teeth. Like rat's teeth. He held her gaze until the car door broke their contact. What mesmerized him was the fact that she'd showed not the slightest trace of annoyance.

That she-wolf wasn't defeated. She was sure to try again.

42

Bazagrá

New Orleans, Louisiana
5:00 a.m., Tuesday, August 30, 2005

Johnson tapped her gently on the shoulder. "Salazar, wake up. We have a report of gunshots. Close by."

"The sun's not up," she said, trying to clear her groggy mind as she peered through the window. "What time is it?"

"Just past five."

She shrugged into her ballistic vest and quickly checked the room to make sure they were leaving nothing behind. "Several shots?"

"The report was very specific. Gunshots in a family residence close to Saint Louis Cemetery," Bull said. "They think it was Bienville Street, but they're not sure."

"That's no help at all!" Charbou complained. "Bienville runs from Saint Louis Cemetery No. 1 to No. 2. They have the same name."

Amaia dropped into the Zodiac and took a seat in the stern next to Bull, who'd already started the motor and was ready to steer them into the street.

"He's still with them? Do we know that?" she asked. "Is he holding hostages?"

"No idea," Bull admitted. "The report wasn't from the ops center. It came from a Red Cross launch passing through the area. That's why they couldn't give a precise location. Lots of their volunteers aren't from the city, and most of the street signs are gone."

They elected to head toward Saint Louis Cemetery No. 1. If the person who'd radioed it in wasn't familiar with the city, he wouldn't know there was another Saint Louis Cemetery; otherwise he'd have given a more specific address.

They reached Bienville and throttled back the motor. Terrified screams from a single-story house told them where to go.

The water was halfway up the house. Faint, flickering yellow light, probably from candles, shone through an open dormer window in the gabled roof. The screams came from there. Bull took the Zodiac to the wall. Bill and Bull leaped out of the boat as Johnson tied up, and scrambled across the tar-paper roof. At Bull's signal, the policemen erupted into the little room. An instant later, they called the others.

The attic, even though it had a window, was actually only a low space between the roof and the downstairs ceiling. Unpainted rafters sloped down to meet rough flooring. Yellowing lumps of spun fiber, now useless as insulation, were stuffed into the corners of the space. An ancient African American man, tiny, wrinkled, and covered with sweat, lay on the plank flooring by the window, gasping and groaning, his right hand clutched to his chest. Amaia assumed he'd been shot, especially because an old woman was aiming a rifle down the steep stairwell, cursing furiously at someone invisible in the darkness downstairs. A little boy, maybe four or five years old, had crawled back under the lowest part of the roof and was huddled against the mass of yellowing insulation, sobbing.

Amaia felt a film of sweat break out over her skin as soon as she got inside. The temperature in the attic must have been well over one hundred degrees. The place stank of piss, sweat, and mold. The only light came from the stub of a candle inside an ancient hurricane lamp at the woman's feet. Her enormous shadow moved across the attic space every time she shifted her position, making it hard for them to see what was going on.

Charbou seized the woman from behind, immobilized her, and disarmed her. His firm movements were assured and unprovocative. She gave up her weapon but doubled her ranting against the unknown intruder downstairs. Alarmed, Charbou pointed his pistol in that direction.

Johnson crouched next to the moaning victim. The old man's clothes were soaked with sweat. Without hesitating, Johnson ripped off the old man's shirt to check for a wound. There was no blood, but it was obvious he'd received a tremendous blow to the chest. Several bright-red marks were evident over a massive bruise.

"This may be a heart attack." Johnson's voice was uncertain.

The old woman was crouched behind Charbou, gabbling hysterically and pointing down the dark stairwell. Bull tried to ask her what had happened, but it was no use. She kept shouting nonsense and pointing down the stairwell.

Dupree stepped back to the window and looked out on a sky so black it seemed as if dawn would never come. He raised his gun so the laser sight on the barrel sent a glowing beam through the darkness, and he pulled the trigger. The tremendous explosion deafened them all. They all turned toward him.

Dupree said nothing, but he had everyone's attention. Amaia doubted anyone could have heard him if he'd been speaking just then, for their ears were ringing from the gunshot. He raised a finger to his lips to command silence; he stepped over the man on the floorboards and slowly approached the huddled boy. He hunched low but his head brushed against the underside of the roof. Keeping the dazzling beam of his flashlight away from the boy's eyes, Dupree spoke quietly. "We're from the police. We're here to help you. You're safe now. Stop crying and listen up. Is there anyone else here?"

The boy wasn't sobbing anymore. He pointed toward the stairs.

"Okay, that's fine, I understand. Somebody's downstairs. But is there anyone hiding up here?"

The boy shook his head and again pointed urgently toward the stairs.

"Did they touch you?" Dupree asked, tapping his own chest.

"Only Grandpa."

"That's good. Stay right there." Dupree moved out from the low space and got to his feet. He holstered his weapon and turned to the old woman. He took her by the shoulders instead of speaking. He guided her away from Charbou and turned her so she could see his face. "How many of them?"

"They took the girls!" she sobbed.

"Who took the girls?" Dupree asked her in a low voice.

The woman replied, plainly terrified but quiet now. "Samedi. Samedi took my girls."

Charbou was surprised. "Samedi?"

"Baron Samedi, *le criminel* Samedi!" she insisted, her voice rising. "Samedi took my babies!"

Dupree and Bull exchanged a nod. Amaia looked to Johnson for an explanation. She was fed up. She'd been obliged to put up with this game of complicit little nods and cryptic remarks for the last three days. She wanted to know what the hell was going on. It was obvious this had nothing to do with the Composer, and it was just as clear to her that both Bull and Dupree had been expecting something like this from the moment the team got to New Orleans.

"Are they down there? Did they run off?" Dupree asked the old woman.

"No, they gone and they carried off the girls, but my man," she said, waving toward the old man stretched out on the floor, "he shot one of them devils. They leave him behind and that one run off to hide down there. I know he down there, I can hear him; he not gonna get far after what my Henry done to him. No way to kill them devils, but my man put him down." Her face was full of fierce pride. "They almost kill Henry for that."

"How old are the girls?"

"Eight and twelve, Diana and Bella, my granddaughters, Jacob's sisters." She pointed toward the dark corner where the boy crouched. "Samedi, he take only girls. He want virgin blood, want to eat their hearts."

Bull nodded, exchanged a glance with Dupree, and motioned toward the ladder.

Charbou looked from Dupree to Bull as he listened to the old woman's incoherent remarks, astonished to see them taking her seriously.

"Hey, can someone explain what the fuck—"

"Keep quiet!" Dupree sternly cut him off and focused again on the woman. Amaia was shocked by Dupree's reaction. He leaned close to the woman to reassure her. "Tell me, ma'am, how many are down there?"

"One! Henry shot him in the leg, the others leave him behind. He down there now, I hear him." She waved a trembling hand toward the stairs.

"Now, think carefully. Is there any other way out?"

"No, we nailed plywood 'cross all the doors and windows, and then we came up here; they made this window up here in the old house 'cause they afraid of floods."

Dupree took out his gun and shined his flashlight down the stairwell. The water was all the way up to the landing where the stairs turned and were lost in darkness. A trail of blood confirmed her story. The quantity on the stairs meant that whoever lost it was in danger of bleeding out completely. Dupree heard water splashing. The movements sent ripples across the surface of the dirty lapping water. Dupree turned to the old woman, pointed toward the far end of the attic, and whispered, "I want you to go over there next to your man and your grandson. Y'all stay right there and keep quiet. You hear?"

She nodded without a word and retreated to settle down next to the old man, who was gasping for breath.

Dupree motioned to Amaia and Johnson. They positioned themselves next to Charbou, who showed his dislike for what was happening by shaking his head and glaring at his partner. Amaia saw he was furious. He planted himself on the stairwell where Johnson sent him, but he didn't object when Dupree and Bull took the lead on the way downstairs.

They avoided the trail of blood as they descended, pressing themselves against the wall as they approached the landing.

"This is the police!"

Charbou pointed to the turn and signaled to Dupree that the suspect was there, just as they'd expected. The water on the ground floor was deep enough to be over anyone's head, so the suspect had to be on the stairs.

"We know you're there, and we know you're hurt!" Bull called out. "Throw your weapons into the water and put your hands above your head, where we can see them!"

Again, they heard the splash of someone wading through the water.

"We're armed and there's no other way out." Bull's voice left no room for doubt. "Don't make this any more complicated than it has to be. We'll shoot you if we have to!"

Bull peeked around the turn in the staircase and pulled back immediately. He gestured and mouthed his report without making a sound: "He's right there. Water up to his knees." He made a fist, extended his index finger and thumb, then shook the hand from side to side to indicate he hadn't seen a weapon.

Dupree turned to pass the information silently to those above. He found that Amaia had followed and was right behind him.

Dupree covered Bull, who pressed against the wall as he descended with his pistol ready. The figure began thrashing wildly as soon as the flashlight beam hit him. He kept his head lowered, and a mop of dirty hair hid his face. He swayed from side to side as if about to collapse. Bull shined the flashlight at the man's feet. The water around him was stained deep red, and each time he lifted his leg, a flash of something stark white emerged from the pool of blood. With his next step, the figure tottered as if about to collapse.

Bull guessed the white object was maybe eight inches long. He hadn't seen it clearly, but it might have been the handle of a knife or small machete. The suspect had no other weapon, or at least he wasn't carrying one, for one hand was against the wall and the other clutched the wooden rail. Bull moved the flashlight beam upward, trying to illuminate the man's face, but the tilted head and mass of hair made that impossible.

Bull realized that the suspect hadn't made a single sound. He hadn't moaned or complained either, even though he was bleeding profusely and having trouble keeping himself erect. Bull aimed the light below the man's waist again, got a closer look, lost his footing, and fell back on his haunches on the stairs.

Dupree rushed down to Bull, training his gun on the suspect as he helped the cop to his feet. They descended side by side and halted two stairs above the hunched figure. Dupree shouted at the suspect to sit down. Above them, Amaia used her own flashlight to illuminate the scene, revealing the suspect's puny frame wrapped in some kind of knee-length poncho. He was bent almost double, and his neck seemed to be sunk between his shoulder blades in an unnatural position.

"It's a woman," Amaia breathed behind them.

Giving no sign she saw or heard them, the agonized creature continued turning in awkward circles, using her long, bony hands to maintain her balance, her overgrown fingernails like dark claws clutching the handrail and leaving deep scratches in the varnished finish. Amaia saw clearly what had so astonished Bull. And when the woman next stepped through the pool of bloody water, the others saw that the brilliant white object they'd mistaken for the handle of a knife was in fact a broken, jagged bone protruding from the bloody flesh of her leg.

"Get me a tourniquet!" Dupree went down the last two steps.

"Oh, my God!" Amaia exclaimed in horror, unable to tear her eyes away from the wound, unable to understand how the creature could possibly stay erect without howling in pain.

"For fuck's sake!" Charbou exclaimed behind her and then pleaded, "Make her stop, goddamn it!"

After twisting a length of soaked cloth above the injury, Dupree grabbed her shoulder, forcing her to turn on her axis. She fell against the balustrade. Bull and Amaia kept their pistols on the woman as Dupree shined his light on her from above. Fighting back his disgust, he stretched his gloved hand toward her face. She recoiled.

"I'm not going to hurt you, I just want to see your face," he said. Amaia heard something in his voice, an emotion that hadn't been there before.

An obscure muttering burst from her mouth. "I'm . . ."

"She said something," Amaia cried. "She's talking!"

They fell silent, trying to catch the thin thread of her voice.

More unintelligible whispering. And again, that whistling intake of breath. "I'm . . . mm . . . mmm . . . dead."

Charbou threw down a strip of cloth found somewhere, and Bull twisted it around the suspect's thigh.

Amaia fixed her eyes on Dupree's face, visible beyond Bull and the woman. "I thought she said . . . that she's dead."

Dupree grasped the dangling locks and pushed them, almost threw them, back. Her face was gray, as if rubbed in ash; her skin was stretched so thin over her bones that it looked like parchment about to rip. There was so little flesh on her skull that they could see the shape of her molars through her cheeks. Her lips were dry and cracked, covered by sores that looked like herpes blisters, and her eyes were huge, bulging with the adrenaline of terror, her thin lids without lashes. But the worst was her expression, a gaze that, despite her fear, was vacant and hopeless.

Dupree dropped to his knees and looked deep into her eyes.

"I'm . . . mm . . . mm . . . dead," the woman said again.

Dupree shined the light into her eyes and saw that her pupils didn't contract. He raised his voice. "What's your name? Tell me your name!"

The woman reacted with a strange expression, as if she'd just awakened or had glimpsed some fleeting reality. She raised her head. Then, between those terribly dry, swollen lips, a white tongue appeared, so covered with mold it seemed coated with cream. Her teeth, the color of cork, looked as if they were about to fall from their unstable places in her diseased gums.

Her lips scarcely moved as a harsh gushing sound heavy with phlegm erupted from her throat. "Méeedora."

The odor from her mouth made Dupree recoil in horror.

“That’s impossible!” yelped Bull. “It can’t be!” He pushed aside the mess of hair that covered the creature’s neck. Her shriveled skin was darkened by a cancerous purple growth, but even so, a tattoo was visible. Elegantly curled letters formed her name. Bull could hardly get the words out. “For Christ’s sake! This is Médora Lirette!”

The woman raised her right hand and placed those five long fingers on Dupree’s chest as he stared at her, not believing his own eyes. “Médora?” he echoed. “Médora Lirette . . .”

The woman replied as if speaking from the grave. Her voice was scarcely audible. “Bazagrá . . . I’m dead, and so are you.”

Dupree’s face lost all color. He gasped as if suddenly deprived of air. He dropped his weapon and with it the lamp he’d been holding on the woman. He raised his own right hand to his chest and grasped her bony claw. He knew he was having a massive heart attack; he was going to say so, but he couldn’t speak. Sweat covered his face. He trembled, shaken by the force of the attack. He fell over backward as if struck by lightning.

43

RETURN

Florida

Brad Nelson poked his fingers under the frames of his glasses and rubbed his tired eyes vigorously. He'd been driving for hours, never stopping, ignoring at least three vehicle prompts to take a break. He couldn't. And besides, he felt great. It was just that his eyes ached from the intense concentration of night driving.

It had been a long drive, but he wasn't thinking of the immense distance he'd put behind him. He was remembering that night in Galveston eight months earlier when everything had gone to shit. Galveston had been a mistake. His life there, his job, the way the place had affected the kids and his marriage. His whole world had collapsed. It was his own damn fault, and he'd been paying the price ever since. He'd traveled a long, difficult road, and the agonizing process of self-examination and reform had taught him much. He'd been lax and careless; he'd been inattentive; he'd completely failed to take charge of his own life. And now he was going to pay for it.

Another little chime sounded—the car was nagging him again to take a break. That meant he'd done another two hundred miles. Nelson checked his watch. He'd get to Sarah's house in just over an hour. She and the kids were probably still asleep. Or maybe they'd be up already, getting ready to leave for school and work. He needed to get there before they left, because he wasn't sure his resolve would last until they got back later in the day. He had to take advantage of the energy that came with making his decision. He muted the chime and put the pedal to the floor. He couldn't stop now, because it was one thing to rehearse it in his head hundreds of miles away, but acting on it was something else entirely. The wry smile on his scarred face looked like more of a grimace. The job ahead wouldn't be easy, but he knew he could rejoice once it was all over. He'd been preparing himself for this for the past eight months.

44

Chaos

Charity Hospital, New Orleans
6:37 a.m., Tuesday, August 30, 2005

Charity Hospital's ground-floor emergency room was underwater. The staff had broken out all the windows along the second-story hall across the front, and the medical team was using the opening as an improvised boat dock to receive the injured. The supervising physician carried out the triage, dictating his diagnoses and instructions.

Their reception was swift, for the FBI team had radioed ahead. Triage started even before unloading. "Male, forty-four years old, tachycardia, pain and pressure in the chest, difficulty breathing, cold sweats, nausea, lost consciousness for up to six minutes but is alert now. Looks like a cardiac seizure. FBI agent involved in hostage rescue. Room 1."

A dozen hands reached out and lifted an unresisting Dupree. He clamped his jaw shut, refusing to groan despite the pain. His face was white as a sheet as they placed him on a stretcher. Johnson swung up out of the Zodiac to follow.

The doctor turned to the old man whom the team had brought with them from the house. "Male, about eighty years old, identical symptoms, no loss of consciousness. Room 3." The wife and grandson followed the patient's stretcher down the hall.

The supervising physician checked his notes. "You radioed you had an injured woman as well?"

Bull jabbed a thumb toward the covered form in the stern. Medical orderlies came aboard.

"Why did you cover her up like that? She'll stifle in this heat."

The staff at Charity had seen almost everything in the previous forty-eight hours, but the sight that met them when the paramedic pulled back the blanket put all that to shame.

"For fuck's sake!" he exclaimed, scrambling back so suddenly that he fell over backward. The stink of putrefaction and mold filled the boat.

"It's a fucking corpse!" another cried.

"No, no, she's alive," Bull told them without looking at the patient. "Kind of, anyway."

"Kind of alive?" an irritated Charbou snapped, glaring at his partner.

The supervising physician took charge. "Get her out of there! Woman, undetermined age, open compound fractures of tibia and fibula, extreme dehydration, extremely undernourished. Note: coming from a hostage rescue: crime victim. Do everything you can. Get it together, people! We've seen worse."

"Not worse than this," a nurse said under her breath.

Amaia looked down the hall. Johnson had stationed himself before the closed door of the room where they were treating Dupree. Charbou was with the Zodiac, trying to convince the EMS team to let him store it with the ambulances on the second floor of the garage. Someone would certainly steal it if they left it unattended.

Amaia urgently needed to question Bull, but he'd disappeared as soon as they unloaded their charges.

She looked around. Waiting rooms had been converted into medical wards and storage areas. Beds, stretchers, and wheelchairs were stacked in the middle of the space and pushed up against the walls. The air-conditioning was out. Windows stood open wherever possible. Elsewhere, the staff had smashed out the fixed panes. The heat and stink were nauseating.

She saw the boy they'd brought with them. He sat all alone on the bare floor by the nurses' station, a plastic action figure in each hand. His lifeless eyes were fixed on the wall before him. She went to him after checking to make sure she could see Johnson from where the boy sat. She had a couple of bottles of water, and she offered him one as she settled by his side. "You're Jacob, aren't you?"

The boy nodded.

She'd been searching for something to say to encourage him to talk, but it wasn't necessary.

"What's your name?"

"My name is Amaia." She solemnly shook his hand.

"That's a weird name!"

She smiled. "Yes, I guess so. It's not from here. It's from somewhere else."

"What does it mean?"

"Mean?" she repeated, caught off guard.

"Jacob comes from the Bible. Bella is 'pretty' in Italian, and Diana was queen of the moon."

Amaia assumed that for a child of his age, a queen and a goddess were practically the same thing. "Bella and Diana are your sisters? The girls they carried off?"

He nodded.

"Where are your parents?"

"They work in Baton Rouge." She saw the distress in his face. "They'll be here soon," he said without much conviction. "Granny told me so."

"It means 'the end.'"

Jacob was confused by her comment.

"Amaia means 'the end' or 'the last.' Some people say it's from the first mother. The earth mother, the mother of us all. She's the beginning and the end."

The boy smiled. "That's a funny name!"

"Yes, I suppose it is."

The child held up his two little plastic figures. One was almost completely yellow, like a big, fat rabbit; the other was a little orange dragon, spitting fire out of the tip of its tail.

"Which do you like better?"

"The dragon," she said without thinking.

"That's Charizard, he flies and burns things up. Pikachu's better than him."

She gathered that Pikachu was the other figure, and she also saw that the boy was relieved she liked the dragon better.

"Okay, then, I like Charizard better."

Jacob held out the toy. "For you!" He placed it on her palm.

Amaia was surprised. She'd assumed Jacob simply wanted to play. But no, he'd asked her to choose because he wanted to give her one of his toys.

"Jacob, thank you so much, but I can't accept him." She turned the little dragon over and saw that Jacob had written something underneath. She pointed to it. "Did you write your name?"

"Uh-huh."

"Do you put it on all your toys?"

"Yes."

"Why do you do that?"

"Diana collects Pokémons too, and she's always saying mine belong to her."

Amaia sat there with her eyes on Jacob as she loosened her vest and searched her pockets. She took out a folded piece of paper, opened it carefully, and showed the boy the photo she'd taken from the conference room the day before. It was a close-up of the mysterious mark along the side of the violin. "Take a look at this. What do you think it is?"

Jacob took the photo and leaned over to study it. "It's a violin that belongs to some kid named Mic."

"Mic? You think that's what it says?"

Jacob nodded. "That's what it says: Mic. It belongs to Mic!"

Surprised by that declaration, Amaia studied the image with the astonishment you experience when someone shows you how an impossible piece actually does fit into a jigsaw puzzle. She looked at Jacob. "How old is Mic?"

Jacob thought about it. "Four. Or maybe five."

"Why do you think so?" she asked. She wanted to hear his explanation.

"'Cause he writes the letters all together. Really little kids always write them separate."

"You're older than that, of course." Amaia smiled. She turned over the dragon and found that Jacob had carefully connected the letters as he'd inscribed his name. "Wow, Jacob, you've been a big help! I wasn't going to accept your Charizard, but you know, I think I will take him with me, after all. He'll be my lucky charm." She refolded the photo and tucked it away along with Charizard. She saw Jacob watching her closely. "I wish I had something to trade you for him."

The boy lowered his gaze. Amaia realized he was looking at the pistol on her belt. "You want my gun?" she asked, surprised.

Jacob nodded.

She assumed a very serious expression. "You know it's a real one, right?"

"Uh-huh."

"Then you know I can't give it to you, because a boy shouldn't go around carrying a real gun."

He nodded, disappointed.

"Why do you want it?"

"Because," he said, starting to tremble and looking away. "'Cause I'm scared."

Amaia followed the direction of his gaze and saw nothing unusual. She hesitated, wondering how she should react, until she finally put her arm around the little boy. She pulled him to her side. "Listen, when I was little like you, I was scared too. But you'll just have to grow up and become a policeman if you want to carry a pistol."

"You're with the police because you were scared when you were little?"

"Yes, I really think so," she declared, realizing she'd just told the truth. "In fact, I'm sure of it."

"And you're not scared anymore?"

"I *am* scared, but now I have this," she said, tapping the pistol at her hip. "And this too." She smiled and pointed to her badge. "These mean I can go after the people who scare me."

Jacob looked doubtful. "And when you catch them, you kill them?"

She had to think about that. Normally she'd have said, *No, a gun isn't for killing; it's only for defending yourself.* She looked down at the frightened child beside her and realized she couldn't give him that pat answer, because it wasn't true.

"Yes. I get rid of them."

Jacob smiled, but he quickly looked down again. "But some of them you can't kill, like that zombie in our house. My grandpa shot it and didn't even hurt it, it just kept marching around like a broken robot." There was real terror in his voice. "What'll you do if the bad guy is dead already or if he's a ghost?"

"Did you get a good look at the people who came into your house?"

"There was two with masks on their faces, another one like that lady, and the ghost. The ghost was their boss."

"Their boss was a ghost? Why do you say he was a ghost?"

"Because he didn't say anything! He told them what to do with his mind. And his face . . ."

"What did he look like?"

Jacob looked down and said nothing for a few moments. She understood immediately afterward that he'd been gathering his courage. He stood up and offered her his hand, inviting her to come with him. Uncertain exactly what he was up to, she took it and followed. He led her four steps toward the nursing station counter, and then she suddenly saw the reason for his furtive, frightened glances. Jacob pointed to the wall and an anatomy poster showing the muscles of the human body. "He was like that."

45

Guardian Angel

Elizondo

Ignacio Aldecoa didn't have an alarm clock. He'd never needed one. He clicked the switch of the little bedside lamp and picked up the watch he'd inherited from his father. It was five o'clock in the morning. He was sure that when he went downstairs, he'd find embers faintly glowing in the dining room fireplace. He hadn't slept a wink that night, for as hard as he'd tried, he'd been unable to suppress the evil of that empty glare. He played the sequence over and over in his mind: the white hand swaying seductively in the air, the thin, almost invisible fabric billowing about the wrist, the matte-black hair of the she-wolf—and that smile.

He wasn't hungry, but he ate all of his usual breakfast, and when he was leaving, he wasn't entirely surprised to discover that for the first time in years, his wife had locked the door. The closest dwelling was a mile and a half away, so they'd never felt the need to lock up. He stood for a few seconds, contemplating the key in the lock and wondering just how much Joxepi had seen. Clearly enough to frighten her. He went out and made sure the house was secure behind him, then went to the sheds. He whistled for the dogs Argi and Ipar, two border collies who were his inseparable companions for sheep herding.

He returned at noon and found Joxepi on the telephone with Engrasi. They'd all gone to the police station the previous afternoon to report the attack. Ignacio understood from his wife's half of the conversation that earlier that morning, the lieutenant had called Engrasi. The video cameras at the border crossing hadn't recorded any vehicle with that license plate. Ignacio shook his head slowly as he cut up the dogs' food over the kitchen sink. He wasn't surprised to learn that either the license plate was phony or that the lieutenant hadn't made the least effort to track it down. Out of the corner of his eye, he'd caught the exaggerated grimace the lieutenant had made to the desk sergeant. The police clearly thought a kidnapping was about as likely as an abduction by aliens. The lieutenant had suggested a little girl's imagination could get carried away, especially if she was high strung.

It didn't matter. Ignacio had already made his decision.

Through the classroom window, Amaia saw Ignacio in the schoolyard. She knew her aunt would be waiting for her at the gate, but she was glad to see him. Serious and immovable as a boulder, he stood under the gentle *zirimiri*. He wore a marine-blue windbreaker and a tilted black beret on which tiny raindrops shone like silver. Ipar was seated at his side, patient and alert. Amaia lagged behind after the school bell rang, letting the crowd of noisy children get out first. Some approached Ignacio, and a couple of them even reached out to try to pet Ipar.

"He bites!" Ignacio gravely warned the most audacious of them.

Amaia smiled at how quickly they snatched back their hands, thinking the dog really was going to attack. When Amaia arrived, Ignacio leaned down to speak to her. "How is your hand?" he asked, studying the gauze pad taped across it.

"Oh!" she exclaimed apologetically. "My aunt took care of it."

Ignacio gestured to the dog. Ipar advanced and started sniffing her. After circling her several times, he went back to heel by the shepherd.

The girl held out her hand and let Ipar sniff the bandage.

"Amaia, this is Ipar. He's a border collie, the best type of dog for sheep herding. These dogs have been in my family for four generations, so Ipar is the great-great-great-grandson of the first Ipar. His nose and ears are extremely sharp. He's always alert. Nothing escapes him, and he's very brave. From now on, Ipar is your dog. He's going to take care of you."

Amaia's face lit up and her eyes widened in astonishment, but then she appeared to have misgivings. "My aunt . . . ?"

"Your aunt agrees. I'll be walking you to and from school for a few days. You can play with Ipar, but don't let the other children touch him. Amaia, Ipar can't have friends. These dogs obey only one person, and you're going to be his mistress. Keep him close always, because as long as he's with you, nothing bad can happen. Ipar wouldn't hesitate to take on a wolf, and he will do whatever is necessary when it comes to defending you."

Amaia looked at Ipar's compact frame and then at Ignacio, and he knew what she was thinking. She'd never seen a wolf. For her a wolf was a savage creature in nature documentaries, as foreign as a Bengal tiger or an African lion. She wanted a better guarantee, so he told her what she needed to hear. "And if the witch comes back, he'll kill her."

"Really?" He heard the plea for reassurance in her voice.

"He'll finish her off once and for all, I give you my word."

The girl didn't smile. She knew this was deadly serious. She put her bandaged hand onto the dog's head and spoke to him. "Let's go, Ipar."

46

Skinless

Charity Hospital, New Orleans
Morning, Tuesday, August 30, 2005

Amaia saw Johnson beckoning to her from the door of Dupree's room as he concluded a conversation with a man she didn't recognize. She headed in that direction without releasing Jacob's hand.

"Do we know anything yet?"

Johnson looked back in frustration at the closed door. "Still nothing. People have been in and out, but they're not telling me anything. I called you over because I have a couple of things to share."

Amaia studied Johnson's face. He was unnaturally pale, despite the heat. His complexion was stark white. Even his mustache, the most distinctive feature of his face, seemed sadly reduced. He was worried about Dupree, and she didn't blame him. It was clear the two were close. Despite Johnson's obvious disapproval of the behind-the-scenes machinations of Bull and Dupree, his devotion to his boss was absolute.

Johnson looked her directly in the eyes, perhaps to interrupt her scrutiny of him. "Did you see that guy I was talking to? That was Lorenzo."

She frowned, perplexed.

"Phil Lorenzo, from Rescue Me. They're based here, remember? They were here yesterday when we contacted them by radio."

She suddenly got it. "Brad Nelson's partner! What did he say?"

"Well, a whole lot, to tell you the truth, but I don't know if any of it is useful. A lot is still unclear. On one hand, he confirms Nelson left the group early once and arrived late another time. In fact, he admitted he covered for Nelson one time, telling Chief Meigs that Nelson was with him, when in fact the man had peeled off early."

Amaia gave him an inquiring look. Were things starting to click into place?

"But he also said Nelson had problems in his marriage, a lot of family matters he had to deal with. Lorenzo likes to think of himself as an understanding guy, says he was drinking a lot ten years ago and his own marriage almost went down the tubes. He got through that, but when he looked at Nelson, he saw his former self. Figured his partner needed protection. When Lorenzo was having a hard time, he was ashamed to own up to his problems. Used to sneak off to Alcoholics Anonymous. Wanted nobody to know, so he made up all sorts of excuses. He admitted that for a long time, he was lying to practically everybody. He claims that's a phase, one you can overcome once you're ready to face reality. 'You take things you're ashamed of and make them things you can be proud of' is how he expressed it. He showed me a lapel pin commemorating a full decade of sobriety."

"So he thinks Nelson has problems with booze?"

"Seems he never asked Nelson directly," Johnson said ruefully. "Just part of being an understanding guy, I guess."

"Oh, that's terrific! So we've got a partner who covers for Nelson because he likes him and assumes he's an alcoholic. That certainly doesn't give us anything new to work with, does it? Except that Brad Nelson had problems with his family, he thought he had to resolve them, and he used that as a pretext to be absent from work. At critical times! And nobody except his benevolent partner knew."

"You still don't believe Nelson's the Composer?"

"Fits of anger correspond much better with the profile of someone with a drinking problem, in my opinion. Alcoholics Anonymous often has meetings in churches. Remember, Captain Reed told us he saw Nelson sneaking into a church, even though absolutely no one thought he was religious."

"Okay. Anyway, I told you I had more than one piece of news," he said, patting the canvas sling with the walkie-talkie at his hip. "There's still no cell phone service, but it seems the hospital's computer system is functional. A nurse told me they have Internet. It's spotty, but they're receiving emails. I got hold of the system password and picked up several emails. It's as slow as molasses; took me practically twenty minutes. One is addressed to you." He took out his BlackBerry and showed her the screen. "It's from a Virgil Landis, general manager of the American Insurance Association."

Johnson steadied his PDA on his forearm so she could read as he summarized the contents. "He goes into detail about the way the association works and what their adjustors do. He confirms that adjustors have access to all the data submitted for policies reinsured by the AIA and that they visit the disaster scenes to assess damage and approve payments. I have to say he was really helpful. The only information he doesn't include is the extract from the personnel files you requested. He can't send that via email because of privacy concerns."

Amaia looked up from the screen. "All right, but that wouldn't have helped us a lot anyway. I think I might have gotten the ages of the children wrong. Because of the victims' ages, I thought he was repeating everything exactly as before, but exact matches probably weren't necessary. If, eighteen years ago . . ." She glanced down at little Jacob, standing by her side. "If he did *all that* and disappeared, even if he managed to establish a new life for himself very quickly, his children would necessarily have to be younger. Jacob was a big help with that. I'm speculating our man has a four- or five-year-old son named Mic, or Michael, or maybe Micah, and it's the boy's violin. The other children might play instruments as well. I think that's why he came back for it in Galveston."

Johnson was willing to play along with her theory. "He saw his son had scribbled on it, and he was afraid that might lead back to him."

Amaia tilted her head, reflecting. "When he leaves a violin at the crime scene, he's not just transforming an ordinary space into a music room. If his children also play the violin, he's trying to make everything match. That would lend credence to the idea that the newer crimes are rehearsals for what he intends to do to his own family."

Johnson mulled it over, nodding. "That's brilliant reasoning. Dupree will be pleased."

Amaia released all the air in her chest in one great whoosh. "I don't know. It's so confusing. I can't tell if I'm thinking logically or my brain's just trying to fill in the gaps with absurd speculation."

"I don't believe we're at a dead end with Landis either. He says that he can't send the information by email, but he also doesn't say he'll need a court order before he'll discuss it. He included his personal phone number in the email, so he probably wouldn't mind having a little chat."

"Sure, but the cell phone towers are down."

Johnson leaned over and whispered in her ear. "Listen, the nurse who told me about the computer system also said the hospital's landlines are working. The main switchboard is jammed; if you pick up a phone out here or in the reception area, you won't get a signal. But they set up a code that gives access to the outside. Zero, zero, one, pound sign. The admin offices on the fourth floor are equipped that way, but they're closed right now." He pressed a ring of odd-shaped metal probes into her palm. "Do you know how to pick a lock?"

She gave him Jacob's little hand in return. "Your nurse is a real gold mine. Or maybe she found you attractive."

He smiled. "I guess I haven't completely lost it, huh?" Even his mustache seemed to have revived a bit.

Light from outside the office window indicated the sun had come up while she'd been in the hall with Jacob. The office windows were still covered, so she couldn't see outside. The blurred view through the horrible plastic sheeting gave her the impression that the exterior world had been dissolved in acid.

It wasn't until after she'd tapped in the phone number that she thought to check the time. The hands of her watch pointed to 7:40. She was going to give it a try anyway. With the one-hour time difference between New Orleans and Washington, Mr. Landis was probably up and about. When someone gives you his private number, it's because he thinks you might want to call.

Landis was indeed up and having breakfast when the phone rang. He didn't seem at all put out by her call.

"It was very generous of you to give me your number, Mr. Landis. I completely understand that my request may have put you in a somewhat awkward position. For the time being, we're looking only for the kind of general information that any personnel department would have on hand. It would help us a lot, because we're in the middle of an extremely important—and confidential—investigation. Well, in fact . . ." She gave a little giggle. "Actually, I shouldn't be telling you this, but we suspect one of your adjustors may be involved in a delicate matter."

Landis was obviously attracted by the conspiratorial nature of detective work; he couldn't wait to give them a hand.

"I've always made it a principle to help the police any way I can, so I'd be more than happy to assist the Bureau."

"You're really very kind, sir. Of course, I'm counting on your discretion, because, going forward, I'm going to have to share certain aspects of the investigation, and since it's such a *delicate* matter . . ." She dangled that last tantalizing adjective before him.

"Of course!"

"One thing first—do all the adjustors travel to disaster sites?"

"Yes, as I explained in my email. They have to confirm and assess the damage if they're going to approve payments from the contingency reserve fund."

"Do they travel all across the country?"

"Well, our adjustors' offices are located in different areas, so each adjustor is more or less responsible for a different region. Adjustors generally work their own part of the country, but if there's a wide-ranging catastrophe, they can be summoned to a different area. Obviously, speedy responses are vital in such situations, so any number of adjustors might be dispatched on temporary duty."

"You said in your email that you never pre-position them when a disaster is expected. Hurricane Katrina, for example."

"We would never ask our employees to put their lives at risk. That would be reckless." He laughed. "And besides, we'd have to raise our insurance premiums if we took that added risk!"

Amaia assumed that was an example of insurance company humor. She pretended to be amused.

"It's enough of a challenge to get them into a disaster area even after things have settled down; and I assure you our professionals face more than enough risk in the course of their work."

"Now, an adjustor could access private information filed in support of a policy—and that could include sworn, notarized statements. Or am I wrong?"

"Correct. If a policy statement is based on fraudulent declarations, the contract is null and void, and the client isn't entitled to compensation. That's in the fine print of every contract. The client signs to certify the accuracy of the information provided."

"All right, that's perfectly clear. Then tell me, do adjustors need any sort of special authorization to access that information?"

"Adjustors are experienced agents, very senior people, so they have full access to any policy we accept."

"The person we're looking for might be between fifty and sixty years of age," Amaia informed him.

"That doesn't refine your search much. Most of our adjustors are in that age range. The AIA appreciates dedication, but we value expertise even more. It takes years of field experience to qualify. We may have one or two who are younger than that, but they're the exceptions."

"If I had to refine it a bit more, I'd probably be looking for someone who was about fifty-five years old. He'd be married with three children, most likely two boys and a girl. And, well—I don't know if your files are this detailed—one of the boys might be named Michael."

"Our information is comprehensive, since we require our employees to take out a policy with us. Come to think of it, about five or six years ago we set up a database with the birthdays of our employees, their spouses, and their children. It's always a nice touch to send them a birthday card."

"Tell me, is your office in Washington?"

"We have regional offices as well, of course. In fact, the Washington office is purely administrative. Our personnel are based out of New York or Austin, Texas."

The connection was obvious. New York was close to Cape May, New Jersey; Galveston, Killeen, and Alvord were in Texas; Brooksville, Oklahoma, was probably an easy day's drive from Austin. Getting from Austin to Florida or New Orleans would be simple. An adjustor could take a flight to somewhere within reasonable driving distance of a forecast disaster.

Amaia hazarded a last request, not expecting much of it. "Mr. Landis, I'm going to forward to you a list of some significant recent disasters, including New Orleans, where a disaster is striking even as we speak. I'm down here helping out after Katrina, so I don't know when I'll be able to phone you again, but I'll do my best to get back in contact. But it may be extremely important for our ongoing investigation to establish which adjustor—or adjustors—visited those specific locations and when. And if any happened to be on leave on those dates. Oh, and if any of them has been on vacation for the past couple of days."

"Um-huh," Landis responded, certainly taking all that down.

She had a sudden inspiration. "And could you also provide the birthdates of any adjustors who fit those criteria?"

"I can."

"How long do you think it will take to gather all that information?"

Landis was quiet for several seconds. Amaia was hoping against hope that he could have it quickly.

"Some of this I can have for you today, but for most of it I'll need to check with our regional HR departments . . . oh, let's say, probably by noon tomorrow."

Agent Stella Tucker noticed that her left leg was numb. She stretched it as much as she could, which wasn't much. She had to get out of the seat in the back of the van, then bend a long way over to stretch her legs. She glanced back at the five men with her in the van and caught every one of them except Emerson quickly looking away and pretending not to have been staring at her butt. Her FBI colleague, seated in the other jump seat, was staring at nothing. She rolled her eyes and massaged her calves to get the circulation going.

The SWAT team leader's voice came through her earphones loud and clear. "He just moved. Still got his hands on the steering wheel, but he's looking up."

"Everybody stay put!" she responded. "Remember, unless something unexpected happens, we wait for him to enter the house. If we arrest him now, even if he's armed, the DA will make mincemeat of us. We wait until he goes inside."

She'd reminded them a dozen times, but she knew all the SWAT team members were on edge. She was just as nervous and irritable as they were. Her legs ached from the perpetual squatting in the back of the van.

Brad Nelson had been sitting in his car, parked in front of his wife's house, for an hour and seven minutes.

He'd driven up, stopped right before the front gate, and killed the motor. She'd been convinced right then that he was going to get out and go to the front door. He'd even pushed open the door on the driver's side, which caused the interior light to go on. But then he'd pulled it shut and stayed inside, intently studying the house. Ten minutes earlier he'd looked up for a few moments as if something had caught his attention, but then he'd knotted his hands together, gripped the wheel, and put his forehead against them.

"My man on the upper terrace says it looks like he's praying," the SWAT team leader told her.

She took that as a telltale sign. Praying before killing would be entirely in keeping with the profile for the Composer they'd assembled from crime scene details and records of Martin Lenx's behavior.

"He's separated his hands and he's looking up again."

She looked through the rear window. She had an unimpeded line of sight to the front of the Spanish colonial home with the broad second-story terrace. A palm tree near the entrance partly masked a walk around that ran to the rear of the house. From her position, she could see the back of Nelson's car but very little of the man himself.

"Stay alert. If he's finished his prayers, he might be ready to go."

Events seemed to prove her intuition correct.

"He's moving again," the SWAT leader radioed. "He's leaning over now, taking something from the glove compartment. It's a gun! Repeat, suspect has a pistol!"

"Everybody stay alert!" Tucker urged again. "Remember, wait until he goes inside."

She saw the car door spring open with such force that it rebounded and slammed back against the emerging driver, who paid no attention. Both of his hands were clutching the pistol, which he extended firmly before him. Leaving the car door open, he hunched over and ran toward the side of the house. Tucker was astonished; she hadn't expected him to go that way. He'd been in front of the house for more than an hour, as if he couldn't work up the courage required. Tucker had expected him eventually to start the car and drive away.

The SWAT leader yelled into his microphone. "Heads up, everybody, he's going to the back! Suspect is armed and heading toward the back door!"

Desperate for air untainted with men's aftershave and unable to restrain herself, Tucker opened the rear door just a crack. Through the early-morning quiet of the street, a thunderous pounding reached her before the voice of the SWAT leader did. "Attention! He's kicking the back door down!"

She exerted command. "Wait! Wait, everybody, until he goes inside."

The next thing she heard was a series of gunshots. She could have sworn there were four, though in the recap afterward they counted five: four from Nelson and one from the SWAT member in the living room forced to return fire.

When she returned to the improvised emergency room, Amaia saw Bull with Johnson outside Dupree's room. Little Jacob was nowhere in sight. Charbou stalked down the hall toward them, clearly furious.

"Where's the boy?" she asked.

"Don't worry, he's with his grandmother," Johnson told her. "Her husband is stable. They've been moved to the third floor."

She pointed to the door. "Any news?"

Charbou answered angrily, glaring at his partner. "No, there's no fucking news, and you know why? Let me tell you, since your boss and my partner have been working behind our backs all the time we thought we were tracking down a serial killer!"

"That's not true. We're after the Composer," Jason Bull countered patiently, keeping his voice low.

"Salazar was on to it from the start, all those little whispers and private conversations. I didn't see it at first, then, yes, I saw it, but I didn't want to believe it, even though she pointed it out. Because not in a million years would I have thought you'd do such a thing!"

Bull looked down, patiently enduring his partner's tirade. When he did reply, it was again in a quiet voice. "You wouldn't have understood."

Charbou glared at him. "I wouldn't have understood. You're telling me I'm an idiot. If there's anything I don't understand, it's why you didn't explain it to me. And you can start by telling me—what in holy hell is that *thing* we brought here in the Zodiac?"

Bull met Charbou's stare with complete calm. "What does she look like to you?"

Not put off for an instant, Bull's partner stepped in close and spit out his reply. "Whatever the hell it is, there's no name for it, and if there is one, I'm sure as hell not going to say it!"

Bull nodded. "Well, that's exactly what she is."

Charbou gave a phony laugh. "Are you trying to tell me that it's a fuckin' zombie?"

"I'm just saying that some things are exactly what they appear to be," Bull replied, still entirely calm. "Sometimes the simplest explanation is the best."

Amaia cut in. "What is Samedi?"

Bull pressed his lips together. "I can't answer that. It's part of the investigation Agent Dupree and I are conducting. I'd need his permission."

Johnson spoke. "His permission? Agent Dupree just had a coronary! Maybe you missed that? He's in there with his life dangling by a thread. I have seniority here, and that makes me the next in command. Tell us! That's an order!"

"You can't order me. I'm not FBI. My cooperation with Agent Dupree is entirely—"

Charbou grabbed him by the throat and pushed him against the wall. Bull didn't even raise his hands to resist. "I went to your wedding! I'm your son's godfather, and you're treating me like this?"

Johnson and Amaia pulled Charbou back.

"Okay," Bull gave in, closing his eyes. Charbou released him and stepped back. "Her name's Médora, Médora Lirette. She was kidnapped ten years ago, right after her sixteenth birthday, during Hurricane Casilda."

Johnson nodded. "Go on."

"I was in the unit that dealt with human trafficking. Médora was the little sister of Jerome Jay Lirette, a drug dealer in Terrebonne, down in the swampland about an hour from here. Jerome had been dealing since he was a little kid, and he was smart. He was never arrested, and he became a medium-sized dealer with a lot of people working for him. He took care of his mother and grandma, and he was particularly protective of his little sister. The same night that Casilda rolled across the marshes, people broke into his house and carried Médora off. The descriptions of the abductors were like those of the people who took Jacob's sisters last night. The intruders took her and two girlfriends who were there for a sleepover, all of them minors."

"Médora was kidnapped ten years ago? Are you sure?"

"Her name was tattooed on the back of her neck, a birthday gift from Jerome. And it was an abduction, not a kidnapping. The perpetrators didn't ask for ransom, because they had no intention of giving her back. Drug dealers usually take care of their own problems, but Lirette notified the police when

Médora disappeared. And not in Terrebonne, where he lived; he came to police headquarters in downtown New Orleans with three lawyers. They wanted to talk to the New Orleans police chief and the district attorney.

"They were sent to me first. Jerome was beside himself. He obviously hadn't been sleeping at all, and all that, that . . . whatever . . . was completely beyond him. He didn't say a word at first.

"He told us someone had 'abducted' his sister. That's the word he used. He didn't say 'kidnapped,' he said 'abducted.' He claimed he knew who had her, and he was ready to swap information about his drug trafficking business in exchange for immunity and help from the police and FBI in finding his sister. You can imagine what we thought. Lirette kept his mouth shut after that, but his lawyers laid it out in black and white. Mr. Lirette understood the seriousness of the matter, they said, but he would give us the goods on important aspects of the drug trade: distribution, methods of bringing the drugs into the country, the names of port officials on the take, and where the merchandise was stored. We knew most of the junk came via the canals or across the swamps, but even so, we couldn't turn down an offer of inside information about the port. They said it was all written down already, and they'd turn it over if we agreed to a deal. They huddled in the chief's office and gave the DA fifteen seconds to leaf through a twenty-page single-spaced statement. It took him only ten seconds. They signed the agreement, handed over the document, and the narc squad got to work right away.

"Jerome's account said that a month earlier, he'd been exploring the possibility of collaborating with a Baton Rouge organization. That's all he knew about them. But Jerome didn't get where he was by being gullible. The questions they were asking made him suspect those people weren't interested in a deal but intended to take over his networks. He broke off the talks. Two nights after that, while Casilda was at her worst, an armed group invaded his house, terrorized his mother and grandma, and carried off the sixteen-year-old sister and her two friends. Lirette wrote that Samedi had taken them."

"That's exactly what Jacob's grandmother said," Amaia commented. "The boy described two attackers with masks and another individual who looked like Médora. He described the attack to me in detail, and when I asked him who was in charge, he pointed to an anatomy poster on the wall, a picture of a human body with exposed muscles and no skin."

"Good God!" Charbou protested. "The kid's imagination is going wild over his grandmother's story. Okay, I have to admit that the sight of our friend Médora would scare the shit out of anyone. And the kid's only four years old."

"Five," Amaia corrected him. "He's a bright little boy. One of the calmest and most credible witnesses I've ever interviewed."

"Oh, great! Now you believe the story of a four-year-old, and that takes care of everything?"

"Five! He's five years old, and I don't see any reason not to believe him!" Amaia angrily spat at him. "Why do people always doubt children? I don't see why Jacob should be any less credible than Jerome Lirette. They were more than happy to take the word of a drug dealer!"

Johnson had a feeling of déjà vu. He was sure Salazar was talking about her own past.

Charbou took her on. "Everybody in Louisiana knows Samedi's a spirit. Baron Samedi is one of those voodoo *loas*, but he's the *loa* of death, an evil spirit they blame for the worst kinds of crimes. We've seen him represented millions of times for Carnival and Halloween. He's a skeleton with broken hips, wearing a sombrero and smoking a cigar; sometimes he wears a tuxedo or tailcoat . . . I'm sure any kid on the street could point him out. He's part of our folklore, like the leprechauns are for Ireland." He turned to look at Bull. "And there's also the myth about the secret organization called Samedi. The Black House or Black Church, some people call it. There's probably not a single Louisiana policeman who hasn't heard Samedi blamed for cases that couldn't be solved. The fact that there've been disappearances has made some folks think it's a pedophile network trafficking in young girls. I don't believe Samedi even exists. It's just another version of the old wives' tale repeated by frustrated cops. It's like the boogeyman. No official investigation has ever turned up a scrap of evidence it exists."

Bull took a more nuanced approach. "I always thought there might be some truth behind those stories. A lot of criminal networks operate in the shadows for years before we can prove they exist. I thought Samedi might be like that. I figured that the stuff about ghouls was just folklore.

"And then along came Jerome Lirette and told us that two nights before, some people broke into his house before dawn, right after a storm. Just like tonight. He and two of his associates were in the house along with his mother, his grandma, his sister Médora, and the two girlfriends. The power was out, and the phone wasn't working, but they'd survived the storm just fine. Then they heard this huge crash. At first they thought a tornado had come along in the wake of the hurricane and busted down the door.

"The first thing the invaders did was grab his associates and kill them execution-style, a single shot to the head. Then Baron Samedi, his very self, walked into the house with three more people. Jerome said they looked 'totally weird,' but he wouldn't give us any details. The thugs rounded up the girls and herded them out of the house. His mother and grandma were screaming their heads off. All this time, the baron, or at least whoever was dressed up as Baron Samedi, stood in the center of the room, enjoying the chaos like it was a show put on especially for him. The older women tried to grab the girls back, but Samedi's people beat up the old ladies. His grandma died on the spot; his mother ended up with a broken collarbone and a broken arm. And Jerome broke down in front of us and confessed he hadn't done a damn thing. He was terrified, literally paralyzed by fear. The intruders left the way they came, and he heard his sister Médora screaming, scared out of her mind, and he couldn't do a thing.

"He told us he could still hear his sister's screams, and they were killing his soul. We gave him a polygraph test, but we needn't have bothered; it was obvious he believed every word he said to us. He was humiliated and in torment; his guilt and shame were obvious. And anyway, no drug trafficker of his stature would turn over half his assets to the DA unless he was serious.

"We verified his story. The police down there in Terrebonne figured it was a matter of a couple of drug gangs settling scores. Jerome had told the sheriff some people had invaded his home, killed his friends and his grandma, and beat up his mother. He didn't mention the abductions. When the sheriff asked about Médora, Jerome claimed she was staying with family in Saint Bernard. The local coroner authorized the transfer of the body of Amelia Lirette, Jerome's grandma, to a local funeral home. We inspected the corpses of Jerome's associates at the Saint Gabriel morgue in Terrebonne. The gunshot wounds corroborated his story. We confirmed that the other two girls were missing.

"We interviewed Jerome's mother in the hospital. That was even more disturbing, because she held nothing back. She described two of the people with the man dressed as Samedi as being the living dead. That's exactly what she told us. So, despite not entirely crediting Jerome's statement, we opened an investigation into the abduction of Médora Lirette and the other girls. We treated it as a kidnapping at first, assuming it was related to Jerome's shady business, especially since we found no trace of the mysterious men from Baton Rouge who'd allegedly contacted him.

"All this led us to think there might be a crime network trying to take over midlevel dealers and their distribution channels, forcing them to cooperate by kidnapping family members. That happens a lot with drug cartels in Mexico, Colombia, and Brazil. We heard plenty of rumors—the Black Church, the Black House, Samedi . . . but the organization was a fantasy. It simply didn't exist.

"Practically every police force in every country has that kind of legend as an excuse for cases they can't solve. That's what we were facing: a dead end. Until an FBI agent suggested a whole different approach, telling us we shouldn't assume it was about Jerome at all. It had to do with Médora." Bull looked at Amaia. "You were right. Dupree and I know each other. From a long time ago."

"Ten years," she said.

He nodded. "Dupree and Carlino were the FBI agents assigned to help us with the kidnapping of Médora Lirette."

Johnson looked puzzled. "I don't know any Agent Carlino."

"That's because FBI special agent Frank Carlino died ten years ago during the investigation, just like Jerome Lirette. It almost cost Dupree his life as well."

47

Petit Bon Ange

Charity Hospital, New Orleans

The door opened. Two physicians came out and looked them over. "I guess you're the people who brought in the freak show," one said.

Amaia didn't understand the joke, if indeed it was one. She gave the speaker a withering look.

He saw it. "No reason to be offended."

"How is Agent Dupree?" Johnson asked before Amaia could reply.

"I have good news and bad news. It looks like your friend had an acute myocardial infarction. He has all the symptoms of a heart attack, but the good news is that it's not a heart attack at all. Your colleague has a Takotsubo cardiomyopathy, colloquially known as 'broken heart syndrome.' The symptoms—chest pains and difficulty breathing—resemble those of a heart attack. It's usually caused by a sudden surge of hormones related to stress. Adrenaline, for instance. The arteries aren't blocked; the heart muscle itself contracts so violently that the left ventricle becomes almost conical in shape. Your friend's heart is literally being squeezed nearly shut in the middle."

Johnson looked at Amaia. He was overwhelmed. "'In the middle,'" he repeated in a strangled voice.

The other physician took up the narrative. "When we examined his chest, we found five closely spaced scars from an old wound. They look like stab wounds, but the CT scan was no help in diagnosing their origin. Maybe you know what happened?"

Amaia turned to Johnson, who shook his head. "No idea. But he did mention an old scar had been giving him trouble over the last couple of days."

"He did," Amaia confirmed. Out of the corner of her eye she saw Bull turn away and look down.

"We were also struck," the doctor went on, "by the resemblance between your friend's scars and the pattern of trauma on the chest of the elderly man you brought in. Five lesions received during a violent blow. Those welts, taken together, look more or less like the arms of a starfish. Did you zap him with a stun gun or something?"

They shook their heads.

"Did you try CPR on him?"

"No," Johnson said. "At first I thought he'd been shot. But when I saw the marks on his chest, we didn't touch him."

The doctor turned to his colleague with a baffled expression. "I was expecting them to say they'd used a defibrillator." He frowned. "That would help make sense of the old man's story. He claims people tried to tear his heart out. The thoracic pressure during a heart attack can be almost unbearable, and that might be what he was feeling when you tried to help him."

"Will you have to operate?" asked Johnson.

"No, the treatment is purely pharmacological. We have medication that can help Mr. Dupree's heart return to its original shape in a few days or weeks. The hurricane complicates everything. We're monitoring him and giving him diuretics and analgesics, but he should be treated with beta-blockers and ACE inhibitors. The hospital pharmacy has exhausted its supplies of the drugs he needs. In normal circumstances, we could get them from another hospital in the city; we'd send a courier to pick them up, and they'd be here in twenty minutes or less. But we don't have a way to dispatch someone, and even if we did, other hospitals are facing the same shortages."

"What are you going to do?"

"Whatever we can. Monitor him and keep him rested, give him painkillers. But that's about all we can do until the situation clears up out there. His heart has to work enormously hard to pump blood, and that causes him intense pain. Perhaps that's where you can help." He took his time to look at each of them. "After we gave your friend our diagnosis and told him the circumstances we're facing, Mr. Dupree told us he intends to leave the hospital. He insisted we release him."

"Wouldn't that be dangerous?" Johnson asked.

"Extremely. Mind you, recovery could happen naturally. But without treatment, if he comes under stress, his left ventricle could rupture. That would mean instant death."

"Then we can't let him leave," Bull said.

The doctor shrugged. "On any other day, I'd keep at him until he was willing to listen to reason, but just look around." He waved at the crowded hallway. "I need every bed, every stretcher. Any physician worth his salt would find a Takotsubo cardiomyopathy fascinating; I'd love to see how it evolves. But right now, we're almost out of resources. We've had to shut down the air-conditioning because the generator has only enough fuel to keep vital systems functioning. There's even talk of evacuating the hospital. I'm not going to keep anyone here against his will. It's up to you to convince him."

"May we see him?"

"They're medicating him right now, but you can go in in a few minutes. Before that, we need your cooperation on another matter. The neurologists and psychiatrists treating the woman you brought in want any additional information you might have. They are literally spellbound by the case." He gave Amaia a wry glance. "Like I said, it's a freak show."

Her expression let him know she still wasn't amused.

"I'll stay here," Johnson said, gesturing toward the closed door. "Just in case."

"I'll go," Bull replied decisively, following the physicians.

"So will I," Amaia said in a tone that left no room for discussion.

"Me too," added Charbou, giving Amaia a defiant look.

"Where did you find this woman?" one of the physicians demanded as soon as Amaia and the cops appeared.

The silence was palpable. The team members' faces were grim. Realizing he'd been too abrupt, the doctor paused and started over. "I'm Dr. Stone, head of neurology." He stepped forward and offered them his hand as he gestured over his shoulder at his colleague. "Dr. Matteau is the chief of psychiatry."

"How's the patient?" Bull asked.

The doctors exchanged a glance. "She's . . . not in bad shape, considering she had a very serious open fracture. We've had some problems treating it. The operating rooms are all downstairs, so they're flooded. When the water started rising, we brought as much equipment as we could to the second and third floors, but even so, our setup isn't really adequate for surgery. They're working only on life-and-death cases." The doctors looked at one another again. "Let's get down to it: you brought her in. The emergency department told us it had something to do with a kidnapping, so we assumed . . . well, was she the victim?"

Now Amaia and Charbou were the ones to trade glances.

"I'm sure you noticed that despite the seriousness of the injury, she wasn't complaining. In fact, she wasn't making any sound at all. We thought she was in shock; some people react that way because they're terrified by the sight of their own injuries. But we've established that she's in a state of complete analgesia. She shows absolutely no signs, physical or neurological, of feeling pain. We think it's probably congenital, perhaps hereditary. It would be helpful if you could identify her. That way we can see if we have the medical history of any of her family members in our files. This is an extremely rare affliction, on the order of one in a million."

Bull nodded. Amaia and Charbou looked down, not in the least surprised.

The physicians exchanged baffled glances once again. "They've realigned the fractured bones and applied a splint to immobilize the leg. We administered antibiotics and bound the wound; nothing more can be done until we have a proper operating room. But that's far from what interests us the most." He invited them to approach a broad plate-glass window behind him.

They stepped forward. The window gave them a view of a poorly illuminated padded cell. The dimness was attenuated only by the daylight filtering through the blinds on their side of the window. A hospital bed was in the center. The woman stood in a corner, her head lowered and her face partly hidden by her tangled mop of hair. The staff had replaced her rough poncho with a blue hospital gown patterned with tiny white flowers; it made her look even more out of place.

"We did everything we could to keep her lying down. We were tempted to strap her down; we had to immobilize her while treating her leg, but then we decided it would be better to release her. We didn't want to have to put her under heavy sedation, because that would have made communicating with her virtually impossible. She's been standing quietly in that corner since then. She's in a semihypnotic state, similar to that of a sleepwalker, but she does respond to simple questions."

His colleague took up the thread. "I was hoping you could help us out. We need to know anything you can tell us. We heard she was involved in a kidnapping. If you can, please tell us how long you think she was held and whether she ever received medical treatment."

Bull swallowed hard. "Well, that's not exactly how it was."

"She says her name's Médora, but all she remembers is her first name. This case is unprecedented. I've been practicing psychiatry for twenty years, and I did major research on Cotard's syndrome, but I've never actually seen a case like this."

Charbou spoke up. "You mean it's a disease?"

"What did you think?" the doctor said with a smile. "No, don't tell me; you thought she was a zombie."

"She said—"

"Of course she did! I know she says she's dead. I'm from Louisiana too. But that is the textbook definition of Cotard's syndrome, also known as the delusion of denial or nihilistic delusion. People suffering from Cotard's syndrome believe they're dead. Did she say anything else?"

"Just a minute," Amaia said. "What does all this have to do with being from Louisiana?"

"Only that I'm perfectly aware of the myth that's behind it. I mentioned that I studied Cotard's syndrome. I published a paper titled 'The Delusion of Denial and the Living Dead.'"

Charbou gave Bull a funny look. "So you think Cotard's syndrome explains zombies?"

"The first case on record was documented by the French neurologist Jules Cotard in 1880. His patient, also female, insisted she was dead. She believed her heart had stopped beating and her organs were decomposing. In some cases, patients are convinced their bodies don't exist at all and that their spirits are wandering. In the most acute cases, the patients experience olfactory hallucinations and smell their bodies rotting. Some even claim to see worms devouring their flesh. All too often, they stop eating entirely and starve to death."

"So it's a mental illness," Amaia said.

"Yes, or it could be physical in origin. Both have been documented. Cotard's syndrome is a harsh and frightening disease, both for the patient and for those who witness it."

"What could have caused it?" Amaia asked. "Is it hereditary?"

"No, it's extremely rare. As for the possible causes, I was hoping you might be able to enlighten us. If we knew where she's been and in what conditions—and her family background—we could try to establish whether others in her family suffer from mental illness, hereditary or otherwise."

"Otherwise?" she asked.

"Toxicological. In some of the documented cases, the delusion may have been triggered by exposure to poisonous substances."

"Self-ingested or administered?" Bull asked. "Is it possible to induce this state?"

The neurologist couldn't hide a grin. "You mean, could she have been 'zombified'?"

Bull refused to be put off. "I'm from Louisiana too."

"We haven't been able to take a blood sample yet because she's lost so much blood. Maybe she's been drugged, but as for 'zombification,' well, there's not enough in the literature to establish that it's even possible."

"Or to disprove it either. Right?"

His colleague the psychiatrist intervened. "A great deal has been written, but virtually none of it is based on science. Neurological damage isn't the only explanation, and I believe we can't dismiss the idea that toxins are affecting her behavior. But certainly not to this extent. As physicians, we're obliged to rule out that possibility, at least for now. Although . . ."

"Although?"

"There's evidence of severe lesions of the corneas. I'd say she's almost blind. We'll have an ophthalmologist examine her, of course. And there are other traces of what appear to be old chemical burns. I'd hazard a guess she might have been addicted to drugs sometime in the past. Either that, or she was subjected to some kind of prolonged treatment. Her arms bear track marks, probable injection sites, skin abscesses, and signs she was bound or immobilized for long periods."

Bull was clearly affected by the psychiatrist's report. "You said you were able to communicate with her, at least a little. What did she tell you?"

The psychiatrist studied Bull for some time. "In normal circumstances I wouldn't reveal it, but you're from the police, and I have the impression this woman could be the victim of a crime. I think you should see this."

The doctor pressed a switch that raised the thin slats of the blinds that kept the padded room dark. He aimed a flashlight beam at the patient. The woman did not react at all. He raised his hand to a small plastic box fixed to the plate glass and lifted its cover to reveal a two-way speaker. "We found that she reacts more readily to a voice than to an actual human presence. This is an intercom like those used to monitor infants." He pressed the button. "Médora."

The figure huddled in the corner showed no sign of having heard him. She remained still.

"Médora."

Nothing. The physician closed the cover of the intercom. "Denial of one's identity is a common symptom of this delusion. Her vision is affected by the abrasions on her corneas, but she may also have a neurological inability to recognize faces, to recall them, or even to identify them as human." He lifted the intercom cover. "How are you?"

The first sound they heard was a sharp gasp; the second was gargling from a phlegm-choked throat. Amaia felt the hairs on her neck rise.

Through her mop of hair, they saw cracked lips covered with sores. Air burst between her lips but otherwise there was no movement.

"I'mm . . . mm . . . mm . . . deeeeaad." The voice could have been either male or female.

"Do you know where you are?"

"I'mm . . .mm . . . deeeeaad," the patient whispered.

"Do you know what happened?"

"Deeeeaad." The voice rose from deep inside her through apparently immobile lips. It had a disturbing, diseased tone.

"Where were you before?"

The patient's body swayed as she transferred her weight from one leg to the other. She seemed about to tumble over, but she stayed on her feet.

"The graaaaave."

Bill leaned over. "Ask her if she remembers where she was before she died."

"Where were you before the grave?" the psychiatrist asked.

Silence. And then a sudden whimper, as if she were going to cry. "I died."

"What happened then?"

"The graaave."

"And then?"

"Sa . . . me . . . di." She wheezed.

"What?" The doctor turned to them. "Did you hear that?"

Bull joined him at the window. "May I?"

The doctor hesitated. Bull gave an inquiring look to the neurologist across the room, who nodded his approval.

Bull's deep voice resounded on both sides of the plate glass. "Médora Lirette!"

The huddled woman seemed to shiver slightly. Amaia thought she was inclining her head as if to hear better.

"Médora Lirette. What did Samedi do to you?"

"Samediii . . . killed me . . . and tooook me from my graaave."

Bull sighed in exasperation. "Who is Samedi?"

The woman turned from the corner where she'd taken refuge, broke into a run, crossed the little room, and slammed into the glass right in front of them. They recoiled in shock. The horribly dry skin of her face was pressed to the glass, and those lips covered with sores left dark smears where the pustules had broken. Amaia was convinced she caught a sharp whiff of the swamp.

"She can't see us," the neurologist told them.

As if to contradict him, those dead eyes scanned the room, stopping to focus on each of them. Médora shut them after that and stood as if turned to stone. She didn't move her lips, but a great groan broke from somewhere in her gut. She trembled.

A clear, childish voice took them by surprise. "He got *mon petit bon ange*."

"Who's that?" Bull insisted.

The woman stood stock still and opened her eyes. Her gaze seemed to pierce the glass window that separated her from Bull. After another moment, without even the slightest twitch of expression, she released a distorted sound, a scream that erupted from the depths of her soul. Again, they heard the childish voice, the cry of a desperate little girl. Amaia was convinced, impossibly, that a different woman was imprisoned somewhere deep inside this pitiful creature.

"Le Grand . . ."

48

Promises

Superdome, New Orleans

After finding Seletha was comatose, Nana and Bobby had undertaken a frantic search along the interior tunnels of the stadium, trying to get to the Red Cross aid station. Their search was an agonizing journey because of the number of people driven into the corridors by the torrents of rain drenching the stadium bleachers, the difficulty of forcing Seletha's wheelchair through the crowd, and Nana's dependence on her cane. Bobby stopped every few steps to try to keep his mother's head upright, but each time, she slumped forward, chin on chest, emitting only guttural sounds.

At last they found first-aid workers in a makeshift station installed in a tool closet, but the paramedics were no help. They confirmed Seletha was in a coma, but their only supplies were aspirin and saline solution. At least she seemed to breathe better when they placed her on a stretcher. They couldn't transfer her to Charity, the closest hospital, until after the storm.

Bobby was desperate. He looked first at his mother, then at Nana and the paramedic attending Seletha. "But we got to do *something* . . ."

The man shrugged.

They ended up spending that night and the following morning there. Nana and Bobby sat on the floor and leaned against the stretcher where Seletha was slowly dying.

The paramedic came to them at one o'clock that afternoon. "We gonna take your mama now. They movin' her to Charity in a boat."

Bobby reached out to help Nana stand up.

"Only one person with each patient!"

"But you can't! Just look at her," Bobby protested, pointing to Nana. "She's sick too, they just operated on her, and she practically can't walk. I can't leave her here by herself!"

The medic was losing patience. "We got more than a hundred people to transfer, and the boat's only got twenty-five seats. Y'all are in the first group 'cause your mama's really sick, but we got other bad cases too. And that one," he said, meaning Nana, "she can take care of herself."

Bobby started to protest again.

"Sorry, man!" the staffer cut him off. "You go right now with your mama, or all three of you wait for another boat. And I can't say when we gonna get one."

Bobby exhaled.

Nana took his hand. "Bobby, darling, you got to take your mama to the hospital. I'll be okay."

"Well?" the medic pressed them.

Bobby took off his knapsack and pushed it at Nana. "You wear it in front, or they gonna steal everything. Don't share the water, you got enough just for you. And the faucets here full of mud." He looked all around, racked by anxiety. "Nana, I want you to stay here close to first aid, and don't you move. You hear me? I'm gonna come back and get you soon as my mama goes into the hospital. I'm gonna come get you, I promise. But no way you should move from here, 'cause if you do, I'm never gonna find you."

Nana nodded, almost overcome.

"Promise me that!" Bobby begged as the paramedics picked up Seletha's stretcher. "Promise me, Nana! Tell me right now you not gonna move from right here."

"I promise," she told him, looking around as she plunged into despair.

49

The Freak Show

Charity Hospital, New Orleans

Johnson was still posted outside the door to Dupree's room. He beckoned to the team, and they went in to see the boss. The room was bare except for five occupied stretchers. Dupree's bed was all the way in the back under a window with smashed-out panes. His lips were dark, almost blue. He was so pale he looked frostbitten, though the film of sweat on his face belied that impression. He was leaning on one elbow and struggling unsuccessfully to get his shirt on.

"What the hell do you think you're doing?" Johnson angrily reproached him. He took away the shirt. Exhausted, Dupree sagged back onto the stretcher. They all saw the ugly constellation of ancient scars on his chest.

"I have to get out of here." They could scarcely hear him. Though he looked ravaged, his determination was evident.

Amaia went to his side. "We'll talk about that in a minute, but I think you owe us an explanation first."

Dupree's eyes closed for a couple of seconds. "That's not so easy . . ."

"I understand that. Lying is always difficult. I don't know what the others think—you can work that out with them one by one—but you should have told me that we were coming after Samedi. I had a need to know. I would have worked just as hard for you, and we wouldn't have wasted time thinking we were tracking down the Composer."

"I wasn't deceiving you. Our priority is the Composer."

"Wrong. That's the excuse, the official mission," Amaia corrected him. "The Composer is your pretext for being here. I don't like being manipulated. I think you should have told me."

Bull inserted himself into the conversation. "Seems to me you've already realized how hard it would have been to explain. We're trying to catch a phantom, we know that. They took us off the case ten years ago, but they never technically closed it. We're not investigating it officially, but we were galled that we never got to the bottom of it. After Agent Carlino and Jerome Lirette died, the higher-ups said it was pointless to continue. But we were certain it wasn't over. We stayed on the alert, sure that he was going to turn up again in the next storm, just like when he carried off Médora Lirette."

Charbou clicked his tongue in annoyance. "I know it's hard; I got friends who lost their partners on duty, and they've never gotten over it. But it seems damn irresponsible to me for somebody to put a whole operation at risk for the sake of a personal vendetta."

Dupree gave him a withering glance. "This operation has never been at risk. We're only a step or two behind the Composer, and he doesn't even know it."

"I agree with Charbou," Amaia exclaimed. "All this time I thought I was here to hunt down the Composer! With all due respect, Special Agent Dupree, you allowed yourself to be distracted. Look at the way Tucker wound up in charge of the Florida operation. She's getting results. We aren't."

Johnson looked down and covered his bushy mustache with one big paw. They all knew he didn't care for Tucker, but they could also see he didn't like the way the case had been handled.

Dupree gazed at them wearily. "Tucker doesn't know a goddamn thing, and I brought you along because I'm convinced you can find the Composer for us. But I needed to understand Samedi too." He closed his eyes and went silent. Seeing him like that, Amaia was reminded of Médora Lirette.

She tried again. "About this woman, Médora Lirette. Are you sure this is the same person? That was ten years ago."

"It's her," Bull declared.

Dupree nodded without opening his eyes. "No doubt about it."

Amaia hesitated, trying to frame her question. "I saw her. She seems . . ."

"Out of her mind," Dupree muttered under his breath.

"When you say that, you mean driven mad by her abductors?"

Dupree nodded. "That's what they do."

"To whom?"

"To the ones they take."

"The doctors said she's mentally ill."

"She is."

"And you think her illness was induced," Amaia finished the thought. "In the early days of psychiatry, the general belief was that the mentally ill were alienated from their own true selves."

"Correct." His voice was a whisper. "I believe that's what happened to Médora."

"How can you be sure?" Amaia demanded, refusing to make allowances for his evident fatigue.

"It's not the first time," he said. He gestured to Bull.

She hammered away at him. "The physicians see two possible origins of her illness, physical or neurological."

"Right," Dupree said. "Mental illness caused, at least in part, by exposure to something toxic."

"They mentioned that possibility. But are you sure we're talking about the same thing?"

"I don't know," he said faintly. "What are you talking about?"

"About what I saw upstairs in a padded cell: a woman with feeble vital signs, absence of ego, a belief she was dead, complete surrender of human awareness—"

"Sure sounds like zombification to me," Charbou muttered.

"You could call it that," Dupree agreed. He was fading fast.

Amaia got down beside his stretcher and bent over him. She noticed that his fingers were curled around a little gray pouch. Dupree jerked it away and hid it under the sheet.

"That's not what I'm going to call it," she told them. "It's not just people from the banks of the Mississippi who've heard of the surrender of will. And I'm not talking about zombification. It's a much more deliberate approach and it's far crueler: brainwashing with drugs. GHB, scopolamine, flakka, even jimsonweed—people call it the devil's snare.

"European police forces have been working hard over the past few years to break up human trafficking networks that subjugate women with drugs, keeping them semiconscious with substances that rob them of their will. Some of their victims knew more or less what was going on. They perceived they were being held as prisoners, but afterward they recalled living in a stupor and dreaming—or rather, experiencing—nightmares that never ended. Most of those rescued were astonished to learn they'd been in a haze for years. They couldn't remember a thing. A few months ago, I arrested a man who abducted women, locked them up, and kept them high on Rohypnol. They were totally at his mercy. And there's scopolamine, the rapist's drug; in some cases it's been used to induce individuals to empty out their bank accounts or give up passwords and identities."

"I'm not disputing any of that," Jason Bull replied, "but maybe you do have to be born along the Mississippi to assume that *poudre de mort*, death powder, reduced Médora Lirette to the condition she's in now. Tetrodotoxin, if you want to use the scientific name. The victims of your trafficking networks regained their self-awareness once they were off the drug. Médora never will. She knows exactly what she's missing."

"Is that what she said Samedi took from her?" Charbou asked.

"*Le petit bon ange.* The good little angel that lived inside her. Her soul."

"Okay now, it seems to me we're getting pretty far off the subject." Charbou was still pissed off by all this. "I'm no FBI super-agent," he snarled at his partner, "but in my opinion it seems pretty harebrained to think that a single incident establishes a modus operandi. Médora disappeared during a natural disaster, but so what? It's crazy to think they were going to wait ten years before doing the same thing again."

Dupree sat up on his stretcher. The agony of the effort bathed his face in sweat.

Johnson was alarmed. "We should let him rest."

Dupree motioned to ask for a moment to recover.

Bull went to his side and whispered, "Tell them, please."

Dupree stared into the invisible distance. Then he told them.

"Hurricane Betsy devastated Louisiana in 1965. The levees broke, the city flooded, people drowned. I was only four. The night the hurricane hit, my father's cousin Nana was taking care of several children in addition to her own daughter: four neighborhood girls, my sister, and me. My father and mother were trapped on Grand Isle. The parents of those girls, like mine, were away, either in Baton Rouge or down on the coast. We were up all night in Nana's attic, which did have a window. A group of strangers invaded the house before dawn, tied Nana and me up, and carried off the girls. It was in the newspapers for years. 'The Treme Six,' they called them. At first, the police treated the case as a kidnapping, but they never found a trace of any of them. Two years later, their names were officially added to the list of people who went missing during the hurricane."

With uneasy glances, they all held their breath, uncertain how to react.

Dupree went on. "But I was there. I was really little, but I know the hurricane wasn't responsible. I saw who did it . . ."

Johnson said what they all were thinking, "Samedi."

Dupree didn't reply.

"How old were the home invaders?" Johnson asked.

"I know where you're headed," Bull intervened. "It happened forty years ago. Thirty years went by between the attack on the Dupree family and the Médora Lirette case. We told you we received instructions to stand down, and that's what we did. But we've been watching. And we're pretty sure Samedi's been back several times."

He ticked them off on his fingers. "On September 20, 1996, a year after Médora Lirette was taken, a fifteen-year-old girl named Andrea López disappeared from a trailer park outside Gretna. Her mother, a crack addict, claimed that Death came and took Andrea away.

"On January 11, 1999, a man was arrested in Acadia Parish and charged with complicity in the disappearance of his two daughters, fourteen and sixteen years old. He was a real scumbag, the sort who'd probably have sold them if he'd gotten the chance, but he kept insisting that armed men led by a demon broke in and carried his daughters off.

"In Estherwood, Samantha Oliver's mother went to the police because her daughter disappeared during a storm. They assumed the girl was a runaway, even though the old woman across the street swore she saw dead men do it. According to her, they were led by Baron Samedi."

Charbou frowned. "If there's somebody abducting girls out there, why would he dress up like a weirdo?"

"To throw people off his trail," Johnson said. "I spent two years investigating religious sects and illegal rituals. I learned back then that in eighty percent of the crimes involving magic or satanism, the magical or supernatural element was used deliberately to confuse people. And it almost always did. Media outlets go wild for that kind of thing. Only about two in every ten cases involved people who really believed that stuff."

Bull nodded. "We don't assume Samedi is an individual. Samedi's more like a cult with a leader, a *bokor*, who puts on that identity to terrify and dominate. This wouldn't be the first time. It's common knowledge that down in Haiti, President François Duvalier sometimes dressed up as Baron Samedi and cavorted on the balconies of the presidential palace. He even went out into the neighborhood to scare people into believing the president himself was Samedi or at least was protected by Samedi. In any case, a witness, no matter how reliable, is immediately discredited as soon as he claims that the death baron carried the girls off. It sounds so absurd that the police turn a deaf ear. If we hadn't been tracking disappearances of young girls that occurred during disasters, we'd probably never even have noticed."

"Sherrington's victimological profile," Amaia mused. Dupree nodded, feeling understood. "You posit the existence of a predator or a facilitator—which would make him even harder to trace."

"A facilitator?" Charbou asked.

"An individual or even an organization," she replied, keenly searching Dupree's face, "dedicated to identifying victims to feed to psychopaths, pedophiles, or collectors who are willing to pay enormous sums for them. They choose victims who are seriously at risk, for example, very young girls or runaways. And now Médora Lirette has reappeared, and she just told us where Samedi is."

"That's exactly why you have to get me out of this place," Dupree said in a strangled voice.

"To go where?" Johnson protested. "I know they've told you how serious your condition is and how dangerous it is to turn down medical supervision."

"They also told me they have no way to treat it. All they could suggest was that I lie here like a log. You have to get me out of here."

Johnson, intent and anxious, covered one of Dupree's hands with both of his own. "And where would we go? For the love of God, Dupree! Things out there have gone to hell since yesterday! The water kept rising throughout the night, and now eighty percent of the city is underwater. The hospitals have run out of medicine. National Guard units from surrounding states have been dispatched, and there's still not enough personnel to deal with this. People are looting supermarkets. There's total anarchy out there. You're asking me to move you, but where could we go?"

Dupree beckoned him close. "If I stay here, I'll die. I need a *traiteur*. You have to take me to the swamp."

Johnson straightened up. He turned to the others. "What the hell is he talking about?"

Bull explained. "A *traiteur* is a Cajun medicine man."

Thunderstruck, Johnson turned back to Dupree and sputtered. "I swear by all that's holy—"

"Let's go," Dupree whispered hoarsely. "And let's take Médora with us." Before Johnson could react, he added, "They can't cure her here."

Amaia gave Dupree a grim look. "We're going after him, aren't we?"

He said nothing.

"That's why you want to take Médora. You think she knows where the girls are. And you're expecting her to lead us there."

Dupree took a deep breath and spoke with great effort. "Ten years ago, we had something that was maybe a lead," he said, his eyes on Amaia. "It led us to a shanty town out in the swamp where we found evidence, a little brooch Médora's mother identified as hers. Solid proof. And that clue took us to an enormous estate, a former plantation abandoned years before. When we got there, we found a fence around it, electrified and equipped with security cameras. We couldn't get a search warrant the same day, because that was the day Jerome Lirette disappeared and Agent Carlino turned up . . ." He looked away, unable to complete the sentence.

Bull continued the account. "I've kept an eye on the place ever since, and we know the estate belongs to a Dutch corporation. In the property records, it's been retitled as Janssen Huis, but originally it was known as Le Grand Bayou Plantation. The Cajuns always simply called it Le Grand."

"That's what Médora said," Charbou confirmed, almost against his own will, "when you asked her about Samedi."

"Do you really believe there's any possibility at all they're still keeping abducted girls out there ten years later?" Amaia asked.

Bull responded, "Why not? We never got a search warrant. And we never mentioned the place in any of our reports. No one's aware we even know about it."

Charbou looked Dupree directly in the eyes. "Bull and I would be outside our jurisdiction."

"Kidnapping is a federal offense. You two would be on my team purely as guides, that's all."

"Listen," Bill Charbou said. "We'll take you to your *traiteur*, and we'll take a look at the house. And if we find nothing, we'll come back to NOLA with leeches up our butts."

Bull was impressed. "I didn't think he'd be able to convince you."

"Yeah, well, I get excited at the idea of sticking my nose outside my own jurisdiction."

All eyes turned to Amaia.

Dupree spoke. "Salazar, what do you say?"

"What about the Composer? We've made a lot of progress here. I believe we correctly refined the profile regarding the ages of the children. Nelson still doesn't fit it exactly. We talked with his partner on the rescue team, who admitted he covered for him. But he also described disorderly, impulsive, and confused behavior that's completely inconsistent with the actions of Martin Lenx and the Composer. The hypothesis that he's an adjustor sent to disaster scenes is starting to look like our best bet. I talked to a senior manager at the American Insurance Association, and in just a few hours, I'll have a list of names we can work with."

"In a few hours?"

"Yes, probably by noon tomorrow. It all depends on my finding a telephone line."

"Give me those hours," Dupree said. "Please."

"What?"

"You're right. I brought you along to track down the Composer. Samedi simply turned up along the way, but now that we're aware of a crime and have the means to pursue the perpetrators, we can't let it drop. I won't abandon you here, and I won't force you to come if you don't want to. But I'm begging you to give me those hours. Give me until tomorrow."

"I have a lot of unanswered questions," she warned him.

"I'll answer them all."

"And I'll ask them all," she said in a steely voice. "Even the most complicated ones. I want the whole truth; if I think for a moment that you're hiding something from me, you can count me out."

"Agreed."

"And we come back to NOLA for the Composer as soon as possible."

Johnson interrupted them. "Bad news!" He was aghast. He held up his BlackBerry to show them the email he'd just received.

Dupree and Amaia looked at him.

"Tucker arrested Nelson in Tampa. They staked out his wife's house and even had SWAT team members stationed inside. Nelson came back from his trip, parked in front of the house and sat in his car for an hour, evidently trying to work up his courage. Then he jumped out of the car, raced around the side of the house carrying his service weapon, kicked in the back door, and went in shooting. He took down the SWAT member in the living room but got a bullet in the chest in return. Nelson's unconscious in the ICU and in critical condition."

Amaia gave Dupree a disgusted look. "Tucker doesn't know a fucking thing, does she?"

50

ANNE-FRANCE

Elizondo

Inspector Anne-France Renaud glanced at her partner and was tempted to slap him out of his seat in their official vehicle. Ludovic was well intentioned, young, cute, and a computer whiz; in fact, they were here because of him or, to be more precise, because of his computer skills. He was one of those odd types who shine at college but remain practically infantile in many other aspects of their lives. He'd just gotten his driver's license, and now he was always begging to drive the way a Labrador puppy whines to be taken out for a walk. Inspector Renaud, in her late fifties, was impressed by his computer abilities and oddly satisfied to be driven around all day by her brainy young assistant. She bragged discreetly about him to her colleagues, even though he often got on her nerves. She'd driven from Biarritz almost to the border, but when they reached the quiet roads of the French Basque Country, she'd slowed down, enchanted by the beauty of the countryside. It lulled her into stopping and turning the driving duties over to him. Their progress since then had been slow but agreeable, but for the last five minutes here in Elizondo, he'd been trying to parallel park on the street that ran along the River Baztán. She'd tried to focus on the charm of the little town as the rising spring mists dissipated in the midmorning sun, but she erupted in a sharp huff of annoyance the second time she felt the rear bumper hit something.

"Good God, that's enough!" she exclaimed, throwing open the passenger-side door and getting out before Ludovic could get the vehicle properly positioned.

She looked at her notes and checked the numbers along the street. The house turned out to be very handsome, just the sort of dwelling she'd have liked to own. The entrance was through an archway into a covered courtyard with stone benches that matched the façade. The upstairs windows were adorned with flower boxes overflowing with bright-pink petunia blooms. The front entrance to the house was a double door of dark wood with heavy iron rings fixed on either side.

"I'll do the talking," she warned Ludovic before she knocked. This was their little game. She knew it would be impossible to keep her smart-ass junior partner quiet, but she liked to goad him to see just how much he'd take.

"Whatever, boss. Just remember my Spanish, Italian, and Portuguese are great."

"But you can't drive worth a damn," she muttered maliciously as she rapped on the door. "And besides, the lady speaks French."

The slim, elegant middle-aged woman who opened the door was dressed in slacks and a high-collared sweater. She wore her hair in a bun. Anne-France smiled, for this was exactly how the inspector had imagined her when they'd spoken over the phone the previous afternoon.

"Engrasi Salazar?"

"Yes. At your service."

"Inspector Anne-France Renaud, French National Police."

"Of course. Did you locate the car?"

Anne-France continued without answering that question. "I assume the girl is in school, as you said. Are the other witnesses here?"

Engrasi nodded and stepped to one side to let them in. A border collie showed his fangs and silently stalked stiff legged toward them. "Don't be alarmed. This is Ipar. He's just checking you out. He'll be done in a moment."

And indeed, a few seconds later, the dog withdrew and stationed himself between them and the front door. The house interior was warm and smelled of wood smoke. As Engrasi ushered them through the living room to the kitchen, Anne-France noticed, perhaps a bit enviously, a couple of wing chairs facing the fireplace where logs were burning merrily. A man and woman stood at the kitchen table, waiting for them. They looked about Engrasi's age. The woman, Joxepi, was short and perky, with close-cropped hair. The man, Ignacio, was tall and sinewy. He seemed very serious, and his strong features evidenced a distinct mistrust of the new arrivals.

"Did you find the car?" Joxepi asked immediately. "Is that why you're here?"

The inspector gave them an ambiguous nod accompanied by a shrug. "Before we get into that, Assistant Inspector Bélanger and I would like to hear your account of what happened." She looked at Ignacio. "It seems that you, Monsieur Aldecoa, had a better view than the others."

"I've thought about it a lot," he said. "I went over it, trying to remember every detail, and now I'm sure that the car went up and down Calle Santiago twice before it stopped. I remember thinking it was a French tourist who'd lost his way and was trying to find the border crossing."

"What happened when the car stopped?"

"I thought the person on the passenger side would lower the window and ask for directions, but the rear door opened instead. Someone inside said something to the child. I didn't hear the voice. The open door partly hid the person, but I did catch a glimpse of the sleeve of a white blouse, loose and practically transparent, and a woman's hand. She was beckoning, trying to get the girl to come closer. Amaia is normally a careful child, but she took a couple of steps in that direction. That's when I shouted a warning and the child froze. Everything happened very quickly after that. I ran toward the girl; the woman stepped out of the car and grabbed Amaia's arm. I got to them just in time to tear the girl out of her grip. I saw . . ." He pointed to the garment Engrasi had laid out on the table. The overcoat displayed a rip that ran the length of the lower half of the sleeve. "The deep scratches on Amaia's hand are still healing. The woman jumped back into the car and they took off."

"Did you get a good look at her?"

"Yes, and I wish I hadn't." His mind presented him with that unforgettable image of the smiling she-wolf. "I described her to the Guardia Civil."

Ludovic spoke for the first time. "Yes, we have their report. Several things caught our attention—" He sounded ready to plunge into a lengthy commentary, but Ignacio's wife interrupted him.

"Did you find the car or not?"

The assistant inspector sighed in disgust. "We are immediately notified of stolen cars via antiterrorism channels. The Guardia sent us a license number that was very close to that of a car stolen in Bordeaux two days earlier. It wasn't detected at the border because the thieves had changed a number on the plate. It wasn't the first time we've run into that trick. But what actually caught our attention was the way they tried to snatch the girl."

Horrified, Engrasi put both hands to her mouth. "You're sure they were trying to kidnap her? It couldn't have been something else?"

Anne-France nodded. "There's no doubt, because Señor Aldecoa's account matches almost word for word those of witness statements in four other cases. Four young girls have been abducted over the past five years, all of them prepubescent, approximately the same age as Amaia."

Ignacio was astounded. "How is that possible? Four girls? This is the first we've heard of such a thing!"

Assistant Inspector Bélanger laid out photographs of the four missing girls. They all had long blond hair, more or less similar to Amaia's, and they clearly resembled one another. The choices hadn't been random. "Three disappeared in different localities in France, and the fourth was taken in Belgium."

"And then what?" Engrasi demanded, anguished. "Tell me they were found!"

Inspector Renaud's grim expression brought out harsh lines caused by years of smoking. "Unfortunately, they have not yet been located."

"But who did this? Who's carrying them off?" Engrasi insisted. "Who was that woman?"

"We doubt she's acting on her own. We believe she's part of a human trafficking ring."

Aldecoa's wife surveyed the visiting officers from head to toe. "And why would that group abduct young girls? I don't understand." Joxepi cast about for an explanation. "Maybe some woman couldn't have her own children, so she's sick, you know, out of her mind . . ."

Ludovic happily stepped into the gap. "We believe it's a well-organized group, but we can't be absolutely sure of their aims. Maybe trafficking in young girls, exotic rites of some fringe cult—"

"Cult?" Ignacio exclaimed, surprised.

"The choice of prepubescent girls is a clue, and we've heard rumors that various quasi-religious groups are active in different areas of France. They present themselves as law abiding, but some have been accused of conducting strange rites supposedly connected to witchcraft. Animal sacrifices and so on."

"Devil worshippers?" Ignacio asked him.

"Hmm," Ludovic responded. "More like our ancient ancestors' witchcraft, I'd say. You know, rites calling upon primal forces; nowadays those could range all the way from extraterrestrial visitors to demons from hell."

Engrasi reacted. "And you think that kind of cult could be operating in this region?"

Inspector Renaud glared at her apprentice and quickly intervened. "We have no proof any such cult exists."

"We haven't disproved it either," Ludovic continued airily. "This whole region, on both sides of the Pyrenees, has been a hotbed of magic for centuries. The Zugarramurdi witch trials, cult practices throughout history, the Inquisition . . ."

"And what do you propose to do about it?" said Engrasi. "The Guardia Civil hasn't lifted a finger!"

"We'll talk to them, of course," Renaud replied. "We will make a point of asking them to keep a close eye on the child, though we doubt the criminals will come back here."

Ignacio shook his head, violently disagreeing. These two officious visitors had no idea of what he'd seen shrouded by the cowl over that she-wolf's head.

Engrasi saw his concern. She asked, perhaps in an effort to lower the tension, "Why are you so certain they won't come back? Did they fail before and not return?"

"They had never failed before."

51

Krewe

Hinterlands outside New Orleans
Afternoon, Tuesday, August 30, 2005

The fierce sunshine rendered the air heavy and humid and threw dazzling reflections across the streets drowned in rippling, muddy water. Dupree had been pale and drenched in perspiration, and the inevitable strain of leaving the hospital via the second-floor window just made his condition worse. They lowered him into a sitting position in the stern, the most stable section, so as to spare him as much as possible from the boat's shocks and jolts. Bull, at his side, steered their craft. Dupree accepted a couple of painkillers from Johnson, downed them with a sip of water, and closed his eyes.

Johnson and Amaia were on one side, and Charbou was in front of them. Médora lay in the prow, wrapped in a sheet from head to foot. Her foul smell wafted through the air as the Zodiac got underway, but at least they could keep their distance.

Johnson checked on their motionless passenger. "Maybe we should loosen the sheet around her face. It's really hot out here."

"No way!" Charbou said firmly. "It's better like this."

Bull's reply was wary, even unfriendly. "Better for who?"

"For me, damn it!" Charbou snapped. "Better for all of us. I swear to God, if I have to look at that thing again, my head's going to explode!"

Nobody challenged him.

Amaia was too full of her own contradictory thoughts to comment. She was still assimilating the news from Florida of Tucker's precipitate action and Nelson's arrest. And the fact that Dupree had convinced them all to head out into the swamp. Bull was on his side; Johnson had shown his loyalty—he'd have followed Dupree without question to the very depths of hell. What really astonished her was that even after arguing against the proposal, both she and Charbou had signed on.

Johnson had gotten assistance from the navy. The dispatcher promised to arrange for an SUV with a hitch and trailer for the Zodiac. Once they'd left the Mississippi and entered the less turbulent canal waters en route to the base, Dupree opened his eyes and looked up. He peered at the members of his crew, one by one, and he grinned. "Hell of a krewe I've got here."

"Goes without saying, cap'n!" Bill Charbou replied.

Bull turned to Amaia, knowing she wouldn't have gotten the joke. "The krewe is the company that builds and rides on a float in the Mardi Gras parade. The captain's the crazy man in charge."

Amaia stared at Dupree. He gave her a wink; he wasn't forgetting for a moment that he owed her, big time. "What is it you want to know?"

Johnson interrupted. "I think you should rest. It's not a good idea to be exerting yourself."

Dupree waved negligently. "I'm fine," he said, even though his pallor and his sweat-bathed face belied that assertion.

Amaia thought about it. She tilted her head to one side and gave him a calculating look. "I want to know lots of things. For starters, what's Bazagrá?" She watched for a reaction. "I think that's what Médora said in the house before . . . well, before your heart attack."

Dupree closed his eyes and nodded. This was clearly difficult for him, but she refused to be put off. She waited patiently, her eyes on Dupree. At last, he answered. "Some think it's nonsense, a meaningless expression like 'abracadabra.'"

"And the others?"

"That it's a curse. An invocation of the devil. Bazagrá, Bazagré, Bazagreá—from Beelzebub, Ba'al Zebub, or Baal, the ancient god of the Canaanites and Philistines."

Amaia continued in a prosecutorial tone, "What are those marks on your chest? They are just like the ones on Jacob's grandfather."

"They're from the man who abducted my sister and cousin that night during Betsy. I grabbed his leg and wouldn't let go. Nana has the same scars."

"All right," she accepted that odd account. "But there's one thing I need you to explain, because it's vital for me to understand. I see how an investigation might be shelved without finding out who murdered a drug trafficker. What I can't get my head around is the fact that the FBI stopped investigating the murder of one of its own."

Dupree straightened up a bit, supporting himself on his right forearm. His features contracted in a grimace of intense pain. He gasped. "It has less to do with the murder than with the way Carlino died."

"I considered that," she admitted. "And I concluded he might have been doing something illegal. Maybe, just maybe, shutting down the investigation was a way to draw a curtain over something scandalous."

Bull couldn't contain himself. "Nothing could be further from the truth! Agent Carlino died in the line of duty. And in a way, so did Jerome Lirette. He died carrying out his duty to his family."

Dupree raised a hand to hold Bull back. "When I joined the investigation, I immediately saw how the account from Lirette and his mother matched my memories of when they took my sister, my cousin, and the other girls. Jerome was getting frantic because the police insisted on treating Médora's abduction as a drug-related kidnapping. But knowing what we were confronting and where to look wasn't enough. Then we found Médora's brooch in that shantytown in the swamp." Dupree took a moment to catch his breath.

Bull took over. "They say the swamp has eyes, and they're not referring only to the animals out there. Lots of Cajuns live there in settlements, in houseboats, or aboard their own boats. But nobody knew anything. We could hardly believe it. The folks in the swamp have a kind of sixth sense; they're always letting the sheriff's department know about outsiders. And they also report things that can't be explained."

Charbou was intrigued. "How's that?"

"Before I joined the homicide squad in New Orleans, I was a deputy sheriff in Terrebonne. Folks there are superstitious, and farther out in the swamps, they're even more so. Living in the swamp gives you a whole different idea of the universe, and it wasn't exceptional for the sheriff's department to have to look into a report that somebody saw a *rougarou* or that *lutins* were active. But in the Lirette family's case, nobody'd heard or seen anything at all. We were surprised."

Johnson spoke. *"Rougarou? Lutin?"*

"The *rougarou* or loup-garou is a swamp monster, sort of like a wolf-man. The *lutins* are a little harder to explain. Folks think they're mischievous spirits, kind of like goblins. And then there's also *fifolets*, the ghost lights over the swamp. Saint Elmo's fire probably, but Cajuns see them as evil spirits, ghosts of the drowned who're drifting in the currents down in the bayous."

Johnson was astonished. "The Terrebonne police responded to those kinds of reports? When I was looking into criminal religious sects, we usually found local authorities more skeptical than not."

"I guarantee you that if you'd been living here for a while, none of it would seem ridiculous. The swamp is alive. If, as a law officer, you work in cooperation with an ethnic group like the Roma or Cajuns or Native Americans, you have to understand their customs, or you'll be completely lost. And besides, it's no secret that south Louisiana is a land of voodoo."

"'Voodoo'?" Amaia echoed him, skeptical. "You mean witchcraft?"

Bull grimaced, uncomfortable, but answered her with great seriousness. "Voodoo is the major religion in countries like Togo and Benin. The Caribbean version is the official religion of Haiti, because the slaves brought it with them from Africa hundreds of years ago. It got mixed up with Christianity and spawned cults. Santería, for example, or candomblé and Umbanda. And, yes," he said, looking at Johnson, "you can bet your life the local police are going to accept calls and reports of any kind of suspicious activity. When a belief system is so deeply embedded in a culture, it's going to influence things. You have to accept some rituals you might normally find distasteful or disturbing, like animal sacrifice, midnight meetings, tomb desecration, corpses stolen from their graves—"

"That'll do." Johnson held up a hand to stop him.

"Jerome screwed up," Dupree said. "His sister had been gone for more than a week, and we'd turned up absolutely nothing. No one had seen a thing, or even worse, if they had—as we suspected—they weren't going to squeal. So, without telling us, Jerome offered a twenty-thousand-dollar reward for information about Samedi. Twenty thousand bucks is a tidy little fortune in those parts. He put out the word he was ready to pay that much, and it spread like wildfire.

"We'd been trying to contact Lirette for hours, with no success. Late that morning, we went to his house. His mother was scared out of her wits, a shotgun in her hands, but she finally opened the door to us. You couldn't blame the poor woman. She told us her son wasn't home. Jerome knew the hospital was going to release his mother that morning, but he hadn't come to pick her up. She was sure something terrible had happened. We thought so too; everybody knew Jerome Lirette was devoted to his family. He wouldn't have abandoned his mother, especially right after losing his sister and his grandmother. We called the sheriff and were about to send search parties out when an anonymous caller told us where we could find his body.

"At practically the same moment, Jerome's mother called us in hysterics with a message her son left for us. We thought maybe someone was playing a practical joke on us. Or somebody interested in the reward had called her with a made-up story. We split up. I went with the sheriff, Detective Bull, and some deputies to where the tipster said we'd find Lirette's body; Carlino went to talk with Jerome's mother."

"It was a trap," Charbou guessed.

"No. No, it wasn't, and that's the strangest part of it. Jerome had left us a note at his mother's house about the reward he'd offered. And we found Lirette's body exactly where the caller said it would be. He'd been decapitated. They'd nailed his headless torso to a tree trunk in a dreary swamp. He was naked."

"What about Carlino?" Johnson asked.

Dupree exhaled completely. "When we got there, Agent Carlino was lying full length on Lirette's porch, a terrible wound in his chest. He was still alive. Six feet away, carefully planted on the top porch step, was Jerome's head. I leaned close to my partner. He was trying his best to say something. The blood gushing from his mouth choked off his words; I tried to stop him from talking, but he was desperate to tell me something. I pressed my ear to his mouth and finally understood what he was saying: 'Lirette is alive.'

"He was talking about Jerome, which was insane, considering that the man's decapitated head was there in full sight. I thought the shock of his injury was making Carlino delusional, so I answered, 'Sorry I was too late. Lirette is dead.'

"He shook his head and coughed up more blood. 'No, no, he's alive,' he said, waving toward the head over on the top step. The cut through the neck was jagged and messy, as if Jerome's head had been torn off instead of cut. I could see tendons and tissue spread out from the neck, exactly what I'd expect to see if a head was ripped off a body. The skin was blueish white, gray in some places. His mouth was half-open, a swollen white tongue protruded from between his lips. His eyes were closed, and there was hardly any trace of the handsome Jerome Lirette I'd known. But it was Jerome, there was no doubt about that.

"And right then, that decapitated head opened its eyes and looked at me. The tongue slipped back into the thing's mouth, and the lips quivered as if it were trying to say something."

Dupree stopped to watch for Amaia's reaction; she nodded, accepting his story without question. "I couldn't take my eyes off it. I was deafened by the mother's screams inside the house and stunned by that vision. My partner grabbed my hand to attract my attention. I leaned over close to try to make out what Carlino was saying. 'Samedi ripped my heart out. He took it with him.'

"I looked down, appalled, at my friend's terrible wound. It looked like they'd blasted him point blank with a shotgun. All I saw was a deep cavity with irregular borders that shivered inward with each breath he tried to take. My partner struggled to speak as I tore off my shirt and stuffed it into the wound. 'If you follow him, he'll tear your heart out,' he said.

"Carlino was alive all the way to the hospital. We drove him to Houma and evacuated him to Baton Rouge by helicopter. I was with him all the way; it took about twenty minutes. He knew he was dying. I kept holding his hand and talking to him; he lost consciousness mere seconds after the helicopter landed. They hooked him up to the emergency room monitors, but it was no use; he was dead. Carlino was a young man, only thirty-three, so the doctor refused to give up. He used the defibrillator several times, but got no result, so he pushed the paddles into the wound to touch the heart muscle. When he did, he couldn't believe what he found. Agent Carlino had no heart."

"That's impossible!" Charbou protested.

Johnson, deeply affected, said, "I don't think Charbou means that this kind of crime—or sacrifice or ceremony, whatever the hell you want to call it—can't exist. But the victim couldn't possibly remain alive for that length of time."

"That's not all," Dupree said unhappily, his failing voice betraying his fatigue. "Agent Carlino's body continued to show cerebral activity for another forty-eight hours. And four days later, the medical examiner had to stop the autopsy because some of his organs reacted to his scalpel as if they were still alive, just as Jerome Lirette's severed head had seemed to be. Both bodies were cremated.

"I delivered a detailed report countersigned by the Terrebonne sheriff and by Detective Jason Bull of the Homicide Section of the New Orleans police. Lirette's mother also made a formal, notarized statement. And for that, they locked her up in a psychiatric ward for a very long time. I saw her just the other day on a balcony in Bourbon Street, but I didn't recognize her at first. From what she said, I don't think she ever recovered." He looked at Bull. "Four hours after I turned in my report, my superior officers summoned me and insisted I rewrite it and omit any detail that couldn't be explained rationally. I did."

Amaia looked away. She, too, knew quite enough about giving accounts that omitted the irrational and inexplicable.

52

Traiteur

The swamp

The SUV and boat trailer were waiting at the naval dock as promised. During the seventy-mile drive southwest along US 90, they'd left Médora secured in the boat, stiff and unmoving as the menacing figurehead of a pirate ship, because Charbou had said he'd rather tie himself to the hood than have her at his side in such a cramped space. The team left the SUV parked outside a deserted settlement of ramshackle houses somewhere near Houma and continued by Zodiac.

The swamp sucked up the daylight as soon as they moved into it from the open water. Amaia had never been in swampland before, but the sensation was similar to being in the forest of Baztán. Dupree's account had transported her through time to the forest and a long-ago night she thought she'd managed to forget. She remembered all too clearly the awesome beauty and harrowing terror of that night, and a shiver ran up her spine.

Dupree's high fever had returned. His forehead was burning hot when they carried him aboard the Zodiac. He had to fight to stay awake, lifting his head from time to time to suggest landmarks to Bull, though knowing they were virtually useless in a vast area where almost all reference points had been swallowed up. The sun, though low in the sky, still burned fiercely. It would set in an hour, and they all began to dread navigating the shaded, overhung domain of the great swamp by night. Amaia felt a chill, and she began to wonder if it was a sign that she too was developing a fever.

Bill Charbou had just suggested returning to civilization when they saw the camp.

It was the strangest place Amaia had ever seen. There were three houses built on pontoons, either anchored to the swamp floor or secured with heavy chains to big trees. Because of the high water, their roofs almost touched the undersides of the high crowns of the trees. Tied up to these improvised floating docks were at least a dozen shrimp boats festooned from stem to stern with strings of lights, the first undamaged watercraft they'd seen for days. People waved at them and called out over the racket of a generator. Amaia heard lively music and voices both young and old.

"How's your mamandem?" people chorused from the rails along the houseboats.

Bill and Bull grinned and gave them the thumbs-up sign. "How's your mamandem?" they shouted back, provoking a happy storm of shouts.

"Mama and them?" Amaia asked Charbou.

"Assistant Inspector, Louisiana is and always has been a matriarchy!"

They tied up to the railing of one of the houseboats, and a dozen hands helped them aboard.

The *traiteur* was a golden-skinned man, his thin body stretched and a bit hunched, as if he habitually leaned over for hours on end. His wide, loose pants with rolled-up bottoms revealed strong legs with bony ankles and enormous feet that scarcely fit into his plastic sandals. He wore a ragged New Orleans Hornets T-shirt. The man's hair was fairly long, and the streaks of gray were particularly striking.

The *traiteur* went aboard the Zodiac to check on the patients. He uncovered Médora and examined her impassively. If his face showed any emotion at all, it was pity. He was very quick with Dupree. He took just a glance before giving a command to the men to lift him out of the boat. Half a dozen shrimpers carried Dupree inside the houseboat. Johnson followed on the *traiteur*'s heels, trying to share the doctors' diagnosis. The *traiteur* paused, surprised Johnson by turning around, and gave the FBI agent his full attention.

"Thank you," was all the *traiteur* said. His gratitude sounded so sincere that Johnson found nothing more to say.

At least twenty-five people, men and women, shrimpers and swamp dwellers, were in the room, which ran the entire length of the deck. Their presence didn't seem to bother the *traiteur*; he acted as if he were alone with his patient.

The *traiteur*'s voice was low, masculine, and gentle, all at the same time. It struck Amaia that she'd like to hear his laughter. The man bent down and disentangled Dupree's fingers from the cord with the little goatskin pouch Amaia had seen at the hospital. He examined it and then placed it on the pillow next to Dupree.

"Do you know what that is?" Amaia whispered to the woman standing closest to her.

"The gris-gris of that man," she responded hoarsely.

Amaia gave her a surprised look, partly because of the answer and partly because she hadn't expected to get one at all.

"His voodoo charm. Somebody who love him very much make it up, for they know he in danger. Without that, the man be dead now."

A completely unexpected low heave of nausea caught Amaia. She seemed to be developing a fever, or maybe the eerie atmosphere in this place after all those hours in the burning sun was affecting her head. She felt a deep pang in her belly, thought for a moment it was her period, but calculated that was impossible. A sharp pain ran down the inside of her thigh and her lower back felt incredibly weak. She tried to ignore what was happening in her body and to concentrate on the medicine man.

The *traiteur* settled on the floor next to the pallet they'd laid out for Dupree. Kneeling on the wooden deck, he placed his hands on the boss's chest, bowed his head and murmured words—prayers, maybe, or incantations—that Amaia couldn't make out. She had no idea where the conviction originated, but in the depth of her being, Amaia understood the man was powerful in the humblest way imaginable; he was a gentle warrior, an unpretentious prince.

The *traiteur*'s hands shifted to Dupree's sides, then his feet, then back to his head. Each time he prayed or performed ritual motions, it was with the same vigor, the same confidence and savoir faire. He applied his palms to Dupree's body as if wrapping him in an invisible blanket to shield him from pain.

He rose and looked about at those present. Dupree lay at his feet, eyes closed and arms resting at his sides. He was no longer sweating. He seemed to be sleeping easily.

"Now we are going to let him work. I treated him; now he has to cure himself."

"He's asleep?" said Bull. It was part question and part affirmation.

"No," the *traiteur* replied. And without further explanation, he looked around at the fisherfolk and commanded them with a gesture to bring Médora into the houseboat.

Not one of them mirrored the pity and sympathy of the *traiteur* when they pulled back the sheet covering Médora. The odor of death spread through the air. Several cried out in horror and fear. They covered their mouths and noses with their hands or the fabric of their T-shirts. Some crossed themselves; others kissed charms or crucifixes.

Médora stood in the middle of the space, only half-aware of her surroundings. The six naked lightbulbs dangling from the rafters swung slightly, flickering to the generator's low, uncertain rhythm and threatening to go out completely. The *traiteur* pushed her hair back to uncover her face, and Médora bowed her head to escape the feeble light. The brittle knots of her mass of hair hung before her face and hid the stiff, dry skin stretched over her skull.

The man's voice was tender. "Who did this to you?"

Her answer was wordless. She released a faint hiss that sounded like air escaping from an inner tube.

The *traiteur* raised his hands ceremonially and placed them on her skeletal shoulders.

Médora jerked away and reeled back a couple of steps, throwing panic into those on that side of the room. The *traiteur* took two strides forward so he was again directly before her. He didn't touch her this time, but he bowed his head and began incanting, utterly motionless except for his lips.

The woman began to sway. Forward and backward, as if a gentle swell were washing through her body, originating at her feet, rising to her knees, hips, shoulders, and neck. She hissed quietly. "Ssssh, ssssh, ssssh."

Amaia watched, spellbound. Never in a million years would she have thought that a body so mistreated, desiccated, and covered with sores could move like this.

"Ssssh, ssssh, ssssh."

She produced a sound that was sort of a hiss and sort of a hum.

"Ssssh, ssssh, ssssh, ssssh."

Her arms swung at her side like dead branches, and the undulation extended upward to include her head, which tilted rhythmically to one side and then to the other, her face concealed by that mass of dry, matted hair.

A subtle modulation, a whistling sound, became audible.

"Ssssh, ssssh, ssssh."

"That the snake," said the woman who'd spoken to Amaia earlier.

Yes, of course it was, how had she failed to recognize it?

Médora hissed and moved as possessed by the snake. The faint warning sign Amaia had perceived earlier now became dire and sinister. Alarms went off in her head and evoked memories of the light in that little clearing deep in the forest, warning her that the gates of hell stood gaping wide. The unexpected vision was so violent and vivid that, without thinking, she started forward to warn the *traiteur*. The woman grabbed Amaia's wrist with her strong fisherwoman's grip and held her back.

The *traiteur* stepped closer to Médora, still murmuring his incomprehensible incantations, and suddenly, smoothly, he took her in his arms as if she were a little girl. The woman's skull settled against his chest. He didn't grip her or constrain her in any way; he embraced her with an intimate, filial motion of real love, of generous protection. Médora slumped in his arms as if all the energy that had sustained her had suddenly drained away. Her arms dangled limp at her sides, her knees doubled, and her feet gave way as her head fell back, revealing to everyone the cruel reality of the death engraved in her features.

The *traiteur* held her and lowered her to the floor with great care. He signaled to the others to cover her with a blanket.

Johnson, Amaia, and the New Orleans detectives approached the man.

"Your friend will be all right," he said, gesturing to the motionless Dupree. "But for her I have no cure."

Amaia gazed at him, unable to comprehend. What, then, had she just witnessed?

He turned to her as if he'd read her thoughts. "The Takotsubo cardiomyopathy is called the broken heart syndrome. That's what happened to your friend. His heart was being squeezed to death in a vise of fear and doubt some evildoer had cursed him with. I can't cure this woman, though, because the root of her disease is not within her."

Bull and Johnson nodded, as if that made sense.

Charbou didn't. "I don't understand."

"He can't cure what she doesn't have," Amaia said. "*Son petit bon ange*, her soul. She said Samedi took it."

Charbou turned to the *traiteur*. "But is that possible?" Even Charbou recognized the man's authority, Amaia saw. Bill had scoffed and doubted right up to that moment, and now for the first time, he'd glimpsed a different reality, one in which other rules might apply.

"She believes it. That's enough," the *traiteur* replied. "Maybe he didn't take it, but he's certainly holding it prisoner. She's his slave, and the place that held it is now empty. She's like a house abandoned by its owner, open for anyone to enter."

"I watched what you were doing," Charbou said, looking down at the woman lying on the floor. "And she is starting to look a little better."

"That is temporary, a momentary relief. The wolf will be back."

Amaia darted a glance at him, feeling a stir of panic at that terrible phrase, and saw that the *traiteur* had noticed her. He was studying her closely.

"The doctors said she's suffering from Cotard's syndrome," Amaia maintained.

"I agree with them," the *traiteur* replied.

Charbou was looking for a reassuring explanation. "So you agree she's mentally ill?"

"Of course. But she didn't make herself sick. *They* made her sick, they induced it, the same as if they'd deliberately inoculated her with a contagious illness."

"It's always . . . okay, now just listen. I'm from New Orleans, I've heard about voodoo and zombies and curses and pincushion dolls for casting spells, all that stuff. But I always thought it was just stories. I never thought . . . And of course I never believed in any of it."

"Whether you believe it or not, it exists. The *bokor* who did this is a priest of darkness, someone who calls on spirits to work evil. The world's phony portrayal of voodoo does contain a grain of truth. It is a religion of spirits. That's what the word 'voodoo' means: 'the spirit who speaks.' And when someone can speak to spirits, he can choose to speak either with the good ones or with the evil ones. Médora has an illness that makes her act and feel as if she were dead. I can't imagine any greater anguish. But her mind won't recover unless her soul is healed. Médora is ill because she believes. The ceremony of zombification is the *bokor*'s way of persuading his victim that she has died, the *bokor* stole her soul, and then he resurrected her dead body. That's why the victim belongs to him."

Amaia insisted, almost pleading, "Dupree said you'd help Médora!"

The *traiteur* pointed to Amaia's abdomen. "I can help you, if you want, but we *traiteurs* have our limits. Taking an antibiotic might be a good idea. You ask Annabel." He pointed to the woman who'd been next to Amaia. "These waters are full of microbes, and the women in the swamp are always getting cystitis."

Amaia became aware that the discomfort that had afflicted her had now spread along her spine. The sharp pains were worsening and she urgently needed to pee—sure signs of a urinary tract infection. She pressed her lips tight and fought against the malaise. "But if you don't help her, she won't be able to help us. We need to ask her questions; the lives of two little girls may depend on what she can tell us."

"I don't think she'll say any more than she already has."

"She hasn't said a damn thing," Charbou declared.

The *traiteur* smiled. "Maybe not in your language, but I guarantee you that the one who was in there," pointing at Médora's supine figure, "did speak."

53

Stella Tucker

Tampa, Florida

Agent Stella Tucker examined herself in the mirror as she washed her hands. Cropping her hair had been the right choice. She never had to worry about it being out of place now. Her skin was properly hydrated, although the tension and violent effort of the preceding hours had left their traces, especially in the hollow circles beneath her eyes. She tried out a smile and was pleased with the result. Her suit was in good shape, although she'd have changed her blouse if she'd had the chance. But it was too late to go back to the hotel. She couldn't make a senator wait.

Director Wilson's phone call from Quantico had taken up valuable time, but she'd enjoyed hearing him praise her work, even though Tucker knew Wilson and Verdon thought she was a bad apple. No reason to worry about that right now. With Dupree out of contact somewhere in New Orleans and his team in disarray, Stella Tucker wouldn't have to work for him again. Given her success running her own team, nobody would deny her that.

A couple of sharp pings announced the arrival of the text message from Emerson she'd been expecting. The senator had just arrived from Washington and was entering the building. His secretary had called an hour earlier. The senator had taken the first available flight and wanted to see her in the VIP room of the hospital where Brad Nelson was being treated. She'd made sure a police officer was posted outside the ICU.

Things couldn't have turned out better in the Nelson case. Twenty minutes earlier, the physicians had informed her that Nelson had regained consciousness. The FBI couldn't interrogate him yet because he was intubated, but the doctors were confident he would recover. It was practically a miracle that the SWAT officer's bullet hadn't killed Nelson, though it had smashed his vertebra, meaning he would probably never walk again. Tucker knew that a dead Nelson would have been an extraordinary achievement, but bringing a serial killer to justice in court would also generate a remarkable amount of publicity favorable to her.

She offered her right hand to her reflection and rehearsed a respectful nod. Not servile, not at all; professional, rather. Neither impressed nor indifferent. Tucker was the FBI agent in charge of the operation that had saved the lives of the family of a United States senator, but that was her duty. She needed to strike a tone between hero and seasoned pro, appropriate for graciously accepting the well-earned gratitude she was expecting from the senator.

54

Fermenting

Elizondo

It was a gesture he found comforting, so internalized that he resorted to it instinctively even in his sleep. This time it failed. He reached out for her furtive warmth and opened his eyes. Rosario was gone.

She wasn't in the house. He knew that the instant he awoke. Even so, he went through the rooms one by one, barefoot, the chill creeping up from his feet. He returned to their room and sat on the edge of the bed, staring at the hollow on her side where she should have been. He bent over the bedside table, pulled open the drawer, and pushed aside the pile of carefully paired socks inside. He took a large yellow envelope from beneath them and put it down next to him on the bed. With a trembling finger, he traced the letters in blue ink someone had used to inscribe his daughter's name. He sighed, deeply upset by Rosario's disappearance.

His wife had stopped visiting the girls' room at night as soon as Amaia went to live with her aunt Engrasi. And she hadn't left the house at night for the past twelve years, not since she was last pregnant.

Sleepless years they'd been for him, as he watched to make sure she was still beside him in bed. He remembered the first time he'd awakened and realized she was gone. He recalled his initial astonishment at finding she wasn't there, his alarm at the prospect of a sudden illness or fainting spell, the worry about a possible miscarriage. After that, checking the house, mastering his panic, and throwing an overcoat over his pajamas to go to the bakery, only to confirm she wasn't there either. Then sitting in the living room, waiting, speculating, tormented by worry and suspicion, staring at the telephone and deciding he'd wait another fifteen minutes before calling the police. Finally, hearing her key in the lock and hurrying upstairs to feign sleep and pretend to wake just as she returned to bed, her body still chilled by the cold of the streets outside.

Then gathering his courage and asking in a tremulous voice, "Where were you? Is everything all right?"

She replied, in a reassuring voice, "Don't worry, I'm fine. I couldn't sleep and I went downstairs for a glass of milk."

Juan couldn't go back to sleep after that.

Rosario continued to leave the house in the middle of the night or the wee hours of the morning at least one night out of ten. She always returned before the sun rose, chilled but serene, to slip into bed and pretend she'd never left.

He'd thought a thousand times of confronting her, racking his brain for a way to bring up the subject. Each night that she left the house, he sat in the darkness waiting for her in the living room, imagining how the conversation might go when she came in and he caught her sneaking back before dawn. She'd be obliged to explain, in that case, and tell him where she'd been and with whom. She'd have to tell him why his pregnant wife had left his side in the middle of the night.

Then came the moment he heard her key in the door. After that, the gentle brushing sound as the bottom of the front door moved across the weather stripping they'd installed to hold in the heat. She gripped the handle to keep it from clicking when she closed the door. Her steps were quiet and cautious as she came upstairs, avoiding the treads that creaked.

Her caution and care not to be discovered were what made him return to bed just before she entered their room. He told himself that her silence was concern, her concealment was composure, and her care to avoid discovery was proof of shame and repentance. That first night had set the pattern, because once she was back in bed, he heard her breathing settle into a regular rhythm and sensed her body relax when she finally went to sleep—that's when he sat up to look at her. His only feeling was gratitude she was with him, gratitude she'd returned. And every time she left the house at night, right up until the day she gave birth, he promised himself he'd reproach her and question her, but that very first night had been decisive, even though he wasn't yet aware of it. He would never say anything.

After all, what was there to say? What demand could he make? For when he saw her sleeping beside him, he still asked himself how such an amazing woman had chosen a miserable man like him. He still couldn't believe it. Engrasi called him an ostrich hiding his head in the sand so as not to see the problems. But Juan felt more like a duck, an ugly duck in love with a swan. He felt invincible next to her, but he didn't forget for a minute that he was a simple man with no culture and little refinement who was allowed to be the consort of a queen. How could he possibly seek to control her? Or oblige her to do anything at all?

The second time she went out, he was so worried that he could think of little else for days. Where had his wife gone, carrying her shoes and with her coat thrown on over her nightgown? Where could a pregnant woman possibly go in the middle of the night in a town where everything closed at nine in the evening? The torment of doubt was driving him crazy. Unable to sleep at night, irritable all day long, he consumed meals that had no taste and became bitter bile when he vomited them up. After Rosario's third nighttime disappearance, Juan decided to consult the doctor.

"Given the unusual nature of this pregnancy," Dr. Martínez had tried to explain, "she may well be finding things very difficult."

"Is it endangering her health?"

"No," the doctor reassured him, "she's healthy, and she's taken my diet advice very seriously. Besides, she's getting a lot of exercise by walking and she hasn't gained too much weight, which would be counterproductive for a pregnancy like this one. The last test results were excellent, but a pregnancy like hers, with its unusual aspects, is not only a challenge for the woman's body, it stresses her spirit and mind as well. But don't worry. Rosario is a healthy woman, and she can handle it."

One night after she returned and her body was beginning to warm the bedclothes, he overcame his inhibitions and whispered in the dark bedroom, "I'm your husband, and I love you. Wherever you go, I'll go with you."

Rosario didn't answer right away. It took so long that he thought she might have already been asleep. Or perhaps she felt so ashamed that she couldn't find the courage to reply. Then with a decisive, alert voice, Rosario replied. "Never!"

He remained awake the rest of the night, staring at the ceiling and turning that word over and over in his mind, wondering what it could mean and what threat it implied. Rosario left the house at night at least once a week during the last three months of her pregnancy, but Juan never said a word to her about it again.

Then she gave birth. His world fell apart, and he knew he was to blame, no one else. Amaia was born as one of a pair of identical twins; Rosario made sure the other one never woke up. Though he'd wanted to believe the horror had been an accident or, as Dr. Martínez said, the result of a postpartum depression that would fade away like a bad dream, there'd been many times in the following months he'd found his wife perched over the child's bassinet. He tried to convince himself this was simply her mother's instinct, the concern that impels so many fathers and mothers to get up at night to make sure their baby is still breathing. But there was something in Rosario's face, in her eyes, something that had nothing to do with care and protection; it was the anxiety provoked by an unfinished task. He saw it and was devastated. Though deep down he knew it would do no good, he whispered words of encouragement, assuring her the baby was fine and nothing was going to happen. He put his arm around her shoulders and persuaded her to return to bed.

He'd made his peace with it by convincing himself night after night that she wouldn't do the unthinkable. Waiting, sitting up in bed when she got up and went to mumble obscure words over the baby, hoping the child was sleeping and wouldn't understand, until finally all those threats erupted into the darkest, blackest catastrophe. On that night, he'd had to remove his own little daughter forever from his house.

Juan was conscious of his own limitations. He was a simple, calm, organized man whose concerns were his work, his family, and delivering on his promises. He'd been like that since early childhood. But some things he couldn't handle, because they were beyond him.

Juan had difficulty with words, and he found it agonizing to identify things by name; he was overwhelmed by the very fact that every object had its own unique name. He was one of those who thought things existed only when they were spoken of, so he could exclude horrors from his life and home by refusing to put them into words. He'd adamantly reproached Engrasi for saying Rosario had been intending to kill Amaia ever since the day the child was born. He hadn't even been aware he was shaking his head in rejection of that thought, for it was too horrible to imagine.

Haunted by fear, he picked up the yellow envelope and lifted the flap to reveal the dark plastic frame that held the X-ray. He pulled it out, dropped the envelope, and held the image against the light. His daughter's skull stood out in profile against the dark background, marred by two wicked white blobs at the points of impact, each surrounded by pools of dark gray showing the extent of the internal hemorrhaging. He squeezed his eyes shut and broke into sobs, flung the X-ray on the bed and got up, resolved to act.

Just as on that night twelve years earlier, he sent up a silent prayer that he'd discover her nearby. He was appalled to find himself hoping she might have broken a bone, have injured herself, or be lying unconscious on the floor of the bakery workshop, anything at all, provided only that she hadn't started going out again at night. He checked every corner of their home, knowing he'd find nothing. He took the keys to the bakery and pulled on his coat over his pajamas. He left the house and walked through the night of a silent, dreaming Elizondo, disturbed only by the sounds of the flowing river. He went to the bakery, seeing from a distance that it was totally dark, but even so, he unlocked the door and looked around. She wasn't there. He slumped against the door, knowing there was nothing more he could do.

He dried his tears, shaken by the clarity of his perception. He had to say it. He was resolute, but even so, when he tried to speak, his voice was inaudible because he was choked with anguish. "Rosario . . . ," he said in a quivering whisper, "Rosario is going to murder our daughter."

Astonished by the brutality of that statement, he covered his mouth with his hands as if trying to hold the words back. Finally, yielding to the inevitable, his arms fell to his sides and a furious animal bellow broke from somewhere deep inside. He realized that he'd always known, and the atrocity had lived in him, trapped only by his refusal to name it. By putting it into words at last, he had conjured it up in all its terrible cruelty. He didn't bother to lock up. He rushed outside, his feet slipping on the wet cobblestones as he raced toward his sister's house.

55

Engrasi

Elizondo

Ipar's ears perked up when Engrasi peeked into Amaia's room. He was up on her bed again, even though Engrasi had provided the dog his own bed on the floor. The sleeping girl had one arm curled around her dog, her hand nestled in the thick fur of his neck. Engrasi knew that as soon as she had left the room earlier that evening, her niece had encouraged Ipar to come into her bed.

Smiling indulgently, Engrasi lifted a finger to her lips as a sign to him to keep quiet. Ipar seemed to understand, for he settled back into place. She leaned against the doorframe, enchanted by the sight of her sleeping niece. A low-wattage nightlight cast its dim glow across the sleeping figure. Amaia must have left it on so she could sleep, or, actually, so when she awoke suddenly in the middle of the night, she'd know instantly where she was and not be scared.

Amaia's hair glinted in golden-blond waves across the pillow. That beautiful hair cascaded to her shoulders, and Engrasi planned to let her grow it out until Amaia asked to have it cut. Such abundant blond hair, like Engrasi's own, was rare in their family. They'd inherited it from Juanita, her mother, Amaia's grandmother. It made the girl stand out from her dark-haired sisters. Rosario had first woven it in long, tight braids and later chopped it off with ragged scissor cuts that left the child looking miserable and abused. That brutality should have set off alarms even then. Engrasi had seen the threat of violence hovering over Amaia: the clothes her mother forced her to wear, the food the child was compelled to eat, the way Rosario had hacked Amaia's hair short to destroy that banner of individuality. Engrasi shook her head slowly, bitterly regretting her own failure to intervene. *So often our failure to speak out against horror makes us accomplices.*

"*Gabon*, Ipar," she called as she closed the bedroom door, sure at least that Amaia felt secure and protected.

Engrasi had been anxious and apprehensive all day long. After the French police officers left, Joxepi had warned her, "You can't leave her alone for a second, Engrasi. Don't let her stick her nose outside unless Ipar is with her. If those people are as dangerous as the French inspector said . . ."

Ignacio, as taciturn as ever, jerked his head in disagreement. "Ipar will give his life to protect her, but the desire that motivates people like that is so deep and vile that no dog can intimidate them."

Engrasi accepted his counsel. She knew he was right.

"I've been thinking for a while of sending Amaia away to study, maybe even outside the country. She was the one to suggest it, actually. She's gifted, very advanced in her schoolwork. Months ago, one of her teachers told her about a boarding school in Pamplona. It has a fine reputation; the coursework is all in English, and she'd be there throughout the week. Some students come home only during vacation. And I could go see her on the weekends."

"After what they just told us, I wouldn't hesitate for a second."

Engrasi had indeed been seriously considering the possibility for some time, not only because of the attempted abduction, but also because she was haunted by what Rosario had said: "If there's one thing I've known since the day that girl was born, it's that we all have a destiny, Engrasi. She'll fulfill her destiny just as I must fulfill mine."

Engrasi went downstairs to the living room. She used a couple of lengths of kindling to light the logs in the fireplace, then went to the sideboard and unlocked a drawer with the key she wore on the chain around her neck. She took out a little black silk bag and brought it to the table. She undid the knots in the drawstring, one by one. She inspected her deck of Marseilles tarot cards with a vague feeling of dread. They were a bitter but necessary pill, considering the seriousness of the consultation she was about to make.

She shuffled the deck deliberately, focusing on exactly how to ask her question. She put the cards down, cut the deck, and shuffled again.

Her deck was so ancient and worn that if she laid the cards out on the table face down, she could recognize each of them by their tattered corners and telltale use marks. When consulting on her own behalf, she used the method of the Roma, who interpreted one after another the ten cards that wound up on top of the deck. She would flip each card over and then set it in place in a pattern that would come to resemble a Celtic cross.

She framed her question and set out the first card, which by the terms of this consultation represented Amaia. The Star, with the image of a beautiful naked woman beneath a clear sky filled with stars; a maiden pours the water of knowledge into a river that vanishes into the horizon. Engrasi smiled; that was her girl, all right. The Star was the essence of youth, beauty, and a luminously pure soul. It evoked the clarity of a nourished mind that could see truth and perceive what others had hidden. It augured a brilliant future, good fortune, smiling happiness, and a beneficent heaven.

She turned over the second card, even though she knew immediately what she was about to see. Death, a skeleton with empty eye sockets, stood on a battlefield, scything off heads. Engrasi held back, reluctant to place the second card in its assigned place above the Star, wanting somehow to keep it from covering the girl sleeping upstairs. She held it up, careful to keep it from touching other cards. After all, this most feared card in the deck didn't always symbolize actual death. Frequently, and probably this time as well, it was a portent of destiny about to reveal itself. It could be a warning of great danger, received in time to take swift action to avoid disaster.

She was anxiously studying the skeleton's empty eye sockets, as if hoping to extract some additional meaning from the shadows within them, when someone pounded on the front door. She was so startled that she dropped the card and saw it land half across the earlier pick, hiding the starry sky and most of the long hair of the beautiful maiden.

The frantic knocking resumed. Engrasi got up; she left the tarot deck on the table but pushed the card showing Death away from the young woman on the Star. Alarmed, she went to the door. "Who is it?"

"Engrasi, it's me, Juan. Please let me in!"

She opened the door and was confronted by the contorted, tear-streaked face of her brother.

"Engrasi, where's the girl?" he cried out.

"Amaia's upstairs, asleep in her room. Juan, do you have any idea what time it is?" She was trying to make sense out of all this.

"I need to see her. She's going to kill her!" he cried as he pushed his way into the house and leaped past his sister toward the stairs. Engrasi followed, trying to warn him. "Juan, don't! Don't open the—"

She caught up with him just as he turned the handle to push the door open. Ipar's snarling muzzle thrust through the door, and the dog's vicious snap barely missed Juan's hand, leaving it wet with saliva.

Juan turned back to his sister, thrown into confusion. "Wh-what's this?"

"That's Ipar," Engrasi told him with great seriousness. "He's Amaia's bodyguard. Let's go downstairs. We need to talk."

Juan stood petrified for several seconds, unable to tear his gaze from the door behind which his daughter was sleeping, guarded by a vigilant dog. He turned to his sister and nodded. He spoke in a very low but determined voice. "I'll sign the papers for Amaia to go to that school. We have to get her out of town right away."

Engrasi had never seen her brother so decided. "What made you change your mind?"

"Rosario is going out at night, the way she did before Amaia was born. It's starting again, Engrasi. If we don't do something quick, she'll kill her." He broke down and sobbed. "Rosario will murder my little girl!"

56

Infection

The swamp
Nightfall, Tuesday, August 30, 2005

Sweaty, nauseated, and cursing her bad luck, she'd followed the *traiteur*'s advice. Amaia's fever wasn't particularly high, but she was shivering uncontrollably and felt an agonizing burning sensation each time she tried to urinate. Fortunately, Annabel had a good stock of single-dose antibiotics to attack the infection.

The fisherwoman stirred the contents of a little envelope into a glass of clean water. "Good drug, this one. Tomorrow you look back on this like a bad dream. I know how it feel, baby. This bad water and all those germs . . ." She handed the glass to Amaia, who downed the contents in one long swallow. Annabel told her to eat something.

The shrimpers and fisherfolk had improvised tables by setting plywood sheets on sawhorses and other assorted pieces of furniture. They brought out dozens of folding chairs. Amaia was going to tell Annabel she couldn't eat a bite, but the tempting odors coming from the kitchen changed her mind. "What smells so good in there?"

Annabel smiled. She was a tall, strong woman, a bit overweight, her shoulder-length hair loose in the front and done up in a ponytail behind. "Ham and shrimp. My man, Clive, and the boys cooking up a jambalaya."

"I've never had that," Amaia admitted. "It smells wonderful." She went to the kitchen, where a big pot on a portable camp stove held a simmering red-tinted mixture. Clive was stirring it with a long wooden spoon and explaining the recipe to Johnson.

"My mama always make it for holidays when I was little," Annabel said, pointing to the pot. "Right now maybe don't look like the time to celebrate, but we got plenty to be happy for. Most of us lost the houses, true, but we save the boats, and they how we earn our living, right? The family is fine, the babies safe, so you know, my dear, we ready to *laissez les bons temps rouler*!"

"You're right. The important thing is that everyone's okay. Were you able to get in contact with the other families?"

"Oh, yes, most of the boats got radios to talk a long way. We get news like that, 'cause out here in the swamp, your telephone don't work much. We get along fine with the radio. Why, today I talk with a cousin of mine in Maine, told him we all right. He worried a lot about us."

That caught Amaia's attention. "How's that possible? A maritime radio usually reaches only a few miles."

"Oh, for sure! But it wasn't on the radio—or, anyhow, not only on the radio. We use the boat radio to contact a shrimper somewhere with his cell phone connection, somebody like Cousin Paula in Cocodrie. We give her the number we want, and she call with the cell phone. Then she put the phone on speaker next to the mic, and we talk like that. Just one problem, though: all the boats on that channel hear you talk."

Johnson and Amaia looked at one another. "Did you hear that?" she exclaimed, delighted by the discovery. Charbou and Johnson were impressed.

Johnson spoke to Clive. "Can you show me how to do that? We need to get in contact with someone. It's important, more important than I can say."

"I got it set up with Paula to talk, round eleven tonight. We can try. But right now the jambalaya ready. You got to eat a jambalaya as soon as you finish cooking it." He waved behind them. "And it look like this crew full of hungry people."

Johnson turned to find a line of Cajun families already lined up along the tables.

Amaia relieved Bull at Dupree's pallet as soon as she'd finished her meal. Johnson and Charbou followed Clive and Annabel to their shrimp boat.

"He hasn't woken up," Bull told her, "but his fever's gone, and he's looking a lot better."

Amaia sat on the floor by the pallet. She stared mindlessly through the windows that gave out onto the dark swamp, that realm of darkness the bayou dwellers claimed was inhabited by the *fifolets*, spirits floating above the dark surface of the water. Tiny *lutins*, spirits of naughty children, danced around them and sneaked up on sleeping people to braid their hair.

She took in the sounds around her. The festive noise of people sharing a meal in the next houseboat reminded her how resilient human beings could be. She heard the regular creaking of the cables securing the houseboats, a slow rhythm set by the waves. And something else, too—a low murmuring, rhythmic, like prayer. She noticed that Médora wasn't in the room.

Peering out the window, Amaia saw the *traiteur* on the back porch, sitting opposite the human wreck that had once been a woman. He was holding her hands and murmuring incantations.

Dupree's voice in the darkness startled her. "What is *Gaueko*?"

She jumped. "You scared me! Are you feeling better?"

"Yes," he said. "A lot better." He wasn't a hundred percent yet, but at least his voice had regained its tone and vigor. "What is *Gaueko*? I heard you say that last night in the dark while we were staring out at the drowned city."

She returned and settled beside him in the dim light. "*Gaueko* is the lord of darkness, the spirit of the night. *Gauekoak* are 'things of the night.' In the little town I come from they have legends about all kinds of magical creatures, but you can sort them into two categories: creatures of the light and creatures of the dark. The *gauekoak* are the shadowy spirits that wander through the streets and the mountains. They're made of night, death, and loneliness, and they're always seeking some unguarded access to creep into a human body. According to the legend, they can go anywhere they please until the sun rises. Then they have to scramble to find caves or rocks where they can hide from the new day. Many people in my region decorate their outside doors with a thistle—the *eguzki-lore*. That means 'the flower of the sun.' The goddess Mari gave it to human beings to ward off *gauekoak. Gauekoak* avoid those houses because the flower looks like a sun. My aunt always keeps one by our front door. Just in case."

"I know what you're talking about," came his voice from the darkness. "Voodoo has an evil spirit called Kalfou who climbs on the chest of his sleeping victim and paralyzes him. The victim's aware of his plight, but he can't escape. My aunt Nana wouldn't let me open the bedroom windows at night, even when it was over a hundred degrees, for fear that I would let Kalfou in."

"I thought you said you were Catholic."

"My mother was. Nana brought me up after my parents died. She took me to Sunday school and confirmation classes. We went to mass every Sunday. But she practiced voodoo as well. Maybe you find that strange?"

"Not at all. My aunt Engrasi has a psychology degree from the Sorbonne, but she consults tarot cards. Not so different."

"And you?"

"I don't believe in any of it. I respect people's faith and their beliefs, of course. An investigator has to. But that's it."

"I suspect you weren't always like that."

"Like you said, you always carry with you the influence of the place where you were born. When you come from a place like Baztán, you accept the people's beliefs. Like accepting Cajun culture out here in the swamp. I remembered the *Gaueko* story last night, when we were looking out at the darkness in New Orleans. I had an intuition then, a superstitious feeling that night creatures would own the city even after the sun rose. What I saw later on just confirmed that feeling. We were lost in the night of Samedi. He'd cursed New Orleans forever."

"But you denied your folklore when we were standing out in the Allens' field in front of that destroyed roof. Claimed you didn't know the legends, said you couldn't remember."

"That was partly true. Those tales belong to a place and time that are no longer part of my life. They're irrelevant, mostly forgotten. It's just that lately, with the Composer's murders and Samedi's return, the old myths keep coming to mind, as if they are connected somehow. It's absurd, I know. Myths from the back country of Spain come from an entirely different world than that of the Composer. But I can't shake the feeling that some malevolent force in my past is haunting me."

Dupree remained silent for a time. "There's a positive side to myth. Legends caution us of danger, but they also suggest ways to protect ourselves and forestall the threat. You might say there's always a 'flower of the sun' to fend off the *gauekoak*. Evil spirits may be powerful, but they're not invulnerable."

She made no comment, for she knew that no *eguzki-lore* in the world could stand up to the evil they were tracking now. After a long pause, she responded with apparent indifference, "They're just made-up stories."

"The other day, after Johnson asked about the region you come from, I got him to tell me more. He described a fertility goddess and the guardian of the woods. Even some kind of enchanted women with webbed feet who dwell in the rivers."

Amaia sniffed. "Sure, and I'll bet he forgot to mention that the fertility goddess is the queen of the witches. In the time of the Inquisition, the poor women who sacrificed to her in hopes of getting pregnant or gathering good harvests were denounced, arrested, and tortured. Any deviation from normal behavior, any absurd little quirk, was used as evidence against them. Most often, they were midwives, they'd decided not to marry, or they spoke to animals."

Dupree clicked his tongue in the darkness. "The Pyrenees had no monopoly there. In all of Europe, in the whole world, including the New World, there was hysteria about witchcraft. The Salem witch trials, for instance. What did the folks back there in Elizondo do to you, anyhow? Why do you clam up whenever you so much as hear that name?"

"I'm not here just by chance, am I?"

"Do you believe in chance? Or coincidence?"

She didn't answer.

He changed the subject. "Do you think human beings are really so different from one another, even when they're separated by thousands of miles?"

"In what respect?"

"It seems to me that people all over the world have the same hopes and fears and ambitions. Mankind's history is the history of our fears. It stands to reason that we'd all create similar legends to give names to those terrors, to try to control them. I believe there's a natural ability buried deep in our primal consciousness, that ferrets out connections, maybe not entirely logical ones. Those connections are hunches, and they're vital for our survival. I believe that a gut feeling is far more important in investigation and detection than hard data. Facts that can't be observed directly but have to be inferred from other, visible evidence. You called them 'latent variables.' Those latent variables told you the Composer had killed before and was rehearsing for a final, crucial massacre, and your insight led us to Martin Lenx. It's like that here. Things you learn here sink into your mind, and they resonate with concepts you're struggling with, deep in your subconscious. They're constantly whispering that there must be a correlation between seemingly unrelated events. Or maybe there's a live link between then and now."

"That hasn't been much use in locating the Composer."

He sighed. "Don't torment yourself. Try to sleep. Early tomorrow morning we'll take the boat out to Le Grand, or what's left of it. And tomorrow will be the time, if ever, that your ability to detect latent variables will be required. For that, I need you to be strong."

Amaia was distressed. "I was so sure of myself . . . But now I see my mind was closed. I was obsessed, but I've lost faith in myself. I wonder whether I've been completely mistaken. Maybe I'm not the tool you need."

A flashlight beam pierced the darkness. They heard Charbou's voice. "Salazar, Johnson's asking for you. He says it's important."

She followed Bill along the pontoon walkways between the houseboats, and then they climbed from one boat to another until they reached Clive and Annabel. The harsh glare of the overhead lamp in the deckhouse made her squint.

"Salazar!" Johnson called out as soon as he saw her. "Annabel's cousin out in the Gulf telephoned NOLA, and we're in contact with the ops center. I've got the supervisor, Bernard Antée, on the line."

Amaia nodded.

Johnson pressed the transmit button. "Bernard, I have Assistant Inspector Salazar with me now. Could you please repeat what you just told me? Over."

A metallic voice spoke through distant static, amplified by the cabin's loudspeakers. "Hello, Assistant Inspector, glad to hear you're safe. Less than two hours ago, a Texas National Guard contingent went into a residence near Jackson Square and found a family of six shot to death. They called us right away, asking to get in contact with the police, and because of what they described, I thought of y'all."

Amaia's jaw dropped. She gasped. In a sudden panic, she moistened her lips and tried to put her thoughts in order, fending off the host of questions that crowded her mind. "Mr. Antée, I have to speak with the group that discovered them. Over."

"Afraid there's just no way to reach them, ma'am. I'll do my best to put you in contact if they call back, but they're combing all the houses in the neighborhood to make sure folks get out. We got teams in from various military units today, and tomorrow morning the evacuation starts. But like I said, when I heard the report that matched your criteria, I tried to collect all available information. I hope I can help you. Um, over."

Amaia released a little huff of air. Well, that was better than nothing. She pressed the transmit button. "What can you tell me? Over."

"Three females, three males. Three victims were young, probably teenagers. One woman was elderly. All shot in the head. And the bodies were laid out side by side, but the team didn't specify in which direction . . . They found a revolver next to the adult male. Looked like he'd dropped it. Over."

"Did they say the residence had been searched earlier? Over."

"They found it marked that way, but the unit code was their own. They were sure that nobody from their division had been there. Over."

"Like in Jefferson," Johnson whispered. "Identical!"

Amaia bit her lip and hesitated before asking. She knew it was unlikely anyone would have noticed, but she had to pose the question. "Mr. Antée, do you recall if they said anything about a violin being in the room? Over."

"No, no mention of anything like that. Over."

"And this is very important, Mr. Antée—could they tell how long the victims had been dead? Over."

"That I can help you with," he replied, sounding pleased to be providing the information. "There's a medic on the team. When they called in, he told us they hadn't been dead more than two or three hours. Over."

Amaia looked at Johnson and Charbou. She pressed the button. "Mr. Antée, do you know what the team did after that? Over."

"They marked it with police tape. Obviously, they couldn't evacuate the bodies or do much else, but the residence is sealed. That's all that can be done for the moment. Over."

"Thank you. You've been a big help. And thanks to you, Paula. Out."

She turned around to find Dupree leaning on the doorframe. She addressed him. "We have to go back! I need to see that family."

He looked at her, considering her request. "The fishermen are getting ready, and we plan to leave before dawn for Le Grand to look for Jacob's sisters. This is our last chance to find them; every hour we delay makes it less likely. I didn't get there in time to save Médora ten years ago, but I think they'll lay low with the girls for a while before they make them disappear forever. I can't give up and leave those children to the same fate as Médora Lirette. We'll search for them, then after that, we'll go back to New Orleans."

"But . . ." She understood Dupree's reasoning, but the news was further evidence the Composer was in New Orleans and she'd been right, after all. She quivered like a bloodhound on a fresh scent.

Dupree saw it. "He's not going anywhere. If he's clever, and we know he is, he'll blend in with the crowd when the evacuation starts. And you heard it from Antée: that's not till tomorrow. They'll prioritize getting the sick and the injured out first. The Composer will be stuck in the city for at least a couple of days. I need you here." He turned and left.

"Agent Dupree!" she called after him.

"Yes?"

"Like I said—Tucker doesn't know a fucking thing!"

He grinned, under the cover of darkness.

57

Occam's Razor

Tampa, Florida

Tucker had been waiting for a while. She was starting to get nervous, and she'd changed her mind twice as she tried to decide whether to remain seated on the Naugahyde sofa or stand by the door. She went to the table where someone had set out coffee, a pitcher of ice water, and a selection of cookies and crackers. She turned back so as not to appear nervous before Emerson, who'd planted himself in an armchair. He was pretending to page through a magazine, but she knew he was watching her every move. Good God, the man was a pain in the ass. She'd just sat down again when a man in a suit, obviously a staffer, opened the door and stood aside for Senator Rosenblatt to enter.

Republican senator for Florida Stephen Rosenblatt cast an impressive figure. Tall and portly, he had the ruddy complexion of someone who loved the outdoors and got too much sun. He was dressed in an elegant, impeccably tailored beige suit that nicely complemented his deep tan. His thick hair was cut short and combed back in a style twenty years out of date. She caught a distinct whiff of the scent of his hair gel.

"Sorry to keep you waiting," the senator said as he sailed into the room. "Afraid I was delayed longer than I expected. The doctors let me in to see my son-in-law."

Tucker smiled as she took the senator's proffered hand, deciding she was going to give Emerson a real dressing down for allowing the senator to get into the ICU ahead of them. Standard procedure was that law enforcement was the first to interview a suspect. She could imagine the reaction of the uniformed cop posted outside the ICU. No one in the state of Florida would dare stand in the way of their senior senator.

Afterward, when she replayed the conversation in her mind, she realized she hadn't caught the senator's reference to his "son-in-law."

Senator Rosenblatt took the sofa without indicating where she should go. His assistant handed him a voluminous file in a maroon binder.

"So you're Agent Stella Tucker, FBI, in command of the operation to safeguard my daughter and grandchildren, which put my son-in-law in the hospital."

She gave him a firm nod, her hands dutifully clasped behind her back.

"Tell me, Agent Stella Tucker, do you think I'm an idiot?"

Taken aback, Tucker looked at him and felt her smile freeze in place. Emerson's ears perked up.

"Of course not, sir," she managed to reply.

"I'm just asking, because you seem to assume I didn't have Brad Nelson investigated when my daughter started dating him. A faceless man with an unconfirmed identity emerges from a burning building and eventually attracts the attention of a senator's daughter. Of course I had him investigated! And you know what? Not only did I find he was clean as a whistle, my people confirmed he was a decent man who'd overcome obstacles few people ever have to face. He and I have been on very good terms ever since. Don't for a moment think I don't know he's got a terrible temper; I grant you he's something of a brute. But so am I, and I respect such men, as long as they're able to maintain control and direct their energy positively. And he'd done that, for years.

"For years! And then, I don't know what happened. Maybe it was his job, maybe he just reached his limits. My son-in-law screwed up with my daughter, and that girl's just as unforgiving as I am. She's made him pay for it ever since, and that's fine with me. But I like Nelson, and he likes me. When he saw his life was going to hell, he came to me like a son to a father and asked for my help. He's been trying to make up for his blowup ever since. He's been separated from his family for the last eight months and getting anger management counseling. He's made his pilgrimages to folk healers, psychologists, and psychiatrists, and they've put him through the wringer with all kinds of therapies, trying to teach him to control that wicked temper of his."

Senator Rosenblatt tapped the binder in front of him. "You've correlated the dates of his leave requests with family murders all across the country. But he was out in the Texas desert or some equally godforsaken place with a support group every single time, doing therapy sessions to learn to control his anger. I know, because I've been paying for them. In this binder I've got all the reports on Brad's progress."

Tucker's mouth opened in astonishment until she realized how foolish she must look. She clapped it shut and licked her lips, thinking fast. "Senator, you're very generous and I admire your big heart. But you need to keep in mind that Brad Nelson was arrested for breaking into the house where your daughter and grandchildren live. He kicked in the back door, sir." She demonstrated the stance, hands raised before her. "I assure you that your son-in-law intended to shoot his family; he gunned down and almost killed a police officer stationed inside the house. Nobody assaulting a house like that has good intentions."

The thing that most offended Tucker was Rosenblatt's response to her earnest explanation. The senator turned to his assistant with an expression of incredulity that showed he thought she was incompetent. He looked back at Tucker, tossed the binder on the table, and addressed her like a clueless adolescent who'd failed to understand a joke. "Brad saw one of your shooters in a black uniform and hood trying to keep out of sight on the upstairs terrace. We all know that the enemies of freedom hate our representative government and especially our freely elected senators. Everybody knows that my family lives here in Tampa. Brad Nelson is an exemplary police officer. He went fully armed into the house, risking his life to defend his family."

Rosenblatt rose and left without another word.

Agent Tucker felt as if her world had just collapsed. Her head spun. She staggered back and dropped into the armchair.

Ready to black out, she was subjected to more humiliation. The staffer leaned over her before following his boss. "You're going to be sued. I suggest you hire an attorney."

Emerson walked out on her as well. "I was against this operation from the start!"

58

A HOLDING PATTERN

Charity Hospital, New Orleans

His tongue flickered across his chapped lips, and he found a little blister at the corner of his mouth. His mind was beginning to clear at last. He wondered how long he'd been unconscious. He couldn't tell how much of his exhaustion and fever was due to illness and how much was the New Orleans heat and humidity. The dizziness and fatigue could have been caused by the struggle of wading through the flood. The familiar rush from sending a family to heaven was gone, replaced as always by a nagging feeling of incompletion. His mission wouldn't be done until he'd redeemed his real family. Maybe the cause of his malaise was the knowledge that time was running out. He knew deep down that each of those families had been a test case, a trial run. But they weren't his own sinful family. Martin had been saving others while his own beloved family continued sinking into depravity.

Fever had been the first symptom, but he hadn't recognized it until the chills began. He'd been finishing up, dispatching the family near the intersection of Chartres and Jackson, when an icy shiver, breathtaking in its intensity, seized him and wouldn't let him go. He pulled up his pants leg and saw why: the bandage on his injured leg was soaking wet. A nasty yellowish ooze from beneath the gauze made it look like some horrible mold was consuming him. The hot, swollen wound had an alarming purple tint. The filthy dressing had become one huge scab. He felt terribly dizzy and weak.

He vaguely remembered wading down the street in the middle of a crowd. Jackson Square? Yes, that was it, one of the few spots of higher ground. After that, something about a boat, a hospital, and the dreamlike sensation of being lifted through a window.

Martin had been sitting on the floor for hours, his back against the wall. At first, he'd accepted the chair offered by a young man accompanying a comatose woman, probably his mother. But dizziness soon overcame him, and he could hardly hold his head up. He'd slid to the floor and leaned against the wall with the old woman's stretcher on one side and the metal IV stand holding drips for both of them on the other.

Martin looked up at the half-full bag. The staff had said the plasma was dosed with antibiotics and tetanus vaccine; the second unit of that solution was draining down the plastic tube and through the needle taped to his arm. He lifted his other hand and touched his forehead. The fever seemed to have subsided. He was still weak, but he felt a lot better. He needed rest. He needed to get some of his energy back. He reached down and gingerly probed the skin around the new dressing. His leg was still inflamed, but it seemed less swollen.

He looked around. The young man who'd given him the chair was weeping aloud, his head in his hands. It looked as if his mother had just died. The hand that dangled over the edge of the stretcher was little more than skin and bones. The medic told the boy they had to remove his mother's body because they needed the stretcher. He removed the IV, left Martin the stand with the drip, and took one end of the stretcher. He and an orderly carried the body away. The young man followed, but Martin knew they wouldn't let him into whatever temporary morgue they'd set up.

He's a good son, Martin thought, and wondered if she'd been a good mother. That conjured up thoughts of his own mother and how he'd dispatched her to heaven. He murmured a brief prayer for her soul.

59

Forsaken by the Saints

Superdome, New Orleans

Nana awoke again, uncertain whether she'd slept for hours or merely minutes. She was too tired and dizzy to try to unzip the knapsack to take out her purse and search for the little gold watch Bobby had told her to keep hidden. Each time she woke up, she found herself bathed in sweat, a sign she was becoming dehydrated. There was little she could do; her blouse stuck to her back, and big drops of perspiration trickled down her chest and belly behind the plastic knapsack she clutched tightly. She cursed the pressing urge to pee that had tormented her for hours. She knew she wouldn't be able to ignore it much longer.

She looked around. She was convinced there were more people now, even though that seemed impossible. She gulped the foul, contaminated air. It stank of the piss, sweat, and breath of thousands of refugees. She was distressed that she was so weak. Perhaps she should finish the last of the chocolate granola bar in the knapsack. Her nausea just made her need to pee all the more.

She'd promised to wait there for Bobby, but that was yesterday, an eternity ago. Another day had begun. She was going to pee all over herself if she didn't do something about it, and that would be awful.

She gripped the head of her cane and put a hand on the shoulder of the man seated next to her. "Please, can you help me get up?"

Her first thought was to go to the nearest toilet. She didn't care if it was filthy. She needed her privacy, even if she had to pee on the floor. *This is teaching me a lesson,* she thought. *Comes a time, from one day to the next, when we find ourselves ready to accept things we swore we'd never put up with.*

The painful journey to the women's restroom took more than half an hour. Even from afar, she smelled the stinking puddle churned by thousands of passing feet. The rubber tip of her cane slipped awkwardly a couple of times, sending her stumbling forward in the slick mess. Groups trying to get into the stadium surged dangerously against those trying to get out, so that for long moments, the jammed bodies pushed and shoved until at last someone managed to wriggle through in one direction or the other.

Nana felt a hot, humid breeze from the outside on her face. It stank, but she preferred it to the fetid air inside. She'd almost reached the exit when somebody elbowed her one way and somebody else shoved her back. Nana lost her cane and fell forward onto her knees, her palms slamming audibly against the concrete floor as she tried to catch herself. A cruel pain shot up from her kneecaps. She'd wrenched her hip. Helpless on the concrete floor, Nana panicked. Overcome and ignored, heedless of the pain, she thought she was done for. She was going to die right there in the press of all those bodies.

A woman pushing past grabbed her under one armpit and yanked her up. The abrupt tug hurt, but it brought her back to her feet and kept her from being trampled. There was no time for gratitude, for the woman immediately disappeared into the crowd. Nana tottered forward, buffeted from one side to the other, her cane lost in the scrum. Her legs ached unbearably. That human tide swept her onward until the stadium vomited her out into the plaza.

She was outside.

The sun burned down from on high. Nana staggered and limped onward, each step threatening to bring her down. Clinging to the railing around the access area, she looked out at her city, and her heart burst with grief. For hours she'd heard tales from arriving refugees, but never in her worst nightmare could she have imagined this hellish sight. Women headed for the stadium dragged desperately crying little children behind them. Filthy, half-naked people stretched out on the ground. Surging water surrounded the stadium and the stench was overpowering. Flies swarmed over the faces of drooling elderly men and women left to their fate. Nana realized that she and they had been abandoned in the heart of their own city.

Without her cane, she could hardly move. She knew she couldn't go back inside. Bobby would never find her now. She was alone. She saw that the open area around the stadium had become one immense toilet. People squatted everywhere, doing their business like animals, heedless of those around them.

Horrified, mad with pain and knowing she couldn't hold out much longer, she stepped out into the area where the lawn had been. The earth squished and yielded underfoot, soaked in feces and urine. She went to the wall, trying to keep from stepping in the worst of it, and wept as she raised her skirt, crouched, and released a stream of pee just as the National Guard trucks roared into the parking lot.

60

Black Mangrove Swamp

The swamp
Wednesday, August 31, 2005

They'd left the Cajun camp before dawn and had navigated through the swamp for more than an hour. Despite the previous day's high temperatures, it was incredibly chilly out on the water. The vapor in the air cloaked them in a film of cold humidity. The sun began to penetrate the swamp, and the dense mist over the surface of the lake started to lift. In that light, Dupree's face revealed how much pain he'd been suffering; as if in compensation, his gestures were imbued with a profound determination and vigor. He whispered directions as Bull steered their craft with the help of two Cajuns.

Seated in the center of the Zodiac, Amaia, Johnson, and Charbou huddled under plastic sheets the shrimpers had lent them. In the prow, the dark figurehead of Médora was positioned as if in the lead. With her was the *traiteur*, who'd insisted on coming with them. They advanced along shores laid waste by the storm and flood two days earlier. Natural features and human constructions were reemerging. The many simple shacks that had previously dotted the shorelines seemed to have been destroyed. The masts of several shrimp boats jutted up from the muddy brown water over the slips where the hurricane had sunk them. Like eerie tombstones they marked the watery graves of their owners' means of making a living.

The sun rose higher and began to heat the swamp. The rising columns of mist were replaced almost instantly by pale humming swirls of mosquitoes above the water. The Zodiac entered a bayou where the brilliance of the morning sky was almost entirely obscured by overhanging branches of trees so stout and tall they'd proven invulnerable to the winds and the flood. The waterway became a tunnel enclosed by dense vegetation.

The current in the bayou slowed as they advanced. Eventually they found themselves in a wide, shallow, virtually stagnant lake. Bull stopped the motor and raised it to keep the propeller from catching the underwater growth. On the far side of the lake, stunted trees populated the marsh, a thick forest so dense and wide, it hid everything beyond. Aerial roots snaked above the water to form the intricate knotted network of a mangrove forest. Amaia caught a flicker of movement in the shadows and reached for her sidearm. A feral hog and half a dozen of its offspring emerged from the brush and peered at the Zodiac.

One of the Cajuns raised his rifle, but Dupree stopped him. "Don't even think about it. The last thing we want to do is let them know we're here."

The dark deathlike figure in the prow twitched. Her wrapping slipped down and revealed a skeletal shoulder. As the sheet slid to the bottom of the craft, they saw the splint and bulky wrapping the *traiteur* had applied to reinforce the metal rod and dressing from the hospital. Médora leaned forward, stretched, and clamped her bony hands on the bow.

Dupree raised a hand to caution the others not to intervene. He needn't have bothered. Collectively, they held their breath, eyes fixed on the bizarre figure. They were repelled but fascinated by the raucous gasping breath she emitted with each tiny movement. Médora raised her rigid injured leg, pushed it across the bulky side of the Zodiac, and let it drop with a sluggish splash. Dupree nodded, lowering his hand, and signaled them to follow her.

The narrow hoofs of a feral hog could canter fearlessly through this marshland maze, but the roots jutting crazily across the swamp offered human limbs no easy purchase. Médora slipped and slid across their knotted, twisted surfaces. She advanced quicker than any of them, her splinted leg lurching perilously. The *traiteur* followed close behind.

Amaia glanced at Dupree, remembering his comments the previous evening. Scrambling after Médora across that twisted structure of branches and roots, they were literally pursuing a zombie. The tangle that resembled glistening, shifting black bones threatened to send them headlong into the muck at any moment.

The intense stench of wet wood, mold, and water both fresh and stagnant filled their nostrils. She tried not to think about the snakes or alligators lurking in these black mangroves. The tree trunks teemed with fire ants and poisonous caterpillars. She did her best to keep her gloved hands close to her sides. This place was hell on earth, and anyone not born to the swamps would never survive them without a guide. She'd lost all sense of time, distance, and direction, because she had to focus on every step she took. The path ahead seemed identical to that behind. She felt a stir of panic at the thought Médora might lose them.

She looked back several times for Dupree. He waved her onward. How had they ever decided to follow a nearly blind woman through this wilderness? Were they going to be trapped here forever?

Fate answered her silent plea. The mangroves thinned and revealed a broad meadow brilliantly illuminated by the intense morning sun. Médora stopped at the limit of the mangrove maze and stood unsteadily looking around. Breathing hard, they stopped to watch her. Amaia was grateful for the sudden gust of perfume from fresh flowers that unexpectedly evoked memories of another meadow in another time. She put those out of her mind and concentrated on their bizarre guide. Médora awkwardly stepped away from the knotted roots and sank knee deep into the green surface that stretched as far as they could see.

Fragrant red flowers swayed above the emerald-colored swamp grass of that wide expanse. At first Amaia thought they were some rare species of orchid, but then she realized they were water lilies, the fleurs-de-lys that symbolized New Orleans.

Progress was slow as they waded after Médora. Dupree advanced to the *traiteur*'s side and conferred with him in a voice the others couldn't hear. The water was thick and lukewarm, an organic slime repugnant to the touch. And then the first thunderclap sounded. It boomed loud and immense, almost on top of them.

Here it comes.

Amaia scanned the sky. A heavy fog hovered some distance overhead. Visibility across the swamp was still unimpeded, but a dense layer of churning low clouds was closing in. What kind of sky was this? The scent of flowers became more pungent and rose around them in a perfumed surge, sweet and hypnotic. As they advanced, the water gradually became shallower. The thick mists closing overhead refracted the brilliant sunshine behind them in a strange, dazzling display that hurt their eyes and nearly blinded them. Another long, rolling burst of thunder shattered the air and continued: one—two—three seconds.

The Lady is coming. The warning echoed so loud in Amaia's mind that for an instant she thought the others could hear it too.

She heard raised voices and turned to look. Dupree had caught up with Médora and now stood in front of her, blocking her advance. She avoided his eyes but sluggishly moved from side to side and peered about as if aware of her surroundings. Confused by the human obstacle in her path, she hugged herself and started rocking back and forth.

The shrimpers had planted themselves at the rear. Bull was talking with them. He turned to beckon to Dupree. Johnson went back to join them.

"We not going any more," the older one insisted. "We finished!"

"But why?" Bull complained. "I don't understand!"

"We not going more, 'cause it too dangerous."

Johnson looked them up and down. "Don't give me that crap. You two are tough swamp Cajuns. You knew we were looking for Le Grand. What's the matter now?"

Clive looked behind them, wanting to backtrack, while the other man replied. "That thunder."

"Thunder?" Johnson exclaimed, amazed. "You fellows are afraid of a storm?"

The older man appeared to take offense. "Not just a storm! The thunder. You call that normal? Look up at the sky!"

They did, and the harsh glare forced them to squint.

"Where the black clouds?" the man challenged. "Where the big old cloud full of water?"

Bull interrupted. "The storm's still far away!"

"No, that storm right here. You not hearing the thunder? The last one make the ground shake!"

"Okay, then, it's right here," Bull conceded. "But so what?"

"That one a bad sign," Clive declared earnestly. "Everybody know that." He turned to the *traiteur*, who said nothing but did nod in confirmation.

Bull couldn't believe it. "Thunder is a bad sign?"

"*That* thunder . . . ," the man said emphatically and pointed up. "The sky ain't dark, not one raincloud. When thunder come out of a sky like that, you better watch out."

His companion confirmed it. "You see and hear a sign like that, you best not go on."

"Ha! And why is that?" Bull mocked them. "What're you scared of?"

The men looked at one another. "They say if you go through the swamp and you hear thunder in a sky with no storm, you turn back. The swamp spirits are in a meeting; you bother them, you cross their land, they put you to sleep for a hundred years. Maybe more."

"Like Rip van Winkle," Dupree commented. They all turned toward him. "Same as in Washington Irving's story."

"There!" Johnson exclaimed. "You see? It's just a made-up story!"

"But," Dupree told them, "Irving took it from mountain legends. People believed it. Folks in different places have different ways of describing the same fears." He glanced at Amaia but saw she wasn't paying attention to their discussion. She was staring distractedly into the distance.

She was remembering thunder from another place and time.

The shrimpers refused to be moved. "All that thunder say we got to stop. We thought we knew where you going, but with that zombie for a guide—"

"She's a woman, and suffering!" the *traiteur* cut him off. "A victim, abducted and held prisoner for ten years. She's still a prisoner. Pay her some respect!"

The Cajuns looked down but didn't budge.

The *traiteur* left and went to Médora's side.

Dupree surveyed the shrimpers and clicked his tongue in frustration. "I don't care. Go back if you want and wait in the Zodiac. We can't waste any more time. The lives of two little girls depend on us."

"No way are we letting these scared hicks go back to the Zodiac!" exclaimed Charbou, who hadn't said a word before this. "As soon as they hear more thunder, they'll take off and leave us stuck here."

Dupree gave the two a questioning look, but neither would meet his gaze.

Bull ended the discussion. "Sorry, friends, but you're going to have to come along. It's too late to turn back now."

"So now you gonna arrest us?" asked Clive. "Or something like that?"

"No," Charbou replied. "But if you two insist on staying here, I'll handcuff you both to one of those trees full of fire ants, and you can wait there till we get back."

That did it. The Cajuns followed the team, though obviously against their will.

The open space ended abruptly at a line of thick bushes that formed a natural barrier about twice a man's height. Another thunderclap sounded overhead just as they reached the thicket. The shrimpers exchanged a pained glance. Médora pushed through the thorny bushes and the others followed. Just beyond the brush, a chain link fence along a berm surrounded a vast property.

"And here you have it," Dupree whispered. "Ancient and venerable, Le Grand Bayou Plantation."

They followed Médora along the perimeter fence. Bull motioned to Dupree, pointing to the security cameras, but on closer inspection, it became evident they'd been out of commission for a long time. They were covered with lichen and obscured by leafy growth. There were gaps in the chain link fence at various points, and the main gate had been mostly wrenched off its hinges. Bushes had been planted on either side of the entrance. The two sections of the gate were chained together and secured with a new padlock.

Médora ignored the gate and instead crawled through the bushes on one side where the fence was torn and there was a low gap wide enough to pass through. Fragile as she was, Médora went to the muddy ground and pulled herself under, dragging her splinted leg behind her. Inside the plantation, the water was knee deep. Water stood stagnating in a broad natural basin. Amaia was sure the area had been planted with marshland cultivars.

It occurred to her that the bayou had been the proprietor before the intrusion of human beings and now had reclaimed its territory. The immobile, dark, and threatening surface of the water was a great black mirror. In the distance, the main house stood on a rise, the only area that hadn't been assaulted by the flood. Dispersed around it and still standing in floodwaters were at least five outbuildings. The first was a single-story rectangle, perhaps an old stable, inside which they could see metal and plastic drums of various sizes and colors piled high. It seemed deserted.

The farther they went, the more evident it became that the property had been abandoned in a hurry. The only vehicle in sight was a jeep with its hood up. They approached cautiously and found the motor covered in mud.

Keeping their guard up, they filed along the berm inside the perimeter, where tall, thick hedges offered concealment from anyone at the plantation manor. Médora stopped there; Dupree and the *traiteur* stood on either side of her. The rest of the team circled behind the outbuildings, then Bill and Bull headed for the main house, dragging one of the reluctant shrimpers along with them.

Johnson and Amaia took the other Cajun to the stables, where there was no sign of recent human presence. They returned, but before they could report, Médora set off again.

A ramshackle structure, perhaps a caretaker's residence, stood awash at the far end of the property. Médora hobbled toward it. Amaia, the *traiteur*, Johnson, the Cajun, and Dupree trailed behind. It was slow going. With every step, their boots sunk into the yielding mess beneath the water. Amaia tried to ignore the sensation that someone or something was clutching at her feet, drawing her down and claiming her as its own.

Another thunderclap burst overhead, generating a shock wave and a rush of air.

She fought against the panic.

The Lady is coming, chanted the faceless chorus in her head.

They finally reached the bizarre building, which had obviously been uninhabited for years. It was an unusually elongated structure. The ground floor had been inundated. Residue left by the flood showed the waters had crested high on the windowless roof.

Thunder roared. Huge raindrops showered down from a sky that was misted and yet still as brilliant as before; the lukewarm water drenched them to the bone in less than thirty seconds.

She's coming. She's here.

61

FATALITY

Elizondo

Amaia Salazar was twelve years old when she went missing in the forest for sixteen hours. They found her in the early morning, eighteen miles north of the place she'd wandered off the path. When they questioned her, she insisted she remembered almost nothing of what she'd gone through. But even so, she could describe in detail all the emotions and sensations, all the feelings and fears that had assailed her as she traversed the forest: the initial panic when she realized that she couldn't find the path, her reasoning that surely she'd be able to find it again, later, having to admit that she'd gotten as lost as one of the little girls in a menacing tale by the brothers Grimm. She clearly recalled the thunderclap that tore through the ether of a gray sky of whipped fog where there was no trace of dark. She remembered the tree, the storm, an eerie presence lurking out of sight, the house, and the man.

The cool late-winter morning could have been like that of any other day on the calendar—but it wasn't. Dense mists spilled down the mountainsides like soapy water dumped from a bathtub. Hiking-club members parked their cars along the sides of the road near their meeting place. People greeted one another heartily as they arrived, as if much more time than just a week had passed since their last outing.

There was something sacred about hiking in the mountains. Those damp, cold days left glistening drops of moisture clinging to her wool clothing, festooning her like tiny jewels.

During the first hour of their march, the hikers spoke very little. They focused on establishing a rhythm and maintaining their pace. They inhaled the chilly Baztán air through their nostrils and exhaled visible clouds through scarf-covered mouths. Trudging forward mechanically meant she had no need to think. Sometimes she would forge ahead, hearing the steps of the group behind her; other times, she would lag and let the others get far enough ahead for her to enjoy the sensation of being alone. The excursions were always similar but never the same. She hadn't known she would enjoy them so much. Nor had she known the day would ever come when she'd have to give them up forever. The forest lulled her, rocked her on its breast, and relieved her of any notion of fear, of shame, of the need for vigilance. More than anything, it banished the thoughts and anxieties boiling in her mind day and night that never allowed her to rest. Only out here did those fears retreat to the obscure realm from which they'd come, making her feel in charge at last.

It could have been a morning like any other, but she knew it wasn't, because it was the last one. She was going away. After she left, she would miss only the forest and her dog, Ipar. Her aunt would visit, but it would be a very long time before Amaia came back to her forest. And there was no way to take Ipar with her. Her eyes filled with tears every time she thought of that. She paused and knelt to hug her dog, pressing her snub nose into the thick fur at his neck. And he huddled close and eagerly licked the tears from her cheeks, as if he had a premonition of the coming separation.

Amaia let the other hikers get ahead of them, so the trail would seem hers alone. She ambled forward and noticed a glint of white in the grass. A wild primrose, so pallid it seemed frozen stiff. *Maybe it's the first one of the season,* she thought, feeling privileged, as if the forest were presenting her with something unique to mark her departure. Ipar, attracted by her curiosity, came up and cautiously sniffed the flower. That set her giggling until she saw he'd inadvertently broken the stem with his snout.

"You're such a clumsy thing!" She knelt, pushed Ipar aside, and tried to realign the flower within the lush crown of green leaves. But she couldn't; the fragile little bud's stem had broken off. She held it delicately with two fingers and frowned at Ipar, a bit annoyed but loving him just the same.

That's when she saw the tree. The bark of its trunk gleamed in the morning damp like a silk dress draped about the hips of a great lady.

Amaia checked to see whether the other hikers were still in sight. They were. She stepped off the trail and had to make her way around the branches of a fallen beech tree and across a wall of tall ferns that stood as if on guard to protect their lady tree from the open space of the trail.

The tree was magnificent in its primitive splendor. Amaia looked up, entranced by its towering height and the clear brilliance of the dew coating its jade-green leaves. The trunk shone. She was captivated by the way its branches proffered shade and calm, creating a sheltered environment where the air was sweet with the scent of clay. Its roots erupted from the earth and wound together beneath her feet in an elaborate mandala, a firm, harmonious structure that spread out from the trunk in every direction. Following a sudden impulse, Amaia stooped and deposited the flower in a hollow at its base. She stood there, surrendering herself to the protective authority of the tree, lulled, happy, and dreamless . . .

She never knew how long she'd stood there, entranced by that maternal presence. But she did remember hearing the thunder and thinking it strange. Ipar's furious growls seemed to come from somewhere far off. Amaia tore her eyes away to break the hypnotic spell of the bewitching tree and looked down. Her head was spinning. She sat, raised her knees, and stared intently at the ground between her heels in an effort to make the world stop tilting.

She raised her head very slowly and saw a hysterical Ipar barking at the thick undergrowth. He bounded forward a few feet and then backed up until he touched her, only to launch himself forward again toward the dense foliage. Amaia moved out from the shelter of the tree and looked up. She and her aunt had a name for what she saw: "whipped fog," a layer of roiling low clouds that infused the air with moisture and hid the sun. She squinted up and heard more thunder.

Bewildered, she looked around and only then became aware of how far she'd strayed from the trail. She could have sworn she'd gone only ten or twelve yards into the forest, but from where she stood, there was no sign of the trail at all. She called Ipar to her side and tried to retrace her steps, but the trail wasn't there. She returned to the tree and tried backing away. She retreated farther and farther, nearly losing sight of the tree, but there was no trail. Alarmed, she went back to the tree.

"Where's the trail, Ipar?"

But the dog's attention was totally fixed on whatever was out there in the thicket. His eyes darted back and forth as he detected the intruder's position. He continued bounding, tracing out a semicircle and barking furiously.

Another thunderclap exploded overhead, shaking the ground beneath her feet. Amaia looked up but saw only that layer of fog obscuring the sky.

The members of the hiking club discovered she was missing when they stopped at ten o'clock for an early lunch. Javier Atienza, the leader, took less than ten minutes to question each of the fifty participants to try to figure out what had happened. He ran his dry palm over his weathered face and cursed himself aloud for failing to pay closer attention. He usually kept a close eye on the child, for Amaia was the only girl who wasn't accompanied. Her aunt, a friend since childhood, had entrusted the girl directly to Atienza because Engrasi's recent knee pain had made walking difficult. She'd confided to him her disappointment that when she'd expressed her wish that the child get out of the house for some kind of activity, he'd suggested one Engrasi couldn't participate in. Atienza had reassured her by promising he wouldn't let the girl out of his sight. He predicted she'd have a good time, she'd discover a world of extraordinary beauty, and she'd make new friends.

Javier felt he'd been correct in two of those predictions. The child was quiet and solitary, but it was obvious she enjoyed the outings. She always carried her camera on a strap around her neck to photograph whatever caught her attention. She clearly liked the activities, but she was very reticent and avoided the company of others.

Amaia preferred to walk a few paces ahead or behind the rest of the group. On the first hikes, some girls her age had approached her and tried unsuccessfully to strike up a conversation. When those kids' parents invited her to join them for the lunch break, Amaia chose instead to go to a nearby tree, lean back against the trunk, and take out the lunch her aunt had prepared. She stared up at the treetops as she ate by herself.

Javier left her alone. He knew there were many ways to commune with the forest; for some people, silence was the key. There was something holy about it, as if a voice hidden in the dense vegetation was whispering words only they could hear. He was sure that in years to come, Amaia would become a solo excursionist. A solitary relationship with the wilderness provides for those rare individuals a happiness beyond words. When they come home, their faces shine as if they've experienced a miracle.

No one remembered seeing the girl after about nine o'clock in the morning. They weren't quite sure, for Amaia often lagged behind to take a picture of something. Knowing that, Atienza had been in the habit of looking back or slowing their progress until eventually he saw her hurrying after them, clutching her camera to her chest. He was fairly certain he'd seen her rejoin them at least once that morning.

Amaia's father set out with a search party before noon. They shouted her name, waded through clearings and thick undergrowth, and checked the brooks and waterfalls, grottos and hollow trees, lean-tos and huts, hunter's cabins, gullies . . . The only answer to their calls was the repeated thunder that boomed from that strangely luminescent white sky.

Night fell. Juan Salazar's blood boiled in anger when volunteers expressed relief that they could discontinue the search. A girl was a girl, they agreed, but this one was odd. The Salazar girl had no friends and never talked with anyone. Besides, all that thunder from a clear sky was a very bad sign, a clear omen that the Lady of the Storms was returning to Baztán.

Juan Salazar thanked the men for their help. They offered excuses and words of encouragement, obviously ashamed to be giving up, but they left anyway. Juan kept at it with a handful of hunters, a couple of shepherds, and Elizondo's Guardia Civil. Javier Atienza was there too, hounded by guilt. He refused to eat, drink, or rest until they found the child. The darkness was total by eight in the evening.

That's when the storm broke.

Ipar knew about storms. Thunder didn't intimidate him and neither did lightning, but he was worried and agitated by whatever was lurking out there in the bushes. The icy rain drenched Amaia. The girl huddled, shivering, under the cowl of her soaking wet jacket. Water gushed over them as if from a broken pipe. Her hand, sunk deep in the dense fur of Ipar's neck, ached with cold. The night was totally black except when bolts of lightning zigzagged across the sky. Driven by their energy, Amaia stumbled onward in an effort to navigate the landscape the flash had etched in her mind.

Ipar knew the child was tired. Often, she sank to the ground to rest. He pressed himself against her to give her his warmth, for her pulse was becoming sluggish and her body temperature was sinking. Amaia hugged him tight, closing her eyes and wrapping her arms around his neck. She drowsed off only to awaken frightened and feverish a few seconds later.

Ipar knew sleeping in the rain was dangerous, but it was almost as bad when Amaia got up again, for she set off in the wrong direction, even though Ipar had tried to direct her every way a sheepherding dog knew how. She kept wandering northward, as though obeying the silent call of the dark herald hiding in the bushes. Something out there was tracking the girl's movements, slipping subtly through the undergrowth. Ipar could do little more than stay close to the poor little thing while carefully monitoring the ominous rustling. He growled and barked from time to time to keep the tracker at a distance. Ipar wasn't going to allow that unseen menace anywhere near his little mistress.

62

LE GRAND BAYOU

The swamp
Wednesday, August 31, 2005

They crept around the structure and came upon the entrance just as Charbou, Bull, and the old shrimper arrived. It was obvious this building hadn't been abandoned like the others; someone had propped the door open with a fallen branch. Médora waded in through thigh-deep water and drew back against the wall like a frightened mouse. Amputated heads of pumas, wild boars, alligators, and crocodiles glowered at them from the dimness. The sight seemed to terrify her. The taxidermy was in terrible shape, ravaged by time and dried out by the high temperature, and the coating of mud and flood residue gave the heads a disgusting, diseased appearance. This place, obviously used as a hunting lodge at one time, had been derelict for many years.

Two large tables stood in the center of the main room, flanked by floating benches. The tabletops were above the water, but the surfaces were thick with mud and slime. Floodwaters had coated the panes of half a dozen windows with filth. Exposed wooden pillars in the center of the vast room held up the ceiling and roof.

A flight of stairs with two landings led up to a loft space where a door stood open. The unmistakable sound of whistling came through the doorway, despite the rain thundering down on the roof. A shirtless man backed through the upstairs doorway, appearing so suddenly they had no time to hide. He was dragging some kind of heavy bundle down the stairs. It knocked sharply against each step. They raised their pistols, waiting for a sign from Dupree.

Médora screamed like an animal caught in a trap. The man stopped whistling, dropped the bundle, and whirled to face them.

The corpse of a young woman with long black dreadlocks slid toward him, her head knocking with a horrible hollow sound each step of the way. His initial impulse was to scramble upstairs, but the body was in his way. Jason Bull fired a warning shot, and one of the shrimpers tried to hit him. They both missed.

The whistler snatched a gun out of his waistband and opened fire with incredible quickness. His two shots blasted some of the old trophy heads, sending a shower of wood chips and sawdust over Médora's head. He darted down the stairs and Charbou jumped him at the lower landing. The two smashed against the wooden banister, which gave way and sent them both plunging into the water. They wrestled while the others shouted, their pistols following the suspect as they called on him to surrender. A gun went off several times, the reports muffled by the muddy water. The whistler went limp on top of Charbou. Bill pushed him off and waded clear of the area where blood was rapidly spreading in the dark water.

Médora had stopped screaming. They turned and saw that the *traiteur* had covered her head with his jacket. She stood motionless against the wall on her thin, fragile legs, scarcely able to stay erect. She rocked back and forth with the hissing sound of a leaky pipe. The dressing of her leg wound was filthy, and a dark red stain was spreading down her other leg.

"Oh, my God!" the *traiteur* cried. He leaped and caught her just as her legs gave way. Kneeling, he wrapped an arm around Médora's skeletal shoulders and fought to keep her head above water. His other hand was trying to stanch the hemorrhaging that spread like red dye up that absurd flowered hospital gown.

In that final instant, a beautiful light flickered in the dying eyes of the girl whose life had been stolen. Médora didn't scream or shout, but her lips moved as if attempting to speak. The *traiteur* leaned close, trying to make out her words. Then her body slipped from his grasp and her abdomen sank into the dirty water. Dupree and Bull went to their knees beside him and helped hold up the young woman's head and shattered frame. The *traiteur* put one palm to her brow and the other to her chest, continually murmuring. He leaned in again and pressed his face close to the woman's mouth. He kept praying for her even after that faint light in her eyes had faded away forever.

Dupree helped him carry her to one of the tables, all the while keeping his eyes on the staircase.

Bull whispered, "If anybody else was up there, surely he'd have shown himself by now."

"If he had a gun, that is," Charbou replied.

They exchanged a complicit glance, went to the stairs, stepped over the corpse jammed against the landing rail, and rapidly ascended. They positioned themselves on either side of the door at the top. They extended their pistols as they peeked inside, took turns checking the interior, and then went in.

Bull came back immediately. "All clear. There's a young man up there, dead, Dupree, and more girls." He gestured toward the *traiteur* and the two shrimpers. "I think they should stay downstairs."

In the attic room, they found five victims, all of them girls. Amaia estimated their ages at between twelve and sixteen. The floodwaters had gone down hours earlier, and though the residue reached almost up to the ceiling, everything was dry. Their clothing and hair had the shriveled appearance of something first soaked and then dried. The humid atmosphere of the swamp and the lower floor were completely gone, replaced by a parched, all-consuming heat. At the doorway and in the center of the room, the ceiling of the cramped loft was high enough for Bull or Charbou to stand upright. The walls sloped rapidly downward, following the slant of the roof, so the team was forced to bend over or go on all fours to investigate. There were no windows. The only furnishings were a dozen or so torn mattress sacks stuffed with Spanish moss, a good-sized table that had lost a leg and lay on its side, and a lit lantern hanging from a nail by the door. That was the only light source. They had to use their flashlights to examine the bodies.

Jason Bull leaned against one of the angled walls, looking like he was about to collapse.

"Are you okay?" Amaia murmured as she passed him.

Bull looked down. "No. How could I be? Five girls, for Christ's sake."

Dupree turned to him. "Six, including the girl on the stairs. He was taking her somewhere. It looks like they were cleaning up." He pointed to the male corpse by the door. The man was slumped against the wall in a sitting position and appeared to have been killed not long before. "They must have argued. Probably because the girls were dead. I think this one was killed by the one downstairs."

Charbou examined the corpses one by one. "Is there any way to find out if Jacob's sisters are here? Do you see any way to identify them?"

Johnson grunted. "They're somebody's sisters and daughters. Isn't that enough? They've been dead for a couple of days at least. No way to tell exactly. They probably died of dehydration in this heat. They didn't get food or water," he said, looking around. "The temperature has been unbearable since the hurricane. Heat accelerates decomposition, so it'll be difficult to determine time of death."

"Since Katrina," Dupree said, leaning over a body. He studied Johnson. "Step aside."

Johnson moved back, and Dupree pulled a body across the floor so that it lay face up. She must have been about thirteen. Dark skin, shoulder-length curly black hair. She wore a pink blouse with red stripes tight against her pubescent breasts. With the greatest of care, Dupree put one of his hands over the other, positioned them over the child's diaphragm, and pressed as if starting CPR. The little girl's mouth opened and emitted a sort of sigh. A white-and-pink froth covered her lips.

Bull and Charbou covered their mouths and noses, reacting to the odor.

"They drowned," Dupree said. "Right here."

Charbou placed a hand on Johnson's shoulder. His voice was rough, especially compared with the intimacy of the gesture. "I didn't mean these victims aren't important. But we have no way of knowing how long they've been here. But we know Jacob's sisters were carried off from NOLA on the night of the hurricane. We got this far trying to track them down, so I'd really like a clue, any clue at all, that suggests they're still alive."

Johnson rose. "You're right. Jacob told me Diana was grounded because she'd dyed her hair at a friend's house without getting their parents' permission. She put red highlights in it. All these girls, including the one downstairs, have black hair."

"Thanks," Charbou responded.

Johnson made a gesture that seemed almost an apology for what he was about to say. "But we don't know how many girls our whistler already removed."

Amaia had gone to the far end of the attic space. She squatted where the slanted roof met the floor to survey the room from that perspective. The waterlogged pallets along the walls seemed to have been hardly displaced at all, but the girls' bodies were scattered. They weren't grouped as if they'd huddled together in fright, which they surely must have. She returned to the center of the space and put up a hand to touch the marks showing the height the floodwaters had reached.

"They got up on the table," she said, lifting it by the broken corner and holding the table balanced upright. "They must have been terrified when water started flowing under the door. It was pitch dark. There's no fuel here for that lantern, so the whistler must have brought it with him. They got up on the tabletop. They heard the storm shaking the building, and meanwhile they were totally in the dark as the water rose, first to their ankles and then to their waists and then to their chests. Terrified prisoners taken from their homes and then battered by Katrina."

She's coming.

"A young girl has no idea who wants to hurt her and who wants to save her. How can she know?"

63

The Forest and Its Master

Elizondo

Ipar padded along beside the girl. She'd said nothing to him for a long time, and that was strange, because she usually spoke to him constantly. He saw her sluggishness and perceived her exhaustion, the way her little body was trembling and the gradual slowing of her heartbeat as her body temperature fell.

When they'd last stopped to rest, Ipar had come to her to offer his warmth. The girl had leaned against him, too drained even to embrace him. She'd stayed like that for a long time, drowsing, half roused by each thunderclap, only to fall again into that deadly lethargy. Ipar barked until she stirred at last. He insistently pushed his nose against her until he finally got her to rise.

Lightning filled the sky, revealing a twisting trail down the mountainside.

"Let's go, Ipar," Amaia managed to whisper.

They began to work their way down the steep slope, through the thick, low bushes that crowded the forest. Ipar again caught the scent of the lurking presence that seemed to have always been hovering just out of sight. That unseen figure had regularly moved ahead of them and holed up in the darkness to wait. Each time they got on the move again, so did their unknown watcher.

Ipar heard a soft whistling sound from the densest stretch of the woods. His ears perked up and he listened intently. It was calling him. The girl tried to stay on the path, but she was exhausted. Cloaked in darkness, Ipar nudged her onto a different course through the thicket.

If they'd thought they were in darkness before, unable to see anything, the wild foliage provided evidence they'd been mistaken. The forest closed about them with every step they took, blocking out even the intense flashes of lightning overhead but providing them an arboreal refuge, for the trees grew so close to one another that only an occasional drop of rain fell from their tops. Their unknown pursuer remained outside the forest proper for the time being. Ipar detected a couple of relatively dry, comfortable spots at the feet of the largest trees, and he guided the girl to one. She sank into her forest bed almost as if arriving home.

Ipar stationed himself at her side in the darkness. That's when he caught the unmistakable scent. He was surprised not to have detected it earlier, although the place was rife with forest smells, including mushrooms, berries, earth, and leaf mold—a perfect symphony of odors.

Basajaun. He must have been there the whole time, for Ipar recognized his scent from distant memory, a revered spirit lost in time. Ipar, from a shepherding race and the offspring of working dogs, had spent his first seven years in the mountains. He knew he'd encountered this presence before. He had no way of determining if by direct experience or if—like so many things he knew and perceived—the knowledge had been transmitted to him in the genes of his race of proud shepherds.

Basajaun was there in the forest with them, and unlike the herald that stank of hunger and anxiety, *basajaun* was untroubled. He moved slowly, partly because of his size but even more because of his nature. His breathing was deep and cavernous, perfectly calm, just like his spirit. Ipar knew this viscerally, instinctively. Ipar was certain he'd heard those whistles before with their reassuring message that the lord of the forest was watching over all.

Amaia's border collie settled down, calm for the first time since they'd wandered away from the hiking trail, for he sensed the master of the forest breathing serenely among the great trees. Ipar remained concerned, for the girl was far from well. Ipar pressed himself against her, trying to transmit his warmth, but especially to let her know he was still there, for even asleep she shuddered, agitated by a terror that denied her rest.

The girl dreamed. She wept as she did.

Ipar licked her burning forehead. She struggled in her nightmare and raised a hand as if to push something away from her face. "I'm just a girl!" she whimpered, still asleep.

In her half-awake state, the girl knew this was a nightmare, but that knowledge offered her no consolation. If she opened her eyes, she'd be lost and surely die. She didn't want to wake, she didn't want to be killed again, and that dilemma made her so terribly sad.

She didn't want to die, but she was terrified of the storm.

The Lady is here, chanted the chorus in her head.

I'm scared! she replied.

The Lady is coming, insisted the child-murdering ghouls, indifferent to her plea.

She scares me! Amaia protested, begging for mercy.

64

Confirming Identity

The swamp
Wednesday, August 31, 2005

Thirteen years later in a dark hunting lodge, the child's anguished plea and the grown woman's explanation became a single voice. Amaia told them, "A child who believes everyone is conspiring to murder her will be terrified even of a rescuer."

Bull heard her clearly but had no idea what she was talking about. Charbou, on the other hand, stared at her, intrigued, both amazed and bewildered.

Johnson started to say something, but with a gesture, Dupree cautioned him to remain silent.

Amaia continued. "They stood on the table, trying to keep their heads above water, until the table leg broke. It's jammed in the corner over there." She pointed in that direction. "The girls fell into the water on top of one another. They did their best to stay afloat, but they weren't strong enough. The water rose and they drowned, trapped against the roof. Eventually it subsided and left them here."

Bull's sudden interruption broke the spell of her story. "It was an accident, then. Nobody goes to all the trouble of kidnapping girls just to drown them. This was a prison. That's probably how the Samedi gang handled Médora and the others. They kept them locked up here and transferred them when things quieted down. Nobody would be likely to think kidnappers would use this place."

"Remember what happened to Médora." Charbou's face was grim. "Maybe these poor children were better off."

Amaia gazed unhappily at the small corpses. "Yes. Maybe the storm saved them from something even worse. The Lady doesn't do things by half measures. That's how she operates."

Johnson raised a hand, cautioning them to be quiet. He cupped his ear and was concentrating, trying to identify something in the distance. It grew louder outside the flimsy wooden walls, and they all heard it. An outboard motor. "His partner's coming back."

The whistler had been moving bodies downstairs, so he must have had at least one other associate. No more than that, they'd guessed, because if there'd been more, a second man would have stayed to help with the bodies. And they needed a means of transportation to remove the dead, so there had to be an associate. The snarl of the outboard approaching the hunting lodge confirmed that much.

They rushed down the stairs, hurrying to forestall any precipitate action by the shrimpers. Clive was downstairs and the *traiteur* was sitting beside Médora, but the older Cajun was nowhere in sight.

"Where's your friend?" Bull called out.

"My man decide to keep watch out there in the bushes. You say somebody probably coming back." He gestured toward the corpse floating at the bottom of the stairs.

"No way we gonna let him surprise us like that one did."

They exchanged alarmed glances. Bull and Charbou rushed to the door, while Dupree, Amaia, and Johnson went to the grime-covered windows. A rifle shot cracked and echoed in the pouring rain. Johnson threw open the window just in time to see a man blasted backward out of an arriving Zodiac. A second man was at the outboard motor. The newcomers had been taken completely by surprise.

"Goddamn it!" Johnson exclaimed.

The second man let go of the throttle, grabbed a shotgun, and fired the first barrel in the general direction of the former hunting lodge. He obviously had no idea where the bullet had come from. He raised his gun again just as the shrimper outside put a slug into his belly. The man clutched his gut and fell forward.

Impelled by inertia, the Zodiac drifted forward and bumped against the lodge. Johnson and Amaia threw themselves over the starboard side as Bull and Charbou climbed aboard on the port side, shouting at the man to put his hands up.

He didn't, and they saw why. He was too intent on trying to keep his guts from spilling over his jeans.

"Take him inside," Dupree ordered. Turning in the direction of the shrimper in the bushes, he shouted, "And you—get out of there and put your gun down! You must have scared off every boar in the swamp!"

They worked the boat along the side of the lodge to the main entrance.

They put what was left of the man onto the second table, next to the one where Médora's body lay. Charbou had improvised a pressure bandage from oily rags in the bottom of the boat. He'd done a fairly good job of stemming the blood flow and containing the victim's intestines. The man was unconscious. He looked about forty years old.

The *traiteur* examined him quickly and shook his head. "I can pray for his soul, but there's nothing to be done for his body. He's bleeding out. He'll die in an hour, maybe less. And it's going to hurt." He turned and went back to Médora.

"Traiteur!" Dupree took his arm and waded with him to the foot of Médora's improvised bier. He pointed to the gunshot victim. "He may be the only one who can tell us where the girls are. They were taken from their homes just like Médora, and they'll wind up like her if I can't get to them. I've been trying all my life to track them down. We got really close when Médora was taken, so close that they murdered her brother and my partner. Dozens of teenage girls have disappeared from their homes since then. Nobody gave a damn about them, nobody cared where they were going to wind up. We're as close as we can be to cracking this case. They had six young girls upstairs. I don't know how many more they have stashed away, but I do know that we're the only ones who're going to do anything about it."

"How is that possible?" the *traiteur* asked.

Dupree looked confused. Amaia was the one who answered. "Come with me."

"What?"

"Come upstairs with me." She pointed toward the attic.

Dupree stopped her. "Salazar, I don't know if that's a good idea—"

"I will," the *traiteur* told Dupree. "I believe your colleague wants to show me something more than just bodies." He followed her upstairs. Dupree went with them.

The lantern was still lit, for in the rush and confusion of the boat's arrival, no one had thought to extinguish it. Its dim reddish light glowed in the asphyxiating space and gave the place the bizarre appearance of a bedchamber for slumbering dolls. All the drowned girls lay on their sides, except for the one Dupree had turned on her back. Their arms were stretched out, and their hair obscured their faces. Each looked as lifeless as the ancient hunting trophies downstairs.

Amaia shined her flashlight across those small corpses one by one. "We are looking for a demon, and his greatest achievement is making us think that he doesn't exist. This kind of predator can stay active for years. He hides his tracks or the bodies of his victims, making them look like disappearances, runaways, accidents, or suicides. He chooses vulnerable girls, black teenagers who are socially marginalized, girls whose disappearances won't be noticed or will seem unimportant. His victims are poor but attractive. The sort of girl who's lucky if her family pays any attention to her; a girl likely to run away because she doesn't like school, her parents are strict, or they don't let her date. Everyone in the town, in the neighborhood, knows about them. Maybe they're outcasts or they shun company because they prefer to be alone.

"That's the kind of girl who disappears during a hurricane, gets swept away by the floodwaters, or goes missing in a forest during a storm. The sort whose name gets added to the list of disaster victims, and no one's surprised. And nobody takes a closer look. Why bother? After all, those girls would have wound up running away from their hard lives and disappearing anyhow.

"He's a monster, and he's making sure he doesn't get caught. He's perfectly capable of masquerading as an upstanding citizen to his dying day. He's not looking for notoriety, because he already has his place. He's a demon hunting down vulnerable souls. Not only does the bastard abduct them, he carries them off like hunting trophies to this miserable shack. And that's only the start of their suffering.

"Do you have any idea how many names are going to appear on the official list when they eventually draw up the death toll for Katrina? Dozens? Probably hundreds? Think of it: this is the perfect time to make someone disappear. That's how he built his empire. That's how he keeps feeding his evil desires. He's a vampire lurking in the darkness."

She paused and met Dupree's steady gaze. She knew she'd recapped every point of his lecture on victimological profiling and Sherrington's pioneering work. She summed it all up. "His satisfaction and pleasure are the same as those of the devil: they come from the fact that we don't believe he exists."

While listening to Amaia, the *traiteur* had visited the corpses one by one. He stepped up very close to Amaia, bent forward, and took one of her hands. Behind him Amaia saw Dupree's silent figure in the doorway. For some reason, she suddenly felt terribly ashamed.

Amaia recoiled and almost snatched away her hand, as if she had a premonition that the contact provided the *traiteur* access to an intimate, half-forgotten secret she desperately needed to hide. But the man held her hand firmly and retained it in a steely grip astonishing for someone so slim. He covered her hand with both of his, as if wrapping it in a broad, heavy blanket.

Truth burst from her with torrential force. "There was a day that a raging storm saved my life."

65

Ipar

Elizondo

The girl burned with fever, trapped in a delirious dream in the shelter of the enormous beech. Her devoted dog stayed at her side and licked away the tears that squeezed beneath her lids.

Amaia was inhaling flour. The finely ground powder with its primal mineral tang infiltrated her windpipe, blocked her sinuses, and made her struggle for air. She knew she shouldn't inhale, but when she desperately tried to breathe, the flour that covered her body also filled her throat, soaked up saliva, and became a sticky paste that made her gag. "I don't want to die! I'm only a little girl!" Every syllable of that stifled cry drew more of the choking, sticky mass into her lungs. Her very cries for help were killing her. A thunderclap left her half deaf. Her consciousness faded. She was sure the end had come, but then moist, warm hands pushed the flour from her face. She blinked in confusion.

"Today's the day, little vixen," Rosario leered at her. "*Ama*'s going to eat you up tonight."

Amaia screamed in terror, and the shriek that tore her throat interrupted the nightmare. She shuddered awake in the dark of the forest. She couldn't see a thing. She thought she must be dead. Deathly cold and delirious with infection, she heard only her own hoarse screams. Her anguished voice was that of a stranger.

Ipar's frantic barking brought her back. Reality intruded. She realized she was lost in the forest and that she was going to die. She was going to be eaten alive.

Scrabbling against the rough bark of the great beech, she made it to her feet. She blindly clutched Ipar's furry neck before taking her first step.

"Let's go, Ipar," she commanded him in that unrecognizable voice.

The dog resisted. He tensed and refused to advance.

Amaia sank to her knees, embraced him, and pleaded. "Please, Ipar, please come on. Let's go. Please!"

Holding fast to his collar, she stumbled forward. This time Ipar didn't resist. He stayed close to his mistress's side but looked back several times, as if trying to signal to the lord of the forest he had no other choice.

Amaia couldn't see a thing. She squeezed her eyes shut for a moment, to see if it made any difference when she opened them again. Ipar guided her steps and managed to keep her from running into the trees. She felt their benevolent, looming presence as she stepped past, but she found herself constantly stumbling over roots, rocks, and the uneven ground. She lost her footing, and Ipar leaped in front of her to cushion her fall and keep her from sprawling headlong. She cried out at the sudden pain in her knees and thighs. She sobbed in anguish and fright. She was unable to get to her feet immediately, and when at last she did, every step was agony, as if sharp pieces of gravel were embedded in her kneecaps. She thought a few times that she could hear the river, but the roar of rain through the treetops overwhelmed it. She had no choice but to struggle onward.

As she advanced, the trees thinned out and the temperature dropped. The sparser cover of the treetops left her feeling abandoned, an orphan, as she emerged from their protective shelter. She staggered out of the forest and was confused by a forceful, prolonged whistle. But had she actually heard it?

Ipar froze in place. Several seconds went by, but the whistle didn't come again. Amaia told herself it must have been caused by the wind. Lightning split the heavens and lit the night. Though half blinded by the intense glare, she saw a trail running across the steep mountain slope and descending toward a hollow.

And something else.

Amaia screamed. Something stood close before her. Ipar bounded forward, barking wildly. Left alone, dazzled by the lightning, she was terrified by the image of the looming dark figure stamped into her mind. She was sure it wasn't benevolent. She'd always known she was condemned to death, and this confirmed the truth of that premonition. Shaking with fever and trepidation, she called her dog. Fear turned to total panic because he wasn't there. Ipar kept snarling and barking on the trail ahead of her. Seconds became an eternity. Suddenly he stopped and rejoined her. She crouched down and held him tight. He'd driven away the creature, whatever it was.

"Don't leave me, Ipar, don't ever leave me!" she begged, weeping, grabbing his collar with both hands.

Before trying to advance, she strained her ears, seeking to detect any presence ahead of them, but the roar of the rainstorm covered every other sound. Ipar growled again a couple of times, but Ignacio had taught Amaia to differentiate between warning growls and Ipar's fierce canine expression of satisfaction at warding off danger.

The trail became steeper, narrower, and more overgrown. She had to hunch over and scramble for handholds to keep from falling. A vast void yawned before her. She was grateful for her mountain boots, for descending would have been impossible with any other footwear. Still gripping Ipar's collar, she was forced to huddle so low she was almost squatting on the trail. Her knees ached, and the bloody scrapes across them cracked every time she bent her legs. In this fashion, they made their way down the trail. Exhausted, Amaia stopped to rest. She looked out across the open space and saw a light.

A house, in the depths of the forest. A house with lit windows. The girl's feverish mind understood this meant people, maybe a phone she could use to call her aunt, a fireplace glowing with warmth. She kept her eyes on it, afraid to blink, afraid the vision would vanish. Ipar perked up, encouraged by the prospect of rescue.

Amaia saw more and more lights as she continued down the slope. Some lined the edges of the property, while others in the yard illuminated the front door and the drive where a number of cars were parked. The sight of all this in the driving rain was unreal. After the dark, the cold, the injuries, the fever, and the suffering, she was flooded with euphoria. She reproached herself. She'd been such a fool to get lost. She'd given up only a few minutes earlier and accepted the fact that she would die in the forest. And she'd been only about half a mile from the house all that time!

Amaia stepped onto the rough cement and took a couple of steps along the firm surface. She sobbed, overwhelmed to have survived and reached safety.

The rain stopped instantly, as if someone up there had turned off the faucet that was pouring torrents from the sky. That abrupt change was eerie and ominous. Ipar halted and so did Amaia. Water drained from the rough road surface into the ditches alongside it. Amaia sighed and was shocked at the sound of her own breath. The rain had deafened her throughout their descent.

A shrill whistle split the air and startled her. She whirled about, expecting to see someone. The piercing sound was so close and insistent that she expected the whistler to be on top of her.

"What's happening, Ipar?" she exclaimed, expecting him to attack.

Ipar wasn't bothered. He stood at ease, in the relaxed posture she liked so much. Alert, completely erect, his pointed ears and his eyes focused in front of them. Ipar wasn't afraid of anything.

The girl wiped away the raindrops caught in her lashes. She walked toward the house.

There were many more cars than she'd thought when she first caught sight of it from the slope above. They must have had many guests. Large, shiny SUVs were beaded with rain. Amaia stopped in front of one, trying to recall what had made her feel so apprehensive. A sudden wave of dizziness washed over her. The world tilted. She leaned against the car to keep from falling.

Another powerful whistle split the air and made her jump. Again, it had come from behind her. She spun about so suddenly that she almost blacked out. She had to grab both Ipar and the handle of the car door to keep from tipping over.

No one was there.

Trembling all over, she secured her grip on her dog and lumbered painfully toward the front of the house.

The stout wooden door was smooth and unadorned. There was no knocker. An overhead light illuminated the entryway. The door was flanked by large earthenware pots holding elegant little trees with reddish leaves. Closely spaced stone slabs provided a path across the neatly cut lawn. Amaia got to the door, found a doorbell, and released Ipar so she could ring it. Suddenly uncertain, she realized she didn't know how to present herself. What do you say when you appear at someone's door after you've been lost in the woods?

She didn't have time to think. The door flew open. She took three or four steps back. A shaft of warm yellow light threw a perfect triangle on the ground.

A young man looked out at her. He wore dark trousers and a white shirt with rolled-up sleeves. The golden light from the hall reflected in his long chestnut-colored hair. He pushed it out of his eyes with his left hand. He didn't seem at all surprised to see her. He smiled warmly, sensually, waiting for her to speak.

"I got lost," she stammered hoarsely, increasingly intimidated. Her fever was rising, and her nausea was intensifying, but she had to explain. "I need to telephone my aunt."

The smile became even warmer. "What's your name?"

Many years later, Amaia would learn this was a pick-up line, a question that was much more than a mere inquiry. It was the opening gambit of a subtle power game.

"Amaia Salazar Iturzueta," she recited. She heard herself sounding like a talking parrot and felt ridiculous. Her cheeks quivered. She sighed, closed her eyes, and tried to calm down.

"Amaia," he repeated, savoring the sounds.

Amaia was only twelve. She liked boys. She'd been attracted to two or three in her short lifetime, but she'd never experienced the sensuality, the tingling, or the accelerating heartbeat this man provoked in her merely by echoing her name. She involuntarily raised a hand to smooth her hair. It was wet, cold, rough, and tangled. She found herself wondering what her clothing looked like, which was a really odd thought at such a moment, but she didn't dare take her eyes off that smile. His lips were thick but masculine. He had perfect white teeth; his eyes might have been brown or green or—no—blue! And something in his serene, worldly attitude held her spellbound.

Suddenly she knew what was odd: he hadn't been surprised. He was acting as if it were perfectly normal for a little girl to appear at his front door late at night, soaking wet, feverish, hurting, and bruised. What he said next convinced her that he'd been expecting her somehow, that he'd been waiting forever for her.

"I didn't think you'd look like this!" he exclaimed in delight.

Amaia shrugged, disconcerted, as a deep fatigue settled over her. She didn't understand any of this. Was he supposed to know her? Had he imagined her somehow? Her fever kept her from thinking straight.

Ipar snarled and barked loud and hoarse in full-throated warning. His sudden change confused her even more.

A faraway lightning bolt backlit the mountain crags' stark profile against the sky.

"Would you like to come inside?" the man asked, still with that inviting smile.

Ipar was furious. Amaia broke eye contact with the man to look at her dog. Ipar crouched in attack position at her side. His soaked fur was plastered down like a sheepskin, and the hair of his ruff stood up where she'd been clutching him. His head tilted and his distrusting eyes were fixed on the man in the doorway. Ipar's broad, furry tail, so similar to that of a fox, curled under his body, and the hair along his back bristled. A ferocious warning growl surged from deep within him.

"Amaia?" the man summoned her.

How she liked the way he pronounced her name, as if no one had ever known how to say it correctly until now. In his mouth, her name was that of the woman she'd be someday, a knowledgeable, sensual lover . . .

She looked up at the enchanting, voluptuous smile that made him seem so eager to please. Then she saw that other figures were clustered behind him. The golden-yellow light upon the man left the others silhouetted and impossible to make out.

Of course he has people here. All those cars . . . they must be having a party.

She started to step forward, but Ipar moved in front of her, pressed her back, and redoubled his loud, fierce opposition.

What's going on with you, Ipar?

Another deafening whistle split the air. A lightning bolt struck close by with a sharp crack. The instant crash of thunder shook the ground, jarred her bones, and made her teeth chatter.

Amaia backed off. The rain renewed and engulfed them.

"Amaia!" the man lured her from the doorway. The smile was still there, but something had changed in his voice. Was he beginning to lose patience?

Captivated by his smile, she kept watching him even as the immense new wash of rain blurred his features. She wanted to go to him. She was ill; she was freezing. His voice attracted her, soothed her. The pelting rain was icy cold.

The Lady is coming, she thought.

Ipar blocked her way. He refused to cede an inch.

Another deafening whistle split the air.

That gorgeous man beckoned to her. "Amaia!" His smile was the same. "Would you like to come inside?"

She wanted to say, *Yes, yes, I would. I do want to go inside.* What other choice did she have? What did Ipar want? What did a stupid dog know about what a girl needed?

More thunder.

She's coming, she heard in her mind.

The charming young man shifted slightly to one side. One of the silhouetted figures stepped out into the golden light.

Amaia gasped in astonishment and convulsed in terror. "Nooo!" she cried from the depths of her being. "No, no!" she screamed at the person standing in the doorway and welcoming her with a smile.

"No!" she cried, stumbling backward one step, then another, then another.

More of them emerged from the doorway as she screamed and backed away. They watched her, amused.

A blast of thunder shook the ground. Dozens of bolts of lightning parted the heavens. The insistent whistling seemed to come from everywhere at once.

She knew.

The Lady is here.

The people by the door, suddenly tired of waiting, surged into the pouring rain and came for her.

Amaia couldn't scream. Terrified and voiceless, she backed away, stumbled over one of the stone slabs of the walkway, staggered, and almost fell. She shut her eyes. At that precise instant, the path was lit by a blinding flash that dazzled everyone, and a tremendous crash of thunder deafened her. She felt only the electric sizzle and powerful impact of the shock wave when the lightning bolt struck.

66

Jam in the Cupboard

The swamp
Wednesday, August 31, 2005

The *traiteur* gave Dupree a warning look before placing his hands on the unconscious man. "I never lie. I can't. I made a pact with God. If anyone's going to lie to him, it'll have to be you."

"No problem," Dupree agreed, suddenly reinvigorated.

The *traiteur* closed his eyes and moved his hands, first across the man's head and then over his abdomen. He peeled away the bulky dressing Charbou had improvised and placed his right hand directly in the wound, moving it with great care and closing his eyes as he murmured an incantation. At last he opened them again, turned to Dupree, and nodded.

The FBI leader leaned over the unconscious man, grasped his chin, and shook it slightly. "Wake up!"

The thug opened his eyes and blinked up in confusion, pressing his hands to his belly and finding the *traiteur*'s hands in his wound.

"Don't move," Dupree told him, covering the man's hands. "This is the *traiteur* of the big swamp, and he's helping you. What's your name?"

"Dominic," came the faint answer.

Johnson peeled off his own jacket, folded it in thirds, and slipped it under the man's head.

The man's mouth quivered in confusion. "It doesn't hurt anymore," he whispered in astonishment.

"But it will, if he stops his spell."

"No," the man pleaded. "Please . . ."

"Okay, Dominic. Is there anyone else here on the property? Are you expecting anyone?"

"No."

"Fine. Where are the girls?"

"Dead. But we didn't kill them," he panted. "The water went up and drowned them . . . during the storm."

"Other girls are missing," Dupree insisted. "The ones they took from NOLA the night after Katrina."

The man squeezed his eyes shut. When he opened them, tears spilled out. "I oughtn't to have got involved. Len convinced me. There was a lot of money. They got here and found the girls dead, Len got really mad, then they told him he had to clean up the mess. That's why he came looking for me. I knew what Len was up to, I was always asking him to get me into it. There's a lot of money, but they're really dangerous, those fellas . . ."

"You mean Samedi?"

He nodded.

"Did you ever see him?" Dupree asked expectantly. "Know who he is?"

The man shook his head and responded with a grimace that was supposed to be a smile. "You got no idea, do you? It's Samedi, man!" He said it reverently, as if speaking of a god.

"The girls from NOLA. Where they at?"

The man closed his eyes, shook his head, and sighed. "I can't say."

"You got enough problems already. Do yourself a favor. You help us, and we'll help you."

"You folks don't understand. They'll kill me."

"You're the one who doesn't understand. I'm gonna be straight with you. You got a really ugly wound down there," he said, pointing to the man's belly and raising his head just enough for him to see the bunched-up rags holding his guts inside his body. "We're miles from the nearest hospital; you gonna be dead in a couple hours if we don't get help. And I'm not moving you out of here long as I think the girls are hidden somewhere in this big old plantation. We're gonna search every container in every storehouse in the place, even if it takes days, and we're not gonna leave here till we find 'em."

Dominic's lips tightened as he looked down at his belly.

Dupree gave a slight nod to the *traiteur*, who responded with a twitch of his hand. Dominic screamed in anguish, and beads of sweat popped out on his face.

"You help us, we get you out of here."

"What they do to folks who cross 'em is a thousand times worse than dying."

Dupree instinctively raised a hand to his chest. His face lost its color as his old scars burned and his heart skipped a beat. He sought to calm himself. "We'll protect you."

"Protect me? What kind of protection? Len says Samedi got people even in the police."

Bull and Dupree glanced at one another. That thought had never occurred to them.

Dupree took out his badge and held it before Dominic's eyes. "We're not police, we're FBI. We can put you in a witness protection program. New life, new identity, far away from here."

Dominic squinted at the badge and thought about it. Dupree turned and nodded to the *traiteur,* who scarcely moved. Dominic howled in pain.

Dupree leaned forward. "They must've got here yesterday or, at the earliest, the day before. The girls upstairs have been dead since the hurricane. Where do they have the girls from NOLA?"

The *traiteur* moved his hands again. It was obvious from Dominic's expression that the pain had lessened.

"You gonna take me away and give me a new name and place . . ."

"I give you my word."

Dominic closed his eyes. "They over in the mansion."

"Our guys went there," Johnson told Dupree, "and it's deserted."

"In the pantry, off the kitchen," Dominic whispered, "they built a false back."

Johnson and Charbou dashed for the door with the two shrimpers close behind.

"Take the Zodiac!" Bull shouted after them.

Dupree studied Dominic. A white guy, more or less Dupree's age, Dominic was getting paler by the minute. His eyes were beginning to take on that faraway look of those already halfway through death's door.

"Samedi came here? Did he see what happened with the other girls?"

"No. He don't come here."

"Who's the dead guy upstairs?"

"Pitt. Vince's brother. S'posed to guard the girls. Said they didn't give him time to get 'em out. Len was pissed off. Shot him."

"And who's that over there?" Dupree indicated the body floating face down at the bottom of the stairs.

"That's . . . that was my friend Vince."

"And your friend was happy enough to whistle while he worked, even after he saw Len shoot his brother?"

"They didn't get along too good." No more explanation than that.

"So the guy outside must be Len."

Dominic nodded. The effort seemed to exhaust him. Dupree leaned to one side and saw that the puddle of blood on the tabletop had seeped over the side and was about to drip into the water.

"Len and Vince brought the girls here. We s'posed to wait here till the coast is clear. Roads are full right now, police, the army, even the damn National Guard . . ."

"Who was going to decide how to move them?" Bull asked.

"They tell Len when it's clear."

"How do they reach him?"

"Len has a phone, always on him. Can't call out. They contact him."

Amaia waded out of the lodge. Len's body floated half-submerged a couple of yards from the front door. She rifled through his clothes and she found the phone in the pocket of his life vest. She regarded it with dismay as filthy water poured off it. She tried without success to turn it on as she went back inside. "It's soaked," she said. "Done for."

Dupree sighed in exasperation.

"Didn't they have any other way to communicate?" Bull asked.

"Don't know," Dominic said. By now he was only intermittently conscious.

"You said Samedi didn't come here." Dupree pressed him. "You know if Len told them what happened to the girls?"

"Yeah. 'We lost our catch,' Len said. Told 'em he blew away Pitt for letting it happen."

The *traiteur*, who'd remained silent throughout all this, unhappily echoed Dominic's words. "'Our catch.'"

They heard the motor of the returning Zodiac. Amaia crossed the room and rubbed grime off the window.

"They have the girls!" she exclaimed.

Dupree, sitting on the edge of the table at Dominic's feet, seemed about to pass out.

"Just in time," the *traiteur* said mournfully, taking his bloody hands out from under the improvised bandage. "Your Mr. Dominic has just passed."

The *traiteur*'s grim stare put an end to the shrimpers' protests when Dupree announced they were going to carry Médora's body back in the captured Zodiac. The memory of the six dead girls left behind was a heavier burden than Médora's insubstantial little corpse, which they'd wrapped in a mattress cover previously stuffed with Spanish moss, but the Cajuns were still visibly relieved when they reached the boat they had left outside the mangrove forest and Dupree tasked them with bringing it back to camp.

Jacob's sisters hadn't said a word since they'd been helped through an opening in the back of the mansion's pantry. They hadn't responded to questions when Johnson and Dupree asked if they'd seen other girls or remembered anything their captors had said. Holding one another by the hand, they answered only with mute nods or shakes of the head. The little one might have been eight or nine; the older one was probably twelve. The little one was alert, the older one lethargic, maybe even despondent. Both were very pretty and very frightened.

Amaia saw that the girls couldn't keep their eyes off the crumpled, shrouded figure of Médora. Amaia moved so as to block their view of the corpse. "Diana is the queen of the moon, and Bella means 'beautiful' in Italian," she said, throwing the girls into confusion.

She undid her ballistic vest and fumbled through her pockets. Her blouse rode up, and she noticed her movement had attracted Charbou's attention. She found the little orange dragon and showed it to them. "Jacob gave me this for you."

"Oh!" they both exclaimed and grabbed for it.

Amaia turned it over to show them their brother's name.

They burst into laughter and tears at the same time, throwing themselves at Amaia, hugging her, almost knocking her over. She had to struggle to keep them all from tumbling backward onto the body. Everyone on board was astonished by the girls' reaction.

"Where's Jacob?" cried the younger girl.

"And how's Grandma and Grandpa?" said her sister.

"They're all fine."

"But Grandpa . . ."

"We took him to the hospital, and he's going to get better. They're all there, together," Amaia reassured them. "And we'll take you there as soon as we can. Jacob said your parents work in Baton Rouge."

They nodded.

"We know their telephone number at work," declared Bella, the older girl.

"It's been kind of hard to make phone calls, but we'll find a way to get in touch with them."

Dupree nodded at Amaia, encouraging her to keep talking and to probe them for information.

Amaia spoke to them. "I need to know if those men hurt you. Or if they gave you any kind of medicine."

"They scared us," Diana declared.

"I'll bet they did! I think you both were very brave, because men like that are really scary. I saw one who was older, and another who was blond and kind of fat. And a bald man and a really tall one. Four in all. Were there any others?"

"No."

"Did you see any other girls?"

Jacob's sisters looked at one another. Diana started to nod, but Bella said, "No, there wasn't any others."

Amaia had noticed immediately upon seeing them that the girls' abundant hair was clean and glossy, as if recently brushed. Their heads were crowned with elaborate plaits that gave way to cascading shoulder-length hair.

"Did you comb your own hair?"

They leaned forward to whisper directly to her. "No."

Amaia huddled with them, trying to think who could have done their hair, for she couldn't imagine that any of those thugs would have bothered—or been able—to fashion such intricate knots.

"It was the *lutins*," Bella whispered. "They combed us while we were asleep."

Diana solemnly confirmed it. "*Lutins* like to braid people's hair."

Amaia chose her words carefully. "The *lutins* were there? Did you see them?"

They shook their heads. Diana ran her fingers through her hair. "We too old. Only really little kids can see them. But we heard them laugh. And they did our hair."

Amaia was careful to keep her voice casual. "And did they talk to you?"

"They don't talk. They just laugh and play. You don't know about *lutins*?" Bella seemed surprised by Amaia's ignorance.

"Sure, I know what they are. It's just that back where I come from, they're called *mairuak*. They're the ghosts of babies who died before they were baptized."

Bella was interested. "Did you ever see one when you were little?"

Charbou, seated on one side of the boat, was following every word.

"Well, I don't really know," Amaia replied. "When I was really tiny, what I liked most of all was to go to my grandmother Juanita's house, a really big place, where she used only the ground floor and the upstairs. I remember there was usually another little girl there who looked just like me. She used to wait for me at the very top of the stairs to the attic, and that's where we played. Later on, I forgot about it. But when I grew up a bit, I remembered, and I told my aunt about the little girl who was always waiting to play with me at my grandmother's house. But my aunt said there'd never been any children there except for me and my sisters."

"Did she talk to you?"

"I don't remember her talking, but she loved to laugh." Amaia smiled at that recollection. "She just wanted to play."

"She was a *lutin*!"

Amaia smiled at Charbou's astonished expression. He reached out and brushed a bit of damp leaf from her face. His touch lasted only an instant, but they both reacted so strongly that the girls sniggered.

"You had something on your cheek," he explained to cover his embarrassment.

Amaia dropped her gaze, and suddenly the girls were all over her, whispering in her ear. "Is that your boyfriend?"

"No!" she told them, making sure that he could hear as well.

The smaller girl peered at Charbou and smiled. "Well, he *wants* to be your boyfriend!"

Charbou grinned.

Johnson saw that Dupree was amused and gave him a thumbs-up. Johnson hadn't agreed with Salazar's handling of the Andrews boy, but he had to admit the woman had a natural empathy with victims. It was a rare gift. The ferocious beast that was Salazar had a gentle side. He was deeply impressed by the discovery and by her persuasive use of her talent.

67

Charizard

The swamp

Amaia hopped out of the captured Zodiac as soon as they got to the Cajun camp. Diana called her back and held out the little orange dragon. "Jacob wanted you to have him. He's your good luck charm!"

Amaia didn't argue. She took her Charizard toy and hugged the girls. It was one fifteen in the afternoon when they tossed the mooring cable to the men waiting to tie them up to the floating pier. They left the girls with the *traiteur*. He'd been silent throughout their voyage, holding vigil over Médora's motionless, shrouded figure.

Amaia got ahead of the others and hopped from one boat to another until she reached Annabel's. She hoped that Landis of the AIA was as interested in helping her as he'd sounded the previous day.

"I thought you said you going to talk to him before noon!" Annabel exclaimed without greeting her. "Paula been standing by for two hours now."

Amaia took the microphone Annabel held out. "Go ahead, Paula. Over."

Landis had just come on the line when Johnson helped Dupree aboard. The boss's face had regained some color, but he still looked ill and extremely tired. Landis's voice erupted through the cabin speakers. "Agent Salazar, I have the data you requested. Over."

Obviously, Cousin Paula had tutored him on radio etiquette.

"I can't tell you how grateful I am, Mr. Landis. Over."

"Oh, no need for thanks. It's not every day I get to help the FBI. The truth is, I've enjoyed it, Agent Salazar. As I told you yesterday, all our inspectors travel to disaster scenes. But none of them was present at all the places on your list. One or two, maximum. But that's not surprising. Our adjustors in the Texas region usually respond to tornado damage, while the New Yorkers see to losses along the east coast. They're familiar with the sort of damage caused by the severe weather common to their regions. Over."

"Can you give me anything about the adjustors' children? Over."

"Nine of our adjustors have three or more children. There are two with sons named Michael. One of those boys is twenty-five, and the other was a two-year-old who died in a car crash. Over."

"And what about their leave requests? Over." She wanted to pressure him.

"Concerning time off, three of our adjustors are on vacation right now, two women and a man. We didn't find anyone whose vacation days coincided with more than one or two of the dates you gave me. Over."

"Is any adjustor currently on vacation? Over."

"I think you can probably count him out," Landis suggested. "He's our youngest adjustor, only thirty-two. Just got married, and he's honeymooning in Hawaii. I also checked their birthplaces," he went on cheerfully. "And not a one of our professionals is a native of any of the communities affected by the disasters you listed. Over."

Amaia sighed, doodling on her notepad. How had it come to this? She'd been certain they'd find something. There had to be a thread she could use to unravel this mess. *What the caterpillar calls the end, the rest of the world calls a butterfly,* she thought. Where, how, and why did our caterpillar put an end to his previous life and transform himself?

Landis reacted to her silence. "One of them does have a vacation home in Galveston. Over."

Amaia looked over at Dupree. "Tell me about that, please. Over."

"Robert Davis. He's a good guy, reliable, very serious. He's been with us for years and years. We're not exactly friends, but we chat sometimes. He'd fit the age profile you mentioned, but that's all. In fact, I wasn't even aware of his second home. It came up in a claim he filed. The property was insured with us, of course. Over."

"What kind of damage? Over."

"Vandalism. But we had to deny the claim. We require a police report, but it seems that Davis didn't get one. Over."

"Robert Davis isn't on vacation right now, is he? Over."

"No, like I said, he doesn't match your criteria. He's one of our best adjustors, and he's reviewing claims in our Texas office. He lives in Austin and almost never goes on vacation. Maybe takes a day or two here and there for personal matters. He's had to use some time recently to take care of his wife, so he wasn't sent to any of the on-site inspections at the places on your list. Over."

"Is his wife ill?"

"No, I'd say that she's in delicate health. Natalie is having a high-risk pregnancy. Because of her age. Over."

"Does he have other children? Over."

"Sure, but they don't match either. Two of them, a boy and a girl, umm . . ." Landis seemed to be checking his notes. "Thomas is twelve, and Michelle is nine. Over."

"Did you say Michelle? Over."

Amaia wrote "MIC" in forceful letters below her more or less heart-shaped doodle. She held the page up so Johnson and Dupree could see it.

"Oh! I didn't notice that," Landis muttered unhappily. "I was looking for a boy. Over."

Amaia grimaced slightly, apprehensive at the possibilities unfolding before her. "Would you happen to know if his daughter plays the violin? Over."

"Both children do. Our employees' kids go Christmas caroling together every year, and the company uses the photos for the next year's Christmas cards. We give each employee several dozen. Free of charge, of course. Over."

Amaia exhaled slowly, mastering her rising excitement. "Do you happen to know how long his wife has been expecting? Over."

"Umm . . . no. But she must be due about now. There's a note here that he's just taken a few days of paternity leave. Over."

The pencil she'd been tapping on her notebook slipped out of her fingers, hit the floor, and rolled under the boat's dash panel.

Landis apologized. "Sorry I didn't notice that before, when you asked about vacations. Our firm doesn't count maternity or paternity leave as vacation time, so it doesn't go into the vacation accounting. Over."

Amaia didn't reply because she was incapable of speaking. Her mind was going a mile a minute, making calculations and checking correlations. Natalie Davis was in her third trimester, so her fortieth week, give or take. Since the pregnancy was problematic, they might have scheduled an early birth, either induced or cesarean. If they'd recognized the pregnancy the first time the wife missed her period, that would have been eight months earlier. Just about the time the murders began—and in the same city where Davis had a vacation home. She turned to Johnson and Dupree.

Johnson raised both hands, four fingers on each, and mouthed, "Eight months."

Amaia pressed a hand to her stomach, feeling an emptiness that had nothing to do with hunger. This was the key piece of the puzzle.

She'd had this feeling before, but it took her by surprise. A discovery made when she least expected it, as she was buckling down to work, determined to gut it out . . . and then zap—a lucky shift, a telling realignment of available and hidden information. "You'll have all the answers if you can formulate the right questions," her aunt liked to say. And suddenly there came the solution, hidden in plain sight.

An expected new birth would complete the cycle. Three children once again, the same mistakes, the same sins and offenses.

"You mentioned he's been with the firm for a long time. How long? Over."

"Just a moment." Landis checked. "Seventeen years. And a half. Over."

Amaia grinned broadly at her colleagues, and they nodded.

She'd correctly predicted the shape of Lenx's new life.

Martin Lenx had murdered his family in a house outside Madison eighteen years earlier. Only six months later, he took a job in Texas with the American Insurance Association. New name, new job, new city, new life—new family.

"Do you know Mrs. Davis personally? Over."

"I've seen Natalie a couple of times at the firm's Christmas parties. Over."

"Would you describe her as an attractive woman? Over."

"Hmm," Landis temporized.

In her two conversations with him, Amaia had learned to recognize that hesitant sound as indicating Landis had an opinion he was reluctant to share.

"I suppose she is attractive, in her own way. She's a very thin lady, in good shape for her age, pretty well preserved. Over."

"I need to know if she's beautiful or at least if she used to be. Over."

"Now, I hope you understand, I'm not saying she's ugly, it's just that . . . well, she's not the sort who would catch your eye. I really think that's mostly because she's so shy. Over."

That fucker! she thought. *He re-created every goddamned facet of the profile.* Amaia pressed a trembling hand to her stomach to counteract the surge that threatened to suck her into the abyss. Her breathing had accelerated, and she knew she risked hyperventilating if she didn't keep it under control.

"Mr. Landis, do you have access to Mr. Davis's claim for the damages in Galveston? The one he didn't pursue? Over."

"Hold on," Landis said. For several seconds, despite the distance and the problematic connections via phone and radio, they heard the distinct clatter of a keyboard. "Aha! Here it is."

"Was it damage to the garden? Over."

"How did you know? Says here, 'Intentional destruction of a landscape of tropical flowers.' Over."

What had Landis said? "He's a good guy, reliable, very serious." Lenx was the stern but understanding neighbor who'd withdrawn a complaint against a boy when he learned the child was having trouble adapting to a new home. The good neighbor who offered selflessly to help the older son after the massacre. *For Christ's sake, he even paid out of pocket to have the crime scene cleaned up! And he insisted on accompanying Joseph into the house.* She could imagine the shock the man must have gotten when he saw Joseph's reaction to the unknown violin.

"Landis, this is very important: do any of Mr. Davis's personal days coincide with the list of days I sent you? Over."

Five seconds went by as he searched the files.

"Oh, my God! They're a perfect match!"

Amaia left the bridge and grabbed the deck railing, seeking warmth to counteract her chills. She was shaking hard, even though the temperature had risen almost into the nineties over the course of the morning. Her hands trembled, and the aching void in her belly filled with certainties as she obsessively went over the new revelations.

Johnson followed her on deck, but Dupree lingered in the cabin to study the notebook she'd left behind. A few scrawled words, a rough sketch of a heart that intrigued him. Usually when someone draws a heart, it looks like a valentine heart, two curves that meet in a point. Amaia had drawn an almost anatomical heart with oddly distorted ventricles and a lumpish apex. Dupree folded the sheet and took it with him.

Johnson stood on one side of Amaia. Dupree took the other. The noon sun reflected from the rippling surface of the water, stirred by the bayou current and the backwash of the hurricane tide returning to the Gulf of Mexico. Amaia wondered how many corpses it was carrying to the depths. Dozens? Hundreds? How many had met a horrible fate during the raging storm? How many had been murdered under cover of the tempest? And how many could have been victims of something infinitely worse?

"We have to go back," Amaia said, looking out into the distance.

"Agent Johnson, please go get Detectives Bull and Charbou. We should all be here," Dupree said.

Dupree studied Amaia as Johnson stepped, and sometimes leaped, from boat to boat. After concluding the call with Landis, she'd called another number Landis had provided, that of the gynecologist treating Mrs. Davis. It was recorded in documents filed with the company's health insurance plan.

Steve Owen, MD, hadn't volunteered any information. He'd insisted on maintaining doctor-patient confidentiality as if his life depended on it. But, even so, his silences and negative answers had given them something to go on.

"It's not that I don't want to help you out. I've cooperated in the past when the Bureau contacted me about other matters, but I can't imagine any investigation that would justify revealing medically privileged information. Maybe if you can tell me what sort of crime you're looking into . . ."

Amaia smiled wryly, wishing she could. *Of course, Doctor! I suspect the patient's husband is a serial killer who murdered his previous family. They'd disappointed him, so he decided they'd be better off in heaven. And since he discovered his current wife was pregnant, he's been reliving that experience, killing families all across the country. If the baby his wife is carrying turns out to be male, he'll kill them both. And the rest as well.*

"All right, then, let's attack it a different way," she'd stubbornly replied. "If I were forty-five years old, the same age as Mrs. Davis, and you were my attending physician, I assume you'd do all sorts of prenatal tests to monitor my health and that of the fetus. Am I right about that? Over."

"That would be the usual course of treatment."

"Tests such as amniocentesis, usually done around week sixteen. I assume one was done for Mrs. Davis. Over."

"You can assume that much. Okay, over."

"And I also have to assume the results were favorable, because the pregnancy hasn't been terminated. Over."

"You may be overstepping your bounds there. Some couples decide to continue a pregnancy, even when amniocentesis results strongly suggest an abnormality. Because of religious beliefs or similar humanitarian concerns. Over."

"Dr. Owen, I believe an ethical physician such as yourself, concerned above all for the safety of his patients, wouldn't have submitted Mrs. Davis to a risky test that might have caused a spontaneous abortion if he'd known in advance she was determined not to terminate the pregnancy even in the worst of circumstances. Over."

Though he gave away nothing in his words, Dr. Owen seemed to soften a bit. "My responsibility is to ensure the safety of both the mother and the developing child, and I did exactly that in this case. As I do with all my patients. Over."

"Did they want to know the sex of the child?" she demanded bluntly.

She must have taken him off guard, for he gave a direct answer. "Mrs. Davis didn't want to know. She wants it to be a surprise on the day of the birth." He covered himself. "I don't think I'm getting into the realm of confidential information when I say that. Over."

But he had. He hadn't said "she wanted" but instead "she wants," which implied Mrs. Davis hadn't yet given birth. Amaia didn't make a big deal of it. She kept her tone entirely casual. "But amniocentesis reveals the child's sex. It's shown in the lab results, or am I wrong? Over."

"That's correct," the physician confirmed. "Over."

"Did Mr. Davis ask for that information? Over."

"I can't answer that. It's confidential. Over."

"No problem. Let's take a different tack. You're not going to tell me, but I'm free to continue making my assumptions, right? Well, my belief is that Mr. Davis expressed a great deal of concern about the progress of the pregnancy, right from the first. Am I right? Over."

"That's hardly unusual, so I have no problem commenting. His wife is no longer young—when it comes to giving birth, I mean. Any husband would worry about a miscarriage. Over."

Or he might pray for one, Amaia thought. *God, take from me this bitter cup!* Aloud, she said, "I believe Mr. Davis pretended he didn't mind when his wife didn't want to know the results, except in so far as they related to the normal development of the fetus. But I also believe that later, when no one else was around, he asked about the sex. And you gave him that information. Over."

Owen tiptoed around that one. "The law provides that the father and the mother have the same rights and obligations concerning a child. Over."

"I suppose the sex of a child shouldn't be terribly important to a father who already has both a son and a daughter; and yet for him it was. My thought is that he wasn't very happy to hear they were expecting another son. I'm sure that seemed odd to you. If he already had a boy and a girl, the sex shouldn't have made any difference, right? You'd probably have found that reaction strange, especially on the part of a man who'd been following the course of the pregnancy so closely. Over."

She heard Steve Owen, MD, sigh heavily. "I will admit you have an impressive intuition and ability to formulate convincing hypotheses. I don't think I would care to be married to you. Over."

They ended the call. Amaia was handing the microphone to Annabel when a woman's voice came through the radio. "Assistant Inspector! Over . . . Assistant Inspector Salazar, this is Paula Thibodaux. Over."

Taken by surprise, Amaia checked with Annabel, who encouraged her to answer. "Go ahead, Paula. Over."

"Maybe this seem silly, but you know I was listening . . . Over."

"Sure, Paula, and I'm really grateful. Is there something you wanted to mention? Over."

"Well, yes, in fact. Listening to that doctor, I remember Cousin Tim's wife say she didn't want to know the baby sex till she had it. We thought it just a shame to visit the hospital without the right present, depending if it was a boy or girl. We figured out we could go and call the hospital florist. They get a list every day of all the new little boys and girls and the room numbers. We just gave her the mama's name and found out she had a girl. Then, we waltzed in there with everything pink—baby clothes, bracelets, cuddly toys, pink flowers even! My sister-in-law still wondering how we knew!" She laughed. "If you want, I can try. Over."

"Great idea, Paula," Amaia responded, beaming. "It's the women's health care center at Seton Medical Center in Austin. Over."

Paula called information and got the number. After a few moments of silence, they heard a dial tone, rings, and an answer. Her voice had a cheery lilt. "Hello, good morning there! I like to send two dozen roses to a Seton patient who just had a baby. Oh, and some balloons, please, but I don't know the room or if it is a boy or a girl."

"What's the patient's name?"

"It's Mrs. Davis, Natalie Davis. I know they expect to induce."

"Well, honey, you're a little bit ahead of yourself. Your friend is scheduled to be admitted the day after tomorrow. But you can pay for the flowers now, and we'll deliver them as soon as the baby arrives."

"Oh, okay, then I have plenty of time to come in and pick 'em myself," Paula chirped. "And I can get the balloons and a nice card too."

"As you like." The florist hung up. Paula giggled. "What you think? Over."

"You're a genius, Paula! Thanks! This is Salazar, out."

68

Is It Night in Baztán Already?

The swamp

Dupree studied Amaia again. She held tight to the deck railing as if it were somehow feeding her inspiration. He moved closer, put his hands out where she could see them, and unfolded the notebook page with her sketch of a heart. "Nice drawing."

"I learned what a heart really looks like when I was twelve. A doctor showed me."

"Mine's a bit more compressed in the middle. Like one of those Japanese octopus traps."

"Takotsubo."

Dupree smiled, giving her that enigmatic look that had so disquieted her at first. This time she didn't mind.

"Tell me, if you had to choose a single image or a single moment to define your experience back then, what would it be?"

She didn't have to reflect. "The night." A pause followed as she digested her spontaneous reply. Dupree knew she'd surprised herself. "I could put up with the daytime, but when the night fell in Baztán . . ."

"And is it night in Baztán right now, Salazar?"

"It's always night there."

Dupree responded with a sad but affectionate smile. "You're frightened, Salazar."

She opened her mouth to answer but couldn't find the words.

"That's why you leave the light on when you go to bed."

She said nothing.

"You're frightened, but you want to see your enemy coming. You're frightened, but you're ready for your foe. That makes you courageous."

She refused to look at him, but Dupree touched her chin gently to turn her head. "I knew it the first time I saw you. You were a student at that conference in Boston. I saw it again in Quantico. You're a born investigator. Keep a check on your arrogance, but a loose one, because unless you let your instincts guide you, you'll be no better than any of the others. And listen to your heart. You're going to be one of the best investigators I've ever had the good fortune to know. Listen to your heart, because that's what you and I have in common with the famous Inspector Sherrington. All three of us had the same experience: our hearts stopped, but for some reason we came back. Each of us had to die and find our way back from hell. That gave us a special advantage. Not only do we know the path to hell and back, we recognize those on that same road."

"It's more of a curse than a privilege," she muttered.

"I need to ask a favor of you. There's someone in NOLA named Nana. She's like a mother to me. Lives in Treme, but she said she was going to stay at the Superdome."

"I don't know if they're keeping a record of people's names, but I can look."

He nodded, aware of how absurdly hopeless that request probably was, but he had to ask. "And now let me tell you a story before we go back. I'll have to give the others a different version later. You'll get used to that. You'll have to do it often enough throughout your career. You'll get used to hiding the truth, because stupidity and intolerance are everywhere, and not everyone sees the world as you do. Make up a lie if you have to, lie to save your skin, to protect justice and the truth. But promise me you'll always remember that those are lies and that you'll keep the truth clearly in mind. And never lie to yourself or to me." He paused. "I'm going to tell you something. Something I know you'll understand."

"First tell me this," she interrupted him. "Are we friends?"

"You can bet my life on it." He took her right hand and placed a little gray bag in it.

Amaia smiled.

69

Witch

Elizondo

When Amaia Salazar was twelve years old, she was lost in the forest for sixteen hours. A shepherd named Julián Andía found her in the center of a field, and for years he insisted to everyone willing to listen that a lightning bolt deposited the child at his feet. They found her in the earliest hours of the morning, eighteen miles north of where she'd wandered off the trail. She was unconscious, her clothing blackened and scorched like that of a medieval witch pulled from a bonfire. In contrast, her skin was white, clean, and icy, as if she'd just emerged from a glacier. She'd lost a boot and most of her clothing was gone. Even though she'd been wandering in the driving rain for hours, she was completely dry. The girl seemed to have arrived riding a lightning bolt like the Basque goddess Mari herself.

Julián yelled, not to alert the others, but because he'd been thunderstruck—figuratively, at least. He was afraid to touch her, because he'd heard that if you touch someone struck by lightning, the electricity can kill you. People said the best thing to do was to poke the victim with a stick or pole to discharge the energy. Only then could you touch the person. The trooper from the Guardia Civil who responded to his shouts told him that was nonsense, that the electricity had already exited the child's body through her feet. The proof was that it had blasted off one boot and left the other in tatters.

The trooper squatted down, checked for a pulse, and found no heartbeat. He and his partner switched off, one doing CPR to keep the poor little thing alive, and the other restraining the father, who tried to throw himself on her as soon as he saw her. He shouted gibberish they couldn't make sense of, like "Those weren't dreams!" and "You were right, they weren't dreams!" and "They weren't just nightmares!"

Julián supposed she'd known she'd be struck by lightning, and her father had turned a deaf ear. Of course, who could blame him? But that didn't lessen the mystery, for the girl's dreams had come true, even putting aside for the moment the fact she'd been transported here by a lightning bolt. He'd seen that with his own eyes.

When they pulled her shredded clothing off her chest, he saw the bizarre shape burned into her skin, a bright-red mark like a jagged lightning bolt, as if the wicked storm goddess had branded the child. And he was confused, unable to understand how she could be so cold to the touch if she'd been struck by lightning. And how was it she was completely dry, even though she'd been in the pouring rain all night long? And then there was that weird thing with the dog a few hours later.

Julián had theories he didn't share with just anyone. He confided only in close friends and family members, reminding them that in the old days, witches would gather at Mari's caves to make sacrifices and ask for favors they couldn't get from the good Lord because what they wanted was so depraved. And everyone knew that one of those caves was always dry. God knows that he, Julián, would certainly rather get soaked to the bone than indebt himself to a witch. He'd always found the little Salazar girl a bit strange, but Julián swore he meant no malice. He had nothing against the poor little thing, and it was far better to be nice to someone like her than to get on her bad side. As his late grandmother used to say—and she knew a lot about it—you don't have to believe they exist, but don't you dare go around claiming they don't.

At the regional hospital, Amaia lay on a stretcher, a sheet covering her torso. The rest of her body, except for her scratched and bruised knees and hands, appeared so starkly white that one might think all the blood had been drained from her body. One nurse was closely monitoring her vital signs, and another checked the reflexes of her pupils every couple of minutes.

Engrasi and Juan Salazar held hands as they peered through the window into the ICU and listened to the emergency room doctor.

"We'll do more tests when she regains consciousness, but from everything we can see, she sustained no serious injuries."

"Why hasn't she come to?" Engrasi asked.

"She suffered a tremendous shock to her system. And let's not forget she was in the freezing rain for all those hours, alone and lost. It's no wonder she's exhausted. She'll be weak and listless for several days. When a person is exposed to extreme stress, the brain starts to shut down most activity so as to focus on surviving. She's completely drained of energy."

Engrasi wanted to know more. "They told us her heart stopped. Is that true?"

"Yes. For a while, at least. We can't know for how long. Lightning discharges a massive electromagnetic pulse in a fraction of a second, and ten percent of those struck by lightning suffer cardiac and respiratory arrest. She's very lucky the troopers on the scene were trained in cardiopulmonary resuscitation."

Engrasi put both hands to her mouth, horrified. The very word "resuscitation" gave her a fright like none she'd ever experienced. If Amaia had been resuscitated, that meant she had died. Her baby girl had died—it didn't matter if it was for only a few minutes or even seconds. Her girl had died, and she, Engrasi, who knew the great danger looming over the child, had failed to protect her. Ignacio and Joxepi were right. She had to take Amaia some place far away, somewhere the valley couldn't reach her.

The doctor was still talking; Engrasi forced herself to pay attention. "She's young and strong. We hope there won't be any aftereffects, but I should warn you that sometimes these victims have seizures, even many days later. They may faint. And it's even more common for them to suffer amnesia. Most individuals struck by lightning don't remember anything of what happened to them before the accident."

"And that strange mark on her chest . . . ," Juan asked, obviously uneasy.

"It's a burn mark. She was extremely lucky, because it's the only one. The air around a bolt of lightning becomes instantly hot and can vaporize water. That's why much of her clothing was torn from her body and she was completely dry to the touch. The electrical discharge of the lightning ran across Amaia's skin, drawing out the red blood cells from the subdermal capillaries and leaving that strange mark. It's called a fractal lightning scar, or a Lichtenberg figure. It will fade over time."

"Can we go inside?" Engrasi asked, glancing in frustration at the observation window that separated them from the ICU.

"Yes. But one at a time."

She looked at her brother. "You go first."

When Amaia awoke in the hospital, she saw her father by her bedside. His face was pale, and his hair, soaked by the rain, was plastered to his forehead. His eyes were red and raw from weeping. When he saw her lids flutter, he leaned forward, his face anguished but hopeful. She was so flooded with tenderness when she saw his expression that she almost couldn't breathe.

"There was a tree, *Aita*, a special one. And then I got lost . . ."

"Don't say anything, *maitia*. Just rest."

Amaia's clear blue eyes glistened with gathering tears. "There was somebody in the forest. Ipar kept him away from us . . ."

A cold chill ran up Juan's back as he imagined the dangers to which his daughter had been exposed. "It's all over, *bihotza*. You're safe now, and you'll be better soon."

"I was cold, so cold, and then I saw the house . . ."

"You went to a house?" Juan asked, surprised.

"There was this man . . . so handsome . . . and people with him . . ."

Juan turned to the side, his heart squeezed by the dark foreboding that had haunted him throughout the day.

"They were . . . bad. I was going to go inside because I was so cold, but Ipar wouldn't let me." She opened her eyes wide, suddenly remembering something. "Where's Ipar, *Aita*?"

Juan tilted his head. *Shit!* He didn't want to tell his daughter the truth. "*Maitia,* Ipar loved you very much. He was a good dog, and he protected you right up to the end."

Amaia gasped, "No!" She broke down, sobbing with a depth of grief and pain Juan had never seen before. His daughter, so given to silent tears, broke into sobs and wails so loud that the nurses came running.

"What did you do to her?" one of them challenged Juan, pushing him away from the bed.

"Nothing, I swear!" he replied, greatly offended. "It's just that her dog . . . died."

"And you couldn't have chosen a better time to tell her? Right now, she has to be protected, man!"

She'd snarled "man" as an insult, but what really angered him was hearing the woman remind him, her father, that his daughter had to be protected.

The other nurse intervened in a calmer voice. "I think your time is up now."

"Let me say goodbye, at least," he entreated them.

The nurse nodded, and Juan stepped forward to Amaia's bedside.

His daughter kept on weeping, but now her screams had turned to whimpers as a torrent of tears flowed from her eyes.

"Maitia . . . ," he whispered, "I have to go now."

Amaia looked at him. There was no sign of reproach in her eyes. She held out her arm, silently appealing for a hug. She loved him, as she always had. Surely, she was going to say so . . .

Juan leaned over his daughter, filled with love and distress, and listened to her.

"*Aita, Ama* was there. She was with that man. They were waiting for me, and they wanted to . . ."

Juan straightened up, pushing his daughter's arm away. His eyes wide open, his heart pounding, he put his mouth to her ear. "Amaia, don't tell anybody. If you love me, do that for me. Don't tell."

The immensity of her love and affection for him squeezed her heart until it ached. But the words to declare her adoration withered and became a painful memory wrapped around her vocal cords. Unable to speak, she nodded, and her silence shrouded the deep, dark secret she would keep for him—the reason she would never love him again.

Juan felt his daughter's face brush against his as she nodded.

When he straightened up, Amaia had stopped crying. She stared directly into his eyes. Juan realized he was seeing the serious, determined face that the adult Amaia would have. He looked away, filled with shame, and went toward the door.

"Agur, maitia."

Three seconds passed before Amaia responded. And when she did, Juan already knew it was a final farewell.

"Agur, Aita."

Engrasi had been watching through the ICU window, and though she couldn't hear anything, she hadn't missed a single gesture. Juan came out to stand beside her, downcast, his cheeks covered with tears. Engrasi didn't look at him. "Was she crying over Ipar?"

"Yes."

"You didn't tell her . . . ?"

"No, of course not!" he flared up. "And don't you ever breathe a word either!"

Engrasi turned a withering glare upon him. He lowered his head again.

"What kind of person would I have to be to tell that child that someone ripped open her dog's belly and nailed him up on a tree at the edge of the forest?" she said.

Juan didn't answer. He was in tears again. Engrasi turned away, disgusted.

"I'm taking Amaia away from Elizondo. Immediately."

"You're right," he answered.

"Maybe you didn't understand me. Once she's released. Amaia's not going to set foot in Elizondo again."

Juan just nodded. "Take her far away. I don't think Pamplona is far enough. Take her, I'll give you the money. But don't ever tell me where she is, because I'm weak, Engrasi, and if I knew . . ."

70

The Violin That Belonged to "Mic"

The swamp
Wednesday, August 31, 2005

Johnson brought Bull and Charbou to the boat.

Dupree didn't wait for them to ask why. "We've got him. The Composer is Martin Lenx, and Martin Lenx has been using the alias Robert Davis. He's an adjustor for the American Insurance Association, specializing in evaluating disaster damage. He got the job six months after killing his family in Madison. He's been using insurance application files to get information: the family names, the number of family members, others residing with them, firearms in the home, ages, accidents—everything. He lives in Texas with his second family. Eight months ago, his wife let him know they were expecting another child, their third. He was at their vacation home in Galveston, next door to the Andrews family."

"The son-of-a-bitch Good Samaritan," Charbou muttered with a glance at Amaia.

Dupree continued. "He has one son and a daughter named Michelle who plays the violin. He used it to set up the Andrews living room as a replica of the music room in Madison. Salazar was right about that. That was his first murder in this series. Must have acted on impulse, without planning, and took an enormous risk. The news of another child put him back in exactly the same situation he'd faced in Madison, and his world collapsed. In his deranged mind, the murders were justified by the Andrews boy's bad behavior. The kid was giving his parents a hard time and went on a rampage in Davis's tropical garden."

"What a fucker!" Charbou exclaimed.

"Davis hired specialists to clean up the crime scene to make sure everything was under control. You can imagine his reaction when young Joseph talked about calling the police back in. And I'll bet his daughter complained when she couldn't find her violin."

"He broke into the house and grabbed it before the forensics team came back for it," Johnson said.

"He must have been out of his mind to use his own daughter's violin," Bull commented. "Why didn't he remove the violin earlier?"

"It was an oversight. He didn't think it through, and he was upset when he realized that with another child on the way, his story was repeating itself. His past was catching up with him. He murdered the family next door, people he knew. Giving into that impulse was a huge mistake. That's how murderers give themselves away; without thinking, they choose victims in their proximity.

"His wife is scheduled for induced labor in Austin two days from now. Salazar and I believe he'll get out of NOLA as soon as he can. He intends to return and kill them all."

"We've finished here," Johnson said. "We have to get back right away."

Dupree stared out across the bayou for a moment. "Charbou, you and Salazar go back to New Orleans with Johnson, try to locate Lenx and follow him back to Texas, right to his front door if you have to. You're going to stop him and arrest him. Detective Bull and I are staying here. We still have work to do."

Amaia had been watching Bull stare at the deck the whole time. He and Dupree were obviously up to something.

Johnson looked first at Amaia and then at Bull. "With all due respect, boss, Salazar's a temporary hire, and Charbou's not even FBI." He turned to Bill. "No offense meant."

"None taken. Truth is truth."

"Salazar is as capable an agent as you've ever worked with. As for Charbou, well . . ." Dupree winked at Bill. "He's from NOLA. He'll save your asses in a city he knows better than anyone."

Johnson had more to say, but Dupree cut him off. "I won't be much help. Yesterday I was half-dead, and getting to Le Grand and back has done me in. I'm afraid the *traiteur* needs to work on me some more. Bull will stay here to help me with the Samedi case. We have six dead kidnapped girls in that lodge and four dead men, three of them shot through the guts. We'll take Jacob's sisters back to the city once it's safe to do so. No way am I going to just leave them here, and New Orleans can't take them in yet. And the *traiteur* wants to do a ceremony for Médora, something he calls the farewell to the flesh. It will allow her to die in peace so her soul can start its journey. Bull and I should stay. After all, we know the family, and we bear some of the blame for her death because we failed to rescue her back then."

"What happened to her is terrible," Charbou said. "But it wasn't your fault, and there's nothing you can do for her now."

"Dying's not easy," Dupree said, staring Charbou down. "And it's even harder for someone like Médora. She spent almost her whole life believing she was already dead. Frank Carlino and Jerome Lirette were a really long time dying after whatever those people did to them, even though Lirette was decapitated and my friend had his heart torn out."

"You really think some people linger after dying?"

"What I'm saying is that some find it hard to leave, especially those who are convinced that somebody's conjuring them back or keeping them from going. Dying is hard. It's like being born; you can do it by yourself, but it's better when you have help, when somebody's waiting for you on both sides." His face was stern. "Bull and I are staying. The rest of you, get your things together and hit the road. Any questions?"

71

Truth and Justice

The swamp

Bull and Dupree stood on the pontoon walkway, watching the navy's Zodiac and its passengers disappear into the distance.

Once the boat's wake had dissipated, Bull took a cell phone from his pocket and handed it to Dupree. "I took out the SIM card and put it in my own phone. Voilà!" He turned it on, and the screen populated with a swarm of icons.

"Good."

"Okay, but now what? Samedi—either the man or the organization—knew Len. They're going to be expecting to hear his voice when they call. And they will call. As soon as something doesn't sound right, they'll hang up. We don't have the equipment to triangulate their location. Considering the state of things, I doubt we'd find any police force in the state able to do it."

"I'm not intending to track the call."

Bull waited to hear more.

"When they call, Dominic will tell them what happened."

"But . . ."

"Samedi didn't know Dominic, Dominic didn't know Samedi. Len was the link between them. Len blew his top when Pitt let the girls drown, and he gunned him down. Len told Samedi they'd lost their 'catch' and he'd killed Pitt for his negligence. I think he got permission to recruit another helper, someone they'd never met. And, lucky for us, everyone who knew the new man is dead."

"Dominic . . ."

"My cover story is that Pitt's brother, Vince, was furious and confronted Len. Put two trigger-happy guys together, everything goes to shit, and both of them end up dead. And now I—that is, Dominic, the only survivor—am answering Len's phone, because I knew they'd call. I'm a reliable guy, very efficient. I finished the cleanup all by myself, and Le Grand's back in order, thanks to me. And I'm waiting for their instructions."

"Not a bad story, but they won't buy it just like that."

"True, and that's why tomorrow we're going back to Le Grand. We'll take photos to submit with my report, and then we'll do what Dominic is going to claim he did, in case they decide to visit or send somebody to check it out."

"Okay," Bull admitted, still not convinced. "But what will that get us? They're not going to spill the beans about their gang to the first person who picks up the phone."

"Of course they won't. I've thought about Samedi a lot over the years, and I know we won't be able to understand them without getting up close and personal. We can't do that unless we join—or unless we *seem* to join—their structure. We need Samedi to believe we belong to Samedi. You heard Dominic: they have people in the police. Maybe really senior people. There's no other way to explain how they've managed to keep active but out of sight all these years." He exhaled sharply. "It has to be done this way, because neither you nor I will ever get the authorization to go undercover."

"They won't agree to meet you for no reason at all."

"You're forgetting about the girls. Samedi knows the two girls from NOLA are alive, because Len told him so. They'll tell Dominic to take them someplace, just the way they were planning."

"And what if they send someone to pick up the girls instead?"

"That's a risk we have to take."

"All right, suppose they agree and set up a rendezvous. If we're planning to arrest whoever shows up, perfect, no problem, but you're talking about infiltrating the gang. What's going to stop them from putting a bullet in your brain as soon as they see you don't have the girls? Why would they trust someone who shows up empty handed?"

Dupree stood grimly silent for several seconds before answering. "You're right, Bull. That's why I'm going to hand over the girls."

72

The Fourth Day

New Orleans, Louisiana
Thursday, September 1, 2005

Getting back to the city was easier than escaping it, but finding the way to their destination was another matter altogether. They came back across the Westbank, crossed the Mississippi at Bywater, and from there, proceeded eastward on foot to get to Jackson Square. Their route, sometimes across highway bridges, other times through chest-deep water, got more and more complicated.

The greatest difference between the city Amaia left and the one she found on their return from the swamp was the sense of absolute desperation.

People had been numbed by shock immediately after Hurricane Katrina hit. It'd been evident from the disbelief in their faces, their incredulity at the sheer brute force of nature. The waters rose throughout that first night, so the day broke to catastrophe. People were initially in a stupor, but the progressive deterioration of the situation established a cycle in which each day, the unprecedented disaster became even worse than the day before.

The third day dawned with no significant change. The flood seemed to have reached its maximum level, though there was still the possibility another levee might give way. Even that wouldn't change things much. Eighty percent of the 170 square miles of New Orleans' terra firma was underwater. The power was out and municipal water plants had shut down. No shops were open. There was no air-conditioning in a city where daytime temperatures regularly broke ninety degrees. Nights weren't much cooler.

The third day was one of hopelessness. Children and the elderly remained on highway overpasses, huddled together or passed out under the cruel sun after three days without food or potable water. Rumors of impending rescue passed from mouth to mouth, fed by reports via the few functioning transistor radios, but no help came.

By the fourth day, madness reigned. The team came back from their time in the swamp to a changed city.

Amaia, Johnson, and Charbou trudged along a highway at five in the afternoon. The sun shone as mercilessly as at noon. Under those brilliant, gleaming skies, the city stank of feces and death. It seemed totally absurd that only a few miles away, international flights were departing on schedule, evening newscasters were prepping to go on the air, and some people were luxuriating in long, hot showers and others were making love.

The great mass of NOLA city dwellers, whose initial reactions to this unthinkable torment had been similar, were now divided like cancerous cells into two equally ghastly camps: those who'd lost all hope and those equally bereft of hope who were also incensed.

Some of the despondent did look up as the team approached. Indifferent voices warned them there was no way out; the road they were on went nowhere. Like all the rest of the streets in post-Katrina New Orleans.

The second group, the angry one, made noise and talked rowdy. They screamed at the passing team, threatening them and demanding attention. At the sight of representatives of the state, they yelled, "Where the help you bastards promise us?"

"They ain't sending help!" ranted one man. "Our USA finally done figure out how to kill us all!"

Charbou looked at Amaia. "You know, they're not wrong. Terrorists blow up the Twin Towers, and the whole country has a shit fit, but a city full of black folks drowns, and who cares? Can you even imagine New York four days after the towers fell if nobody went to help?"

Amaia nodded. "This is unbelievable."

Another, smaller group emerged, a breed of determined trekkers. They were scarce and increasingly infrequent, but all the more extraordinary for that. Some were women with infants in their arms. Others were squalid men pushing supermarket carts heaped with the most bizarre assortment of objects imaginable. Shirtless old men, badly sunburned, staggered along carrying shopping bags with photo albums and wedding mementos. They all shuffled drearily and stopped only to shade their eyes and squint into the distance. They resumed their strange pilgrimage like dead souls in Dante's *Inferno,* damned to walk day after day but never arrive at their destination.

The team had just waded through waist-deep water to access one end of an I-10 overpass. Once up on the road's surface, they took time to dump the water and muck out of their rubber boots and dry and check their sidearms. Johnson and Charbou took turns in the lead as they proceeded along the highway. Amaia kept relatively close to them, listening to their conversation. Charbou pointed south. As he turned to look, Johnson suddenly jerked and fell headlong. Amaia halted, confused, not knowing whether Johnson had fainted or simply slipped. Half a second later, she heard the echoing report of a gunshot. Charbou grabbed her arm and pulled her down. Another bullet whizzed overhead.

"They're shooting at us!" Charbou shouted as he crawled past her toward Johnson. Amaia had already taken cover behind the concrete barrier along the edge of the overpass.

"I'm pretty sure it came from that building," she said, pointing past Charbou. "Wait until I give the signal."

"Hurry up!" he shouted, shielding Johnson with his own body.

Kneeling, she raised her pistol above the barrier, shouted to Charbou to go, and discharged a full magazine toward the building without aiming at anything in particular, her only objective being to cover her teammates.

Charbou got up just enough to grab Johnson under the arms and haul him to the side of the road. He fell heavily at her side with Johnson on top of him. Covered in sweat, the FBI agent was clenching his jaw and sucking air noisily through his nostrils, struggling against the shock of being shot.

Amaia checked the wound. He'd been hit in the left shoulder just at the edge of his vest. His arm was twisted at a strange angle, and she suspected damage to the bone and tendons. She dumped out the contents of her knapsack, grabbed a cotton blouse, and pressed it against the wound as she ran her fingers across his back, checking for an exit wound. There was none.

"It's not serious, Johnson. The slug's still in you, I can feel it under the skin. I think the bone is broken, but there's not much blood. You'll pull through this one."

Johnson didn't answer but he turned his head, looking around at their exposed position on an empty highway bridge where each end sloped down to the water.

Amaia read his mind. "Stop it, Johnson, don't even go there! We're going to get you out of this, you understand?"

Charbou straightened up a bit, trying to see where the shots had come from. He slid back down again. "Looks like they've stopped. Probably weren't expecting return fire." He pulled the radio out of its sling. "Attention, code three. This is Detective Bill Charbou, we have an officer down, repeat, *code three*. We're on the I-10 overpass over Elysian at Tonti Street."

The reply was immediate. "Ops center here—"

Another voice interrupted. "Detective Charbou?" The speaker sounded alarmed. "Is Detective Bull the wounded officer?"

"No, it's Johnson, the FBI agent. He took a slug in the shoulder."

The radio went silent for several seconds. This time the reply was from the operations center. "Backup is on the way. Hold tight."

In less than ten minutes, a New Orleans police launch roared up to the point where they'd climbed onto the span. The speed of the police response seemed to reassure Johnson. He was still in pain, but his face had regained some color. He called Amaia and Charbou over as the paramedics tended to his injury.

"You guys have to keep going," he said, dropping all formality and looking Amaia in the eyes. "They've been told to transfer me to the military base. Once they have me stabilized, they'll evacuate me with the other injured and the last remaining families. You can't waste time escorting me across the city. Not now that you're so close."

Amaia nodded. She'd have made the same call. They couldn't give up.

The rescue team took good care of him, bandaging the wound and improvising a sling for his useless arm. When they'd finished, Johnson beckoned to Amaia with his good arm.

"Guess it's only fair," he said, making an effort to smile. "You tracked him down, he's yours. Go take him out. But remember, you'll be on your own. If you report it now, they won't care that you're hot on his heels. You'll get one of two responses: If they even agree to hear you out, they'll ask for details, evidence, and justification for what you've done, and Lenx will be long gone by the time you get to Texas. Or they'll be too busy to listen to you until it's too late, and Lenx will get away. The Composer wins either way."

She nodded.

"And another thing."

"Dupree," she anticipated him. "He's not coming back, is he?"

"No," Johnson admitted unhappily. "But he knows what he's doing."

The paramedics lifted the stretcher to take him to the launch, and Johnson admonished her again. "Remember! Don't report in until it's all over!"

Charbou succeeded in convincing the crew to drop them at the edge of the French Quarter on the way to the base. From there it was a simple matter to get to Jackson Square and Chartres Street. She and Charbou went upstairs, looking for the apartment where the Composer had killed a family two days earlier. Just as the operations supervisor had warned them, almost nothing had been done. The door and windows were cordoned off with the familiar crime scene tape and seals marked with the date and time. And there was the orange *X* advising anyone without a sense of smell there were six corpses inside.

Charbou cut the seals with a razor-sharp switchblade, taking care to damage them as little as possible. He stepped back and looked at Amaia. She nodded. He took a deep breath and pulled up his shirt to cover his nose and mouth. Even before aiming her flashlight into the room, Amaia heard the buzzing of flies swarming over the bodies.

She moved the beam across the corpses, resisting the urge to flail her arms to shoo away the flies trying to settle on her skin. She looked back at the door, yearning for better air. She almost broke and ran to get the reek of decay out of her nostrils, to escape the sight of death and shut out its presence.

She controlled herself. She took a stance at the feet of the victims, bowed her head, and prayed silently for the repose of their souls, something she'd never done before at a murder scene. She had an intuition that this was important because she was now in command. She was responsible to them in a way she couldn't put into words. She prayed intently and took the time to do it right. And she would do the same for the rest of her life, each time she found herself in the presence of a murder victim, because every individual deserves respect. She needed to comprehend each victim and make that person her own. She would forever establish an intimate relationship with the slain in order to merit the mantle of a righteous avenger of the murdered.

When she'd finished her prayer, she took a deep breath through the blouse fabric over her mouth and sank into contemplation. She allowed the foul odors to fill her nostrils. The air gradually became more bearable, but she kept her face covered. She couldn't concentrate with flies crawling across her face.

The victims were laid out with their heads toward the north. They were arranged in order of age, and the killer had taken the cord he'd used to tie them up, just as at the earlier crime scenes. But he'd been far less careful. Either that, or some of the family members had struggled against the binding, for at least two of them had dark bruises on their wrists or ankles. The father was the first body lined up in this montage of mortality, and the pistol lay by his right hand. Then, in order, the grandmother, the wife, two teenagers, and a child. A violin had been left against the wall, just beyond the mother's head. Amaia took out her mobile phone. It showed no connection, but it was still working, because she'd recharged it at the Cajun camp. She took several photos, gesturing silently to instruct Charbou how to light the scene.

Jackson Square was jammed. Crossing it, they saw that the cathedral's main door was open. Candles at the altar provided the only illumination inside. The flickering light was sufficient to make the elaborate gold decor gleam and reveal the flags of Spanish Castile, England, and France flapping slowly near the door, the Stars and Stripes at the fore. That chronological display honored the colonial settlers of the land. Hundreds of people were inside, completely filling the cathedral.

Charbou saw the direction of her gaze. "Do you want to go in?"

She suddenly felt uncomfortable. "No, no—why would I?"

"I don't know," he said. "It's just that I saw you praying for that murdered family."

"Travis," she corrected him.

"What?"

"The family's name is Travis. I hadn't planned to pray, but I think it was because I knew their name. I was trying to make peace with them, to say goodbye to them, to preserve their name. To keep them from being reduced to anonymity."

"I meant no disrespect. Praying was the right thing to do, there's nothing stupid about it. Maybe I'm the one who should go in there to give thanks. The bullet that hit Johnson was meant for me."

Surprised, Amaia stopped and stared. "You say that because he was hit while turning around?"

"I'm saying it because it's true. The shooter was a police officer. I'm sure of it."

Amaia's jaw dropped. She could hardly believe her ears. She took his arm and pulled him over to the stairs so they could sit down.

"You remember what Robin Hood and his boys told us the other day?" Charbou said. "They said armed groups were shooting at black folks."

"You think they were targeting you because you're African American?"

"The boys weren't just making it up. I've been hearing the radio reports. It's true. Gunfire aimed at unarmed people, always black, on bridges and elevated highways."

"This city is in pure anarchy. But you were between Johnson and me. They could have hit any one of us."

"There was something strange when I radioed it in. Before the ops center responded, someone else cut in, somebody who knows us well enough to assume the white man down was my partner Bull."

"You think they were gunning for the two of you?"

"No idea. Dominic said police officers were members of Samedi. He couldn't have been talking about beat cops. They'd have to be more senior."

Amaia looked up at the sky. It was just past seven in the evening, and the sunlight was nearly gone. "We're close to the hotel, and it looks as if the French Quarter's hardly been touched. You think the city's oldest bordello is still open?"

The sky was purplish blue when they got to Dauphine Street at twenty past seven. The big green doors to the hotel were shut, and the flag display across the balcony had disappeared.

Amaia went to the main entrance and squinted through the crack in the door. It swung open suddenly, and she found herself face to face with one of the sisters who owned the hotel.

Without a word, the woman rushed out and enfolded her in a mighty embrace. "Oh, thank the Lord! I'm so glad you're okay—where your other friends at? I got really worried when y'all didn't come back."

"They're fine, all things considered," Amaia managed to reply.

The proprietress released her and hugged Charbou just as heartily. "But y'all come on in!" she said when she let him go. "I got to lock up. They's people out there who would cut our throats just to get in." She hauled them inside and bolted the door.

"You still have customers in the hotel?"

"Bless you, yes. Most don't have any place to go back to. Others was afraid to go out; they's awful stories going round about what's going on out there. And I had friends turning up here 'cause they got nowhere to go. I had to put them in your friends' rooms, but I still got yours." She smiled. "I was sure you was gonna come back."

"Can we stay here?"

"You still my guests. Of course you can."

"Just one night."

"Stay long as you want. Practically nothing left to eat, but me and my sisters gonna stay here long as it takes. On the radio today, they say the government worried 'bout Lake Pontchartrain. If it spills over, the center of New Orleans gonna be underwater too. They say it's gonna take months to pump out the water and fix the levees. They talkin' 'bout an evacuation, an official one, with soldiers going round to force people out of they houses."

"We heard that too."

"Well, I'm tellin' you, I'm gonna wait right here till they come, but I ain't gonna leave my hotel a minute before that. This is our home and our living; I ain't gonna walk off and let any bunch of savages set it on fire and burn up all we got."

Amaia and Charbou glanced at one another.

A big smile broke across the hotel owner's face. "But I'm such a fool! Here I am going on and on, while y'all must be exhausted. Let me take you upstairs." She picked up a lit candle from the reception counter. "One little problem is you got to share the room. I don't have another one."

She accompanied them upstairs and showed them to the room. She lifted the candle high so they could see the inside. After sleeping at a shrimpers' camp, in an abandoned house, and in the hallway at Charity Hospital, the room at the Dauphine was a dream of beautifully appointed tidiness. Looking back, Amaia was surprised to realize how quickly she had accepted and adapted to the misery of their circumstances over the past few days.

"Like I said, we 'bout out of food, so I can't give you breakfast. They's a candle and a little box of matches to relight it if you have to. But here's something

I think you gonna like." She ushered them into the bathroom and held the candle overhead.

Amaia peeked over her shoulder and smiled as their hostess continued. "Before the hurricane got to us, Grace, my sister, had the good sense to fill all the bathtubs right to the top. Be careful with it, because it's got to do for everything. Washing, drinking, you name it. It's not warm, but you got clean towels."

Peeling off the clothes she'd worn since Katrina's arrival was like shedding an extra skin. Amaia placed the folded photograph she'd been carrying on the shelf alongside Jacob's tiny orange dragon. She smiled and then inspected her nude body in the mirror. Her arms and neck were tanned. She rubbed her belly, grateful that Annabel's antibiotics had purged her of the infection. A half-full bucket of water was enough to fill the stoppered sink. The cake of lilac soap delighted her with a fragrance she wouldn't have even noticed in ordinary circumstances. Washing carefully, she discovered bruises and scrapes she hadn't known she had. Another half bucket of water was enough to wash and rinse her hair. She didn't dry herself because she wanted to preserve that delicious, cool cleanliness. It seemed an eternity since she'd felt this good. She put on clean panties and a T-shirt.

"Your turn!" she called and made way for Charbou.

He went into the bathroom and left the door slightly ajar, so flickering candlelight filtered into the bedroom.

She lay stretched out on the bed with the window wide open, listening to Charbou slosh water in the tub and sink. She had a vision of him sniffing the soap just as she'd done. A warm breeze came through the window, carrying the echo of a faraway saxophone. She smiled, delighted that someone in all this darkness was still making music. She got up and leaned on the windowsill to listen. *Two kinds of folks never leave New Orleans: musicians and ghosts.*

She turned her head and saw Charbou reflected in the mirror. His body was bare, shining wet, and redolent of lilac soap. He was as gorgeous as a classical statue. He met her gaze through the reflection. Amaia grasped the bottom of her T-shirt and pulled it over her head with one smooth move; turning to meet his eyes, she got up, stepped out of her panties, and went naked to him.

The specter had stayed away from Amaia's dreams for some time. That night, Amaia sensed a presence by the bed, watchful in the darkness, intrigued by the defiance of the little one who stubbornly kept her back to the door as if proclaiming, *I'm not afraid of you.* Yet she *was* afraid, and they both knew it. The menacing presence bent down close to Amaia, opened her fearsome lips, and exhaled hot breath across the nape of the child's neck.

You're wondering why I didn't gobble you up? I can, you know. Anytime I want. Maybe you think I'm crazy?

Amaia jerked awake in the darkness, thinking she'd sensed a hostile movement. Her eyes opened on absolute blackness. She cursed herself for neglecting to leave her flashlight lit in the bathroom. She fumbled across the bedside table until she found it and then switched it on, holding it low so as not to wake Charbou.

He was sound asleep. She watched him for a few moments but again caught a hint of movement. Outside, beyond the window. That's what had awakened her. She switched off her light, got out of bed, drew aside the curtain, and peered out. Across the street, the heavy curtains of an upstairs dwelling were parted and tied back. Two tall French doors were open wide, and the golden light within revealed a richly decorated room. An ancient man wrapped in a bathrobe was reading in the light of an eight-armed candelabra. Behind him, the gilded titles on the spines of the books in a ceiling-high bookcase gleamed and reflected the warmth of the flickering candles. Amaia watched him, spellbound by a feeling of otherworldly beauty.

"Salazar," Charbou called from the darkness behind her. "Come back here to my bed."

She laughed. "*Your* bed?"

"I'm in it, you're not, so it's my bed. Come here."

"Only if you stop calling me Salazar. It makes me feel like I'm talking to a cop."

"And what am I?"

"A lover," she answered. "Or did I get that wrong?"

"Come over here to my bed, woman, and you'll find out."

73

Gris-Gris

New Orleans, Louisiana
Friday, September 2, 2005

The sun rose just past six thirty, and the temperature was already above eighty degrees. Charbou lay in bed, watching Amaia get dressed. He saw her put the leather cord with the goatskin pouch around her neck.

"Man must think a whole lot of you. He gave you the charm that saved his life."

She rolled the leather pouch between her fingers, pressed its smooth surface, and felt its crisp but yielding contents. It produced a faint crackling sound when she squeezed it. "What do you think's in here?"

"Seeds? Maybe coffee beans, incense, dirt from a grave, powder of ground human bones," he said with a smile. "You know, the usual Louisiana mélange. It all depends on the intent."

"The intent?"

"It depends on whether the giver wants to hurt you or help you. I don't think you have to worry about that stuff, though. We already saw it's a terrific antidote to heart troubles."

"If this is really what kept Dupree's heart going, what's going to happen if he's not wearing it?"

He shrugged. "That . . . is definitely a question."

Amaia examined the bag, frowned, and slipped it into her T-shirt. "I don't believe in charms."

"Then why wear one?"

"For the same reason I'm carrying Jacob's dragon. I believe in faith. Not a personal faith of my own, but I respect the power of other people's beliefs. Empires have risen and fallen on the strength of faith. You could claim that the man we're after is a person of deep religious conviction. In fact, when you think about it, his beliefs are absolute."

Charbou gave her a thoughtful look. "You're very clever, Assistant Inspector Salazar."

"What's this?" she challenged him. "Now I'm Assistant Inspector Salazar again? I thought complimenting my intelligence was part of the Charbou Method."

He placed a hand to his chest, pretending to be hurt. "The Charbou Method? That's what you think I'm up to?"

"I think I had your number from the very first day. You're every woman's boyfriend."

"That might have been true then, but I think Jacob's sisters were closer to the mark. I heard what they told you." He took her by the waist and looked down at the contrasting colors of their skin. "Don't you think we make a handsome couple?"

She didn't reply.

"I'm being honest. I'm telling you what I think. But you must already know it, since you apparently have a superpower that allows you to read minds and predict what people will do."

"That's not a superpower." She was amused, remembering Dupree's comments about what made her different from others.

"And what makes you say our man is still in NOLA? How do you know he hasn't left?"

She sat on the edge of the bed to think about it. "Because for him, the *timing* is just as important as what he does. It's been eight months since he learned his wife was going to have another child. He's been waiting. For a while, he hoped she would miscarry and he could avoid his destiny. It would be a touch of bad luck for her, but for him, a sign that God was sparing him. He's been rehearsing his ultimate crime, practicing on families he thought deserved to be dispatched just as much as his first family did. But he's not going to rush it. For some reason, it's important to him for every single element to be in place. Each and every sign has to be present, otherwise, his crimes would be senseless, nothing more than banal murders."

"He doesn't believe he's committing murders?"

"No. Remember, he's a psychopath. To him, his first family was no more than a failed laboratory experiment. He threw it out and started over. But he has something he believes in. He's a fanatic. You should never underestimate the power of people's beliefs. I'm betting Lenx is still here; for a murderer, New Orleans is the perfect place to be, because thousands of homes have been affected by the hurricane. It's a simple matter for him to select families that fit his criteria, so he can keep rehearsing. Time's running out, though, and his moment of truth is near. I think that in some curious manner, he's intimidated by the thought of acting against his own family. He'll stay away from home right up to the end because he doesn't want to be there for his son's birth. He'll return to dispatch them all, in keeping with his ritual. No hurricane or tornado will be required once he's targeting his own family."

She got to her feet, buckling her belt, and changed her tone. "And after that he'll disappear, just the way he did eighteen years ago."

"You're going to be someone people love to hate."

She smiled. "Why do you say that?"

"Because you're going to be a really good cop, a celebrity detective who tracks down all the high-profile nutcases. The people will adore you, but your colleagues will hate you."

She threw a pillow at him. "Never!"

"As if you have a choice!"

The hotel sisters winked at Amaia as they escorted them to the door. After the farewells, Amaia and Charbou walked eastward. They were going to try to reach the Superdome before the sun was at its zenith. They'd heard via their radio that the president was expected in New Orleans that day. A massive, coordinated overnight evacuation effort had already transferred about twenty-three thousand citizens from the Superdome to Houston's Astrodome, six hours away. Bus caravans would continue to depart throughout the morning.

74

Accepting the Inevitable

Superdome, New Orleans

Nana heard the murmur of voices all around her, like a menacing swarm of wasps. Only the garbled metallic announcements from the PA system interrupted the churning, muttering cadences of those lost souls. She looked toward the flaming sun as it rose, and the harsh light brought tears to her eyes. They trickled down her cheeks. She'd been awake all night, seated on the sidewalk with her back against the metal railing.

She was in agony. Pain consumed her, sinking its malevolent teeth into her knees, her hips, her ankles, her back. Her slightest movement precipitated intense, searing torment. She focused as best she could on regulating her breathing and staying absolutely still, for only by remaining motionless could she avoid triggering the pain. The soldiers had been barking orders through megaphones at the people lining up to get on buses parked along the broad plaza. Men and women of all ages dragged sacks and garbage bags full of their worldly possessions, and sleeping children lay limp and heedless across those bulky bags. Soldiers shepherded them from one place to another and forced them to move their possessions. The people did as they were told, submissive as sheep.

Nana didn't want to leave NOLA. She wanted to go to her house. She could endure discomfort and wait for the electricity to start working again; she could stay busy scrubbing away the mud. She would dry things out. In her time at the stadium, she'd heard all kinds of tales about what Katrina had done to New

Orleans. But Treme was a solid, well-built quartier, and its sturdy houses had come through earlier storms unharmed. No, she wasn't going to leave her city. She would sit right here until somebody with some clout told her she could go back home. Exhausted and inert, she took her last two pills; they stuck to her palate and eventually dissolved into a bitter mess. Her mouth was so swollen and her tongue so dry that she couldn't even swallow.

A young man in a Red Cross jumpsuit approached her. "Are you alone, ma'am?"

She tried to answer but no words came. Instead of speaking, she broke down and started crying. She'd lapsed into crying jags on and off through the night, but they hadn't done her any good. Embattled and surrounded, she was as determined to survive as ever, but she was so terribly tired. She didn't have the strength to react. She was appalled to find herself an old woman, drained of energy, unable even to talk.

The young man handed her a bottle of water, but she couldn't lift a hand to accept it. He loosened the cap, placed it in her lap, and moved on. When she eventually stopped sobbing, she lifted the bottle and drank, careful to take tiny sips. She felt better immediately. Such a damn thing—she hadn't even realized she was dehydrated! She finished the water, set the bottle on the ground, and then, clinging to the metal railing, struggled inch by painful inch to her feet.

She hurt all over, and her head was spinning. She nearly lost her balance, so she tightened her grasp on the railing. If she fell, she'd break a bone or worse, and then she'd die like a poor old turtle left upside down to dry out in the sun.

Nana hung on the railing for more than an hour before working up the courage to cross the crowded plaza to where the lines for the buses were forming. Maybe somebody over there could tell her something. Step by step, squinting against the intense sunlight, she set out. She clenched her jaw. Her vision blurred. She was dizzy, nauseated, and in pain.

"Nana!" someone shouted.

Nana kept moving forward, unable to stop.

"Nana, it's me!"

She managed to halt. Her old eyes, afflicted by the light and burning with misery, opened wide.

Bobby hugged her so hard she lost her balance, but he held her up. "Oh, Nana, I'm so sorry, I couldn't get here till now. Nana, Mama Seletha died yesterday. I don't even know where they gonna take her or when we gonna have a funeral." His voice was broken and exhausted, hoarse and unrecognizable. He gestured toward the stadium. "I looked all over for you in there. I thought maybe they took you out with the first buses."

"Bobby, let's go home."

Bobby's face was grief stricken. "Nana, the house is gone. The flood went all the way up to the upstairs floors in Treme. They ain't no neighborhood left. It all washed away."

She tried to negotiate. "But the water goes down. It always goes down after the storms."

"Nana, the levees broke and the water gonna stay right where it is. They ain't even any way to get there, 'less you got a boat."

Nana was distraught but she refused to be defeated. She couldn't imagine her little house underwater, her kitchen obliterated, the album of clippings she'd left on the table washed away . . .

"Nana, it's over. We got to go."

"But maybe the storm gonna give my things back . . ."

"Storms don't give nothing back, Nana, they take and take, till everything gone."

She broke into sobs again and pressed her face into the young man's chest. He held her with great tenderness. Gradually, comforting her the whole way, he guided her toward the place where thousands still stood in line, waiting for the buses that would take them away from their homes, many of them forever.

The plaza around the Superdome was filled with distress. Amaia saw thousands of people standing in the beating sun, all looking around with no idea of what they were seeking.

The stifling heat intensified the stench of body odor and mold. The damp bundles people were hauling stank. So did Amaia's clothes. She felt the fabric stiffen as it dried against her skin. Their feet sank deep into the muck as they approached the structure.

Angry shouts in the crowd brought her out of her reverie. The people had been waiting for hours, and only six buses had departed that morning, all for Baton Rouge. Thousands waited to be transported, to be taken anywhere at all.

Ten buses drove up at about six o'clock in the evening. People roused themselves, got up, and pushed toward the loading area, pressing the dense crowd already there against the barriers the National Guard had installed. Heated arguments broke out as people disputed places in line. The soldiers guarding the buses watched blank faced and didn't intervene.

Amaia had asked around, only to find that no log or register had been kept. It was impossible to determine the whereabouts of any individual. So much for Dupree's request, and she was beginning to lose hope for herself and Charbou. "It'll be days before we get out of here!" She was dismayed by the spectacle, the sluggish arrivals and departures of clearly inadequate numbers of buses, the understandable anger of those left standing.

Charbou lit up, looking into the distance at a uniformed police officer talking with the soldiers. "I know that cop. Wait here." He dashed off toward the far end of the plaza, not waiting for a reply.

He came back right away, grabbed Amaia's hand, and pulled her to the far end of the access road. "These buses are going to Houston," he explained. "They're more or less shifting refugees from the Superdome to the Astrodome in Houston. My friend says we should go around to the back. They're giving priority to the most vulnerable—the sick, the elderly, and families with children. Once they get a bus almost full, I can get you on board. People will get mad when they realize you weren't in line. Don't say a thing. Just put your head down and climb in. Don't engage with anybody."

She stopped short and dropped his hand. He took a few more steps, carried by his own inertia, then came back to her.

"But what about you?" Amaia demanded, even though she knew the answer. She'd seen it in his eyes that morning when they were splashing toward the Superdome.

Charbou had helped a man wading along the street with two tiny children in his arms and a small boy walking beside him. A woman behind them stumbled and fell headlong into the water. When Charbou helped her up, Amaia saw that she looked like Oceanetta. Charbou was shaken by the resemblance.

"She'll be fine," he'd told Amaia, referring to his aunt. "Old girl's tough as nails and resourceful." He'd marked his words with a decisive nod, but Amaia knew he was boiling with anger, deeply affected by what was happening to his city.

Charbou surveyed the chaos reigning at the Superdome plaza. "I can't leave, Amaia."

"But . . ."

"It won't be easy to get you on a bus. Wrangling two seats would be practically impossible."

"That's not the reason," she contradicted him.

"No," he admitted. "It's not just that. I swore to protect my city, and now bastards are shooting at innocent people and thousands are still trapped. Right there in the Superdome, men have been beaten to death. NOLA is going to pieces. If I get on a bus, I'll be a rat abandoning a sinking ship."

She reached out and covered his mouth with her hand. He kissed her fingers and then took her hand between his. "I got to stay. This is my home. I'm a New Orleans cop, and I can't leave my people defenseless. And you got no time to lose. The only way you'll ever catch him is by getting there ahead of him. We don't know if that's even possible, but you have to try."

She nodded, understanding.

"Go. Track him down. Take him out."

"Like a bloodhound?" she suggested, trying to make light of it.

"You're no bloodhound. You're my supercop."

They went around the rear of the bus, where the police officer was waiting. He beckoned to them.

Two armed soldiers were posted at the rear door as another pair worked their way down the waiting line, choosing priority evacuees. One approached Bobby and Nana. He saw Bobby was holding her up. "Is that your mama?"

Bobby nodded.

"You two get on the bus."

A chorus of protest broke out. The soldier ignored it and continued down the line.

Bobby staggered forward carrying Nana. At the bus door, another soldier gestured toward a pile where people had abandoned the bundles and plastic bags they'd dragged across the city for days.

"No more than one small item per person," the soldier ordered. "Take your documents, your medicines, only the most essential things. They'll give you everything else you need when you get to Houston." Bobby turned to show the little pack hanging behind him. The soldier checked it quickly and with a jerk of his head sent them on board.

Amaia saw transparent plastic sacks filled with photographs, some still in their frames, kids' toys, stuffed animals. Black-and-white images burst into her mind. She shuddered and shook her head, trying to clear it of those blurry black-and-white photographs of Nazis forcing Polish Jews to abandon their possessions in the Kraków ghetto.

Amaia turned to Charbou. "My pistol! I can't identify myself; Lenx might be in line, maybe even on the bus. Even if he isn't, when I tell them I'm FBI, I'll have a hell of a time explaining later why I didn't ask for help or use military channels to contact Quantico. I can't give up my gun."

Charbou's expression was earnest. "He won't take it from you."

"How can you be sure? He's searching everyone they let on the bus."

"Just look at him," Charbou said. "He's a young guy, pretty much a kid playing soldier. He doesn't know if he's in the USA or Afghanistan; it's all the same to him. He's treating these people who've lost everything like scum. And then look at you—white girl, pretty, and he's going to make you ride in a bus full of black folks. Give me your ballistic vest, and maybe he won't even notice."

Appalled, she stared at him. "But what are you saying?"

He was deadly serious. "Do what you need to do. And don't let him take your weapon."

She turned to study the people in line. A woman was approaching the bus, held up by her teenage sons. She was weeping bitterly.

One of the soldiers peered at her. "What you crying for, ma'am? We're rescuing you."

She lifted her head and stared him in the eye. "That really what you think, son?"

An hour before midnight, one of the soldiers motioned to the policeman, who signaled her to get on the bus. Charbou grabbed her by the waist and quickly kissed her. "Go, supercop. Go get him!"

She returned the kiss, pressed herself against him, pulled away, and hurried to the bus without looking back. Her money, cards, and badge were carefully tucked away, but as Amaia had feared, the soldier saw the pistol holstered at her belt. "Miss, you can't get on the bus carrying a weapon."

"I have a permit," she murmured, doing her best not to call attention to their exchange.

"That doesn't change things. Those are the regs. No weapons. You have to leave it here."

She shut her eyes and then—feeling as low as she ever had in her life—she opened them, looked into his eyes, and pleaded in a whisper, "Listen, I'm all alone. Two times they nearly raped me, and this was what saved me." She waved a hand toward the worn faces of sleeping passengers pressed against the windows. "I can't go in there without protection."

The soldier looked in the direction she was pointing. Two seconds passed, and they seemed like an eternity. Then he looked away and waved her on board. Amaia stepped up and took an aisle seat, the only one left. She scanned the crowd outside and caught a glimpse of Charbou just as the bus pulled away.

He raised one hand and kept it high until the bus disappeared from sight.

The woman sitting in front of Amaia reached into her blouse and took out a photo. She held it up so the young man beside her could see it. The image was of a teenage girl with dark eyes and long, curly hair; a girl seated beside her, younger, was looking up at her adoringly. Both were smiling. The elderly woman kissed the photo and began to weep.

"It's all gonna be all right," he consoled her. "You gonna be with me, and I can take care of you till we come back home."

"Promise me that," the old woman begged.

"I promise you, we gonna come back home."

Amaia shut her eyes.

The trip to Houston took six hours. Registration and accommodation at the Astrodome took another two. She walked out then and, in twenty minutes, found a taxi. The driver told her the car rental agencies had no more vehicles but took her to a used-car lot operated by a friend of his. On the strength of her FBI badge and still valid Massachusetts driver's license, the owner agreed to a one-way lease at an exorbitant rate, provided she deposited the equivalent of ten days' rental and returned the car to his brother-in-law's lot in East Austin.

The three-year-old Lexus had no navigation system, but he told her all she had to do was get on Highway 290 and follow it to Austin.

Three hours later, as she was approaching the capital, she stopped at a service station to buy an Austin map. It turned out that the address Landis had given her wasn't in Austin proper but in Lakeway, a municipality twenty miles west.

It was almost noon when Amaia pulled up before an impressive two-story house on a residential street just three blocks from the town center. She got out, surveyed the carefully landscaped yard, and noticed oil stains on the concrete driveway in front of the vast garage. It was obvious that someone regularly left an automobile parked outside, but the car wasn't there now. She stepped into the yard to take a closer look.

A woman pushing a baby carriage passed along the sidewalk and went up to the house next door. Amaia was glad she'd made herself more or less presentable in the gas station bathroom and put her blond hair up in a ponytail. Her blouse was relatively presentable, much more so than her stiff, stained trousers. She hoped the Lexus she'd rented in Houston would help vouch for her.

"They're not home!"

"Oh, hello—I was coming to visit Mrs. Davis. I promised Natalie I'd come by before she had her baby. I just drove a whole bunch of miles to see her, because I wanted to surprise her with a present."

That was the technique—provide details only a close friend would know and information that would explain her obvious fatigue.

The neighbor swallowed it. She picked up her baby, left the stroller by her front porch, and smiled as she walked to the fence between the two properties. Amaia was grateful the woman couldn't come any closer, considering that her trousers still smelled of muck.

"Oh, so I get to share the good news! Natalie's still in the hospital. She had a cesarean the day before yesterday!"

Amaia smiled automatically and realized the operation must have taken place just shortly after her conversation with the doctor. "Oh, heavens! But I thought she was supposed to go in this afternoon to be induced!"

"Well, that's how it goes; Mother Nature has her own way of doing things. The first birth is usually the hardest, and later ones go a lot quicker. My Jeremy got here a week early, didn't you, darling?" She kissed her baby.

"All right, then! Would you happen to know where Thomas and Michelle are?" she tried. "I think Mr. Davis is on a trip." She was sure that a sharp-eyed neighbor would know if he'd returned.

"Yes, that's how it is, that job of his. The children are with Catherine, Natalie's mother. She came to stay and help out with the new little one. I saw them leaving for the hospital this morning."

"Do you happen to know if the baby's a boy or a girl?" Amaia headed for her Lexus. "I'd like to buy the right color balloons at least."

"A boy, but you know, it really didn't matter to them. It was more important for the baby to get here safe and sound. After all, they already have the other lovely two."

"She's at Seton Medical Center, isn't she?"

"That's right."

Before turning the key in the ignition, Amaia lowered the car window. "Please, if Robert turns up, don't say anything; I want to surprise them all at the hospital!"

The neighbor nodded, smiled, and gave her a little wave.

It took Amaia almost half an hour to get to the hospital. She hadn't taken into account the possibility of an earlier birth, and she was praying there was no way Lenx could have found out. She went to the front desk. "I'm here to see Mrs. Natalie Davis. She was scheduled to give birth today, but it seems things went quicker than expected. By almost forty-eight hours!"

The receptionist's fingers clattered across the keyboard. "Mrs. Davis and the baby have already been discharged."

"But that can't be! I came here straight from their house, where I heard her mother and the children left this morning to visit her here."

"Hold on just a minute." She telephoned the maternity ward for a quick consultation, nodded, hung up, and confirmed the news. "You're right, her family did visit this morning. They left together about an hour ago."

Amaia spun about and raced out of the hospital.

75

Inattention

Elizondo
Friday, September 2, 2005

Engrasi left the funeral home. She shouldn't have come, but no one was going to keep her from saying farewell to her brother—not Rosario or anyone else. She was forced to put up with the disgusting spectacle of Rosario playing the bereaved widow. By the time Flora and Rosaura came to speak to her, she'd already decided to leave.

"*Ama* is having a terrible time, she's suffering so much," Rosaura exclaimed. "You have no idea, Aunt Engrasi." She burst into tears. "Oh, Auntie, maybe it's better for you to hear it from us before somebody else tells you!"

Flora spoke up. "*Ama* left your name off the list of family members in the obituary."

Engrasi saw Rosario slyly swivel around in the front pew to watch as Engrasi crossed the room to check the board where the obituaries were posted. And it was true; though she was Juan's only sister, her name wasn't listed with the rest of the family, which included even cousins and distant relatives.

Flora tried to explain it away. "Please, please, don't be upset, Auntie! You know how she is, and with *Aita* dying, she's acting even more bizarre. She's taking it a lot harder than we expected."

Ros hugged her. "Auntie, you have every right to be upset, and on any other day, I'd let the two of you have it out, but today we're begging you not to get into an argument. We loved our *aita*, and we don't want a big fight to spoil his funeral. That shouldn't be how everybody remembers him."

"Don't bother your heads about it," she said. She departed without another word, leaving her nieces both dismayed and relieved. Engrasi had no stomach for this. She'd come back later, once this circus was finished.

She was plunged in thought on her way home, feeling unhappier with every step she took.

How foolish she'd been! Amaia had refused to come back, and Engrasi had almost convinced herself the girl had made the wrong choice. Engrasi hadn't said anything, of course, for she'd taken Amaia's side years before and would always support her niece, whatever happened. Secretly, she'd feared the day would come when Amaia would regret not having been here to say farewell to her father, on this day when reconciliation was no longer impossible. Engrasi realized now that by attending the funeral, she herself had made the wrong choice. Her name wasn't the only one missing. Amaia's name wasn't listed either, as if she'd never existed, a ghost from the past who'd been wiped from memory.

Engrasi crossed the river and stopped where Amaia used to linger, next to the sign with the name of the bridge: Muniartea. The cool, sweet, early-September breeze off the river stirred her hair and disengaged a strand from her loosely gathered bun.

No one should have to die in late summer, not on a day this beautiful. A proper script would call for a protagonist to pass away in the depths of winter. She turned toward the former Calle del Sol, which merited its name that day. At home she closed her front door behind her, then sank down on the stairs and wept. She was unable to find the energy to do more.

She'd loved her brother. They'd often had their differences, and sometimes they'd gotten furious at one another, but that was what happened with people bound by deep affection. Everyone who knew Juan agreed he'd been a fine person, a good man. Of course, those who spoke of him that way hadn't a clue about his other attributes, those which she knew all too well. Sometimes it wasn't enough to be good; one had to be righteous, and her brother Juan hadn't had the courage to mete out justice. He'd allowed his own good nature to contaminate him and turn him into a tame, indulgent plaster saint. He resolutely avoided confrontation at all costs in order to preserve a fictitious stability.

Juan hadn't had it easy. Amaia's prolonged silence had hurt him terribly. His favorite daughter was the sweet child who'd spent so many hours at the bakery watching him work. The child had often danced the "Emperor Waltz" with him, her little feet planted firmly on his shoes. She'd drawn bright-red rounded hearts for him, as all daughters who adore their *aita* should do.

Amaia hadn't always been completely estranged. She'd written to him often in the early years of her exile, her childish letters full of scribbled hearts and declarations of love. Engrasi showed them to Juan but kept custody of them so as to make absolutely sure Rosario never got her hands on the letters. Later, in her teenage years, the letters had become less frequent, and after Amaia went to college, they'd ceased entirely. Amaia had returned to Spain from the United States two years earlier and joined the Pamplona police force. She'd lived in Pamplona since then but had never returned to Baztán or contacted her father. Those had been difficult years. Bedridden at home and then later in the hospital, her brother had moaned, "Amaia isn't coming back, is she?"

Engrasi had been so grieved to see him that hollowed out by his illness. She'd been tempted to lie and spin out some pious falsehood. But she'd made it a point of pride never to lie to Juan. She'd always told him the truth, even though sometimes it caused her anguish. He needed to hear it from her, because good-natured persons like him frequently deceive themselves. They console themselves with pious crap to help them endure an otherwise unbearable existence.

Engrasi wasn't in the world to serve as his fairy godmother. Even when they were children, she'd worked to keep her brother's feet on the ground, and she wasn't about to change just because the end was in sight.

"Amaia won't be coming," she confirmed.

He'd pursed his lips unhappily. "Does she know . . . ?"

"Yes, she knows."

"Will you give her a message from me?"

She didn't like that. "Juan . . ."

"Tell her I've always loved her, and I beg her to forgive me."

"Juan, the fact that a father loves his daughter is not the kind of message you should be sending from beyond the grave."

"But you will tell her?"

"I will, but not for you. For her. And I won't push her too hard to forgive you. Amaia has been trying to forgive you all her life. Her heart has been set on it, and for a while, I thought she'd managed it. But forgiving, like forgetting, isn't an act of will, Juan. A person can't just decide. Your girl's a survivor, and the incredible strength that's kept her alive won't—can't—compromise with the truth."

She'd sat with him for hours, recalling their childhood together, singing old songs and recounting family stories, right up until he drifted off. After that, in his final hours, Rosario had refused to leave his side and hadn't allowed anyone else to accompany him.

The phone rang. Engrasi left her place on the stairs to answer it.

It was Ignacio. "Engrasi, were you at the funeral home? A neighbor said she saw you arrive but you weren't there for long."

"That's right. Rosario left me off the list of family members in the obituary. She excluded Amaia as well."

"That was wicked."

"Yes, well, that's nothing new. I decided it was better to leave than give her the satisfaction of heaping one misery on top of another. Losing my brother was more than enough to deal with. I'll go back later. The undertaker agreed to call me as soon as they leave."

"Well, you weren't there very long, so I guess you didn't have time to see the people who attended."

"Well, no."

"There were some women, not from the town, who kept close to Rosario. At first I thought they might have been her sisters from San Sebastián . . ."

"Her sisters cut her off completely years ago."

"Right, you told me that, and that's why I took a closer look. And . . ."

"Yes?"

"Engrasi, I saw the woman who tried to snatch Amaia thirteen years ago. The she-wolf."

Engrasi held her tongue long enough to choose her words, because asking Ignacio if he was sure of something could be taken as a grave insult. A man of few words, he never wasted his breath, and his every utterance was decisive. Even knowing that, Engrasi took the risk. "Ignacio, are you sure?"

"As sure as I know God exists."

"It was a long time ago."

"Thirteen years, but that makes no difference, Engrasi. And when I say she was the same, I don't just mean that she has aged well. You'd swear she's the same age now as she was that day."

Engrasi lapsed into silence as she tried to grasp what he was saying. "Ignacio, I believe you," she said at last. "But there has to be some explanation, don't you think? Maybe she's that woman's daughter."

"That's what I thought at first. But I went up to express my condolences to Rosario, just to get a closer look. The woman recognized me, just as I recognized her."

"Did she say anything?"

"No, but she smiled at me. Engrasi, the sight of those teeth was burned forever into my memory. Little baby teeth, like rat's teeth."

The funeral director telephoned at ten o'clock to tell her everyone had left. She waited until half past, using the time to fix herself a thermos of coffee. She wasn't intending to sleep. Salazar family tradition dictated that the dead mustn't be left alone on their first night. The custom was ancient, its origins lost in the mists of time. Engrasi considered herself a modern woman, but her mind was large enough to encompass traditions, including the conviction that the soul does not immediately depart from the mortal remains. She viewed dying as a process. At first, the vital force ebbs away and the guiding spirit begins to disengage, proof that death is approaching. After that come hours of bewilderment, difficult and gloom ridden, until the soul at last sheds its receptacle like a butterfly leaving its cocoon.

Pray for us sinners, now and at the hour of our death. It's telling that in all religious traditions there exists a prayer or ritual appealing for protection during the process. One isn't born in an instant, nor does one die in an instant. Arrival and departure are both processes that must be respected. Like the multitudes of women who preceded her, Engrasi would watch over her beloved dead.

"You just have to do what you have to," she told herself, gathering courage before she left the house.

Juan dead was hardly Juan at all. Dressed in a suit she'd never seen him wear, he looked pensive and terribly serious, not like himself at all. Only in his lips did she catch a hint of that charming, sincere, and childlike smile she'd always loved.

She heard a whishing sound behind her. Like a gathering wind.

Rosario.

Engrasi turned very slowly and there she was. Dressed in deep mourning from head to foot, Rosario was the embodiment of elegance. She'd stopped just inside the swinging doors that were still slightly stirring. Beyond the moving doors, Engrasi caught sight of the dark silhouettes of Rosario's escorts.

Rosario's smile, practically a leer, was inappropriate considering they were in a funeral home and her dead husband was lying there in his coffin.

"All right, then," Rosario said. "Where is she?"

Engrasi took a deep breath of air heavy with the smell of funeral home flowers. "Where's who?"

Rosario refused to be provoked. "You know who."

Engrasi forced herself to rise to the occasion. She smiled. "Did you seriously expect to find Amaia here?"

"I know she's here. That little girl can't keep from coming to say goodbye to her *aitatxo*."

Engrasi remained quiet, trying to evaluate and understand the weight and importance of each move, each act, and each word. "She's not here, Rosario, and she's not coming back. And I intend to outlive you to make sure that when she does at last return to this valley for a burial, it'll be for yours."

A hateful grimace twisted Rosario's mouth. Engrasi could have sworn that Rosario gulped and panted like an animal before snarling, "Don't give me ideas, Engrasi. It wouldn't be the first time we gutted her guard dog."

Engrasi felt her knees weaken. She clutched the edge of her brother's coffin.

"You whore!" she lashed back, trembling with fury. "I'm no dog. If you come after me or the girl, I'll tear your head off. I make that vow on the sacred memory of my brother, who was kind and good-hearted enough for the both of us. I'm not Juan. I've got all the macho brutality he lacked, along with enough psychological resilience to live with a clear conscience after murdering you. I will kill you, Rosario, and I won't lose a wink of sleep over it."

She was trembling like a leaf exposed to a blast of wind, and she kept herself upright only by holding on to her brother's coffin, but her words burst forth with more than enough force and conviction to convey her threat.

Rosario's sneer vanished. She jerked her hands and head ever so slightly in some kind of nervous tic. She turned and pushed the swinging doors. The shadows awaiting in the gloom closed around her.

A single savage scream echoed in the exterior hall. After that, nothing. A slight draft, a breath of wind; then the exterior door slammed shut, and only emptiness remained.

Engrasi exhaled and inhaled deeply as she tried to control her tremors. She looked at her brother.

"Juan, I don't know if I ever mentioned it, but your wife is a witch. A real, honest-to-God witch."

76

METALLIC BALLOONS

Lakeway, Texas
Saturday, September 3, 2005

Martin Lenx, who'd been Robert Davis for almost two decades, pulled to the curb in front of his home, just as Brad Nelson had done a few days earlier in Florida. Like Nelson, he took some time to study the front of the house. But unlike the policeman, he wasn't plagued by doubt. He wasn't nervous or afraid of being rejected. He was a bit tired, that was all. The bus out of New Orleans had taken forever to get to Baton Rouge, and it had been no simple matter to find a car to rent for his return home. He ached to go inside, take a long hot shower, and sleep for ten hours. But he couldn't permit himself those luxuries. He'd planned everything: the timing, the words to chant, his return, the birth, the trip home from the hospital, everybody together in the living room, asking Michelle to play something on the violin . . . But the unexpected early arrival of his son had thrown it all into high gear. God was giving him a push. He leaned forward, just as Nelson had, his arms against the steering wheel to support himself. And he, too, tried to pray.

But he couldn't.

His wife's car was parked in the driveway again, and he saw the ugly oil stain under the rear of the vehicle.

He'd told her a million times not to leave her car there. Natalie had been sloppy and negligent for quite some time now. Martin hadn't wanted to accept the evidence of his own eyes, and he'd told her how to do things until he was blue in the face, for God's sake! They had a three-car garage! Did she even understand English anymore? And after she got pregnant again, she'd really let herself go.

It used to be that she would take the trouble to pull the car inside, at least when she knew he was returning from a trip. Okay, he had to admit that she wasn't expecting him back today. He'd managed to phone her at the hospital, and after pretending to be sorry he'd been away and saying how wonderfully happy he was about the baby, he'd promised he'd get back the next day.

Martin ruefully shook his head as he contemplated his wife's car. A sardonic smile spread across his face.

She'd pulled it forward on the driveway a bit, not much, just enough to leave almost enough space for his mother-in-law's SUV, which sat with its rear wheels on the sidewalk. If this continued, before long they'd have two oil stains instead of one.

The sun reflected off the metallic balloons crowded against the back window of the SUV. "It's a boy!" was printed across their fat faces. He had another son, a new one, and that fact, far from pleasing him, just proved to him that God was putting him to the test again.

Martin Lenx leaned over and unlatched the briefcase on the floor in front of the passenger seat. He took out his revolver. Stretching his legs and lifting his butt off the seat, he tucked the gun under his belt, hidden by his shirt and perfectly tailored jacket—*Now slightly rumpled,* he criticized himself. He used the linen square from the breast pocket of his jacket to wipe his glasses, then he folded it and carefully returned it to its place. He ran a hand through his crew-cut hair and got out of the car.

He didn't go to the front. He went around the house to the kitchen instead. He had the key in hand, but there was no need for it; yet again, Thomas or Michelle had left the door unlocked. He snorted in disgust and drew air sharply through his nostrils.

Martin closed the door carefully behind him and threw the deadbolt. He wasn't about to risk a surprise visit from the woman next door.

There was the distinct smell of baby, even in the kitchen. He was surprised by that confirmation that the extraordinary event had taken place. The scent signaled the arrival of a tiny new creature, a real miracle. At any other time, it would have been a promise of fulfillment. The new arrival would normally have been a holy gift.

The moment Lenx had learned his son was in utero, he recognized the divine omen. That herald of the Last Days had lifted the scales that had covered Martin's eyes for so many years. Anguished, he'd asked himself if this was to be the inevitable pattern of his life. Perhaps he really was cursed. Victimized by his family's many sins, he had been forced to pray for their souls. But when God closes a door, he opens a window. Martin Lenx knew what he had to do: start over. Next time everything would be better.

He heard his family whispering in the living room. Perhaps the baby was sleeping. He took out his revolver, held it behind him, crossed the hall, and stepped into the living room.

The backs of his children's heads were visible above the U-shaped sofa, which was facing away from him. They were on either side of his mother-in-law. Natalie sat across from them. Totally captivated by her newborn son, she didn't even look up as he lifted the gun and aimed it at his mother-in-law's head. That was the required order; she had to be the first to die.

He heard the click of a pistol being cocked behind him.

Amaia pointed her gun at his head. "Martin Lenx, this is the FBI. Drop your weapon and raise your hands!"

Martin grimaced in displeasure.

Catherine, Michelle, and Thomas scrambled away from him in terror and huddled around Natalie and the baby on the far end of the sofa. The baby bawled and so did his mother-in-law. Natalie trembled violently, but the strongest reaction came from his older son, who planted himself in front of the others and glared defiantly at his father.

Little Michelle exclaimed, "Daddy, what's happening?" She could hardly get the words out.

Martin looked at them. He smiled sweetly. "Nothing, darling, nothing at all."

Amaia was outraged. "Shut up, Lenx, and do what I say!"

Don't let him talk to them!

"Seems there's been a mistake. My name is Robert Davis, and I don't know anyone named—"

"That's enough! Not another word!"

The women whimpered. The girl and the newborn shrieked and wept.

"Reassure your family. Now!"

"Just huddle down, darlings, like quiet little mice," he said. "This will be over soon."

The teenage son was the only one to disobey.

Keep calm. You've almost got him.

"Martin Lenx, drop your gun and raise your hands. This is your last warning!"

Martin didn't drop his gun, but he slowly raised his arms and turned to face her.

No, no! This is going wrong!

Martin was moving—*He shouldn't be moving*—he was turning; he wanted to see her.

Martin was fifty-five but he was slim and fit. She could tell that he was trying to appraise the situation to see if she had backup.

"Don't move!" she ordered him, holding her pistol outstretched in both hands and pointing it at his face. The usually reassuring feel of the grip brought her no comfort. She'd practiced hefting the two-pound Glock a thousand times, but suddenly it seemed a dead weight. Perspiration ran down her ribs and between her breasts.

Martin was an expert at assessing risk. He had a keen understanding of probability. He wouldn't have managed to stay invisible for eighteen years if he'd been stupid or reckless. He saw there was no one else. If there had been, they'd already have shown themselves. She was alone, and judging from her voice, she was young, almost certainly a rookie. Her body smelled of stress and something distasteful and pungent . . . What was it?

Amaia saw that the teenage boy was going to be trouble. He stood poised and challenging, glowering at his father with fierce hostility. The anger couldn't be new. That distrust and scorn comes alive as boys become men and cease to be blinded by infantile adoration and unconditional love. There's a lot of talk about parents' love for their children, but no one loves as unreservedly as a child. And for that same reason, no one is as judgmental as a teenager.

The young man spoke. "I knew it all along. You really want to kill us, don't you, *Daddy*?" The "Daddy" cut like the lash of a whip.

By shifting his position, Lenx forced her to move. She wouldn't be able to handcuff him unless she was behind him.

Handcuff him? Are you kidding? He's still armed! He hasn't dropped his gun!

"Martin Lenx, drop your weapon. I won't warn you again!"

"Daddy!" the boy insisted.

"Be quiet, Thomas," Lenx answered, turning slowly, this time toward the boy.

"I'm not going to be quiet!" the boy snapped. He took a step toward his father.

"Thomas, please!" his mother pleaded in terror.

But the boy took a second step. His sister and grandmother reached out for him, their extended arms waving like tendrils as they sought to restrain him.

"Is that why you go into Michelle's room at night?"

"Shut up!" Lenx commanded him, now facing his son. Only the sofa separated them.

"Did he come into your room?" the wife exclaimed, looking at their daughter. Natalie's plain, almost-ugly face lit for a moment with a particular beauty. Amaia saw the clear resemblance between mother and son.

The girl sniveled and nodded unhappily. "He scared me . . ."

The wife's face twisted in disgust. The son's expression was one of condemnation.

"For God's sake!" Lenx exclaimed, annoyed. "She's my daughter. I would never touch her! You people are even more perverted than I imagined, if you think such a thing." He lowered his arms and looked down at the pistol as if realizing for the first time it was in his hand.

"Lenx, raise your hands! *Now!*" Amaia shouted, ready to fire.

But Lenx was staring at his teenage son, as if they were the only ones in the room.

"Oh, no," Thomas said. "You wouldn't lay a hand on her. But nothing would keep you from murdering us all. I've known that for a long time now."

"Shut up!"

"You killed the Andrews family just for practice. That's why Mic's violin disappeared."

"Silence! Thomas, shut your mouth!"

"You don't love us," Thomas declared without emotion, as if simply reporting a fact.

You don't love me, complained the tiny girl in Amaia's mind.

"Enough!" snarled Lenx, growing more furious.

Enough! her mother told her, slowly coming closer.

"You've *never* loved any of us," Thomas said.

You've never loved me, nine-year-old Amaia said.

"I've never loved my family?"

He's going to murder his son, just the way she was going to kill you. He's going to shoot him point blank.

"I said put down your gun!" Amaia shouted, moving to the side so her pistol was in Lenx's line of sight.

Martin Lenx heard her, and her voice returned him to reality. Instantly he turned and fired.

His shot caught her in the chest with tremendous force. She toppled over backward, landing half in the living room, half in the hallway. Confused but still conscious, she heard shouting. In the commotion, she was vaguely surprised to realize she felt no pain; the sensation was more like drowning. She opened her mouth, desperately seeking air to counter the expanding emptiness within her. And that's when the pain came. She gasped in terror and looked down. A small dark spot, no larger than a coin, had blossomed on her chest exactly where—she knew it with total certainty—her heart was located.

This is shock from the impact. Shock. You've read about shock a thousand times, stop thinking about the bullet in your body.

She tried to lift her hand to the wound, and she realized she was still clutching the Glock. It occurred to her, as if in a dream, that her firearms instructor would have been proud. "Always keep a tight grip on your weapon, as if they're going to try to take it away from you," Salvador had lectured her on the firing range in Pamplona.

What a strange thought to have while dying. With her other hand she touched the point of impact, dimly regretting she'd left her ballistic vest in New Orleans.

Yelling. She heard yelling somewhere far away. The sofa blocked her view, but she heard the son shouting for help. Gasping, she leaned on her forearm. She held her breath because with every gasp, the pain returned, a pain so intense her vision dimmed and she almost passed out. But she couldn't do that. *Never give up, that's the second rule when you get shot.* Clutching the pistol, she dragged herself back into the room, giving in to the urge to glance at the floor where she'd been standing when Lenx gunned her down. There was no blood. The slug hadn't exited her body. In her delirium, she had a vision of a metal round lodged next to her heart in a tangle of destroyed tissue and blasted arteries.

Get hold of yourself. You're in shock.

Her ears roared with the wild pumping of her little roebuck's heart.

If you give into the panic, your heart will go wild and you'll have a heart attack, and after that . . .

She struggled to lift a hand to her wound. She pressed it, and pain shot through her. But instantly the pain lessened.

Amaia wormed her way across the floor, pushing herself forward with her elbows and heels, spurred by the boy's shouts and the women's screams. She sensed the world darkening and ebbing away. The huge surge of adrenaline constricted her vision and imposed a partial blindness that was like peering through an ancient telescope.

She reached the sofa. She needed to get to her feet, but she knew she had to keep pressure on the chest wound. She put her pistol hand over the back of the sofa and struggled to her knees. Lifting her head was a mistake. The attack of dizziness almost knocked her over. Sweat poured out of her. She knew she couldn't make it to her feet. She advanced on all fours, then leaned on the sofa, dizzy and lurching and resisting the urge to breathe deeply. Inhaling the oxygen she so desperately needed would double her up in pain and make it impossible to regain her vision. Even in her feverish haze, she knew a deep breath would kill her outright.

Lenx was astride his son, holding him down, trying to aim as they struggled for control of the revolver. The mother and sister screamed hysterically. Amaia raised the Glock toward Lenx. In normal circumstances, that would have been the time to squeeze the trigger. But she didn't have a clear shot; she might hit another member of the family. She hunched to the floor, trying to refine her aim, but her straining muscles gave way. She fell forward, next to Lenx, who was still struggling with his son. The baby cried. Amaia gave up on her chest wound and put that hand to the floor for support. A wave of nausea hit her, and her stomach heaved. Unable to raise her pistol, she pushed herself forward, pressed the Glock against Lenx's lower leg, and pulled the trigger.

Martin Lenx howled, thrashed like an animal, and grabbed his exploded calf. He fell to one side, and she saw shattered bone fragments and white tendon tissue bloom in blood like a horrid flower through the hole she'd blasted in his carefully pressed trousers. He dropped his revolver.

Forget the weapon; handcuff him first!

She crawled on top of Lenx, squatted astride him, savagely twisted his arms, and cuffed him. She fumbled blindly in search of the revolver, which Thomas was regarding, transfixed. She jammed it into her own waistband and waved the boy away. Only then, shaken and soaked in sweat, did she collapse next to Lenx.

The family had fled. She heard their voices from somewhere far away. They were calling the Lakeway police. Lenx glared at her, silent, motionless, lying face down with his hands cuffed behind his back. He radiated that moral superiority of his, even covered in blood.

"For the love of God, that stink . . . is piss!" he said, recognizing the stifling reek of ammonia.

Dizzy, gasping, she stared at him. She was about to faint.

"You idiot!" she managed to say. She refused to faint.

He was right. It stank in the room. She raised the hand she'd had pressed to her wound. The blood was as black as a moonless night or a long-dead corpse. That was a bad sign. But her breathing had begun to ease. She pushed aside her blouse, probed the entrance wound, and was astonished by her discovery. With a jerk she pulled out the little goatskin bag, perforated, with a foul black liquid seeping from it. She sniffed it and it filled her nostrils with the disgusting odor of putrefaction and death. The bullet, a dark, copper-colored slug, gleamed in its center like a precious gem in a pool of petroleum waste. Astonished, Amaia touched the bruised and aching spot on her chest. She was unharmed.

She turned toward Lenx and was amazed by the accuracy of her own prediction. His hair was the same, and he wore an unremarkable suit tailored with the same fussy precision as eighteen years earlier. He hadn't even changed the style of glasses he wore, which were now hanging askew from one ear.

A man of fixed habits.

Evil habits.

She spoke. "Martin Lenx, I arrest you for the murders of your mother, your wife, and your children in Madison, Wisconsin, eighteen years ago; for the murders of the Andrews family in Galveston eight months ago; for the murders of at least six families in different locations across the country; and for the attempted murder of your family today in Lakeway, Texas. You have the right . . ." She finished advising him of his Miranda rights and then, with some difficulty, savagely twisted a lamp cord around his thigh to keep him alive. Minutes later, the Lakeway police entered the room.

77

A Regular Guy

Washington, DC
Friday, September 16, 2005

Amaia sat in the visitor's chair in CJIS director Jim Wilson's office, working her way through a pile of statements and case summaries. The director had chosen a navy-blue suit for the occasion. Not a good idea; too little color. Verdon, leaning on the full-length window overlooking Pennsylvania Avenue, was far more impressive than his boss. He had the self-assured air of a military officer. Agent Johnson sat beside Amaia in the other visitor's chair.

Amaia initialed pages and scribbled her signature at the end of each of a dozen documents, put down the ballpoint pen, and glanced over at the packed suitcases she'd left just inside the office door.

The CJIS director followed her gaze. "Are you sure you won't change your mind and stay with us?"

She handed over the documents. "One hundred percent sure."

"I really must insist. It would greatly benefit the Bureau if you'd reconsider our offer and agree to stay."

"My father died in Spain while I was in New Orleans," she said, offering no further explanation. That was the first time she'd put it into words, and perhaps for that reason, it carried sufficient weight and emotion to put an end to the negotiation.

Wilson studied her thoughtfully. He decided she'd turned the Bureau down because she'd been under terrific stress and affected by her father's death. "I understand. Maybe later. But we'll need for you to consult with our forensic psychologists. For them, having a type like Lenx—alive—is a godsend for behavioral analysis."

"Naturally."

Wilson checked her initials on each page and her signature at the end of each document. The shit had hit the fan within the Bureau when the media hailed her as a lone-ranger vigilante. He faced down the critics, emphasizing that the operation had resulted in the apprehension of a killer who'd been on their most-wanted list for a long time. They hadn't even dared to complain that the collar was made by a temporary agent handpicked by Aloisius Dupree for his elite special operations team.

The greatest challenge had been trying to talk her out of returning to Spain. He'd done his best, trying directly and indirectly to impress upon her the vital importance of presenting her to the media as a regular FBI operative.

She'd refused to hear of it, so they made a deal. She'd agreed to appear at the press conference with Johnson, who had his arm still in a sling, and Verdon, the director of the Criminal Investigative Division. In a dark suit with an FBI lapel pin, she was the very image of the no-nonsense professional.

The television at her back now was playing the video of the press conference on a continuous loop.

The arrest of Martin Lenx, dubbed the Family Executioner by the press, was the lead story on news programs, and Amaia knew that a number of producers were trying to dig up enough information for a documentary about the case that had riveted the whole country. There was global interest because of the cold-hearted murder of his first family and his obsession with re-creating every aspect of his former life.

His wives were surprisingly similar. He'd fathered the same number of children, of the same sexes and in the same birth order. He'd glided from a job as an unimpressive office administrator to that of a faceless adjustor at a reinsurance firm. Discreet, formal, and obliging, he was a man of few words, but discriminating and educated.

But what most amazed people was the fact that Martin Lenx hadn't altered his appearance in the least. He continued to wear his hair razor cut and extremely short. He presented himself in the same correct but inexpensive business attire, the same boring ties, even the same style of horn-rimmed glasses. He'd continued attending Lutheran religious services and participating in church activities. He'd even bought and then replaced the same make and model of car.

Director Wilson turned off the video. "Well, Agent Salazar, you'll have plenty of time to watch yourself on television. They'll be talking about you for months: the agent who arrested the most elusive serial killer in recent history. You have plenty to be proud of."

"Thank you, sir, but I was just doing my job."

"Modesty doesn't become you, my dear. Your name will go down in the FBI annals as one of our best agents, the survivor of a point-blank gunshot who arrested a serial murderer of families." He winked. "And all under my command!"

She inhaled—even though deep breaths were still a bit painful—and nodded without comment.

Director Wilson hadn't finished. "When I was informed of your audacious analysis of the case, I told Dupree, 'Brilliance is no excuse for insolence.'"

"I didn't intend to be insolent."

"Don't deny it, Salazar. You can't help it; you just are. But you certainly had the appropriate teacher. What can you tell us about Agent Dupree?"

Amaia nodded slowly, putting her thoughts in order. It was important to keep her narrative straight because she'd already given her version a dozen times, both verbally and in writing, and she'd probably have to do so at least as many times more. "The last time I saw him, Agent Johnson, Detective Charbou, and I were leaving for New Orleans on his orders, because the operations center had reported a crime that matched the modus operandi of Martin Lenx. Agent Dupree was recovering from a heart attack, and Detective Bull stayed with him. A few hours earlier, we'd located the place where girls who had been abducted during the storm were being kept. The girls weren't there, but the evidence we found suggested that a certain Dominic Darrel was involved in their abduction. We believe that Darrel, a go-between, probably took them to Baton Rouge to turn them over. Dupree may have told Detective Bull to follow that trail after we left for New Orleans."

Wilson made a curious gesture as if he were rolling up wool thread in a ball. "Right, yeah, sure, I know all that. Just as you said in your report, same as what

Johnson stated. We don't have a statement from Detective Charbou, because it's been impossible to locate him. Things in New Orleans are still pretty complicated, and communication is down much of the time. But I suspect that if we could contact him, he'd say the same thing."

Amaia looked down for a moment, trying not to remember Charbou declaring he was setting off on his own to serve his city.

Wilson consulted the case file. "Dupree suffered some kind of heart seizure. Can't be exactly sure what kind, of course, because we don't have the medical report or any way to get in touch with the doctors who treated him. Charity Hospital was completely evacuated only days after he was there. But even though Dupree had been admitted to the hospital while assigned to investigate the Composer, he decided to go to the swamp," he read from the report, "'because the boy Jacob Emerit heard the abductors mention the place.'"

"That was Special Agent Dupree's call."

Johnson raised his good hand, asking to be recognized. "The hospital was minimally staffed. They had only about fifteen hours of diesel for the generators. There were no surgeons, and the pharmacy was empty except for a few sedatives and some aspirin. Agent Tucker had just informed us of Brad Nelson's arrest in Florida. We thought the case was closed, and we were trapped in a city that had reverted to the Stone Age. Dupree thought we should pursue the case that had been thrust upon us."

"Right!" Verdon's voice thundered from his place by the window. They'd almost forgotten he was there. "Hurricane Katrina and the New Orleans catastrophe turned into a perfect alibi. No doubt about that! Oh, hold on, excuse me, rewind. Did I say 'alibi'? I meant 'justification.'"

He slowly and deliberately approached the director's desk, letting the silence hang in the air. He stood next to Wilson. "Agent Dupree disappeared, and he's still missing. Can you explain that?"

"Um, well," Amaia said hesitantly, looking at Johnson. "We don't have to remind you how complicated things are down there right now. We had to risk our lives to get out of New Orleans, and Agent Johnson was shot on our way back. Agent Dupree was seriously ill when we left him with Detective Bull and the medicine man in the swamp, the best qualified caretaker we could find."

"And Dupree said he'd return to New Orleans when he recovered," the director prompted them.

"Once it was safe to travel again," Johnson replied. "With all due respect, I don't think those conditions have been met. You have no idea what it's like. The city's getting worse with every passing hour. The place is sheer misery. They keep finding bodies, people who were trapped in their homes when the water rose and others who died of thirst up on the highway overpasses. There's no water, no food, the temperature stays close to a hundred degrees, and snipers are shooting at whatever they want." He indicated his shoulder. "New Orleans is hell on earth right now."

"Confirming exactly what I said," Verdon recapped. "The perfect alibi."

Johnson's sharp sigh filled the office. But an FBI agent wounded on duty could probably expect to be allowed a bit of leeway.

Verdon looked away.

Wilson took up the thread. "The same 'justification' you offered for not getting in contact, not calling for backup, not informing us of your newly discovered suspicions . . ."

Amaia was fed up. These people were at it again with the ridiculous rhetorical games they enjoyed so much, and she'd had enough. She didn't see what they were getting at. They themselves had been intent on drawing up an "official version."

"Are you suggesting our procedures were irregular? Because if you are—"

"Again, with all due respect, Directors," Johnson interrupted her. "There was no proof. We had nothing: No crime scene analysis, no comparative prints, no ballistic evidence, we couldn't compare physical traits, voices, or handwriting, and we had no witnesses and absolutely no technical support. The bodies of his most recent victims are rotting away even now at crime scenes nobody's been able to examine. The technical evidence available to us led Agent Tucker to arrest Nelson, and we lost all communication after that. Assistant Inspector Salazar got to Lenx purely by following her instincts as an investigator; she—and she alone—was the one who tracked him down. She's already reported that the first time she knew for sure Davis was our man was when she got to his house and met his family. Up to that point, there was nothing solid to report. Just as she was speaking with the wife and kids, Lenx arrived, intending to murder them. Thank God Salazar was there, because otherwise, Lenx would be just as invisible today as he was for the last eighteen years."

The senior officials' expressions made it plain they didn't buy a word of it.

Verdon took time to study Johnson and Salazar. "We did manage to locate the Emerit family. Our agents interviewed Jacob Emerit's grandparents at length. The woman insisted that Baron Samedi carried off her granddaughters, her husband shot a zombie, the intruders hurt the old man while trying to rip his heart out of his chest, and one of the agents who came to rescue them collapsed with a heart attack."

Johnson didn't budge. Amaia merely lifted an eyebrow.

"And, of course you've never heard of a criminal gang called Samedi," Director Wilson added.

Amaia angrily shook her head.

Verdon opened the manila folder that lay on the desk and handed Amaia and Johnson copies of a report. "This is from the sheriff in Baton Rouge."

Amaia and Johnson scanned the document as Verdon summarized it. "Yesterday before dawn, Detective Jason Bull from the New Orleans Police Department called for backup at a shooting incident outside the city. The detective later stated he'd gotten there by following the trail of a man suspected as an accessory in the abduction of Bella and Diana Emerit. He'd gotten into difficulties, couldn't locate the man, and then—as if by the grace of God—he happened to witness the delivery of the minors to an armed group that opened fire as soon as he identified himself. He believes he wounded at least one of them. The suspect, Dominic Darrel, and his associates fled. The girls are safe. They're being held for observation at a hospital until their parents can get there."

"Was Agent Dupree with Detective Bull?" Johnson asked.

Verdon gazed steadily at Johnson, his head tilted skeptically to one side. He exhaled fully before replying. "No. The detective said he'd left Dupree in the care of a Cajun medicine man out in the swamp, because Dupree was too weak to travel. The Terrebonne sheriff just reported that the houseboat where this *'traiteur'* was staying apparently sank. The sheriff says it probably went down during Katrina, but it's hard to tell. They didn't find any bodies inside, but the hurricane tide pushed tons of water and muck through there on its way back to the Gulf."

Amaia sighed. "I don't know what to say. I hope Agent Dupree got to safety and you can locate him soon."

"Obviously," Wilson replied.

She dropped the subject. "Are we finished here?"

They gave up, rose, and exchanged handshakes in farewell. Before she could exit the office after Johnson, Verdon stepped forward and blocked her way. “Brilliance or insolence?”

She gave him an angelic smile. “A hunch, that’s all.”

The two senior officials stood in silence after the door closed. The woman’s electric presence hovered in the air.

Wilson was the first to speak. “Maybe it’s just as well she’s leaving. She’d have kept causing problems.”

Verdon gave him an incredulous look. “Are you kidding? Eighteen years, Wilson,” he declared, rubbing his colleague’s face in the FBI’s failure to locate Lenx. “Eighteen!”

Wilson’s lips tightened, a sign he regretted his comment. “No, you’re right. It would have been better to have her on the team. She’s insolent and brilliant, but given enough time, we could’ve put her in her place.”

“Uh-huh. The way we did with Dupree, right?”

EPILOGUE

Pamplona
November 2005

Amaia's mobile phone lit up with an unknown number. She answered it anyway.

Dupree's voice came to her from all the way across the ocean. "Is it already night in Baztán, Salazar?"

Amaia smiled. Then she told him.

A NOTE FROM THE AUTHOR

I began writing this novel on April 16, 2017, in room 105 of the Dauphine Orleans Hotel in New Orleans, where I was staying, and I finished it on July 16, 2019, in the same place.

The headlines appearing in the novel were based on the article "Remembering Hurricane Betsy, a New Orleans Nightmare," written by journalist Mike Scott, in the *Times-Picayune*, May 31, 2017.

The emergency calls cited in the novel are taken from actual calls made to the 911 emergency center when Hurricane Katrina passed through Louisiana.

ACKNOWLEDGMENTS

To the city and good people of New Orleans, to those on the official lists of victims of Hurricane Katrina, and to those who disappeared, for their courage and immense love for NOLA. For standing up to hardship and returning. I've traveled the whole world over, but my home is still in New Orleans.

To Elizondo and the Baztán Valley, the places I return to in my dreams, for inspiring me.

To Manuel Anguita Sánchez, president of the Spanish Society of Cardiology, for our fascinating conversation about broken hearts and creativity.

To Oriol Carús, my guide to New Orleans, for his invaluable assistance.

To the United States Coast Guard, the true heroes of this story.

To the firefighters, the New Orleans police, the Louisiana State Police, and the emergency services, for never giving up.

To the Presbytère museum, near the Cabildo in New Orleans, and its permanent exhibit about Hurricane Katrina.

To the New Orleans daily newspaper the *Times-Picayune*, which was a great resource for writing this novel.

To the Judicial Police of Navarra for their courteous attention and unfailing help.

To the FBI regional office in New Orleans, destroyed by Hurricane Katrina and its aftermath.

To the Dauphine Orleans Hotel and its phantom fiancée.

To Charity Hospital—its eerie, abandoned, but still-standing structure continues to remind us that misery, struggle, and triumph must never be forgotten.

To Moe, the New Orleans taxi driver who lost both his taxi and his house in the Ninth Ward during Hurricane Katrina and asked me to put them in the novel.

To the New Orleans Saints and the Superdome. "I'm no angel—I'm a saint!"

To the musicians and the ghosts who never left New Orleans.

To the whole team at Destino; I'm going back to Gryffindor.

To the goddess Mari, as is only fitting, for all tempests belong to her.

GLOSSARY

agur. A traditional and often honorific salutation that can mean "hello" or "goodbye."

aita. Father.

aitatxo. Daddy.

ama. Mother.

Awright! "All right!" Said in response to a greeting in New Orleans.

basajaun. In the Euskara language, "the lord of the forest." An anthropomorphic creature of Basque and Navarra mythology, generally benevolent, who maintains the balance between humans and nature. The name given to the killer in *The Invisible Guardian,* book one of the Baztán Trilogy.

bayou. From the Choctaw expression *bayuk,* meaning "creek" or "stream." A Louisiana term for an expanse of flowing water in a swamp region.

Bazagrá or Bazagreá. Name of a voodoo demon, derived from Baal and Beelzebub. It appears in ancient Sumerian. The Old Testament renders it as Baal. An incantation used to invoke a curse.

bihotz. "Heart" in Euskara.

bitxito. "Little insect"; used to refer to naughty children.

bokor. A male sorcerer in voodoo. A voodoo sorcerer "marked" with *bokor* is one who practices *lukumi* (the snake) evil magic and *conga* (the rainbow), which involves mostly protective or healing spells. A sorcerer initiated in both types of magic is said to "serve with both hands."

crawfish boil. Crayfish dish cooked in a kettle; a familiar and much-loved traditional meal prepared in the family, outside with friends, or on one's own street.

eguzki-lore. The thistle; a protective talisman of Basque mythology. Its resemblance to the sun confers it protective powers against the creatures of the night, particularly against witches and their spells. It is placed on the doors of houses and stables to defend those places.

fifolet. False fire or Saint Elmo's fire. Mythical blue lights that float above the Louisiana swamps; according to tradition they are the spirits of those who died in the swamps. An alternate version from the days of piracy in the region describes *fifolets* as spirits who guard treasure buried in the swamps by pirates.

gabon. "Good night" in Euskara.

Gaueko. In Basque mythology, the lord of darkness, the spirit of the night.

gauekoak. "Those of the night" in Euskara. Includes dark creatures as well as evil ones, from witches to elves, wandering spirits, and demons such as the *inguma*, a figure common to various cultures, the most ancient of which appeared in the Sumerian civilization. See *The Legacy of the Bones*, book two of the Baztán Trilogy.

gris-gris. A protective amulet in voodoo.

How's your mamandem? Literally, "How's your mama and them?" A common greeting in Louisiana, most frequently between friends in New Orleans, first asking about one's mother and then about all others.

ipar. "North" in Euskara.

itxusuria. "The corridor of souls" in Euskara. The exterior space between the wall of a house and the line left in the ground by water dripping from the eaves. Traditionally the place where unbaptized infants were buried, for they weren't accepted into Catholic graveyards. See *The Legacy of the Bones*, book two of the Baztán Trilogy.

jambalaya. Traditional Louisiana dish of stewed greens, shrimp, and ham; other variations are possible.

krewe. "Crew," but in this case, all those aboard a Mardi Gras float in a Louisiana carnival parade, always captained by a madcap whose orders are strictly obeyed.

laissez les bons temps rouler. Traditional New Orleans phrase from Cajun French that has become the motto of the city: "Let the good times roll."

loa. In the voodoo religion, a spirit intermediary between human beings and the supernatural entity known as Mawu or Bondye, a god inaccessible to humans. The *loas* are the minor gods in contact both with human beings and with the supreme god.

lutin. A mischievous spirit, usually a child who died before receiving baptism. A deep-rooted belief among the Cajun people of the swamps. Only those younger than two years can see them, though anyone can be subject to their pranks. They're believed to carry out mischief and are particularly known for their delight in braiding the hair of sleeping individuals as well as the manes of horses and dogs' fur.

mairu. "Unchristian" or "unbaptized" in Euskara. Ghosts of infants that are buried in the *itxusuria*; they are usually devoted to protecting the home. The infants' bones are prized for the practice of sorcery because of their magic soporific powers.

maitia. "Darling" or "beloved" in Euskara.

maudit. "Cursed" in French.

rougarou. Creature of Cajun myth. Lives in the swamps and resembles a wolf-man (in metropolitan French, "loup-garou").

Saints/Santos. The Saints are a New Orleans professional football team. The Superdome is their home stadium.

shotgun. Type of residence typical to Louisiana, especially in New Orleans, that is lengthy and narrow like the path of a bullet.

traiteur. Witch doctor, male or female, practicing Cajun magic; they heal with prayers, incantations, and the laying on of hands. They are regarded as saintly, profoundly spiritual men and women.

ttuku-ttuku. "Gossip" or "blather" in Elizondo, Baztán province.

zirimiri. "Gentle, constant rain" in Euskara; it's typical of northwestern Spain and so fine that it's almost invisible to the eye.

ABOUT THE AUTHOR

Photo © Alfredo Tudela

Dolores Redondo is an internationally bestselling author who studied law and the culinary arts before writing the Baztán Trilogy (*The Invisible Guardian*, *The Legacy of the Bones*, and *Offering to the Storm*). The successful crime series set in the Basque Pyrenees has sold over 2.5 million copies in Spanish, has been translated into more than thirty-five languages, and was adapted into a popular film series available worldwide on Netflix.

Twice nominated for the CWA International Dagger Award and a finalist for the Grand Prix des lectrices de ELLE, Redondo was the recipient of the 2016 Premio Planeta—one of Spain's most distinguished literary awards—for her stand-alone thriller *All This I Will Give to You*. It has also been optioned for feature film and television development and will be translated into eighteen languages.

Readers who want to learn more about Dolores Redondo and her work can do so by visiting www.doloresredondo.com/en.

ABOUT THE TRANSLATOR

Photo © 2017 Steve Rogers

Michael Meigs reviews theater and translates literature from French, German, Swedish, and Spanish. He won the annual American-Scandinavian Foundation Translation Prize in 2011, as well as the biennial Lewis Galantière Translation Award of the American Translators Association in 2020 for his version of Dolores Redondo's *All This I Will Give to You*. Since 2008 he has published the online journal *CTX Live Theatre*, which is dedicated to live narrative theater throughout Central Texas. He served for more than thirty years as a diplomat with the US Department of State and was assigned abroad with his wife, Karen, and their children in Africa, Europe, South America, and the Caribbean. He has graduate degrees in comparative literature, business, economics, and national security studies. He's a board member of the Austin Area Translators and Interpreters Association and of Gilbert & Sullivan Austin, and a member of the American Translators Association, the American Literary Translators Association, the American Theatre Critics Association, and Swedish Translators in North America.